THE BESTSELLING NOVELS OF
Tom Clancy

THE TEETH OF THE TIGER

A new generation—Jack Ryan, Jr.—takes over in Tom Clancy's extraordinary, and extraordinarily prescient, novel.

"INCREDIBLY ADDICTIVE." —*Daily Mail* (London)

RED RABBIT

Tom Clancy returns to Jack Ryan's early days—in an extraordinary novel of global political drama.

"AN OLD-FASHIONED COLD WAR THRILLER."
—*Chicago Sun-Times*

THE BEAR AND THE DRAGON

President Jack Ryan faces a world crisis unlike any he has ever known.

"INTOXICATING . . . A JUGGERNAUT."
—*Publishers Weekly* (starred review)

RAINBOW SIX

Clancy's shocking story of international terrorism—closer to reality than any government would care to admit.

"GRIPPING . . . BOLT-ACTION MAYHEM."
—*People*

continued . . .

EXECUTIVE ORDERS

Jack Ryan has always been a soldier. Now he's giving the orders.

"AN ENORMOUS, ACTION-PACKED, HEAT-SEEKING MISSILE OF A TOM CLANCY NOVEL."

—*The Seattle Times*

DEBT OF HONOR

It begins with the murder of an American woman in the back streets of Tokyo. It ends in war.

"A SHOCKER!" —*Entertainment Weekly*

THE HUNT FOR RED OCTOBER

The smash bestseller that launched Clancy's career—the incredible search for a Soviet defector and the nuclear submarine he commands.

"BREATHLESSLY EXCITING!" —*The Washington Post*

RED STORM RISING

The ultimate scenario for World War III—the final battle for global control.

"THE ULTIMATE WAR GAME . . . BRILLIANT!"

—*Newsweek*

PATRIOT GAMES

CIA analyst Jack Ryan stops an assassination—and incurs the wrath of Irish terrorists.

"A HIGH PITCH OF EXCITEMENT!"

—*The Wall Street Journal*

THE CARDINAL OF THE KREMLIN

The superpowers race for the ultimate Star Wars missile defense system.

"*CARDINAL* EXCITES, ILLUMINATES . . . A REAL PAGE-TURNER!" —*Los Angeles Daily News*

CLEAR AND PRESENT DANGER

The killing of three U.S. officials in Colombia ignites the American government's explosive, and top secret, response.

"A CRACKLING GOOD YARN!" —*The Washington Post*

THE SUM OF ALL FEARS

The disappearance of an Israeli nuclear weapon threatens the balance of power in the Middle East—and around the world.

"CLANCY AT HIS BEST . . . NOT TO BE MISSED!" —*The Dallas Morning News*

WITHOUT REMORSE

The Clancy epic fans have been waiting for. His code name is Mr. Clark. And his work for the CIA is brilliant, cold-blooded, and efficient . . . but who is he really?

"HIGHLY ENTERTAINING!" —*The Wall Street Journal*

Novels by Tom Clancy

THE HUNT FOR RED OCTOBER
RED STORM RISING
PATRIOT GAMES
THE CARDINAL OF THE KREMLIN
CLEAR AND PRESENT DANGER
THE SUM OF ALL FEARS
WITHOUT REMORSE
DEBT OF HONOR
EXECUTIVE ORDERS
RAINBOW SIX
THE BEAR AND THE DRAGON
RED RABBIT
THE TEETH OF THE TIGER

SSN: STRATEGIES OF SUBMARINE WARFARE

Nonfiction

SUBMARINE: A GUIDED TOUR INSIDE A NUCLEAR WARSHIP
ARMORED CAV: A GUIDED TOUR OF AN ARMORED CAVALRY REGIMENT
FIGHTER WING: A GUIDED TOUR OF AN AIR FORCE COMBAT WING
MARINE: A GUIDED TOUR OF A MARINE EXPEDITIONARY UNIT
AIRBORNE: A GUIDED TOUR OF AN AIRBORNE TASK FORCE
CARRIER: A GUIDED TOUR OF AN AIRCRAFT CARRIER
SPECIAL FORCES: A GUIDED TOUR OF U.S. ARMY SPECIAL FORCES

INTO THE STORM: A STUDY IN COMMAND
(written with General Fred Franks, Jr., Ret.)
EVERY MAN A TIGER
(written with General Charles Horner, Ret.)
SHADOW WARRIORS: INSIDE THE SPECIAL FORCES
(written with General Carl Stiner, Ret., and Tony Koltz)

Created by Tom Clancy and Steve Pieczenik

TOM CLANCY'S OP-CENTER

TOM CLANCY'S OP-CENTER: MIRROR IMAGE

TOM CLANCY'S OP-CENTER: GAMES OF STATE

TOM CLANCY'S OP-CENTER: ACTS OF WAR

TOM CLANCY'S OP-CENTER: BALANCE OF POWER

TOM CLANCY'S OP-CENTER: STATE OF SIEGE

TOM CLANCY'S OP-CENTER: DIVIDE AND CONQUER

TOM CLANCY'S OP-CENTER: LINE OF CONTROL

TOM CLANCY'S OP-CENTER: MISSION OF HONOR

TOM CLANCY'S OP-CENTER: SEA OF FIRE

TOM CLANCY'S OP-CENTER: CALL TO TREASON

TOM CLANCY'S NET FORCE

TOM CLANCY'S NET FORCE: HIDDEN AGENDAS

TOM CLANCY'S NET FORCE: NIGHT MOVES

TOM CLANCY'S NET FORCE: BREAKING POINT

TOM CLANCY'S NET FORCE: POINT OF IMPACT

TOM CLANCY'S NET FORCE: CYBERNATION

TOM CLANCY'S NET FORCE: STATE OF WAR

TOM CLANCY'S NET FORCE: CHANGING OF THE GUARD

Created by Tom Clancy and Martin Greenberg

TOM CLANCY'S POWER PLAYS: POLITIKA

TOM CLANCY'S POWER PLAYS: RUTHLESS.COM

TOM CLANCY'S POWER PLAYS: SHADOW WATCH

TOM CLANCY'S POWER PLAYS: BIO-STRIKE

TOM CLANCY'S POWER PLAYS: COLD WAR

TOM CLANCY'S POWER PLAYS: CUTTING EDGE

TOM CLANCY'S POWER PLAYS: ZERO HOUR

Tom Clancy's Op-Center™

CALL TO TREASON

Created by

Tom Clancy and Steve Pieczenik

written by

Jeff Rovin

BERKLEY BOOKS, NEW YORK

TOM CLANCY'S OP-CENTER: CALL TO TREASON

A Berkley Book / published by arrangement with
Jack Ryan Limited Partnership and S & R Literary, Inc.

PRINTING HISTORY
Berkley edition / July 2004

For information address: The Berkley Publishing Group,
a division of Penguin Group (USA) Inc.,
375 Hudson Street, New York, New York 10014.

ISBN: 0-425-19546-5

BERKLEY®
Berkley Books are published by The Berkley Publishing Group,
a division of Penguin Group (USA) Inc.,
375 Hudson Street, New York, New York 10014.
BERKLEY and the "B" design are trademarks
belonging to Penguin Group (USA) Inc.

PRINTED IN THE UNITED STATES OF AMERICA

10 9 8 7 6 5 4 3 2 1

Acknowledgments

We would like to acknowledge the valuable assistance of Martin H. Greenberg, Ph.D.; Larry Segriff; Denise Little; John Helfers; Brittiany Koren; Victoria Bundonis Rovin; Roberta Pieczenik, Ph.D.; Carl La Greca; and Tom Colgan, our editor. But most important, it is for you, our readers, to determine how successful our collective endeavor has been.

—Tom Clancy and Steve Pieczenik

ONE

Georgetown, Washington, D.C.
Sunday, 9:22 P.M.

Combat was not easy. But it was easier than this.

General Mike Rodgers stood with a Scotch in his hand, wishing it were a double and that he were free to slug it down. If he were in a dark saloon with Colonel August or one of his buddies from the Department of Defense, he would. Then he would nurse the sweet buzz with a beer chaser. But he was not with his colleagues. He was at a black-tie party in a three-story town house on N Street in the exclusive Georgetown section of Washington, D.C. The first-floor ballroom was crowded with nearly two hundred politicians and socialites, attorneys and foreign dignitaries, business leaders and television news executives.

They were all gathered in small groups. Though actively engaged with the people nearest them, each individual was also listening to what was being said in the groups around them. Rodgers could see it in the way their eyes moved. They always shifted slightly in the direction they were listening. Some of these silver-haired blue bloods possessed recon skills that would be the envy of CIA field ops.

On the battlefield, a man knew who the enemy was. At a party like this, alliances could be made and remade during the course of an evening. That was true throughout Washington, but the density of power brokers from so many arenas made it more likely here. In combat, a soldier knew when the fight was over. In Washington, the conflict never ended. Even at Op-Center, where Rodgers was deputy director, friendships were routinely tested by strong differences of opinion over high-stakes operations. Trust was frayed by competition for assignments. And loyalties were challenged and often destroyed by downsizing and bureaucratic squabbles.

The conditions at Op-Center were the reason Rodgers had come to this party. Since the disbanding of Striker, Op-Center's rapid-deployment force that had been commanded by Rodgers, the general had been organizing an in-house human intelligence unit. He was not enjoying the work as much as he had hoped. Rodgers was a man of grapeshot and action, not observation and note-taking. The work was essential. It just was not for him. To make things worse, his efforts cut into the jurisdiction of Bob Herbert, Op-Center's chief of Intelligence Operations. The strain on their relationship was subtle, but the impact was not. There was no antagonism; to the contrary, they were extremely cautious around one another, like outfielders going for a high fly ball and stopping short, letting it drop between them.

When an aide to Texas Senator Don Orr had called to say the senator was interested in exploring professional opportunities, Rodgers agreed to come. So far, the three-term, fifty-eight-year-old senator had not said much more than a big, "Hello, General! Thanks for coming," before being swallowed by the party. The white-haired rancher-turned-politician said that to virtually everyone as he moved from group to group, shaking hands and kissing cheeks. All of them, Rodgers suspected.

Rodgers did not follow him, as several others were doing. Subtly, of course. They wanted to be noticed and introduced to people. They wanted to be legitimized, like made men at a meeting of the dons. Rodgers did not know any of these people, and so he stood near the wet bar, chatting with one of the two bartenders. As a grandfather clock tolled the half hour, a woman approached from the side.

"There is only one thing worse than being a Washington outsider," she said as she asked the bartender for a Coke.

"What's that?" Rodgers asked, glancing at her.

"Being a Washington insider," she replied.

Rodgers smiled. There was a hint of Vietnamese in her strong, cultured voice, but the rest of her was pure Beltway insider.

"General Rodgers, I'm Kendra Peterson, the senator's executive assistant," she said, extending a slender hand. "I'm happy you could make it."

Rodgers's smile broadened as he shook her hand. The woman was in her mid-thirties and stood about five foot seven, with dark skin, exotic eyes, and straight black hair. She had the cool poise of someone who knew things. She was dressed in a strapless navy blue satin gown with a wide, translucent sash. Her wardrobe was seductive, but her expression said she was not interested, whoever you were.

"I'm pleased to meet you," Rodgers said. "I was beginning to wonder why I was here."

"I knew there wouldn't be much chance for you to talk to the senator, but I wanted you to get a feel for the kind of people we work with."

"I see. Care to tell me why?"

"The senator is interested in you," she said.

"But you're not at liberty to tell me more," Rodgers said.

She shook her head once.

"I've heard rumors the senator plans to make a third-party run for the White House," Rodgers went on. "Are they true?"

The woman smiled evasively. "Would you be available to meet with the senator tomorrow afternoon?"

"I might be if I knew why," Rodgers said. "I don't like to go into situations unprepared."

The woman took a sip of her drink and turned toward

the room. "This town house was built in 1877, four years after Georgetown was incorporated into the District of Columbia. Do you know what it was worth then?"

"Probably less than this party cost," Rodgers said.

She grinned. "Somewhat less. Just under five thousand dollars, according to the tax rolls. Seven years ago, at the beginning of his third term, the senator bought it for $2.7 million."

"Your point being—?"

The woman fixed him with those fascinating eyes. "The house was built by a sea captain who never intended to live in it. He willed it to his granddaughter. He knew it would appreciate far more than anything else he could leave her. That is how the senator feels about his political future. What we start here will increase geometrically over the years to come."

"With respect, everyone says that," Rodgers told her.

"The senator has a voting record."

"I know. I looked it up," Rodgers said. "It's conservative and protectionist, with a heavy helping of big stickism."

"Are those very different from your own beliefs?" she asked.

"Not necessarily," Rodgers said. "But you knew that, didn't you?"

"The senator has powerful allies and extensive resources," Kendra admitted. "General, people have a great deal of respect for you. The senator will need an adviser like you." The woman leaned close. "Someone who has experience in the field, off the field, and is fearless in both arenas. Someone who also has experience in intelligence. You are uniquely qualified."

"Thanks," he said. After weeks of feeling like a bastard son at Op-Center, that was good to hear.

The woman finished her Coke. She set the glass on the counter. "General Rodgers—I'm tired."

"You don't look it."

"I feel it," she said. "My staff and I put a lot of weeks into this party. Now I'm going to slip away and get some sleep."

"Actually, I'll be leaving right behind you," Rodgers told her. "Can I give you a lift?"

"You're sweet, but Mr. Carlyle, the senator's driver, is going to take me home. Besides, you should stay and be seen."

"Doing what?"

"Talking to people."

"Your 'extensive resources' probably told you I'm not very good at that," Rodgers said.

"We heard that," she admitted. "We also heard that you're a quick study. It would help us all if the power brokers started to associate your face with this group."

"A soldier who is seen is a target," Rodgers said. "I prefer high ground or a trench."

"Even in peacetime?" she asked.

"Is that what this is, Ms. Peterson?" Rodgers asked.

"Kendra," she said.

"Kendra," he nodded. "I see a lot of mobilization out there."

"I suppose there is no such thing as neutrality in Washington." She laughed. She removed a PalmPilot from her purse. "Would three P.M. tomorrow suit you to meet with the senator and Admiral Link?"

"Admiral Link," Rodgers said. "I know that name."

"Kenneth Link, the barrel-chested gentleman speaking with William Wilson," she said. "Crew cut, red bow tie."

Rodgers turned. "I see him. I still can't place him."

"He's the former head of Naval Intelligence, later director of covert ops for the CIA," Kendra said.

"Right," Rodgers said. "Now I remember. I saw him at a number of NIPC meetings." The NIPC was the National Infrastructure Protection Center. Based at FBI headquarters in Washington, D.C., it was founded in 1998 to bring together representatives from various U.S. intelligence agencies, as well as experts from private-sector think tanks. The NIPC was chartered to assess threats against critical infrastructures in energy, finance, telecommunications, water, and emergency services. "He was always complaining about special interests and compromise."

"The admiral does not believe in making concessions where national security is concerned," the woman replied. "Do you think you would have a problem working with him on a daily basis?"

"Not if we agree that there's a difference between national security and paranoia," Rodgers said.

"What is the difference?" she asked.

"One is a door that has a lock, the other is a door that's completely unhinged," Rodgers replied.

"I like it," she said. "That's something you can discuss together—assuming three o'clock is convenient."

"I'll be there," Rodgers said.

"Good." She tucked away her PalmPilot and once again offered her hand. "Thank you for coming, General. I hope this has been the start of a long and rewarding relationship."

Rodgers smiled at the woman as she withdrew. He did not watch her go but turned back to the bar. He replayed their brief conversation as he finished his drink. The young woman had basically confirmed that Senator Orr would be ramping up a new party and running for president. Rodgers would enjoy being a part of that. His own politics were a little right of center. It would not be difficult supporting the Texan's vision. Rodgers thought back to the early months at Op-Center when he and Director Paul Hood and Bob Herbert moved the newly chartered domestic-crisis organization into a two-story building at Andrews Air Force Base. They staffed the dozen departments with top people like Darrell McCaskey from the FBI, computer genius Matt Stoll, political liaison Martha Mackall, psychologist and profiler Liz Gordon, attorney Lowell Coffey III, and others. They built Striker and recruited the late Lieutenant Colonel Charles Squires to lead it. They saw their initial areas of responsibility expand from a national to an international arena. Those were exciting, rewarding times. There was also a sense of personal evolution for Rodgers. The warrior who had fought in Vietnam and had commanded a mechanized brigade in the Persian Gulf was running special ops missions in North Korea and the Bekaa Valley, rescuing hostages at the United Nations, preventing a new civil war in Spain and nuclear war between India and Pakistan.

He was making a difference.

Now I'm recruiting spies and analyzing data, he thought. It was honorable work, but there was a big difference between commanding and supervising. What was it the Chinese leader Liu Shao-ch'i had said? The true leader is an elephant. The rest are just pigs inserting scallions into their nose in an effort to look like one.

With a nod toward the bartender, Rodgers turned back to the room. There was nothing in here that appealed to him. Not the glad-handing, not the eavesdropping, not the neediness, and not the facades. But Rodgers was definitely beginning to smell onions in his own nose. It was time for a change.

Rodgers would talk to Senator Orr and Admiral Link, but first he wanted to talk to Paul Hood. For there was one concession Mike Rodgers would never make, however bored he became. It was a concept he did not think many people in this room would understand.

Mike Rodgers put loyalty above all else.

TWO

Washington, D.C.
Sunday, 11:18 P.M.

There was a time when the Liverpool-born William Wilson could not have afforded to stay in a landmark hotel like the Hay-Adams, with its view of the White House, the Washington Monument, and Lafayette Park. Or been invited to a Georgetown party hosted by a United States senator. Or been picked up by a woman who looked like this one did.

What a difference two billion dollars makes.

The lanky, six-foot-three-inch Wilson was the thirty-one-year-old inventor of the MasterLock computer technology. Launched five years before, it used a combination of keystrokes, visual cues, and audio frequencies to create hack-proof firewalls. Not content with revolutionizing computer security, Wilson bought the failing London Merchant-Farmer Bank and made it a European powerhouse. Now he was about to go on-line with MasterBank, an on-line service that invested in European businesses. Wilson had come to Washington to meet with members of the Panel of Economic Advisors of the Congressional Committee on Banking Financial Services. He intended to lobby for an easing of foreign direct-investment restrictions that were put in place during the War on Terror. That would remove hundreds of millions of dollars from American banks and stocks. In exchange, Wilson would guarantee an equal investment of hundreds of millions of dollars in American companies. That would keep cash flow circulating in the United States, though the bulk of the profits and tax benefits would still be his.

The stunning young woman had approached him early in the evening, just minutes after he arrived. She was a reporter. After assuring him that she was not angling for an interview—her beat, she said, was the environment and meteorology—the woman asked if she could stop by later in the evening.

"I'm drawn to men who create technological quantum leaps," she said.

Who could resist a come-on like that?

Two hours later Wilson left the party with his two bodyguards and driver. He had agreed to meet the woman at eleven P.M. There were paparazzi outside, and Wilson did not want to be photographed leaving with anyone. The world was a conservative place. He preferred to remain a champion of the financial and science sections, not a libertine of the gossip page.

Wilson had the top-floor Federal Suite, and his bodyguards had the adjoining Presidential Suite. Motion detectors had been installed outside Wilson's door and on the floor of the balcony. If anyone tried to enter without being announced, vibrating wristbands would silently wake the bodyguards.

Wilson had ordered a 1970 Dom Perignon from room service and a light gray beluga caviar. He had candles delivered, along with a dozen roses for the bedroom nightstands. He opened his bow tie but left it hanging around his neck and sprayed a hint of Jivago Millennium above the collar. He probably did not need any of that. After all, he had made a technological quantum leap. But growing up the son of a pub owner, it made him happy to smell something other than ale and cigarettes. It made him even happier to be with women who did not smell of them.

His guest arrived on time and was announced. One of the guards met her at the elevator and escorted her to the suite. Wilson met her at the door with a rose. It made her smile. The rose seemed to disappear.

They ate caviar on toast tips. They drank champagne. They stood close on the balcony and looked out at the White House. They did not say much. She seemed content just to be there, and he was delighted to have her. As a distant church bell sounded midnight, they went quickly from the balcony to the authentic Hepplewhite mahogany settee to the bedroom.

The woman blew out the candles on the dresser, set her purse on the night table, and pushed him back on the king-size bed. She was as assertive as she was beautiful. Wilson understood that, and he went along with it. To succeed in her business, at her age, took confidence. She was showing that now.

"What can I do for you?" he asked.

"Just lie there," she replied as she settled on top of him.

He looked up at her and smiled. She moved her fingers down his arms and pushed them to his side. She placed her knees in his open palms and dragged her long nails across his chest, along the side of his neck, his scalp. Her toned body moved in excited spasms, like a whip. Shining through the window, the lights of Lafayette Park showed Wilson occasional flashes of cheekbone and shoulder.

Lady lightning, Wilson thought. *With thunder rolling from deep inside her.*

Champagne always brought out the Byron in him. Wilson was about to share his little metaphor aloud when his companion suddenly leaned across his chest and pulled a large, full pillow from behind him. She dragged it across his face and then leaned into it, hard.

"Hey!" Wilson shouted. He repeated the cry but lacked the breath to say more. He shut his eyes and closed his mouth and tried to push up with his head. His neck cramped painfully, and he stopped.

Wilson's hands were pinned by the woman's knees. He

struggled unsuccessfully to raise them while he wriggled helplessly from side to side. He screamed into the pillow, hoping his bodyguards would hear him. If they did, he did not hear them. He heard nothing but bedsprings laughing beneath his head, his heart punching up against his throat, and his own thick wheezing as he fought to draw breath. His hands throbbed and the flesh of his belly and thighs burned where it rubbed hers. The pillow was wet with perspiration and saliva.

This is a game, Wilson thought hopefully as rusty circles filled the insides of his eyelids. *This is what turns her on.*

If it was, he did not approve. But he did not dwell on that. His thoughts were not his own. Wilson's head filled with visual doggerel, images that came from other times and places.

And then, suddenly, the slide show stopped. His face cooled, his mouth opened wide, and his lungs filled with sweet air. He opened his eyes and saw the woman. She was still perched above him, a slightly darker silhouette than the ceiling above. His eyes were misty with sweat. They smeared the woman as she bent close. The park lights sparked off something else, something in her hands. He tried to raise his arms to push her back, but they were still pinned. He couldn't speak or scream, because he was still desperately sucking air through his wide-open mouth.

She moved closer and put the palm of her left hand against the bottom of his nose. She pushed up.

"What—?" was all he could say as his head arched back. He cried out weakly, but he sounded like a pig calling for dinner.

Or a man having sex, he thought. *Christ.* The bodyguards would not come, even if they heard him.

A moment after that, Wilson felt a cool sting in his mouth. He felt the weight of the woman leave him. He saw her get up. But that did not help. Within moments a cold, tingling numbness moved down from his ears along the sides of his neck. It filled his shoulders and arms and poured across his chest like an overturned bucket of ice. It tickled his navel and rolled down his legs.

This time there were no mental images, no struggle. The lights, and his lungs, simply snapped off.

THREE

Washington, D.C.
Monday, 8:02 A.M.

Op-Center was officially known as the National Crisis Management Center. That was what it said on the charter, on the small brass sign beside the front door, and on the badge Paul Hood had just swiped through the lock to enter the lobby. Which was why Hood felt a little schizophrenic when he arrived and there was no crisis. He felt paradoxically relaxed and anxious.

Roughly half of the seventy-eight employees at Op-Center were dedicated to intelligence gathering and analysis. The other half handled crises that were imminent or had already gone "active," as they euphemistically described rebellions, hostage situations, terrorism, and other crises. When half the team was idle, Hood worried that someone on the Hill would notice. The intelligence community could learn something from Congress. With nothing more than newspapers, gossip, and intuition, they profiled people and agencies with eerie accuracy. After that came the auto-da-fé. After *that*, people who once moved through the corridors of power became consultants. Hanging out the shingle saved face. What they really were was unemployed.

Hood did not know what he would do if the Inquisition came for him. Ironically, he knew how to stop it. Prior to joining Op-Center, Paul Hood was a two-term mayor of Los Angeles. He got to know a lot of people in the movie industry, and he learned that many of them were extraneous. If they did not find fault with perfectly fine scripts, there would be no reason for them to be employed. The United States military had somewhat the same mentality. Military intelligence financed "cheerleaders," as they called them. These were both indigenous and undercover teams that fomented conflict around the globe. "Counterfeit mobilization," they called it. A world at peace did not need increased military spending. And a downsized military would not be prepared to handle a real war when it arose.

There was some sense to the Department of Defense policy. However, counterfeit mobilization only worked one way for intelligence agencies. You had to pick a foreign national, frame him, and have your guys smoke him out. As much as he hated the sense of entitlement diplomatic plates gave diplomatic personnel, Hood had a problem with that. First, it tied up personnel from watching for real spies and saboteurs. Second, it could begin a pattern of escalation abroad until you actually turned allies into enemies. Third, it was wrong. It was not fashionable in Washington, but Hood believed in the Ten Commandments. He did not always keep them, but he tried. And bearing false witness was one of the *You shall nots.*

Hood greeted the guard, used his card to access the elevator, then descended one level to the heart of the National Crisis Management Center. There, Hood passed windowless offices that were set off a circular corridor of stainless steel. He reached his own wood-paneled office, near the back. He was greeted by his assistant, "Bugs" Benet, who sat in a small cubicle located to the right of the door. The young man was busy at the computer, logging the reports of the evening crew.

"Morning," Hood said. "Anything?"

"Quiet," Benet replied.

Hood already knew that, more or less. If there had been any kind of significant development, nighttime director

Curt Hardaway or his deputy Bill Abram would have notified him.

"Did you hear about William Wilson?" Benet asked.

"Yes," Hood replied. "It was on the radio."

"Heart attack at thirty-one," Benet said.

"Sex is among the most strenuous physical activities, up there with full court basketball and rock climbing," Liz Gordon said as she walked by.

Hood smiled at the psychologist. "I'll bet you wouldn't have said *that* at the Brookings Institution."

"Probably not." Liz smiled as she continued toward her office. The thirty-five-year-old woman had given up a post at the independent research and policy institute to take this job with Op-Center. Initially, Hood had not put much faith in profiling. But Liz had impressed him with her insights about leaders, about field operatives, about soldiers, and about Op-Center staff that were bending under personal and professional stress. She had been especially helpful with Hood's fourteen-year-old daughter, Harleigh. The eldest of his two children had been among the hostages taken by rogue peacekeepers at the United Nations. Liz had given him solid, effective advice about dealing with her post-traumatic stress disorder. The psychologist had also helped Hood reconnect with his twelve-year-old son Alexander after the stressful divorce from Sharon.

Hood shut the door, went to his desk, and input his personal computer code. It was not the name of his children, or his first pet, or the date he started working here. Those were things that a hacker might figure out. Instead, it was Dickdiver, the main character of his favorite novel, *Tender Is the Night.* It also made Hood smile to key it in. Hood and his long-ago fiancée Nancy Jo Bosworth had read it to each other when they first moved in together. When there was still magic in his world and romance in his heart. Before stolen software designs compelled Nancy to run off without telling him why or where. It took almost twenty years for Hood to find her. It happened by accident, during a trip to Germany on Op-Center business. Nancy told him she had wanted the money for them but grew ashamed. Since she could not return it, she kept it for herself.

Old feelings returned for them both. Though the passions were not acted upon, they helped to undermine what had been a colorless, rebound marriage to Sharon. While Hood was alone now, the F. Scott Fitzgerald novel was still the key to a sublime place, the last time Hood was truly happy. The password was his way of remembering that every day.

Hood started going through his E-mail. He used to come to the office and read the newspaper, then answer phone calls. Now the news was on-line, and the telephone was something you used in the car or at lunch. GovNet, which provided Op-Center's secure Internet access, was devoting a lot of space to Wilson's death on their welcome screen. That was not surprising, since his firewalls made it possible for most government agencies to link what had formerly been dedicated lines. They were reporting that he had gone to a party at Senator Don Orr's town house, left around ten-thirty, and went back to his suite at the Hay-Adams. A woman had come to visit him. According to the hotel, she arrived at eleven and left around twelve-thirty. The concierge reported that she had been wearing a block print coat that came down to her knees and a matching crocheted hat with a black ribbon. The wide brim was dipped low. Obviously, she did not want to be recognized. That was not unusual. Many officials and businessmen had trysts in local hotels. They did not want their guests to be identified or photographed by security cameras. Typically, hotel management respected the desire for privacy by allowing expected visitors to pass without scrutiny.

The Metropolitan Police did not know who the woman caller was. She had given a name, Anna Anderson, which had led them to an elderly woman who was clearly not the perp. She may have selected the name as a joke, a reference to the woman who claimed to be Anastasia, the daughter of Czar Nicholas II. The security cameras in the hotel lobby and on the street showed her leaving unhurriedly and walking down Sixteenth Street, where she was lost in the night. Visitors like her seldom used valet parking. They did not want their license numbers traced. Washingtonians assumed that everyone, from waiters to cab drivers, was looking for a payday from a tabloid newspaper or television show. More often than not they were right. The police assumed that Wilson died after the woman left. Otherwise she could have called 911 and then slipped away. This belief was reinforced by the fact that there did not appear to be anything suspicious about Wilson's death. He had perspired heavily—presumably from the exertion—and the bed suggested "an active evening," as one source put it. Though Wilson was young and had no history of heart trouble, many forms of heart disease could slip past a routine electrocardiograph. The autopsy would tell them more.

There was nothing exceptional in the E-mails. A few résumés from agencies and private businesses that were being downsized. Op-ed pieces from the left, right, and center. Requests for interviews, which Hood routinely declined. He was not a self-promoter and saw no benefit to giving out information about how Op-Center worked, or with whom. His E-mail even contained links to password-protected web sites of individuals who were willing to provide intelligence from various countries and foreign agencies. He forwarded these to Bob Herbert. Most were con artists, a few were foreign agents trying to find out about Op-Center, but occasionally there were nuclear scientists or biotechnicians who genuinely wanted to get out of the situations they were in. As long as they were willing to talk, American operatives or embassy officials in their countries were willing to listen.

Hood was about to access his personal address for private E-mail when Bugs beeped him. Senator Debenport was on the line. Hood was not surprised. It was budget time on the Hill, and the South Carolina senator had recently replaced Senator Barbara Fox as the chairman of the Congressional Intelligence Oversight Committee. Those were the officials who kept track of what the federal intelligence agencies did and how much it cost.

"Good morning, Senator," Hood said.

"That may be true somewhere," the sandpaper-voiced senator replied. "Not in my office."

Hood did not ask why. He already knew the answer.

"Paul, last night the CIOC Budget Subcommittee agreed that we have to work out a strategic retrenchment," Debenport told him.

The CIOC's euphemism for budget cuts.

"We took a four percent hit last fiscal year and six percent the year before that," Hood told him. "What's the damage now?"

"We're looking at just upwards of twenty percent," Debenport replied.

Hood felt sick.

"The night crew is going to have to cut its staff by fifty percent. I know that's a lot, but we had no choice," Debenport went on.

"What are you talking about? You're the head of the damn committee."

"That's right, Paul. And as such I have a duty that transcends my personal feelings about the value of Op-Center's work," Debenport said. "It will be my call where to make the cuts, though I want your input and I will rely heavily on it. We would prefer you work backwards. Make your way back to Op-Center's original configuration."

"Our original configuration had a military component," Hood pointed out. "That's already been cut."

"Yes, and those funds were reallocated to General Rodgers's field personnel," Debenport said. "That's an area we feel should undergo deoperation. We looked closely at the internal breakdowns of the other intelligence groups. The Company and the Feds have those areas covered. Merge that post with the political officer."

"Senator, how much are you taking from the CIA, the FBI, and the NRO?" Hood asked.

"Paul, those are all older, established—"

"You're not cutting them, are you?" Hood asked.

Debenport was silent.

"Senator?"

"If you really want to know, Paul, they're getting a small bump," Debenport told him.

"Amazing," Hood replied. "How much time did they spend lobbying the committee?"

"They did the usual PowerPoint dance, but that wasn't the key to the increase," Debenport said. "Those boys grabbed a lot of Homeland Security detail out of the gate. We can write those budget request entries in ink."

"Because of a buzz phrase," Hood said. "We might have been in a position to reorient ourselves if our attention hadn't been on stopping nuclear war between India and Pakistan."

"Yes, and frankly your success is part of the problem. You've shifted the majority of your operations from the United States to other countries—"

"At the president's request," Hood reminded him. "He asked us to augment Op-Center's domestic agenda after we stopped a leftist military coup in Russia."

"I know the history," Debenport said. "I also know the future. The voters don't much care whether Moscow turns Red again or Tokyo is nuked or Spain falls apart or France gets hijacked by radicals. Not anymore. Foreign aid resources are being downsized across the board."

"Your constituents may not care, but *we* know that what happens there affects what happens here," Hood said.

"That's true," Debenport said. "Which is why the mandate the president gave you is not being changed."

"Only our funding. We're supposed to do the same job but with eighty percent of an already stretched budget."

"American households are having to do more than that," Debenport said. "As a senator, I also have a responsibility to help alleviate that burden."

"Senator, I appreciate your position, but this isn't right," Hood said. "I used to work on Wall Street. I run a trim operation, leaner than the agencies that are getting an increase. I intend to request, in writing, a hearing of the full CIOC as permitted under charter—"

"You can have it, of course. But you will be wasting your time and ours," Debenport said. "This decision was unanimous."

"I see. Let me ask you this, then. Is the CIOC fishing for my resignation?"

"Hell, no," Debenport said. "I don't run when I can pass. If the committee thought you had overstayed your welcome, I'd tell you."

"I appreciate that," Hood said. "Did you discuss any of this with the president?"

"That's my next call. I wanted to tell you first," Debenport said. "But whatever his feelings, he has no veto power. He doesn't even have a political majority on the committee."

"So that's it."

"I'm sorry, Paul."

Hood was angry, though not at Debenport. He was upset with himself. He should have smelled this one in the oven. He thought the departure of Fox was a signal that things were going to get better. And maybe they had, in a way. Fox did not see why Op-Center was necessary at all. She believed that the overseas intelligence activities of the CIA and the FBI were sufficient to keep America safe. Of course, she was also one of the senators who had put the bulk of America's spy capabilities into electronic intelligence. That was a huge miscalculation. If there were no operatives on the ground to pinpoint the mud huts, bunkers, apartments, cars, and caves for audio surveillance and spy satellites, a lot of what was called "incipient hostile intent" went unnoticed. That was when surgical covert activity became a War on Terror.

Still, Hood had hoped that Debenport would fight harder to keep Op-Center fully staffed.

The senator hung up, and Paul sat there, looking at the last E-mail he had opened. It was from the CIA Office of Personnel Security, Department of Communication, regarding updated procedures for the evacuation and decontamination of juveniles in the event of a biological attack on child care facilities serving the intelligence community. It was an important document, but it emphasized the gulf between the agencies. Op-Center did not even have a child care facility.

Hood closed the E-mail and brought up the budget file. He called Op-Center's CFO Ed Colahan and asked him to come to his office. He had come in early. Colahan knew their current fiscal year gave them another six weeks of business as usual. He wanted to be ready for whatever the CIOC decided.

Hood knew he would not be ready for this.

The question Hood had to address was whether to cut personnel from most or all of their ten divisions or whether to eliminate one or two departments entirely. He knew the answer even without looking at the figures. He also knew which departments would get him close to twenty percent. One of them would cost him efficiency.

The other would cost him a friend.

FOUR

Washington, D.C.
Monday, 8:20 A.M.

When Don Orr was a little boy, he used to look forward to June 22, the day Miss Clarion's twenty-two-student school closed down for the summer. He did not dislike school. Just the opposite. He loved learning new things. But the first day of summer vacation was special. He would get up at sunrise. With an olive green baseball cap pulled low over his forehead, he filled his father's canteen and slung it across a small shoulder. He made three or four peanut butter and jelly sandwiches and pushed them into a knapsack, along with a package of oatmeal cookies and a compass. Then he took a shovel from the tool shed. That was for beheading rattlesnakes if he encountered any. Holding the shovel like a prophet's staff, he walked out from the family's cattle ranch in Kingsville, Texas. He walked into the hot, windless plain to think about everything he had learned that year. Being alone like that for a day helped to burn the important things into his brain. He had learned in Bible class that this was what Jesus had done, and Moses before Him. The young boy felt that the walk would help to make him a stronger, better man.

He was right. Don Orr did that for ten years running, from the time he was eight. What he did not know, until years later, was that for the first two years, his father had one of the ranch hands follow him. The tradition ended in 1967, when Orr turned eighteen and joined the air force. Orr knew what it was like to walk and ride. Now he wanted to fly. But the air force had other ideas. They wanted him to work with his hands, like he did on the ranch. Just two years earlier, the air force had established RED HORSE units: Rapid Engineer Deployable Heavy Operational Repair Squadron, Engineering. These were divided into two squadrons: the 555th Triple Nickel and the 554th Penny Short. They assigned Orr to one of these. After nine weeks of training at Cannon Air Base in New Mexico, the young man was sent with the 554th to Phan Rang Air Base in Vietnam. There, his specialty was drilling wells to obtain drinking water, a skill he had learned on the ranch.

Orr did one tour in Vietnam and a second in Thailand. He was sorry he never saw combat. Like breaking a horse, herding cattle, or hauling yourself into the baking summertime wilderness, war was the kind of intense challenge that burned things into a man's head, muscles, and heart. That was one reason Senator Orr had always gotten along with combat veterans like Admiral Link. Risk-taking had been hardwired into the systems of those men.

It was not risk-taking but a sense of duty that had inspired Senator Orr to found the United States First Party six months before. Each of the two major parties was like a Third World country, a collection of ideological warlords with only one thing in common: an overwhelming dislike for the other party. There was no singular, driving philosophy. It was discouraging. Orr's idea was simple. The United States needed to become what the Orr Ranch was, a powerful spread run by men of vision. The nation should not be run by parties that burned up their energies playing a tug-of-war for inches. National growth should not be determined by an international consensus or by despots who bullied us with goods, from lumber to steel to oil. The USF Party would provide that. Orr had influence, resolve, credentials, and an American bloodline unmatched by any third-party leader in the past. The effort would also be good for Don Orr. The senator had influence on the Hill, but he did not have control. He was affiliated with good men, but he was not surrounded by them.

That would change.

The senator arrived at his office in the Russell Senate Office Building. Completed in 1908, the Beaux Arts structure was just a short walk north of the Capitol, bounded by Constitution Avenue, First Street, Delaware Avenue, and C Street NE. The senator's office was just off the magnificent rotunda and had an inspiring view of the Capitol dome. It was also just two blocks from Union Station.

"That proximity gives me a comfortable exit strategy," the outspoken senator liked to joke with reporters. When Orr first came to Washington, the *Dallas Morning News* sent him a coach ticket. The newspaper worried that he represented a nineteenth-century Manifest Destiny ideology in a more heterogeneous twenty-first-century world. The *Dallas Morning News* was wrong. He had nothing against a melting pot. He just wanted to make sure that the United States, and not radicals and petty tyrants, controlled the flame. Orr believed that Americans wanted that, too. On warm spring days, when his schedule permitted, the senator would do a short version of his childhood walk. He would take a brisk walk to the station and just stroll around, listening to what voters were saying. Then he would buy a bottle of water and walk back, letting their comments settle in along the way. It matched the E-mails and letters he received from his constituency. Americans embraced globalization, but they wanted a world that was fair. The United States made other nations rich by purchasing their cars, steel, oil, and electronics. We provided them with free military protection. In exchange, most of those countries gave local manufacturers tax breaks while imposing heavy tariffs on American goods. Even Orr's family business had suffered. Cattlemen in Australia, Canada, and Brazil paid their hands far less than American workers received. Many of those ranchers fed their cattle with cheap grasses instead of expensive, healthier grains. It was increasingly difficult to conduct business in that kind of marketplace. Orr intended to change that. He would insist on equal access to foreign markets and matching taxes on imports. If he did not get it, the door would be closed. Critics said he was being naive, but Orr believed that princes and prime ministers, presidents and chiefs would find the world a less comfortable place without American markets—and protection.

The senator had been up late the night before, talking to opinion makers, fellow politicians, and business leaders. Most of those people were friends and allies. A few were not. They had been invited to see how Orr and his colleagues felt about their protectionist activities.

One of those outsiders was the late William Wilson.

Orr heard about Wilson's death from Kat. As his driver moved through the thick morning traffic, Orr phoned Kendra Peterson to discuss the news. They both knew that Orr's office would receive calls from around the world looking for comments about Wilson's death last night. The woman was already at her desk helping to answer calls from reporters, commenting about the genius of Wilson's MasterLock and lamenting his passing. She promised that the senator would have a statement later in the day.

Arriving at the office, Orr discovered that the press were not the only ones interested in speaking with him. Detective Robert Howell of the Metropolitan Police phoned the senator's office shortly before nine. The senator respected law officers of any stripe. He took the call. Detective Howell sounded tense.

"Senator, we understand that Mr. Wilson attended a party at your residence last night," the detective said. "Can you tell me anything about what Mr. Wilson did or who he may have spoken with?"

"We had two hundred guests, Detective," Orr said. "I

noticed him chatting with a number of guests, but I did not pay him particular attention. He left alone, around ten-thirty," Orr said.

"You noticed his departure?"

"Only because he came over to thank me," Orr said. "The Brits, like Texans, have manners. To save you time, I do not know what he said to other guests and I did not notice if he was drinking or what he was eating. I presume toxicology reports will tell you that."

"Yes, sir. Do you happen to know if Mr. Wilson arranged to meet anyone after the party?" Howell asked.

"I do not," Orr replied. "The newspaper said that he entertained a woman in his suite and died of an apparent heart attack sometime during the night. Do you have any reason to suspect otherwise?"

"Not at this time," said the detective.

"I'm happy to hear that," the senator said. He did not want a scandal attached to his name.

"But if someone *was* with him and failed to summon medical assistance—perhaps because she was married and feared publicity—that individual might be guilty of involuntary manslaughter."

"I see. Don't you have video from the hotel security cameras?"

"We do, but the woman was extremely careful not to show her face," Howell told him.

"Which makes you even more suspicious," Orr said.

"It does make us interested in her," the detective agreed. "Senator, would it be an imposition to obtain a list of your party guests?"

"It will be an imposition if my guests are harassed by the police or the press," Orr told him.

"We are only interested in locating the woman who was with Mr. Wilson last night. Our questions will not go beyond that."

"In that case, my executive assistant Kendra Peterson will provide you with a list," Orr told him.

"Thank you, sir."

"Is there anything else we can do for you?" Orr asked.

"Nothing that I can think of right now," Detective Howell told him. "I appreciate your cooperation, sir."

"It was my pleasure, Detective."

Orr hung up the phone and sat at his desk made of rare Texas aspen. It was the same desk the revered Sam Houston had used when he served in the Senate. As Orr had expected, the conversation with Detective Howell was direct but respectful. The D.C. police were good that way. They knew that politicians could shape innuendo as if it were plastique. Investigations were handled with exceptional care. Hopefully, William Wilson's death did not become a distraction for the media. The senator had a plan, a vision for the United States, the unveiling of which was one of the worst-kept secrets in Washington. For the past several months Orr had been organizing funds and personnel to establish a new force in American politics. In two days he would acknowledge what many had suspected: that he would be making a serious third-party run for the presidency. He would make the announcement at a press conference at seven A.M. the next morning, when it was six A.M. in Kingsville. That was when he had first announced his intention to run for the United States Senate, with a big Texas sun rising behind him. The press conference would include an invitation for all Americans to join him at the USF Party's first convention, to be held later that week in San Diego. There, they would define the party's platform and name its first candidates for president and vice president of the United States. Orr did not intend to repeat the mistake of other third-party founders. He was not doing this for personal advancement, for revenge, or to appeal to a radical fringe. The USF was here for people who believed that the interests of America came before the needs of partisans.

Orr looked out the window at the Capitol. It was a bright day, and the 288-foot-high dome gleamed white against a cloudless sky. The senator still felt humbled to see it, to be part of an unbroken chain of leaders dating from the Founding Fathers and the Continental Congress in Philadelphia. The dome was a daily, iconic reminder to him of why he had come to Washington: to serve the electorate fearlessly. To uphold the Constitution with his energy, his heart, and his judgment. If he did that successfully, he would continue to serve here. If he failed, he would go back to ranching.

Either way, Don Orr won.

Either way, he was still an American.

FIVE

Washington, D.C.
Monday, 8:24 A.M.

When is a postal carrier not a postal carrier? That was what Ed March had asked his old friend Darrell McCaskey to help him find out.

The two men had been college roommates at the University of Miami. While McCaskey was recruited by the FBI, March was asked to become a police officer with the U.S. Postal Service. For over ten years, March's beat had been child pornography. Then the Internet virtually ended that use of the mails. He was shifted to Homeland Security activities where most of his time was spent doing the ABCs—alien background checks—of individuals who regularly sent packages to nations that sponsored terrorism. March was currently involved in a stakeout involving a postal carrier who was suspected of helping a certain individual bypass the ABC system by collecting packages from a specific drop box and bringing them directly to the overseas pouches. These were believed to contain materials that could not be sent via E-mail attachments: stolen documents, currency, and possibly computer components.

Right now, March did not want the mailer. He wanted the carrier so he could confiscate the truck before the package could be off-loaded. If the address on the parcel inside was the same that had been found in a terrorist hut in Gunong Tahan, the carrier would be persuaded to turn future packages over to the CIA before they were sent overseas.

March had backup a block away in an unmarked car, but he needed McCaskey to tell him whether he was being watched while he watched the mailbox and carrier. March had been in this location for several days, waiting for another drop-off. It was not uncommon for spies and terrorists to work in partnership with observers. These persons kept a careful eye on nationals in their employ. As often as not, nationals turned out to be double agents. Especially when they had been found out.

Posing as a flag vendor with a small white cart, March was standing on the corner of Constitution Avenue. Mailboxes were potential receptacles for bombs, and this was one of the few locations the USPS had left operational. The postal service police believed that the mailer came over the Potomac from Arlington and dropped it off on his way to work at the Embassy of Malaysia on Massachusetts Avenue. That was ascertained by following the staff members home and seeing who passed this way. There were two potential targets.

One of them had mailed a package at the box forty minutes earlier.

McCaskey was sitting cross-legged on a small bench closer to the Lincoln Memorial. Early-morning tourists and joggers moved by in all directions. McCaskey noticed them all to see if any came by again. That could mean they were watching the mailbox, looking for enemy recon. McCaskey also watched for the glint of binoculars or anyone who had a good eye line with the box.

In McCaskey's hand was one of the greatest surveillance props ever invented: the cell phone. A user had to concentrate in order to hear, so passers-by assumed the caller did not see them. Pickpockets loved cell phones for that reason. McCaskey missed nothing, even as he pretended to talk to his wife, Maria. In fact, former Interpol agent Maria Corneja-McCaskey was sitting beside him on the bench. That irony was not lost on either of them. Mc-

Caskey had always feared that Maria was too wedded to intelligence work to have time for a marriage. That was the problem with McCaskey's first marriage. He had married a fellow FBI agent, Bonnie Edwards, and had three kids with her. Bonnie quit to be a full-time mother, and McCaskey took a promotion to unit chief in Dallas to pick up the financial slack. A subsequent promotion took him to D.C., which was good for McCaskey but not for the family. In the end, after eight years of marriage, the McCaskeys agreed to a divorce. The children visited their father during school vacations, and McCaskey went to see them whenever he could get away. They lived outside of Dallas, where Bonnie had married an oil executive with three kids. She seemed to like her very Brady life.

The dueling careers had come between McCaskey and Maria once, when they first met in her native Spain. They had reconnected when McCaskey was on a mission in Madrid. Maria had agreed to give it up and move to Washington.

Now his beautiful, dark-haired wife was helping him with a stakeout. She woke up smirking. Though Maria was in character now, pretending to be an artist sketching the Memorial in pastel, the bemused look was still there.

"Honey, I am so incredibly bad at having these fake conversations," he said into the deactivated phone. "Pausing and pretending to listen to someone." He paused and pretended to listen. "Then laughing disarmingly." He chuckled. "I'd rather be in a firefight."

"You may have an opportunity," Maria said from the side of her mouth. "Three o'clock, nanny with a stroller."

McCaskey glanced over as the young woman passed. She had Asian features. She was dressed in a Georgetown University sweatshirt and jeans and was absently rocking a charcoal-colored Maclaren stroller with a hood.

"I don't think so," McCaskey said.

"Darrell, there's no baby in the stroller," Maria said.

She put the ivory-colored chalk back in the wooden carrying case.

"I know," he replied, still pretending to talk in the phone. "There's a shopping bag in the stroller. It's probably got everything she owns. Look at the laces of her Adidas. Broken and knotted, hole on one side. The foam handle of the stroller is torn. It was probably discarded. She's homeless."

"Or pretending to be," Maria said as she selected a navy blue stick to lay in shadows.

"It's possible," McCaskey agreed. He looked toward the lawn beyond the path. "I'm more concerned about the guy sitting on the grass with the laptop."

"The man in the windbreaker?"

"Yes."

"Why?" Maria asked. "His back is to the mailbox."

"But the web cam is not," McCaskey said. "He could be teleconferencing, or he could be watching the mailbox."

Just then the mail carrier pulled up in his small local-haul truck. A lanky, blond-haired young man emerged carrying a white plastic bin and stepped over to the mailbox. McCaskey continued to talk on the phone as March moved his cart so he was closer to the mail truck. The carrier did not seem to notice. He knelt, opened the front panel with a key from the ring on his belt, and slowly scooped the contents into the container. He appeared to be looking for something. When he found it, he swept the rest of the mail in quickly and shut the box. Evidently, that was all March needed. He stepped from his cart and intercepted the mail carrier. McCaskey saw March show the carrier his badge, but he could not hear what was being said. The carrier made a disbelieving, then angry face and shook his head. March was insistent as he got on his cell phone and made a call. He was summoning his backup.

The mail carrier moved toward the truck, still holding the bin. March grabbed his arm and said something.

"Hey, will someone call a cop!" the carrier shouted.

The man with the laptop turned. So did the homeless woman. The two of them started to rise.

"Are both of them in on this?" Maria said.

"I don't know," her husband said. "Stay here." He got up and walked toward them. He was still holding the phone to his ear.

The man with the laptop had folded it away, slipped it into a shoulder bag, and also walked toward the mail truck. The woman was quickly pushing her stroller toward March. Other people stopped and watched from a distance.

The carrier attempted to pull his arm free. He yanked harder than March's grip required, upending both the carrier and the bin. The woman with the stroller started running to where mail had been strewn across the street. McCaskey also rushed over. He got there first and, crouching, began pulling mail toward him. Most of it was picture postcards along with a handful of letters. He was looking for an oversized envelope or small parcel with a South Pacific or Far Eastern address. He found one, a fat manila envelope with a Kuala Lumpur address. McCaskey pulled over other letters so this one did not seem to be all that interested him. Maria, sitting close by, was watching the homeless woman.

The mail carrier hurried over. "Thank you, sir. I'll take those," he said, reaching for the letters.

"And I'll take those," March said as he leaned over the mail carrier and wrapped a thick hand around his key ring. He flipped the small metal latch and pulled it free. The ignition key to the truck was on the ring.

McCaskey released the mail. He stood and watched as the carrier put them back in the bin. Then the young man went to collect the rest of the mail. The homeless woman was on her hands and knees, also gathering pieces. The carrier went to take them from her and, with a snarl, she slapped over the bin and its contents. The package bound for Malaysia went spinning back onto the street. The woman scrambled after it. The mail carrier did not go after her.

McCaskey did.

"Hold on!" McCaskey yelled after her.

The man with the laptop was closer. He intercepted the woman as she tried to get away. March did not see him. He was busy waving over a blue sedan. There was a brief struggle, but the man with the laptop got the mail. The woman sped away as McCaskey arrived.

The large envelope was in the man's hand, folded in half. "I've got it all," he said to the mail carrier.

"Thanks. I'll take it," March said, walking over.

"Glad I could help," the man with the laptop said. Then he turned and walked away.

McCaskey had an uneasy sense about this. He waited anxiously while March flipped through the few pieces of mail. He reached the envelope addressed to Malaysia. He held it so McCaskey could see. It had been torn open.

"Shit," McCaskey said.

The carrier was no longer a problem. One of the plainclothes officers had him in custody and was taking him to their car. They had to stop the man with the laptop and the homeless woman.

McCaskey and March exchanged looks. March set out after the man with the laptop. The other plainclothesman followed when the carrier was secure in the sedan. McCaskey turned toward the field that stretched to the Lincoln Memorial. The homeless woman was at the edge of the lawn, digging around in her stroller. If she were stowing the contents of the envelope, they would have a problem. They had no right to search her belongings. If she had a weapon, they could have an even bigger problem. There were hundreds of potential hostages out here.

The former FBI agent walked quickly toward the woman. He still had his cell phone. He pretended to be deep in conversation and walked into the woman. Her stroller was upended, and the contents spilled onto the grass.

"I'm so sorry!" McCaskey said, tucking the cell phone in his pocket as he bent to help retrieve her belongings. Among the clothes and a water bottle were passports from different nations.

"Stay away!" the woman shouted, pushing him back.

McCaskey did not have to yield. Not anymore. He moved to confiscate the evidence of either theft or passport forgery.

With a cry of rage, the woman drew a double-bladed knife from a sheath on her forearm. The leather hilt was in the center with a serrated blade on either side. McCaskey backed away, and she approached him, her legs wide as she slashed left and right. They were not the wild moves of a homeless woman but the centered attack of a trained fighter.

The former FBI agent did not carry a handgun. Only Op-Center field agents were issued firearms, and the shotgun he kept at home for intruders would not be appropriate in a situation like this. He watched as she cut from left to right and back in a dead-horizontal line waist-high. He had to get close to the hand with the knife and do a forearm break. That meant cupping her elbow in the palm of one hand and pushing up and placing another hand on the inside of her wrist and pushing down. The wrist strike would numb her forearm and cause her to drop the knife. The trick was not to get stabbed in the process.

McCaskey kept his hands level with the slashing blade. He did not blink. That had been part of his training. He had to wait for her to do so, then he would—

The homeless woman suddenly flew to her left as a wooden case of pastels smacked into the side of her head. The knife dropped as the woman fell to her knees. Maria was still holding the handle of the box tightly. She brought it back for a second blow, driving the brass hinges into the back of the homeless woman's head. She fell forward on the lawn and landed on her face.

"I have always felt that aikido works better in the dojo than in the field," Maria said.

"Not everyone carries a combat-ready art box," McCaskey said.

The homeless woman's eyes were shut. McCaskey put an index finger under her nose to make sure she was still breathing. Then he retrieved the knife and passports and motioned for the tourists to move away. Security officers from the Lincoln Memorial were running over.

Maria picked up her art kit. "I knew she was bad when she picked up the letters," she said.

"Why?"

"Homeless women don't use apricot-scented shampoo. That's why I watched you instead of Ed."

"I appreciate that, hon," McCaskey said. He looked back toward the street. The plainclothesman was escorting the man with the laptop toward the sedan. The man was complaining loudly. March was walking toward the lawn. When he arrived, McCaskey handed him the passports and knife. March called his dispatcher and asked for emergency medical technicians to care for the woman.

"These are impressive," the postal officer said. "Thanks. Both of you."

"Glad we could help. What have you got on him?" McCaskey asked, nodding toward the man with the laptop.

"He didn't stop when we asked him to," March said.

"Is that a crime?" Maria asked.

"No. I've got a feeling he's hiding something," March said. "I want to have a look at the computer."

"You are permitted to look at his computer files because of a feeling?" Maria asked.

"No," March said. "We are permitted access to his computer under Section 217 of the USA Patriot Act. Suspected computer transgression, possible web cam surveillance of federal officers near a national monument is a crime. No court order required to investigate."

"He may not have known you people were federal officers," McCaskey pointed out.

"Perhaps," March said. "But we have reasonable cause for suspicion. He handled the parcel from the embassy, and he did not stop when we asked him to, repeatedly. If he's innocent, it's a minor inconvenience, and we'll apologize. If he's guilty, we may save lives."

McCaskey made a face as the security officers from the Memorial arrived. March showed them his badge, then asked them to watch the woman. He said an ambulance would be arriving in just a few minutes.

"Look, I've got to put this baby to bed," March said. He offered his hand to McCaskey and Maria in turn. "I can't thank you enough. If you ever need anything, just shout."

"I will," McCaskey said.

Op-Center's top cop felt as though he should say something more on the man's behalf but decided against it. Ed March had a point. He also had the law on his side. McCaskey himself had thought the man might be involved in this. That, too, had been a feeling. Sometimes, lawmen had to act on that.

McCaskey had parked on C Street. He walked back with Maria. His wife was scowling and complained that this was what Spain was like under Franco.

"If everyone *El Caudillo* arrested had actually been guilty of crimes, Spain would have been a nation of felons," she said.

"The situations are not the same," McCaskey said. "Franco was a tyrant. Ed is a good officer trying to protect American lives."

"This is how good officers become tyrants," she replied.

"Not always," he said with more hope than conviction.

The American system was not perfect, but as they drove

to Op-Center, McCaskey took comfort in a slogan that had been written on the blackboard of a Community Outreach Theory class he once took at the FBI Academy in Quantico. It was a reassuring quote from Jefferson: "The boisterous sea of liberty is never without a wave."

SIX

Washington, D.C.
Monday, 9:02 A.M.

Mike Rodgers pulled into the Op-Center parking lot moments after Darrell McCaskey arrived. Their reserved parking spots were side by side, and McCaskey waited while Rodgers got out. The spots were numbered rather than named. If security were ever compromised and someone rigged a car to explode, the assassin would have to know which vehicle he wanted. That was why Rodgers had started leasing cars every six months instead of buying them. He had made a number of powerful enemies abroad with his Striker assaults. The general was not paranoid, but Bob Herbert once told him that Washington, D.C., had over five hundred freelance "street potatoes," as they were called. Individuals who watched the comings and goings of government officials and reported the information to foreign governments. That data could be used for everything from blackmail to murder. Changing cars, like alternating the routes Rodgers took to work, was just good sense. Of course, the general half-expected to open the newspaper one morning and read about some poor joker with his last car getting blown up in a driveway or sniped at in a shopping mall. Then again, Rodgers always checked the provenance of his vehicle. He did not want to end up with a car that had been rented by an embassy employee or drug dealer who was someone else's target.

"Did we both sleep in?" Rodgers asked.

"Nah," McCaskey said. "Maria and I were on a stakeout for a friend with the postal service."

"Some careless spy using the same drop box more than once?" Rodgers asked.

"Sort of. He was passing material to the carrier to bypass security inspections," McCaskey said.

Our own people betraying us, Rodgers thought. Whenever he heard something like that, the general felt every civilized inhibition slide away. He would have no trouble executing someone to whom a payday mattered more than his country. "Did you get them?"

McCaskey nodded. "Maria had the spook spotted from the start. That lady's intuition is amazing."

"Jealous?" Rodgers joked.

"No. Proud. I went after a guy who was web camming the Lincoln Memorial. He turned out to be undercover with Homeland Security. I swear, we've got more cops here than gangsters."

"There are still plenty of bad guys to round up," Rodgers said as they entered the building.

"I know," McCaskey said. "But when counter espionage units start taking friendly fire, it's time to rethink our overall policy. We should be doing more of what you're doing, training personnel to operate abroad and targeting ETs."

ETs were not just aliens, they were exported terrorists. When Striker had been replaced by a human intelligence unit, the mandate was to infiltrate and undermine foreign operations before they became a real threat.

Rodgers did not disagree. But the intelligence community had spent decades relying on increasingly sophisticated ELINT—electronic intelligence—such as intercepted phone and E-mail messages, spy satellites, and unmanned drones. Human intelligence was deemed too risky and unreliable. Foreign nationals who could not be hired outright had to be blackmailed into cooperating. That was costly and time consuming and required a sizable support system.

Even then, the nationals could not always be trusted. Ramping up HUMINT operations also took time and ingenuity. In the interim, United States intelligence operations had assumed a posture similar to the Soviet approach of defending the homeland during World War II. They threw every available body at the problem in the hope of stopping it.

The men emerged from the elevator and went in separate directions along the oval corridor. As deputy director, Rodgers's office was located next to that of Paul Hood in the so-called executive wing. The only other office in that section was that of attorney Lowell Coffey III. McCaskey, intelligence chief Bob Herbert, computer expert Matt Stoll, psychologist Liz Gordon, and political liaison Ron Plummer were in the operations corridor. That was where all the real work was done, according to Herbert.

When Rodgers passed Hood's office, Bugs Benet asked the general if he had a minute.

"Sure," Rodgers said. "What's up?"

"The chief wanted to talk to you," Bugs replied.

"All right. When?" Rodgers asked. Hood's door was rarely closed. It was closed now.

"He said you should go in when you got here," Bugs told him.

"Thanks," Rodgers said. He walked past Bugs's cubicle and knocked on Hood's door.

"It's open," Hood said.

Rodgers went in.

"Good morning," Hood said.

"Morning," Rodgers said.

Hood rose from behind his desk and gestured toward a leather sofa set against the inside wall. Rodgers walked over and sat. Hood shut the door, then joined Rodgers. His expression was curiously neutral. Hood was a diplomat, but he was usually open and empathetic. That helped people trust him, and that made him effective.

"Mind if I help myself to coffee?" Rodgers asked.

"No, of course not, Mike," Hood said. "Sorry I didn't offer. I've been preoccupied."

"I can tell," Rodgers said. He went to the coffeemaker on a small, triangular, teakwood corner table. "Want any?"

"No thanks. I've already had enough to float a horseshoe," Hood told him.

"What's going on?" Rodgers asked as he poured.

"I spoke with Senator Debenport this morning," Hood said. "He wants me to make deep cuts."

"More than the four percent we just gave him?"

"Much more," Hood told him. "Five times more."

"That's ridiculous," Rodgers said. He returned with his mug and took a sip. "You don't trim that kind of money. You amputate."

"I know," Hood said.

"How far from that figure can you move him?"

"He's not going to yield a dime," Hood said.

"Balls. Everything is negotiable."

"Not when you're a politician in the public eye," Hood said.

"I guess you would know."

"I do," Hood said. "People want to feel secure, and CIOC wants to give that to them in as showy a way as possible. That is where the money is needed."

Rodgers was starting to get a very uneasy feeling about the direction of this conversation. Hood was not asking questions; he was making statements, as though he were building a case.

"Anything that has a redundancy somewhere else in the intelligence system has to go," Hood went on.

"My field unit," Rodgers said.

"Yes, Mike."

There was something in Hood's voice that said he was not finished.

"And me?" Rodgers asked.

"They want me to merge the political office and deputy director's post," Hood told him.

"I see." Rodgers took a short swallow of black coffee. Then another. "Ron Plummer is more qualified for my position than I am for his," he said. "When do you want me to clear out?"

"Mike, we need to talk about this—"

"Talk to Liz Gordon. That's what she's here for."

"No, you and I need to work this out," Hood said. "I don't want our friendship to end."

The sentiment made Rodgers squirm. He was not sure why. "Look, don't worry about it. I'm probably overdue for a change. The army will reassign me. Or maybe I'll do something else."

"Maybe we can outsource some of our intel or recon activities, work with you on scenarios for the crisis sims," Hood said.

"I'd rather look at other options," Rodgers replied.

"All right. But the offer stands."

"Was there an offer?" Rodgers asked. "I heard a 'maybe.' "

"It was an offer to try to find projects—"

"Busywork, you mean," Rodgers said.

"No," Hood replied. "Assignments for a uniquely skilled intelligence professional."

Rodgers took a swallow of coffee and rose. He did not want to talk to Paul Hood right now. He had no doubt Hood fought to keep him. Perhaps he had even threatened to resign. But in the end, Hood chose to stay on and confront his "friend" with hard facts and cold efficiency. "When does the CIOC want me out of here?"

"Mike, no one *wants* you out of here," Hood said. "If they did, we would have done this when Striker was officially disbanded."

"Right," Rodgers said. "It's the position that's being eliminated not the man. I'd like to resign rather than being downsized. That has a little more dignity."

"Of course," Hood said.

"How long will Plummer need to take my post?"

"Two weeks?" Hood guessed.

"Fine," Rodgers said and turned to go.

"Mike—"

"I'm okay," Rodgers said. "Really."

"I was going to say that it has been a privilege working with you."

Rodgers stopped. *Screw this*, he thought. He was a soldier, not a diplomat. He turned back. "Would it be a privilege to resign with me?" he asked.

"If I thought that would have changed Debenport's mind, I would have done it," Hood told him.

"As a maneuver," Rodgers said. "A tactic. What about standing shoulder-to-shoulder as a point of honor?"

"To me, falling on my sword would be vanity, not honor," Hood said. "It would be an act of surrender."

"Backing a friend and coworker?"

"In this case, yes," Hood said.

"Jesus," Rodgers said. "I'm glad I didn't have guys like you watching my ass in 'Nam. I'd be under a pile of rocks somewhere."

"This isn't combat, Mike. It's politics. People fight with words and access. They don't die. They get marginalized, they get recycled, they regroup. It's the nature of the beast. Some people do it for ego, and some do it for principle. I took this job to serve the people of the United States. That is sacred to me. I won't give it up to make a dramatic statement. One that won't change a thing."

"Is that how you view loyalty, Paul? As a dramatic statement? Was I just being dramatic when I helped save your daughter in the UN takeover?"

"That's not fair," Hood said. "We've been in the line of

fire for people we don't even know. We agreed to do that when we went to work here. We agreed to protect our nation and its interests."

"I don't need the sermon," Rodgers said. "I've served the country for my entire adult life."

"I know, which is why you should understand what it means to work for a government agency," Hood said. "Op-Center has this much in common with the military. We are impacted by political trends and public whim. Whoever sits in this office has to work with whatever he is given. And with whatever is taken from him."

Rodgers shook his head. "That's what the Vichy collaborators did when they capitulated to the German invaders."

Hood's expression was no longer neutral. He winced, as though he had taken an uppercut square in the chin.

"I'm sorry," Rodgers said. "I did not mean to imply that you're a coward."

"I know," Hood said.

An uncomfortable quiet settled upon the room. Hood stood. He walked toward Rodgers and offered his hand. The general accepted it. There was surprising warmth in Hood's handshake.

"If you need anything, let me know," Hood said. "Or you can talk to Bob, if you prefer."

"I'll talk to you," Rodgers said.

"Good." Hood held on to Rodgers's hand. "Mike, I need you to believe something. This place cost me my family. If it costs me your friendship, I'm going to have to live with that. If it costs me your respect, I'm going to have to live with that, too. But I want you to know that leaving here would have been easier than what I just did. You talked about loyalty. I did what I believe was right for Op-Center, not what was convenient or comfortable or even best for me."

"I believe you, Paul," Rodgers said. "I just don't agree with you."

"Fair enough," Hood said. "But you need to know this,

too. If there were a resistance movement fighting the CIOC, I would join it."

"We can start one," Rodgers said. "I'll have some free time."

"I doubt that," Hood said.

"We'll see," Rodgers said and withdrew his hand. He felt much better having taken a swing at Hood's piety. He saw the man's point, but he still did not agree with it. Friends stood by friends. Period.

Rodgers left and went to his own office. Or rather, Ron Plummer's office. He already felt uncomfortable here, like a noncom cleaning out the locker of a dead soldier. He forced himself to look beyond this, to the meeting with Senator Orr and whatever lay ahead.

A little anarchy, Rodgers hoped.

He was in the mood.

SEVEN

Washington, D.C.
Monday, 9:27 A.M.

Hood was about to buzz Ron Plummer when his outside line beeped. He glanced at the Caller ID. It was his former wife. He did not feel like talking to her now. The conversations were usually difficult. Sharon was still bitter because he had not been around very much since they moved to Washington. Hood was angry because she had not supported the work he was doing at Op-Center. But none of that mattered. The call could be about the kids.

"Good morning, Sharon," Hood said when he picked up the phone. He tried to sound pleasant.

"Hi, Paul. Do you have a minute?"

"Sure," he said. Sharon sounded unusually relaxed.

"I need a favor," she said. "You met my friend Jim Hunt."

"The caterer."

"The home party restaurateur, yes," she said.

Hunt was someone Sharon had known for years, dating back to when she had her own cooking show. They used to have an occasional lunch together. Now the kids told him they were having frequent dinners together.

"His son Franklin will be studying poli-sci at Georgetown in the fall," Sharon went on. "The school will give him college credit if he interns in a political institution over the summer. Is there anything he might be able to do at Op-Center? He's a very sharp young man, Paul."

Hood's former wife, who had always resented the hours

he spent at Op-Center, was asking him to help the son of her boyfriend get an internship there. And she happened to make her request on a day when Hood had been ordered to lay people off. Bob Herbert once said that CIA stands for Convergent Incongruities Abound. That certainly applied here.

"Does he have any particular interests?" Hood asked. He did not really care, but he needed to think for a moment. Did he really want to do this?

"He is a student of languages and maps," she said. "He speaks French and is learning Japanese. In fact, he's been teaching Harleigh basic Japanese grammar. But he would be happy to work anywhere, in any capacity."

"I'll ask around," Hood told her. He would, he decided, though Op-Center rarely used interns, and only then as favors to influential members of Congress. "I just want you to know we had some major cutbacks today. So it may be difficult to place him."

"He wouldn't require compensation."

"I understand," Hood said. "What I mean is that people are going to be preoccupied."

"Okay," Sharon said. By the way she dragged out the second syllable Hood could tell she was not happy with that answer. "Can I have a time frame? If Frankie can't intern with you, he'll have to look into other places."

"Give me a day or two to see how the new landscape looks."

"A day would be good," Sharon said. "That will give us time to explore other options. Thanks."

She did not ask about the layoffs. To her, Op-Center was The Enemy. It had been the rival for her husband's affection. Now it was like an organ donor, dead except for whatever his former wife needed from it. Sharon had also said "us" not "Jim." Hood was a little jealous, not because Sharon had found someone but because she was involved in Jim's life. She was engaged in a way she had never been with Hood's work, she was simpatico. Even the kids were hitting it off. He should have been glad for them all, but he was not.

They chatted a little about the kids. Sharon said that Harleigh seemed to be doing better and had actually picked up the violin again. Alexander was playing too many computer games, listening to too much rap, and not paying enough attention to his grades. Hood said he would stop by and have a talk with him Tuesday or Wednesday. Sharon said Tuesday would be fine, that she was helping Jim on a catering job that night. Then she hung up.

Hood actually envied Sharon. She had an old friend to go to, someone who had known her even longer than Hood. For all he knew, Jim Hunt may have gotten divorced because he learned that Sharon was free.

Hood sat back and listened to the quiet. A decibel lower, and it would be death. Rodgers probably had not spoken to anyone about what happened, but intelligence people knew when the geometry of a room had changed. That was their job.

Hood wished he had someone to talk to. He had never felt more alone than he did at this moment. And he suspected that there were going to be rough hours ahead, when Lowell Coffey and Darrell McCaskey and especially Bob Herbert found out about the cutbacks. And the loss of Mike Rodgers.

Hood had never been one for self-pity. Adults made choices and lived with the consequences. But he had never been cut off from a support system.

That was how I ended up marrying Sharon, he reminded himself. Nancy Jo had left him, and he married the first woman who made him forget the hurt. Unfortunately, Sharon did not fill the void.

He wanted to talk to someone. Not a professional but a friend.

Hood considered calling Ann Farris. The former Op-

Center press liaison had pursued Hood for years. Hood was married while Ann worked there, and after the divorce, there was no danger, no edge to the relationship. There was only Ann's need. Hood did not care for the divorced young mother enough to be with her, which was why he did not call her now. It would not be fair to Ann.

He thought about calling Daphne Connors. However, several dates with the public relations queen had told him they could never be more than friends. In every restaurant they went to, at the movies, at each bar they visited, Daphne always had one ear on the conversation taking place beside or behind her. She never stopped looking for new accounts or useful intelligence to service existing clients. Hood may be a workaholic, but Op-Center did not come with him when he left the office.

Hood was tempted to call Sergei Orlov, head of the Russian Op-Center in Saint Petersburg. The men had been good friends since working together to thwart the coup against the Kremlin. But Sergei was not the kind of man you talked to over the phone. He was the kind of man you sat down with over a huge bowl of uha—fish soup—and vodka shots taken from twenty-five-gram glasses.

Okay, Hood thought. *There's still a lot of work to do.*

Unable to think of anyone he particularly wanted to call, Hood placed the call that had to be made. He asked Ron Plummer to come and see him. Plummer was a team player. He would feel uneasy about Rodgers's resignation, but he would assume whatever responsibilities Paul Hood asked.

As he punched in Plummer's extension, Hood found himself suddenly feeling very insecure about his own future. It was in the nature of men to want to build things, not oversee their downsizing. Hood had always envisioned Op-Center as an increasingly vital part of the intelligence and crisis management community. What happened today was not a move in that direction. It was not about making Op-

Center more streamlined, about reducing bureaucracy and internal redundancies. The NCMC was being gutted. Hood would still have a great deal of work to do, but how important would that work be? Where would it take Op-Center? Where would it take Paul Hood personally?

"That's up to you, isn't it?" he asked himself aloud, to chase away the silence.

Hood asked Plummer to come in. He would deal with the situation one minute at a time. After all, this was what Op-Center was about.

Crisis management.

EIGHT

Las Vegas, Nevada
Monday, 7:43 A.M.

The five-story, white-brick Atlantica was one of the older, less flashy hotels on the southern end of the Strip. There were no dancing fountains, no caged jungle creatures, no landmarks re-created half-scale. When the hotel opened thirty-seven years before, it was, as the flashing red neon sign in the window announced, *Deluxe!* Now it was simply convenient, located close to all the major casinos.

The Atlantica was also relatively inexpensive. Tourists came here looking for a place to drop their stuff before heading to the larger hotels to gamble or see shows. As a result, there were a lot of tourists and constant activity. It was easy to be anonymous here. That appealed to Tom "Melter" Mandor.

The thirty-seven-year-old drove his white Toyota van to the third level of the parking structure. He pulled into a space overlooking the hotel, then undid the seat belt, lit a hand-rolled cigarette, and waited for Richmond. He tapped his fingers on the steering wheel. It was idle tapping but not impatient. Mandor was never in a hurry. During the twelve years he had spent working as an oil rig roughneck, Mandor had learned to take things easy. All the workers had. Otherwise, the downtime would have driven them mad, and the bored, isolated oilmen would have torn each other apart. It was during his three years on the Alaskan North Slope that Mandor had met Michael Wayne Richmond, who drove an oil truck for the Trans-Eastern Shipping Company. He shuttled crude oil to ships that went to South Korea and Japan. That was where the men had come up with the business plan for their new line of work.

Richmond's vintage Thunderbird pulled up fifteen minutes later. The five-foot-ten Mandor left the van and went down the concrete stairs. This was his partner's contact, and he had not wanted to go in without him.

It was already hot, over eighty-five desert-dry degrees. Even though it was cool and dark when he had left his home on the northwestern shores of Lake Mead, he was glad he had worn Bermuda shorts and a white T-shirt.

Las Vegas was not an early rising city, but the man they had come to see was from Maryland. He was still on East Coast time. There was no one in the small casino of the Atlantica. Mandor waited at the entrance, looking at the slot machines as though he were trying to decide whether to play. There was a large, convex mirror in an overhead corner. It allowed the people at the hotel desk to see into the casino. Mandor used it to watch the lobby. The tall, powerfully built Richmond was on the house phone, beside the small bank of elevators. When he hung up, Mandor walked over.

The men did not acknowledge one another. There were security cameras in the lobby, by the casino. They walked to the elevators, and Richmond touched the button. When the door opened, both men stepped in. Richmond pushed the button for the fifth floor. When they arrived, he turned left. Mandor went right. There was a security camera inside the elevator as well. There were no security cameras in the fifth-floor hallway. When the door shut, Mandor turned and followed Richmond.

"How was the drive?" the bald-headed Richmond asked over his shoulder.

"Sweet," Mandor replied as he caught up to his partner.

He gave him a pat on the shoulder. Mandor liked his old friend, and he respected him. "There was no traffic at this hour."

"Yeah," Richmond said. "I made it from Oceanside in four hours flat."

Richmond lived in a small cabin high in the Coastal Range of Southern California. He built the place himself four years ago. After years of freezing his ass in Chicago—where he was one of five kids raised by a single mother in a one-bedroom walk-up on the South Side—then as a driver in Alaska, Richmond wanted to live in consistently warm sunshine. That had been Mandor's desire, too, though he had always wanted to be on the water.

Richmond did not know Eric Stone, the gentleman who had contacted them. All Stone said was that they had been recommended by Pete at the oil company. Peter Farmer was the foreman on the last rig where Mandor had worked. Richmond had recorded the conversation, and let Stone know it. Richmond made Stone state that he was not a government agent and this was not a sting.

The men knew what this was not. They did not know what it was. Richmond had called Pete to make sure Stone was legitimate. Pete said he was, though he did not know what the man needed.

They stopped in front of room 515, and Richmond knocked. Mandor pushed his shoulder-length salt-and-pepper hair behind his neck. He did not like to wear it in a ponytail. He did not like restraints of any kind. That was how he ended up in the oil business. Back home in Toledo, Ohio, when he was twenty, he had beaten up Noel Lynch's former boyfriend when he found them together. Rather than face charges and possible jail time, he fled to Mexico and then to Venezuela, where he was hired to work on an offshore rig. He loved the challenge. He actually enjoyed facing the battering winds, the savage cold, the endless hard labor. When that got routine, he traveled to Alaska.

When that ceased to challenge him, he and Richmond came up with their new gig. One that had no overhead, was advertised by word of mouth, and was not taxed. They provided muscle for anyone who needed it.

The men had started doing that in Alaska. When environmentalists tried to block the tanker trucks or impede access to the rigs, the two men would cart the organizer away—or his wife, if she had come with him—and persuade them to take their grievances somewhere else. Roughing them up cost less than attorneys and was quicker and more effective. It also circumvented the police, whose arrests merely delayed the protests but did not eliminate them.

The work proved to be lucrative and something more. While Mandor was working in Punta Cardon, he learned that Noel had married the stupid jock he'd taken apart. Probably because she felt sorry for a guy who now had only one functioning eye. Each time Mandor hit someone, he was smacking that swaggering linebacker. Some people would call that sociopathic. To Mandor, it was cathartic. He felt that if everyone enjoyed their work as much as he did, the world would be a better place.

The door opened, and a short, well-dressed man stood inside. He was in his late twenties or early thirties, with straw-colored hair and a baby face.

"Mr. Stone?" Richmond said.

"Yes. You are Mr. Richmond?"

Richmond nodded. Stone looked at Mandor.

"Mr. Mandor?"

"Yeah," Mandor said. He could not say "*Yes sir*" to this kid.

"Come in," Stone said as he stepped aside.

Richmond entered first. "So how do you know Pete?" he asked as he stepped into the small foyer.

Mandor walked in, and Stone shut the door behind him. The room was medium-sized, with a king-size bed, a kitchenette, and a small dining area. The drapes were drawn, and all the lights were on.

"Before I answer, would you mind if I did a Raw scan?" Stone asked.

"What's that?" Richmond asked.

"A check for radio waves," Stone said. "I want to make sure you're not broadcasting to someone on the outside."

"Fair enough," Richmond said.

Mandor shrugged.

Stone went to the luggage stand at the foot of the made bed. He removed a device that looked like a small flashlight with an earplug. He put the plug in his ear and slowly shone a cone of pale yellow light down each man in turn. He seemed satisfied with the results.

"Would either of you care for something?" Stone asked. "A beverage?"

"I'm okay," Richmond said.

"Me, too," Mandor told him.

"Tell me about Pete," Richmond went on.

"Peter is an old friend of my employer." Stone drew a cell phone from the inside left pocket of his tailored black blazer. "You may phone Peter if you wish. He will vouch for us."

"I already spoke to him," Richmond said. "He told me you were okay, but he did not tell me who you work for. Or what you want."

"Or what it pays," Mandor added. That was the only thing he cared about. If the price was right, he would pretty much do anything for anyone.

Stone sat in one of two wicker chairs beside a small dining area table. He invited the other men to sit. Richmond took the other chair. Mandor perched on the edge of the bed.

"I work for a gentleman who is an intelligence officer and political activist who has a great many supporters in the international business sector," Stone said. "Peter

Farmer is one of those men. When the time comes to tell you more, you will be very proud to be a part of what we are doing."

"Will we?" Richmond said laconically.

"That's assuming we decide to become a part of this," Mandor said. He did not know what Richmond was thinking, but Mandor did not agree to anything blindly. "You want us to trust you, but you're not trusting us."

"An employer's prerogative," Stone said.

"We're not employees yet," Mandor said.

"True," Stone said. "Let's see if we can remedy that."

Stone was smooth, probably a lawyer. Mandor did not like him. The young man smiled confidently as he slipped a slender hand into his shirt pocket. He withdrew a small manila envelope and placed it on the table. The package clanged lightly.

"There are two keys inside," Stone said. "One of them operates a charcoal gray Dodge van on the bottom floor of the parking structure. The van is in your name, Mr. Richmond. The second key opens a safe-deposit box at the Las Vegas International Trust and Fund Company on Flamingo Avenue. Inside the box is twenty-five thousand dollars in cash. That is half the payment you will receive for what will be three days' work. Would you like to hear more?"

Richmond and Mandor looked at the envelope and then at each other.

"Why the van?" Richmond asked.

"The windows are dark and bulletproof," Stone said.

"Go on, Mr. Stone," Richmond said.

"You have a cabin in the mountains in Fullbrook, Mr. Richmond," Stone said. "There are no neighbors for acres in all directions."

"Right. People come up to look at the view from the ridge some nights, but not often."

"Can they see your place from there?" Stone asked.

"Not at all."

"Good. In two days, at six in the morning, you will receive a call there," Stone said. "You will be asked to drive somewhere, pick something up, and return to your cabin. You will wait there until you are told to drive somewhere else. When that is finished, your work is finished."

"That's it?" Richmond said.

"More or less. For you." Stone looked at Mandor. "You will be needed in San Diego. You'll be working security detail. You won't need to do anything except sit, most of the time."

"That is still pretty vague, Mr. Stone," Mandor remarked.

"We've only just met."

"So all we get is a good night kiss," Richmond joked.

"Yeah," Mandor laughed. "I'm assuming it's outside the law, this thing we'll be doing."

"Laws are sometimes inadequate to deal with reality," Stone said.

"They still put your ass in jail for breaking them," Mandor said. "Mr. Stone, twenty-five grand apiece is real good money, I'll give you that. And I appreciate careful security measures. But secrecy bothers me. A lot."

"Then you have the option of walking away," Stone said.

"Both of us?" Richmond asked. "Because I'm okay with trusting you."

"This is a two-hander, a job for men who are experienced and cool under pressure," Stone said. "I've checked both of you out, Mr. Richmond. But if you have someone else in mind—"

"That won't be necessary," Mandor said. "I'm in." A man did not make money by being cautious. If Richmond was comfortable with this, Mandor could live with it.

"I'm glad to hear that," Stone said. "And don't worry, gentlemen. As you said, Mr. Mandor, the money is good.

Beyond that, however, I must tell you—the upside is truly exceptional."

"Are you saying there will be more work?" Richmond asked.

"That's only a small part of what I'm talking about," Stone assured him. "You can't appreciate, yet, how significant your contribution will be. When you do, you will be justifiably pleased."

"It may sound shallow to you, but being well compensated is all the pleasing I need," Mandor said.

"That isn't shallow at all, Mr. Mandor," Stone said. "It's one of the reasons this nation was founded. So that men would be free to pursue financial achievement."

Mandor liked the sound of that. Greed as patriotism.

The meeting wrapped quickly after that. Richmond and Mandor chatted briefly as they walked toward the elevator. Richmond had taken the envelope and put it in his shirt pocket.

"Kind of a toady, don't you think?" Mandor asked.

"Completely," Richmond said. "Which is why he must be sitting next to some pretty serious power. That's the only way a toady gets to swagger like he did."

"I'm with you on that."

"Let's go down separately," Richmond said. "We can meet at the van he's giving us."

"Why? You think this is a setup?"

"I think it's legit," Richmond said. "But we still don't know who he is, or if there are other guys watching him. If there are, they may want to grab us, see what he said. If that happens, one of us needs to be a floater."

A floater was a roughneck term for a jack-of-all-trades who hovered around a group on a rig. He only pitched in when necessary, usually when someone got hurt or a piece of equipment failed.

Richmond had a good point, so he went down first.

Mandor followed a few minutes later. They met by the charcoal gray van.

"How does it look?" Mandor asked.

"As advertised," Richmond said. "The floor is raised slightly in back. There's a big hollow space under there."

"What do you think it's for?" Mandor asked. "Drugs? Illegals?"

Richmond shrugged. "Does it matter? I've gone through the border checkpoint on I-15. No one ever stopped me."

Mandor leaned close to his partner. "What about a whack?" he asked in a loud whisper.

Richmond was silent for a moment. "Okay. What about it?"

"This is hit-level money. We've never gone there. Do we want to start?"

Richmond looked at his friend. "We get caught for some of the other stuff we do, it's ten to twenty years. At our age, there ain't much difference between that and a life sentence. I don't have enough to retire. Do you?"

"No."

"Then I say what the hell, we do this. We just watch every step and be a little extra cautious along the way."

Mandor pulled a cigarette from his shirt pocket and lit it. Richmond was right. What did it matter? Mandor asked himself. Every job has its risk. He had faced danger every day on the rig, from fires to pump room explosions to metal fatigue that could have resulted in the breakup of the platform. If he were a factory worker, he would face accidents or being laid off. Every day, every breath carried risks. Very few of them offered these kinds of rewards.

"I'll tell you what," Richmond said after thinking for a moment. "Let's have a look at the cash. That will make you feel better."

"Okay."

"We'll leave the van here for a day," Richmond said. "I

don't want our friend to think we're careless or predictable. You can come back for it later."

Mandor agreed. They went to their own cars, left the parking structure, and drove to Flamingo. Mandor fired up a second cigarette while he made his way through the thin, early-morning traffic.

There was no logical reason not to go ahead. Pete Farmer had effectively vouched for Stone. The guy was trusting them with a lot of cash. All they had to do for the rest—and more to come, apparently—was to follow instructions. It sounded easy, like connect the dots. There was just one thing that bothered Mandor. It bothered him more than the other jobs they had taken over the years. Mandor had liked and trusted those other people, the bookies who sent them to collect overdue debts, the mobsters who needed bagmen. He understood them. Eric Stone was a mystery.

But as Richmond had said, they would move one step at a time. In the end, they had one advantage over Stone.

If things went south, they could always put *him* in that special storage compartment.

NINE

Washington, D.C.
Monday, 10:59 A.M.

It was one of those days. A day when Darrell McCaskey was working for everyone but his employer.

When McCaskey worked for the FBI, the agents and field directors called things like this tactical exchange activities. TEA time was when operatives for one law enforcement agency or intelligence group were loaned to another organization. Sometimes it was an official and open-ended seconding, such as General Rodgers being assigned to Op-Center. More often than not, it was unofficial, for a day or two, such as Darrell giving a hand to the postal police.

Or being asked just a few hours later to help Scotland Yard investigate the sudden death of William Wilson. Detective Superintendent George Daily, of the Special Branch of the Criminal Investigation Division, had been asked by the assistant commissioner to rule out the possibility of any "mischief." McCaskey and the fifty-seven-year-old Daily had worked together ten years before on an international investigation of the abduction of Chinese-American and Hong Kong women. They were being taken to China to help populate a generation that had been gutted by strict birth control policies. Beijing began to worry that there would not be enough children to staff the military and workforce in the twenty-first century. The ring was broken, though the government officials were never punished.

"I'm sure the D.C. medical examiner knows how to do her job," McCaskey told his old acquaintance.

"No doubt," Daily replied. "But questions are already being asked, given Mr. Wilson's standing. The AC would feel very much better if someone with experience in criminal matters had a look."

"Do you have information that Mr. Wilson was the target of any particular group?" McCaskey asked.

"There is no such indication whatsoever."

"So this is a cosmetic application," McCaskey said.

"Hopefully, yes," Daily replied. "None of us wants to find evidence of criminal activity in this matter."

McCaskey looked at his watch. "Tell you what, George. I'll make some calls and get myself invited over this morning. Do you want me to call you at home when I'm finished there?"

"Please," Daily said.

"Same number in Kensington?"

"What was it your Western cavalry used to say? They would not be back 'until the enemy is captured or destroyed.' I'll be here until the cavalry drags me away or my wife tosses me out."

McCaskey laughed. He enjoyed Daily. The man took his cases seriously, but never himself. McCaskey also envied the detective's relationship with his wife. When they were working in London, Lucy Daily was openly proud of the work her husband was doing. A childhood survivor of the blitz, Mrs. Daily was a strong supporter of law and those who maintained it.

McCaskey hung up, then called his contact at the FBI, Assistant Director Braden, to get him into the coroner's office. Braden understood the drill and arranged for McCaskey to meet with the medical examiner. The Bureau had a lot of clout with other local offices and set up a meeting for 12:30. McCaskey left his office at once. On the way out, he saw Bob Herbert and Mike Rodgers talking outside Rodgers's office. Herbert looked uncharacteristically sullen. The intelligence chief had lost his wife and the use of his legs in the Beirut embassy bombing in 1983. Tucked in a high-tech wheelchair, Herbert did everything with passion. He laughed hard, fought doggedly, took field assignments whenever possible, and had an explosive lack of patience for bullshit. To see him this quiet was disconcerting.

"Good morning," McCaskey said as he passed.

Herbert's back was to McCaskey. The intelligence chief grunted loudly but did not turn.

McCaskey stopped. "What's wrong?"

"Obviously, you didn't hear," Herbert said. His voice was a gloomy monotone. "Mike Rodgers got canned."

McCaskey's eyes shifted to the officer. "For what reason?"

"I'm budgetary fat," Rodgers said.

"You're saying that Paul signed off on that?" McCaskey asked.

"He signed off on it and delivered the message personally, without offering to resign in protest," Herbert said.

"That would not have accomplished anything," Rodgers said.

"It would have made me respect him more," Herbert replied.

"It also would have been easier," McCaskey pointed out.

Herbert wheeled around. "Are you sticking up for him?"

"I didn't realize we were taking sides," McCaskey said.

"We're not," Rodgers said with finality.

Herbert continued to brood.

"It may be a stupid question, Mike, but how are you with this?" McCaskey asked.

"I'm a soldier," he said. "I go where I'm told."

That was what McCaskey had expected Rodgers to say.

The general let you know what he was thinking. But with rare exception, he did not let you know what he was feeling.

"Will you stay with the army?" McCaskey asked.

"I don't know," Rodgers said.

"Jesus!" Herbert said. He was no longer brooding. "I can't believe we're hanging here, calmly discussing the *screwing* of a friend and coworker."

"We're not," McCaskey said. "We're talking about his plans."

"Darrell, the man has no plans; he was just fired," Herbert said. "As for you, you're a company boy, you've always been a company boy, and you'll always be a company boy." Herbert pushed on the hard-rubber wheels of his chair and turned. "You may be next. You need to grow a pair, my friend," the intelligence chief added as he maneuvered around McCaskey.

"Really?" The former FBI agent dropped a strong hand on Herbert's shoulder. He gripped it hard and stopped the intelligence chief from leaving. "Yeah, I'm a team player. Always have been, always will be. Battles are won by artillery working in tandem, not by loose cannons."

"What is that, a quote from the FBI manual?"

"No," McCaskey replied evenly. If they both got angry, this would get ugly. "That's a personal observation from twenty years of stakeouts, undercover stings, field work, and saving the asses of rogue warriors who *thought* they could handle entire operations by themselves."

Herbert thought for a moment. "Okay. I deserved that. Now, take your hand off my shoulder before I go rogue warrior on it."

There was a disturbing absence of levity in Herbert's voice. He knew he had been the target of McCaskey's remark and did not like it. McCaskey let go and stepped to one side. Herbert wheeled away. McCaskey would try to talk to him when he got back. Herbert's temper had a way of subsiding as quickly as it flared.

Other Op-Center personnel had maintained a discreet distance from the three men. They moved through the corridors in silence, their eyes down or facing straight ahead. But this was an intelligence-gathering organization with sharp political hearing. The employees did not miss much.

"Sorry about that, Darrell," Rodgers said. "Bob's angry."

"He's Bob," McCaskey replied.

"True."

"Look, you've got things to do, and I've got to be somewhere," McCaskey said. "Let me know when you're free for a beer."

"The end of the week should work."

"Sounds good," McCaskey said and shook Rodgers's hand. It seemed a remarkably anticlimactic gesture after all these years and all they had shared. But this was not the time or place for good-byes.

McCaskey hurried down the corridor to the elevator. He got in his car and switched on the new FIAT device, the Federal Intelligence Activity Transponder. It was a chip built into his watch and activated by pulling the stem and twisting it clockwise. The signal was monitored by all mobile metropolitan and state police units. It was basically a license to speed or leave the scene of an accident. It told the authorities that the car was on time-sensitive government business and could not be stopped. The FIATs were introduced two years before so that unmarked Homeland Security officials would not be stopped or detained. Though McCaskey was not on a high-priority mission, Scotland Yard was an important ally. He wanted to get them what they needed as quickly as possible.

Wilson's body had been taken to the Georgetown University Medical Center on Reservoir Road. That was where the medical officer was conducting autopsies while the coroner's office was being modernized. McCaskey went downstairs to look at the body with Dr. Minnie Hennepin.

The middle-aged woman had red hair and freckles. She was wearing a sharply pressed lab coat.

"I guess this is what the Feds refer to as 'cover your ass,'" the slender woman said as they walked down the concrete stairs.

"There's a little of that in everything we do," McCaskey admitted.

"May I ask why Scotland Yard did not simply send over one of their own investigators?"

"The press would have been all over that," McCaskey said. "It would be positioned as suggesting a suspicion of wrongdoing. British authorities want to put their minds at ease and also be able to tell Wilson's shareholders that someone with criminal investigation experience had a look at the body."

"You understand, Mr. McCaskey, that there was no evidence of lacerations or contusions other than what I would characterize as the natural result of an exuberant sexual encounter. We also did a very thorough toxicological examination. I'm not sure what's left."

"You checked for every chemical that could produce results consistent with natural organic failure?" McCaskey asked.

"Everything from formaldehyde to pancuronium bromide," Dr. Hennepin said. "We found nothing."

"Some of those chemicals dissipate very quickly."

"That's true, Mr. McCaskey. But they would have to be of very low dosage and injected relatively near to the heart in order to be potent," the doctor said. "I did the pathology for that area of the body, looking for evidence of hypodermic trauma. There was none."

"In the armpit?" McCaskey asked.

"Yes. I also checked the femoral artery, since that would be a rapid delivery system for chemicals."

"Well, I'll have a look at the body anyway," McCaskey said. "You never know what will turn up."

"Frankly, I'll be interested to see a nonmedical approach to a cadaver," the doctor admitted. "Have you done this sort of thing before?"

"I've sent a few people to the morgue but never had a look at them after they've made the trip."

They reached the basement, and she turned on the light. The morgue was smaller than McCaskey had imagined, about the size of a bedroom. There were six stainless steel coolers on one wall in two rows of three. Cases filled with chemicals and equipment stood against the adjoining walls, and a lab table with a deep sink and a computer sat along the fourth wall beside the stairwell. Three autopsy tables filled the center of the room, each beneath a low-hanging fluorescent light.

"Do you want him out of the cooler?" the woman asked.

"That won't be necessary," McCaskey said. "Do you have a light we can bring over?"

"Yes," she said.

McCaskey had been around death before. Too much, in fact. But that had been in shoot-outs or entering a drug den when someone had just ODed. However sad, however tragic, there was drama in the exit. It was the last act of a life. The exchange with Dr. Hennepin had been casual, as if they were deciding what to do with refrigerated leftovers. In fact, they were. There were no pyrotechnic or emotional fireworks, no memorable or even unmemorable gestures. Just the muted echo of their footsteps and low voices, and their curiosity, which hung in the air like buzzards.

The doctor pulled the heavy handle on cooler number four. Billionaire Wilson was not even in number one. Leftovers and one notch below the bronze. The morgue was one hell of an equalizer.

There was a rush of cool air and a smell like raw lamb meat. The body had not yet been embalmed. Dr. Hennepin slid the slab from the cooler. Then she got a workman's light from one of the cabinets and hung it from the handle of the cooler above. It was not an elegant setup, but it did the job. She also brought over a box of latex gloves. They each donned a pair. Starting at the head, she rolled back the white sheet that covered the body. There was a large Y-shaped incision in the trunk. The area well outside the cut was purple. It shaded to surrounding flesh that was yellowish white. Instead of being sutured, the area had been covered with adhesive tape. The cut had been made through the white tape. After the autopsy was concluded, the wound was closed with a series of clasps built into the tape.

"That's enough," McCaskey said when she reached the waist. Since she had already looked at the femoral artery, he was not interested in any region that far from the heart. The first thing he did was look at the eyes.

"A drug might have been applied by eyedropper," he said. "You often find broken blood vessels from the pressure of holding open the lids."

"This is a little far from the heart," the doctor pointed out.

"Yes, but a megadose of coenzyme Q10 could have been given that way—"

"Causing an infarction that would impact the heart quickly and directly," the medical examiner said.

"And Q10 would not turn up on a routine toxological scan," McCaskey added.

"How did you find out about the coenzyme?"

"I investigated a doctor who killed a patient with whom he was having an affair," McCaskey told her. "When we had enough circumstantial evidence, he confessed and told us how he did it. In this case, though, the eyes look normal."

They did not feel normal, however. The ocular muscles had begun to tighten, setting the eyes stiffly in their sockets. It was like working on a mannequin.

"May I borrow your microlight?" McCaskey asked.

"Yes," she said, taking the tiny, powerful flashlight from her vest pocket. She handed it to him.

McCaskey angled the head back slightly and shone the light up the nose. The veins of the nasal passage were another area where a killer might have made an injection. The skin did not appear to have been broken.

"Do you need any of the cartilage retracted?" the doctor asked.

"No. There would be a small clot if he had been injected here."

"And you know that because—?"

"Junkies," McCaskey said. "There are a number of places they inject themselves so the track marks don't show."

"Interesting. I had heard of them using the areas between the fingers and toes," the doctor said.

"Yes, but law enforcement can see those. That would give us reasonable cause to conduct a search."

"Fascinating," the medical examiner said.

McCaskey moved to the mouth. He checked the cheeks. There were no scars, nor any along the gums. Then he checked under the tongue. It was swollen with uncirculated blood. That made the veins underneath it particularly visible. One of them appeared to have a prick mark.

"Look," McCaskey said.

He pinched the tongue between his index finger and thumb and shone the light into the cavity. Dr. Hennepin looked in.

"I see it," she said.

The medical examiner retrieved a scalpel and a sterile test tube from the autopsy table. She also grabbed a small tape recorder. Narrating her activities for the official autopsy record, she carefully sliced a piece of skin from the area. When she was finished, she clicked off the recorder.

"I'll get this to the laboratory at once," she said. "It will be about two hours before I have the results."

"Thanks. I'm going to keep looking, if that's all right."

"Of course," she said. "Just don't make any incisions."

McCaskey said he would not.

The doctor went upstairs to arrange for analysis of the tissue. That left McCaskey alone with the cadaver. The former FBI agent found no other marks on the upper half of the body. He covered Wilson with the sheet and returned him to the cooler. He closed the door.

Wilson was not doing drugs. They would have shown up on the initial lab report. So would injections of insulin or some other medication. Unless the man had nicked himself on a fish bone at the party, this probably meant that someone stuck him under the tongue.

If William Wilson had been murdered, Washington would be turned into a pop-culture Dallas with public and private investigations and endless conspiracy scenarios about who killed the Internet tycoon.

The medical examiner returned. She took McCaskey's cell phone number as well as his office number and promised to call as soon as she heard something. He thanked her for her help and asked for her complete discretion.

"The autopsy results will be sealed," she said, "though in my experience that's as good as saying we have something to hide."

"In this instance, we may," McCaskey remarked.

As he left the medical center, McCaskey found something ironic in how this had unfolded. Something that even Bob Herbert might find amusing.

That for a few hours at least, the quintessential team player would be working on this case alone.

TEN

Washington, D.C.
Monday, 11:00 A.M.

As the press secretary to Senator Donald Orr, twenty-nine-year-old Katherine "Kat" Lockley typically reached the office around seven-thirty each morning and stayed until seven or eight at night. That was fine with her. She loved her work. But it was intense and exhausting, and a midday lunch break was not a luxury, it was a requirement. She liked to get out of the office, go to the Green Pantry down the street, stock up at the salad bar, and do the *New York Times* crossword puzzle while she ate. Forty-five minutes. That was all she required to recharge her brain.

She would not be getting away from the office today.

Kat did not care about William Wilson personally. The two had barely made eye contact at the party, let alone spoken to one another. When she turned on the BBC news at six A.M., as she did every day, and learned of his death, Kat's only concern was for Senator Orr and how the software magnate's death would impact them. As someone who greatly admired the senator, Kat would have to work hard to keep the focus on politics, not gossip. As the daughter of one of Orr's oldest friends, Lieutenant Scott Lockley of the RED HORSE unit, it was also Kat's pleasure to help the senator.

Kat mentally composed a press release as she showered, made notes as she dressed, dictated the final draft as she drove to work, and plugged the digital tape recorder into her computer when she arrived. The voice recognition program transcribed her words, and she edited them while she phoned the senator. It had been a long night of meeting and greeting, and he was still asleep when she called. He listened to the news without comment, a talent good politicians practiced even in private conversations. Kat E-mailed the text of the press release to the senator's laptop. He approved it, and the short statement was E-mailed to the press by eight A.M.

Although the media reported that Wilson had been with a woman he apparently met at the senator's party, neither Kat nor Kendra knew who that was. The official party photographer had E-mailed all the images he took the night before, over two hundred of them. Wilson spoke to a number of women. He left alone. That fact was included in the press release.

At the Columbia School of Journalism they called this "drawing first blood." You did not wait for reporters to come to you. You went to them and established the parameters of the dialogue. Kat had the senator state, "I have never been interested in the private lives of private citizens, so I will only comment on the man as I knew him: through his work." She had made a point of specifying "private citizens" in case it ever became necessary to attack the personal activities of a fellow politician. Kat did not want to have their moral stand in this instance misunderstood as general disinterest in the morality of public officials.

After sending out the press release, Kat fielded calls literally from A to Z, from Blue Danube Radio in Austria to ZBC Television One in Zimbabwe. There were also interview requests from all the American network morning and evening shows. Kat declined to make the senator available to everyone but *CBS Evening News* and *Nightline*. That would give them several hours to find out more about what had happened to William Wilson and to formulate a response. She E-mailed that information to the staff.

Senator Orr sat in his sunny, wood-paneled office with Kendra and Kat and decided that Kat's plan was a good one. The senator would stick to the day's schedule. Wilson had not been a friend to the American economy. The only reason the Englishman had been invited to the party was so that key Washington bankers could make his acquaintance and try to discourage him from his Eurocentric banking plans. It was a delicate thing, mourning a man whose invention had improved everyone's quality of life but whose politics were aggressively anti-American.

"I *am* curious, though, about who he might have met at the party," the senator had said. "Any ideas?"

"I had the photographer send over his shots from last night," Kat said. "He talked to a number of women, most of them married."

"Which could be why there are no clear video images of her from the hotel security system," Kendra remarked.

"She didn't want to be identified," the senator said. "Well, hopefully, it will not be our concern after today."

"Which is why I've instructed the photographer not to provide any of those pictures to the press," Kat said. "The fact that he was here shows that you were trying to be a mediator. That's a good thing. Photographs of Wilson at the party will create a different impression."

"In what way?" Kendra asked.

"I call it the stink of Pulitzer prize," Kat replied. "What's the first thing you think of when I say 'John F. Kennedy?' The Bay of Pigs invasion? The Cuban Missile Crisis? Marilyn Monroe?"

"The Zapruder film," Kendra admitted.

"And what do we remember Dallas for?"

"I get it," Kendra said, nodding.

"Death resonates, unnatural or otherwise, and pictures

reinforce that," Kat said. "Pearl Harbor, the World Trade Center, the *Challenger* and *Columbia*—the emotional power of the end of something overshadows whatever else it stood for. Images strengthen that impact."

"But there's something we want to strengthen," Kendra said. "The difference between what Wilson stood for and what the senator and USF stand for. Wouldn't this be a good opportunity to do that?"

"It would be convenient, but not good," Kat said. "There is a certain level of tawdriness in how Wilson died. We want to stay clear of that, especially if it turns out he was canoodling with someone from the gala."

"Couldn't we use that to cheapen him and his ideas?" Kendra asked.

"That would cheapen us, I think," Kat replied.

"Yes, I have to agree with Kat on that one," the senator said.

Kendra nodded. "Okay," she said. "I was just asking."

Kat did not always like Kendra's go-for-the-throat thinking, but at least the woman did not take the rejection personally. She was here for Senator Orr and the USF, not for herself.

"There is also the chance that late-night comics turn on Wilson and his lover in a day or two," Kat added. "If that happens, we risk becoming part of the joke right when we are holding our convention."

"Another good point," Orr said.

"So how do we exploit the media exposure we'll have tonight?" Kendra asked. "If the senator condemns Wilson, he'll appear heartless. If he praises the man, we lose credibility. If he goes into his stump speech, then we're *obviously* exploiting the media exposure. Could we move the announcement of a presidential run?"

"Ouch," Kat said.

"Why?" Kendra asked.

"That would keep Wilson alive," Kat said. "Wilson's death and the senator's candidacy become a run-on sentence, inseparable."

"I see it as planting flowers in fertilizer," Kendra said. "Something wonderful coming from shit."

Kat frowned.

"Who cares if we are linked to Wilson?" Kendra continued. "I see that as a good thing. Wilson's ideas were very bad for America. The USF is good for America."

"But we'll be linked to his death, not his ideas," Kat said. "We'll be seen as vultures, opportunists."

"Just having the senator on one of those shows will be perceived that way, won't it?" Kendra asked.

"Not necessarily. The senator will be seen as a diplomat. He can say things like, 'Mr. Wilson and I had a different worldview, but his contribution to technology was invaluable,' or, 'Mr. Wilson was embarked on a path I opposed. His genius was in other areas.' You start with the negative to make an impact, then sugarcoat it so you seem magnanimous."

"I am magnanimous," Orr teased.

The women laughed. It was true. Orr was a politician. Typically, that was not a good fit with idealism or philanthropy. All a philanthropist had to do was convince himself that something was worthwhile and make it happen. An elected official had to convince others, and there was often a considerable gulf between conscience and compromise. A man like Franklin Roosevelt may have felt it was the right thing to free Europe from Hitler. But he needed Pearl Harbor to make that happen. John Kennedy may have thought it was a good idea to send people to the moon, but he needed the threat of a Soviet space platform to get the funding. Fortunately, the senator cared more about getting his message across than about winning the White House.

"I agree with Kat," Orr said. "I don't want to dance too

enthusiastically on the man's grave. But I do like Kendra's idea of making some kind of announcement as soon as possible. Kat, what USF personnel are we looking at today?"

"Just two," Kat said. "A military adviser and an economic guru."

"The military adviser is General Rodgers, the deputy director of Op-Center?" Orr asked.

"That's correct, Senator."

"He took our boys into North Korea, India, Russia, the Middle East to stop things from blowing up," Orr said. "That's good. It would make a good counterpoint to what Wilson stood for. Kat, would you give him a call and find out what he thought about the party, see if there's anything we'll need to show him or tell him to make him more comfortable?"

Kat said she would do that at once.

The media portion of the meeting was over, and Kat left the senator with Kendra. She returned to her office, pausing only to make sure the other staffers did not discuss William Wilson with the media. Orr's personal staff of three men and four women were pretty sharp. Kat did not think they would have done that. But the D.C. press corps was smart, too. They had back-door ways of asking questions. "*I'm not at liberty to say*" could be written as "*so-and-so refused to comment*," which suggested that there was something to hide. For Orr's staff, the correct response to all questions about Wilson was, "*Would you like to talk to Ms. Lockley*?"

Throughout the morning, several people had wanted to talk to Ms. Lockley. She would call back later and tell them that the senator had nothing to add to the statement he had made that morning. Right now she needed to talk to Mike Rodgers. She called his cell phone and introduced herself. The general seemed happy to hear from her.

"Are the senator and I still on for this afternoon?" he asked.

"Absolutely, General Rodgers. The senator is looking forward to it. In fact, he wanted me to call and find out if you need anything. Additional information, a brand of cigar, a favorite beverage."

"Actually, there are just two things I want," Rodgers told her.

"What are they?" Kat asked.

"I want to meet a man with vision and the courage to see that vision through," Rodgers said.

"You will definitely find that."

"I believe I will," Rodgers said. "I have read about the senator, and I admire the values for which he stands. The other thing I want to find is a man who is willing to listen to the people around him."

"General, I just came from a meeting with the senator. I assure you, he listens *and* he hears."

"Then I look forward to meeting with him, and hopefully to working with him," Rodgers replied.

"May I ask a somewhat personal question, General?"

"Sure."

"Are you eager to make a move at this time?"

"If it's the right one," Rodgers told her.

"I'm glad to hear that, sir," Kat told him. "We all look forward to seeing you again."

The woman hung up and relayed the information to Senator Orr. He was glad to hear how the general felt.

"He sounds like our kind of fighter," Orr said.

Kat was glad to hear the senator excited. In a day that offered their first major challenge on the national stage, it was reassuring to find a potential ally.

Now it was time to call back the rest of the reporters who wanted to talk to the senator. First, however, she made another call. One that was more important to her.

She phoned the Green Pantry and ordered a turkey club sandwich.

ELEVEN

Washington, D.C.
Monday, 12:53 P.M.

On the way back to Op-Center, McCaskey stopped at a gas station market for lunch. He got a hot dog and a Mountain Dew. As he stood outside eating, he glanced at a rack of newspapers. The headlines of the *Washington Post*, *USA Today*, and a handful of foreign papers were all about the untimely death of William Wilson.

When he was with the FBI, McCaskey attended a class in ATT—antiterrorist tactics. The teacher, psychologist Vic Witherman, was an expert in what he called countdown profiling. Witherman maintained that it was possible to spot a terrorist who was within minutes of launching an attack. There was a dark brightness in their eyes, undistracted purpose in their step, a confident boast in the way they held their head and shoulders. It was the posture of a demigod.

"It comes from three things," Witherman had said. "One, of course, is adrenaline. Two is the fact that they are out of hiding for the first time in months, maybe even years. But three is the most significant of all. They possess what no one else has: knowledge of the future."

McCaskey was struck by that observation. But today was the first time he had ever experienced something similar. If he was right, he knew what tomorrow's headlines would read.

McCaskey's cell phone beeped as he was getting back into the car. It was Dr. Hennepin.

"It took exactly fifteen minutes for the laboratory to find

something that did not belong in a man's mouth," she said. "Traces of potassium chloride."

"Which is used for what?" McCaskey asked.

"Executing criminals by lethal injection," the medical examiner told him. "It stops the heart."

"Is there any way our subject could have acquired that substance naturally?" McCaskey asked. He was careful not to use William Wilson's name, since this was not a secure line.

"Only if he had been eating dog food and certain brands of weight loss bars and dietary supplements," she said. "I did not find anything in the contents of his stomach that indicated he had eaten any of the above. Moreover, in the case of the bars and supplements, potassium chloride would have been detected in conjunction with potassium citrate or potassium phosphate."

"The sample you found was pure."

"Yes," she said.

"So he was murdered."

"Unless it was self-inflicted."

"Which does not seem likely," McCaskey said. "Who has to be informed about this?"

"I have to send a report to the Metro Police superintendent of detectives and a copy to the MP forensics office," she replied.

"When?"

"As soon as I can write it up," the doctor told him. "They should have it within an hour."

"Can you write slowly?" McCaskey asked. "I have to get back to my office and give Scotland Yard a heads-up. There may be individuals they want watched before the information becomes somewhat public."

"All right," she said. "I'll have them run tests for other coronary inhibitors. That should take an extra hour."

"Thanks, Dr. Hennepin," McCaskey said. "Will you be able to forward a copy to me?"

"Sure."

McCaskey thanked her again.

Op-Center's top policeman was already on the road before the conversation ended. He did not want to call Op-Center or Scotland Yard from the secure cell phone in the car. He was not thinking about the empowerment he gained by possessing foreknowledge. Right now, the former FBI agent was thinking about everything that would have to be done to find the individual who had gone to William Wilson's room and apparently assassinated him.

Upon arriving at Op-Center, McCaskey went directly to his office, shut the door, and called George Daily. The detective superintendent was less surprised than McCaskey had expected.

"It's more credible, frankly, than hearing that he died of heart failure," the British investigator remarked.

"I'm going to meet with Director Hood as soon as he's free," McCaskey said. "Do you want to approach the Metropolitan Police, or would you prefer that we work on your behalf?"

"We'd best do both," Daily told him. "When the press gets hold of this, we will be pressured to take a direct hand. In the meantime, it would help enormously if you would earmark areas that we will need to examine. Local police can be very territorial about their sources and the interrogation process."

"I'll make sure you are represented, Detective Superintendent," McCaskey promised.

"How long do we have until this news becomes public fodder?" the Englishman asked.

"The medical examiner is going to forward her updated report in about ninety minutes," McCaskey said. "Fifteen minutes after that, most of Washington will have heard the news."

Daily sighed audibly. "You know, it used to be *panem et circensis,* bread and circuses, that kept the populace happy.

Now it is cell phones and the Internet. They allow us to savor the blood and pain of others in real time."

"Not everyone does that," McCaskey said.

"Indeed we do," Daily declared. "Some of us don't enjoy it, I'll grant you, but most do. Recidivism, it seems, is not just for criminals. Society itself has retreated to barbarism."

The harshness of the condemnation surprised McCaskey. He did not want to believe that the majority of people were rubberneckers at best and moral savages at worst, that they were no different than killers or molesters who could not be rehabilitated. He had always felt that society was basically sound, that it needed only occasional tweaks from people like himself and Daily to stay on course.

This was not, however, the time to debate philosophy. McCaskey rang Bugs Benet to find out if the boss was free. He was. McCaskey said he would be right over.

As the former FBI agent hurried along the corridor, he realized there was an aspect to foreknowledge that Vic Witherman had missed. Terrorism was easy. All it took was a moment of angry resolve to tear things down. Keeping things together required courage and commitment.

Humanism. *That* was difficult.

TWELVE

Washington, D.C.
Monday, 1:44 P.M.

Paul Hood called around to find out if the department heads in nonclassified areas needed an intern. They did not. Lowell Coffey said he would be happy to work with a legal trainee. Frankie Hunt did not fit that profile. Kevin Custer in Electronic Communications said he would take on someone with interest in the field. Otherwise, it was a waste of everyone's time. Other division leaders said more or less the same thing. Hood could have pushed them, but he did not. As he made the calls, he had already decided he did not want the kid working at Op-Center. Someone who helped a friend was "a nice man." Someone who helped his former wife was "a man with guilt." Someone who helped the lover of their former wife was not a man at all.

Working behind the scenes at Op-Center instead of in the light at Los Angeles City Hall had tempered Hood's healthy but modest narcissism somewhat. But it had not quite turned him into a masochist. Sharon, on the other hand, was mossy with fresh self-interest and vanity. She felt her former husband owed her time, effort, and attention, and she was determined to collect.

Hood would wait a few hours before calling Sharon. That would make it seem as if he had made more of an effort than he had. At least he did not have a lot of time to think about it. Hood had spent a lot of time with CFO Ed Colahan working on the budget cuts. There was not a division of Op-Center that would be unaffected. Matt Stoll's computer division would lose six of its twelve employees, Herbert would lose one of his six intel analysts, and the field force Mike Rodgers had assembled would be eliminated. Operatives like David Battat and Aideen Marley would be recruited on a case-by-case basis. Lowell's four-person legal office would be cut to three. Custer would have to release one of his four electronics surveillance people. The night staff would also be reduced. Each time Hood okayed a cut, he knew he was not only affecting an employee but national security. Op-Center had established a singular way of working. Homeland Security could not simply reassign those tasks to the FBI or CIA; Hood and his people had the trust of agents at Interpol, at the Russian Op-Center, at other agencies around the world. Time, personnel, and funds were required to maintain the quid pro quo nature of those valuable relationships. The cuts were going to impact that severely.

Darrell McCaskey walked in just as Colahan was leaving with his laptop.

"How are you holding up, Paul?" McCaskey asked. He shut the door behind him as the CFO left.

"When I was mayor, I had to cut billions from the Los Angeles city budget," Hood said. "That was politically painful but faceless. Each stroke of a key today was someone I know." Hood sat back. McCaskey looked preoccupied. "You heard about Mike Rodgers?"

"Yeah. Bob was so mad he nearly ran me over."

"I haven't heard from him yet," Hood said.

"He's laying low till he cools off," McCaskey said. "He should be in to see you some time next week."

Hood smiled. "What can I do for you?"

"Ironically, you're going to need to loan me out for a couple of days."

"What's up?"

"I think William Wilson was murdered."

Hood's smile evaporated. "Jesus."

"Yeah. This is going to be a big one."

"How did you get involved?"

"Scotland Yard asked me to bird-dog the autopsy," McCaskey said. "I went to the Georgetown medical center and had a look at the body. The ME missed an injection in the root of the tongue. We sent a skin sample to the lab. There was a concentrated trace of potassium chloride, a drug that can be used to stop the heart."

"That's damned impressive, Darrell."

"Thanks."

"Have you informed the Yard?" Hood asked.

"I did," McCaskey said. "They're going to work through the British embassy to get their own people involved. Until then, they asked if I would be their point man on the investigation."

"What are we looking at, time-wise?"

"Three or four days," McCaskey told him.

"That's when media attention will be at a saturation peak," Hood said.

"I know. The good news is, public attention got us more money after the North Korean incident," McCaskey said.

"That was a very different time, when Congress regarded the old institutions as tired, not blue-chip solid," Hood said. "This is going to be a big, public investigation. If Op-Center is on the news every night, the CIOC may see that as a ploy for fund retrocession."

"Please. The CIOC can't be that naive."

"Not naive, Darrell. Suspicious."

"Of what? They know we have to help other agencies if we want their assistance," McCaskey said.

"You're assuming that we're supposed to survive," Hood said. "The CIOC and our older brothers may have other plans."

"Staggered dismantling," McCaskey said.

"It's possible," Hood said.

"Okay," McCaskey said. "Assume the other agencies *are* leaning on the CIOC to cut us back—"

"I don't have to assume that," Hood told him. "They are. Senator Debenport told me."

"In that case, we should not get locked into a siege mentality," McCaskey said. "We should lean back, put our assets in peoples' faces. Senator Debenport will probably be thrilled to take a corner of the spotlight. What politician wouldn't want to be seen as a crusading crime buster?"

"He'll say 'Cheese' and maximize the benefits of that exposure," Hood agreed. "And when the lights go off, he'll turn to me and say—prodded hard by the other agencies—that there is obviously too much fat on Op-Center's bones. He may ask for additional reductions."

"The electorate wouldn't stand for that, especially if we're working on a high-profile case."

"The voters might surprise you," Hood said. "They want to know that government agencies are doing their jobs. Our job is crisis management. Finding the killer is a Metropolitan Police matter, not a hostage situation or terrorist threat. Voters also don't like it when the rich get special attention. Finding the killer of a European multibillionaire who was trying to take money from American banks, and jobs from our shores, is not as important as making sure landmarks and airports are secure."

"I can't believe our society has gotten *that* self-absorbed," McCaskey said. "I refuse to believe it."

"Oh, we have," Hood assured him. "We once saw endless possibility and opportunity in all directions except down. That was the American definition of beauty. Do you know what happens to the narcissist who stops feeling beautiful?"

"Yeah. He gets botox treatments."

"No," Hood said. "He gets scared that he's going to lose everything else."

"He does that, or America does that?"

"Both, I suppose," Hood replied.

McCaskey looked a little sad. Hood did not like where this was going. The next visit would be from Liz Gordon, who would chat and probe and try to determine if he were acting out.

Maybe with good reason, Hood thought. "Darrell, look. I'm not asking you to have a seat in my bunker."

"I know that, Paul—"

"My personal concerns don't change the fact that the threat to Op-Center is real," Hood went on. "We lost a fifth of our budget today. We can't ignore the possibility that there will be additional cuts."

"I agree."

"At the same time, we have to do what we can to help our colleagues," Hood continued. "All I want you to do is fly as far under the radar as possible."

"In D.C.?"

"I know," Hood said with resignation. "Just be careful. If your name gets attached to this, I don't want any interviews. Make sure your Yard contact understands the low-profile agenda, and maintain minimal C and C with your colleagues at the Bureau."

C and C was contact and collaboration. It described the friendly enemy status of relations between rival domestic law enforcement and intelligence groups. Most international agencies got along fine.

"I will go out in stealth mode," McCaskey promised.

"Good. And when you nail the guy who did this, we'll have another look at how to play it with Debenport and the CIOC."

"*Bring me the head of Alfredo Garcia*, and then we'll talk."

"Something like that," Hood said.

"Sounds good. And chief? I know it's been a tough morning. If I came on a little hard, I'm sorry."

"You asked the right questions at the right time," Hood said. "If I can't take that, I don't deserve to be in this chair."

McCaskey smiled. It was good to see that.

When McCaskey left, Hood told Bugs to hold his calls for five minutes. Then he rubbed his forehead and thought again about the situation with Frankie Hunt. If it were about his son, Alexander, Hood would not have failed to get him an internship. Sharon knew that. So she would know that her former husband had given this minimal effort—if that. Would the little bit of self-respect he gained be worth the little bit of self-respect he could give?

Hesitantly, as though it were a coiled snake, Hood reached for the phone. He began making more calls, in a less ambivalent voice than he had used that morning.

THIRTEEN

Washington, D.C.
Monday, 2:17 P.M.

The telephone call came from Detective Robert Howell of the D.C. Metropolitan Police. Kendra Peterson took it in her office. The detective asked to speak with the senator. He would not say why. Orr was working in the sunlit conference room with Admiral Link and Kat Lockley. Kendra conferenced in the senator, then joined them. Orr put the call on the speakerphone. His American flag tie was loose, and his shirtsleeves were opened at the cuffs and pulled back along his forearms.

"Senator, before the news hits the grapevine, I wanted you to know that William Wilson appears to have been murdered."

Howell said it quickly, efficiently, and unemotionally. The impact was like Franklin Roosevelt describing the day that would live in infamy.

"How did it happen?" Orr asked. He realized he had to take charge of the discussion. Everyone else was too stunned.

"Mr. Wilson was apparently given an injection of a heart-inhibiting drug," Howell replied.

"Presumably by the woman he met in his hotel?" Orr asked.

"That is our assumption. We'll require fine tissue analysis beyond the scope of the original autopsy to determine what the heart muscle may have absorbed. That will take several days of extensive circulatory analysis."

"Detective, this is Admiral Ken Link. Was the new evidence discovered after the autopsy was completed?" he asked.

"Just a few hours ago, Admiral," Howell said. "The medical examiner tells me that a gentleman from Op-Center had a look at the body and discovered the puncture mark."

"Op-Center? What were they doing there?" Link asked.

"I don't have that information, sir," Howell said.

"And they found this wound in the presence of an ME?" Link pressed.

"Yes. Why?"

"I wouldn't trust those spy boys to run a fair Bingo game," said the Oregon-born officer.

" 'Those' meaning from Op-Center?" Howell asked.

"Yes, sir."

"Do you have reason to suspect they would falsify something like this?" Howell asked.

"Their budget was gutted this morning," Link replied. "Paul Hood needs something to get back in the game."

"Including sabotaging a body on short notice?" Howell asked.

"Jury-rigged sabotage is what field operatives do," Link pointed out. "Detective, I'm not accusing Op-Center of wrongdoing. I am only saying that the timing is suspicious."

Kat touched the mute button. "Ken, we can ask Mike Rodgers about that when he gets here."

"That may not be wise," Link said.

"People, we're getting ahead of ourselves," Orr said. The senator deactivated the mute function. "Detective Howell, what kind of scrutiny is this office facing?"

"I honestly don't know, sir," Howell told him. "We need to find that woman. If he met her at a bar on the way home, or if he called an escort service some time during the day, then obviously you're clear. If she was one of your guests, then I'm afraid the paddy wagon will kick up some mud."

"Understandable," Orr admitted. "You have the guest list from the party."

"Yes, sir. We are in the process of interviewing the attendees."

"Detective, I truly appreciate the call," Orr said. "If we hear anything about the mystery woman, I will certainly let you know."

"Thank you, Senator. I will do the same."

Orr terminated the call. He sat back and crossed his big arms. "Who is she? Any thoughts, guesses?"

No one spoke. Orr was not surprised. When Ken Link worked at the CIA, Op-Center was perceived as a rival. The former admiral had an opportunity for payback and took the shot. There were always potential enemies among allies, and no one wanted to say anything that might backfire. Washington was a town of two degrees of separation. Between the four of them, they had known everyone at the party. Everyone at the party knew virtually everyone in D.C.

"All right then," Orr went on. "Kat, does this change our strategy for the interviews tonight?"

"Not as far as the comments about Mr. Wilson," Kat replied. She looked over her notes. "When asked about the death you were going to say, 'As an inventor, Mr. Wilson left behind a significant technological legacy.' Two mentions of his credentials as a scientist to suggest that Wilson was no banking genius. I do not see why we need to change that."

"I agree, but the murder charge is sure to come up," Kendra said. "The senator will need to address it."

"I would deflect it with a boilerplate comment about the charges being hearsay or a police matter," Kat told them. "Get in and out, say something that doesn't invite a follow-up."

"Why?" Kendra asked.

The question surprised Kat. "Because the press would

love to link the senator or any public figure to a homicide," Kat said.

"We're already linked," Kendra pointed out. "Wilson was dead within two hours of leaving the party."

"Where are you going with this, Kendra?" Orr asked.

"The USF will have a platform built on the commonsense rights of American citizens. That includes justice for all and a presumption of innocence. Let's be proactive about that. Tell the interviewer that innuendo is impertinent, intolerable, and eroding our society. That the quest for sensational headlines is counterproductive to the dignity inherent in our judicial system."

"That's like trying to reason with a cheetah or shame a snake," Kat said. "A predator can't change what it is."

"Let them hiss. I'm talking about presenting our courage," Kendra said. "We can't be afraid to take on the press, and this would be a good time and place to marginalize them."

"I agree that the point is worth making," the senator said thoughtfully. "But the immediate aftermath of Wilson's death is probably not the best time."

"You'll have the nation's ear," Link said.

The admiral did not usually weigh in unless he felt strongly about something. Orr could not remember a time when his inner circle was this divided. Kendra was sitting ramrod straight, her expression tense. Kat was drumming her pen on her pad. Link was hunched over the table as if he were playing a naval war game, staring at a map and toy battleships. Orr did not know whether it was the pressure of the upcoming convention, the shock of the latest revelation, or both. He could not let himself be affected by either of those. As president, which he hoped to be, Orr would have to respond to greater crises with vision, intelligence, and poise.

"Ken, are you at all concerned that we will appear opportunistic or defensive?" Orr asked.

"Not especially," Link replied. "Speaking the truth aggressively is a mark of confidence. As for opportunism, it's the media that is taking advantage of you. You're only getting this particular airtime because of Wilson's death."

"The audience will perceive the media as neutral," Kat insisted. "They are the medium. We are the message."

"I agree completely," Kendra said. "Which is why we have to defend the women who were at our party. Otherwise, we will be perceived as using this misfortune just to get the senator's face out there."

"Kendra, none of our guests has been charged with a crime," Kat pointed out.

"But all of them, you and I included, will be investigated by agents of the law *and* by the press," Kendra said.

"Both of which are Constitutionally protected activities," Kat said. She regarded the senator. "Sir, I agree that there is mutual exploitation going on. We can use tonight as a staging area for the convention and use the convention to build our platform. To do more tonight is ghoulish."

"That's a strong word, Kat," Link remarked.

"Isn't that what we're talking about, generating strong reactions?"

Orr could see this getting personal. Kat was very protective of her public relations activities, and both Link and Kendra liked to be involved in everything. Until now, they usually agreed.

The senator looked at his watch. "People, General Rodgers will be here soon. I suggest we do the following. I agree with Kat. I do not want to come on too strong tonight—about Wilson. But I do see one way in. This is a Metro Police matter. A federal agency like the National Crisis Management Center has no business being involved. General Rodgers works for Op-Center. He will know what is going on. *That* is something we can be aggressive about."

"Right," Kat said admiringly. "That will also shift the attention from us onto some vague conspiracy theory."

"That's a good one," Kendra admitted.

"Ken, do you know anything more about this budget cut?"

"No. I saw it in the Congressional Intelligence Oversight minutes."

"What other agencies were hit?" Orr asked.

"None," Link told him. "They all received bumps, in fact."

"So this is a big wrist-slap for Hood," Orr said. "Kat, research the NCMC and talk to Senator Debenport. He's the head of the CIOC. See if you can find out, informally, what precipitated the cut. That might be useful in the general election. Debenport will have to explain why he is putting our nation at risk. I'll find out what I can from Mike Rodgers."

"Senator, the CBS people will be here in a half hour to set up," Kat said.

"I'm sure General Rodgers won't mind a brief interruption." Orr rose. "Thank you, all. This has been very stimulating."

The conference room emptied quickly, and the senator went to his office. A sense of order had been restored, but one that was laced with healthy tension. The interns, assistants, and secretaries felt it and stayed focused. This was how Orr liked it. Direction with a whisper of urgency, purpose without desperation.

Of course, things might not remain this way. But that was all right, too.

Senator Orr shut his office door. The heavy silence felt good. He enjoyed it for a moment, then listened to the phone messages his secretary had passed on. He returned just one, a call to his wife. He wanted to tell her about William Wilson before she heard it on the news. Valerie Orr spent most of the year in Texas because she disliked catty Washington society. The senator missed her but was glad she chose the ranch over D.C. If anyone ever insulted her or talked about her, he would give that individual an old-fashioned switch-whipping.

As he sat down to review General Rodgers's dossier one last time, Orr thought about something his father used to say on the ranch. Whenever money or water were precipitously low, Jeremiah Orr would push an ever-present plug of Red Man chewing tobacco between his cheek and gum, look down at his feet, and say to no one in particular, "I still like our position a whole lot better than the cows.' "

Come what may, Senator Orr liked a good challenge. He liked testing his own ideas and hearing the ideas of his team. He liked his position.

He liked it a lot better than William Wilson's.

FOURTEEN

Washington, D.C.
Monday, 2:59 P.M.

To most outsiders, the Capitol and the office buildings that serviced it defined the phrase *corridors of power.* For over a century, ideas that had first influenced the world, then dominated it, were debated here. Refined here. Presidents were humbled here or declared war here. Laws were passed or revoked here, causing ripples that affected every life in the nation, through every federal, state, and local court. Art and expression were financed here or restricted here.

What Mike Rodgers saw were not COPs. Whenever he had business here—which was mercifully rare—Rodgers felt as though he were entering an abattoir. Fortunately, until this morning, he had not been a very fat cow, so the blades did not usually affect him. But this was where budgets were hacked, policies were eviscerated, good ideas were whittled to nubs, and wise or well-intentioned men and women were cut down at the knees or decapitated.

Vietnam was lost here, not on the battlefield.

The Capitol was about power in the same way ice hockey was about travel. There was a lot of aggressive, muscular movement but very little progress. It was odd. Rodgers did not even see the white of the dome and columns as much as he saw the dark recesses and shadows that creased and abutted them.

Rodgers hoped that Senator Orr could change those impressions.

Military reservists were stationed outside the building, and Rodgers acknowledged their salutes as he was checked through. He went to Senator Orr's first-floor office and was buzzed in. He did not need to announce himself. A security camera above the door did that for him.

Maybe they should call it the corridors of paranoia, he thought. He glanced along the hall. Security was an important issue. But he did not think it was necessary to have a camera above each door. The money the government spent on this surveillance system would be better spent on one or two good Special Ops agents who could track and eliminate assassins.

Rodgers refused to let any of this flavor his opinion of Donald Orr. Men could not be held accountable for the transgressions of their peers.

A sharp young female receptionist sat behind a mahogany desk in the small waiting area. The woman had already come from around the desk. She welcomed Rodgers with a large smile and a strong handshake.

"General Rodgers, thank you for coming. The senator is expecting you," she said. The woman entered a code into a keypad by the six-panel cherry wood door. This opened into the main offices. "May I get you coffee or a soft drink?"

"Black coffee would be good. No sugar."

She walked him through a short maze of desks and cubicles to the senator's closed door. She knocked and was told to enter. The big Texan rose and walked from behind his desk. His eyes were squarely on the general.

"The man who prevented World War III," Senator Orr said. "Twice."

"I'm hardly that, but thank you," Rodgers said.

"General, modesty is forbidden on the Hill," Orr said. "We passed a law against it, I think."

"I'm only visiting."

"Doesn't matter," Orr said as the men shook hands. "I

hear tin horns every damn day. When you've got Gabriel's trumpet, play it."

Rodgers felt old calluses on the senator's palm and undersides of his fingers. He knew that the Orr family was in ranching. He was glad to see the senator had not been too privileged to work.

"Besides, I'm hoping we can convince you to stay," the senator went on. "Please, sit down," he said, gesturing toward a leather armchair.

The receptionist returned with Rodgers's coffee. He had not even seen her slip away. She set it on a glass-topped teapoy in front of the chair. Steam rose from a navy blue mug with the Camp David logo in gold. The logo was set facing Rodgers. It was just a cornet semiquaver but unavoidable.

A barrel-chested man entered as the receptionist left. Rodgers recognized him from the party.

"Admiral Link," Rodgers said, rising.

"Sit," the admiral said. He shut the door behind him before shaking Rodgers's hand. He swung an armchair around so that there were three chairs in a circle. "Good to meet you. Sorry we didn't have a chance to talk last night."

"Those things are always so unmanageable," said the senator, taking a seat. "Not like a good cattle drive."

"You should hand out electric prods," Rodgers said.

"Best idea I've heard in a while." Orr laughed. It was a genuine laugh, not a performance.

"I heard about William Wilson on the drive over," Rodgers said. "Has there been any fallout?"

"Not yet," Orr said. "I have to do a live segment on the *CBS Evening News* in about twenty minutes, though. I'll know more after that. Hopefully, you'll stick around so we can talk more. I don't want to rush this."

"Of course," Rodgers said. "I have to tell you, though, Senator. I'm not really sure what 'this' is."

"A new political party, a new way of doing business in D.C.," Orr told him. "You have heard this before, I'm sure."

"So often that I've stopped listening," Rodgers admitted.

"Most Americans have tuned out, General Rodgers, which is why we need to get their attention. We need to make a dramatic new start fast, no wasted time." Orr leaned forward in his chair. "I am about to announce my candidacy for the presidency. I will be asking the admiral to be my running mate. None of that will surprise anyone. However, what I will be asking for in my acceptance speech will be different from typical convention rhetoric. I will demand what we are calling FAIR change. That's *full American infrastructure reform*. Everything from the judicial system to Social Security will be reorganized to serve the people who need them."

"That's going to take clout and money," Rodgers said.

"The funds will come from misguided programs, such as the billions we spend annually in unappreciated foreign aid and foreign products," Orr said. "If other nations want access to our consumers, it will cost them in tariffs. As for clout, I'll get that from the people of this country. We've forgotten the electorate, General Rodgers. If necessary, we will hold monthly plebiscites to decide issues. Representatives who oppose the wishes of their constituents will become former representatives."

"It's a program with hair on its chest, I'll give you that," Rodgers said.

Orr sat back. "But?"

"I'm from 'show me' Missouri by way of hell," Rodgers said. "I'm a starry-eyed pessimist."

"I like that," Admiral Link confessed.

"Hope for something good but expect the worst," Orr said.

"I would say 'anticipate it,' " Rodgers said.

"Sam Houston was like that, and look what he accomplished," Orr said. "He built a state."

Rodgers grinned. "But then, he was from Texas. I'm from Connecticut."

Orr smiled broadly. "Texas is a state of heart, not just geography. General, we're a little different from you, the admiral and I. We are cautious optimists about how FAIR will be received. Regardless, once our campaign is under way, I will need a military adviser, one with chops. A man who has been out there getting his hands dirty and who also understands intelligence work. One who will become the secretary of defense in an Orr administration."

"You are uniquely qualified," Link added.

"I'm also a little confused," Rodgers said. "Are you making me an offer?"

The senator laughed. That one was a short stage laugh. "As I said, Texas is in here." Orr touched his chest. "I watched how you walked into the office. That's the way I want my cabinet members to step to a podium."

Rodgers was flattered and also suspicious. Either Orr was hooking him for some other reason, or he was exactly as he said: a straight-shooting politician.

"General, may I ask how things are at Op-Center?" Link said.

"Why?" Rodgers asked. "What have you heard?"

"Not much," Link replied.

"In D.C.? That's unlikely," Rodgers said.

"He's got you there, Ken." Orr laughed, once again for real.

"Touché," the admiral said. "The truth is, we just heard they're spearheading the investigation into the murder of William Wilson."

"Really?" Rodgers said.

Link was watching him. "You seem surprised."

"I am. Who's the point man?"

"I don't know. But whoever it is, he's good," Link

replied. "He's the one who found signs of trauma under the tongue that the medical examiner missed. He turned this from a heart attack to a homicide."

"I see," Rodgers replied.

That sounded like a street-smart "get" by Darrell McCaskey. Op-Center must have become involved at the request of Interpol or Scotland Yard.

"General, we heard that the CIOC has instructed Op-Center to make budget cuts," Link went on. "Why would Director Hood take on an outside project like this in an environment trending toward austerity and realignment?"

"You would have to ask him," Rodgers said.

"Of course," Orr said. "Ken, you're asking General Rodgers to breach departmental confidentiality—"

"Actually, it's more than that," Rodgers informed the men. "This morning I learned that I am part of those bottom-line reductions. My tenure as deputy director is effectively over."

"They asked for your resignation?" Orr asked, surprised.

"Two weeks from now I'm either working with you or back at the DoD in some other capacity."

"Now that's a kick in the damn teeth," Link said. "They ship out an American hero, then help to investigate a decadent British billionaire."

Orr's phone beeped. He answered, listened, said he would be right there. "I'm expected in the conference room for a pre-interview with Mr. Dan Rather's associate producer," he said. "General, will you be able to stay for a bit? This should not take more than fifteen minutes."

"Of course," Rodgers said, rising as the senator did.

Orr left the room and shut the door behind him. Rodgers sat back down. Link was looking at him. Rodgers took a sip of coffee.

"General Rodgers—Mike, if I may—do you mind if I ask you something personal?"

"Go ahead."

"Do you feel betrayed by Paul Hood or Op-Center?"

"I wouldn't go that far," Rodgers replied.

"How far would you go?"

That was a loaded question, Rodgers thought, though he was not sure what exactly it was loaded with. He knew at once that this was not idle chat.

"I don't feel good about the way things happened, but this was an assignment, a tour of duty," Rodgers replied. "For whatever reason, that job is over. I'm ready to move on."

"That's a healthy attitude," Link said.

"Thanks. Now I'd like to ask you a question, Admiral."

"All right."

"Does it matter how I feel about Op-Center?"

"Not in terms of your working with us," Link said. "It's more a question of helping them."

"I'm not following."

"Paul Hood is moving them into a very dangerous place, not just for him but for us," Link said.

"Why us?"

"It's a question of appearances," Link told him. "If the NCMC is ham-fisted about their investigation, it's going to slop all over us, all over our guests, and all over our convention."

"Why do you assume it will be handled badly?"

"Because Op-Center is suddenly very shorthanded," Link said. "Let's say that Individual X has taken on this assignment. He still has to perform his other duties, plus whatever new duties he inherits due to the cutbacks. I don't have to tell you that in a reduced-personnel environment in the military, standard operating procedure is to shoot every door in a house and see which one groans. If Individual X is forced to take that approach here, we may suffer unwarranted hits."

"Possibly. But the hits should not be serious."

"When you're launching a new political party, any stain

on your credibility is serious," Link said. "It scares away donors. Also, I've spoken to a number of people on the Hill. They wonder if Hood may be using this action to try to retrench, to fold the idea of international criminal investigation into crisis management. He did something like that before."

"Actually, we backed into that one by stopping a missile attack on Japan," Rodgers said. "The president asked us to take on additional responsibilities."

"I understand that the situations are different," Link said. "So are the times. The CIA was moving from human intelligence to electronic intelligence. Data was falling through the digital cracks. Op-Center was there to catch it. The Company won't let that happen this time."

"Okay. Even if that is true, why is it our concern?" Rodgers asked.

"Because the perception is that Paul Hood may have manufactured a situation," Link replied.

"Horseshit," Rodgers snapped. He hoped this perception was not something Link had whipped up. It was contemptible. "I know the people at Op-Center. They would never do that."

"Other people aren't so convinced," Link said.

"What people?"

"Influential people," Link replied. "People who have the ear of the CIOC and the president. What I'm saying, Mike, is that it is a bad situation all around."

"Okay, it's bad. Why share that insight with me?"

"I think you should talk to Hood," Link said. "Tell him that the way to help Op-Center is to soft-pedal this."

"Soft-pedal. Do you mean bury?"

"I mean they should let the Brits handle this through channels. They should let the Metro Police work the investigation."

The Metropolitan Police were efficient, sensitive, and discreet. Their footsteps would not splash much mud.

While Rodgers did not believe that Hood was doing this for the reasons Link had stated, there was no doubt that the presence of a crisis management organization would leave a much bigger footprint.

"There's something else to consider," Link went on. "The CIOC can effectively dissolve Op-Center tomorrow simply by downsizing the budget to zero. If Hood steps on FBI jurisdiction, that could happen. Be a friend to him. Suggest to Hood that he reconsider his involvement."

"I'll think about it," Rodgers said.

The subject was not raised again.

The men talked a little about the USF and the convention, and Link shared a list of politicians and business leaders who were privately committed to lending support to the party. It was impressive. He also gave Rodgers a CD containing USF press releases and internal directives to bring him up to speed.

Donald Orr returned, and so did a sense of balance. The senator said the interview had gone very well, that he had told CBS that they should wait for an official statement from investigators before speculating about the death of the man he described as "Britain's gift to Europe." That was one of Kat's phrases, Orr said, and he liked the point it made.

As Rodgers conferred with the men, he found himself very relaxed with Orr and very suspicious of Link. The Orr-Link dynamic was not good cop, bad cop. It was more honest than that. Orr was like the white hat sheriff who would face a gunslinger on Main Street at high noon and let him draw first. Link was the deputy who hid behind a window with a rifle, clipped the bad guy in the shoulder, then went over and stepped on the wound until the man told him where the rest of the gang was hiding. Both approaches were strategically valid as long as you were not the target. Rodgers knew where he stood with Orr. He was not so sure about Link. There was a fine distinction between being employed by someone and being used by them. It was up to the integrity of the employer and the dignity of the employee to see that the line was not crossed.

Rodgers left, promising to call the men with his answer in the morning. He wanted to join them. The idea was exciting, and it was a new experience for him. Still, Rodgers was not certain what to do. It would mean leaving the military for something that was wildly uncertain. On the other hand, what in the world was not uncertain? When Rodgers woke this morning, he was still the deputy director of Op-Center.

As Rodgers walked to his car, he found himself feeling surprisingly bitter about his dismissal. Why would Hood fire him, then put a high-overhead individual like Darrell or Bob Herbert on an off-topic investigation? It wasn't exactly disloyal, but it did suggest some sadly screwed-up priorities. And what about the idea that Hood might use this to help Op-Center? Though he did not for a moment believe that the evidence would have been falsified, as Link suggested, perhaps Hood would in fact seize on this to help redirect an ailing Op-Center.

That's the beauty about being deputy sheriff, the general decided. The sheriff was the big symbol and the big target. He had to get out in the street and confront the outlaw. He could not snipe at him from safety, and he did not have time to run a psy-ops campaign.

Clearly, Kenneth Link's years as the director of covert operations for the CIA had not been wasted. As Rodgers drove into the heavy traffic and rust-colored sunlight of late afternoon, he decided he would have that talk with Paul Hood about the William Wilson investigation.

FIFTEEN

Charlottesville, Virginia
Monday, 4:18 P.M.

When April Dorrance was a young girl growing up in rural Sneedville, Tennessee, on the Virginia border, her father collected discarded appliances and fixed them for resale. That was the kind of thing a skilled and resourceful African-American man had to do in the South in the early 1970s to feed his family. April loved playing house with the appliances before they were repaired. She also enjoyed watching her father work. She loved seeing his huge hands manipulate fine wire and tools. He always explained what he was doing and why.

"That was how my pop taught me," Royal Dorrance said one night in their small cabin with its corrugated tin roof.

"And is that how his father taught him?" April asked.

"Yes ma'am," he replied.

"Who was the first one who learned it?"

"That would be my granddad, Mr. Walter Emmanuel Dorrance," Royal told her. "He was a private with the 803 Pioneer Infantry during World War One. Big segregated unit, meaning they only allowed black soldiers. He learned all about engineering when he fought in France."

"He went to school in a war?" April asked.

"In a way, Precious," her father said. "He had to learn things to survive and to help his friends survive."

"Does that mean war is good?"

"Sometimes," he said. "We're free because of a war. And a lot of things get invented to fight wars."

April never forgot the idea that war could be a positive aspect of civilization.

When April was a little older, not quite eleven, she began coming home from school and fixing some of those appliances herself. She loved how proud her father was when he came home with a new truckload of goodies. After his death, she continued in the family business to help support her mother and younger brother. With the help of her high school science and shop teachers, the young woman earned a scholarship to study electronics at the University of Tennessee College of Engineering in Knoxville. April excelled and graduated in 1984 from Cornell University with a Ph.D. in QuASSE—quantum and solid state electronics. She was immediately recruited by the CIA. April agreed to go to work for them because of the challenge, the job security, and the fact that it was close to her mother and brother. She went to work in a secret research laboratory located in Richmond, Virginia. The facility was actually below Alexandria, in a bunker below the University of Richmond. Only the UR president, select members of the board of trustees, and the UR chief of police knew they were there. No one knew what they did there. A large annual endowment bought their disinterest.

And April Dorrance got to learn and grow because of war.

The eleven-person staff of the School, as they called it, tested new forms of electronic jamming, surveillance, and triangulation equipment for use by mobile forces during combat. A university was the ideal place to do that, since computer and telecommunications use on campus was constant and typically cutting-edge. There were always students who brought with them the latest laptops, cell phones, and other portable electronics. The kids owned everything a modern soldier, spy, or terrorist might possess. Probably more. The School staffers liked nothing more than field-testing prototypes on unsuspecting students and teachers. It was like *Candid Camera*, watching them as they tried to figure out why their cell phones were suddenly talking to them in Bantu, the language of April's ancestors.

The problem with the School was the burnout factor. It was intense work done in windowless surroundings for long hours. It was impossible to have a social life. It was also difficult to leave. The CIA had control over the kinds of positions one could seek after leaving their employ. They did not want confidential information finding its way into the private sector. An electromagnetic inhibitor that could plant false readings on enemy radar could easily be built into an automobile to befuddle police radar. April did not want to work for a government contractor who would demand the same extended hours and would not have the kind of budget or resources she had at the School. That left teaching. April had bought a house in Goochland, halfway between Richmond and Charlottesville. She simply drove twenty miles in the opposite direction each morning to teach microelectronics at the University of Virginia.

But people who had worked with April over the years often called her to consult on specific projects, and she was happy to do so. The government still possessed the best toy box on earth.

Nonetheless, the call was unexpected.

The caller left a message on her cell phone, which she returned on a more secure landline in her office. It was not the caller who surprised her. Though the two of them had never worked together, they had met on a number of occasions. What surprised April was what the caller wanted. The government had hundreds of these weapons stored in military and intelligence warehouses around the globe. Then again, April understood that they might not have one exactly to these specifications. She also knew that sometimes goods had to be acquired "off the books" because the system had "moles and holes," as the caller referred to them.

April could deliver it, of course. And she would, because she trusted the caller and their mutual friend.

Besides, it was fun and lucrative. Just like working on the old Formica-topped kitchen table in the cabin in Sneedville.

April was informed that the components would be delivered to her home that evening, and she was to assemble them for pickup the following morning. That was more than enough time. These weapons were increasingly modular. Not like the days when Private Walter Dorrance had to use a mallet and spare train rails to fashion replacement cranks and ballast for the Allies' twelve-inch Mk4 siege Howitzers. He certainly did not get paid as well as she did, either. This one would buy her mother a new car.

And maybe do some good. Because war could be a force for good.

Even a war that was only one bomb long.

SIXTEEN

Washington, D.C.
Monday, 5:22 P.M.

When Darrell McCaskey worked for the FBI, he nurtured relationships with the press. McCaskey did not believe it was the right of the public to know everything that was going on in law enforcement. But reporters had sources who were otherwise unavailable to the Bureau. Information was the coin of the realm, and to find out what journalists knew, McCaskey often had to trade confidential data. Happily, he was never burned. Trust was the foundation of journalism—between reporter and subject, medium and audience. Throughout his years with the Bureau, McCaskey had encountered a handful of agents he did not trust for one reason or another. Yet he never met a reporter who went back on his or her word. Results were the foundation of crime fighting,

The guest list for Orr's party, published in the *Washington Post*, differed from the guest list given to McCaskey by the Metro Police. The newspaper had a list of everyone who was invited. The police had the list of people who had actually showed up, as tallied by the invitations turned in at the door.

There were four names on the invite list that did not show up on the attendance list. Mike Rodgers was on both lists. McCaskey could not imagine why the general had been invited.

Rodgers was out of the office, and McCaskey left a

message on his cell phone. Then he called the *Washington Post* reporter who had covered the event. It would be necessary to talk to everyone who was there and also get an accurate head count; someone might have slipped in through the kitchen or a side door or walked in on the arm of a senator. McCaskey also wanted to find out who Wilson was seen conversing with. That was something a journalist would have noticed.

Bill Tymore was the *Post* business reporter who had attended the party. He had come as the date of Kendra Peterson, Senator Orr's executive assistant. Tymore agreed to talk if McCaskey agreed to keep him in the loop, off the record. McCaskey did not have a problem with that.

"Before you ask, I've been seeing Kendra for nearly a year, she does not expect preferential coverage, and I left about a half-hour before Wilson did so I could write my article," Tymore said.

"So you don't know who might have left to visit him."

"Or if anyone did," Tymore pointed out. "I have someone looking into the local escort services. One of the girls might have been paylaid en route and an assassin put in her place."

"Paylaid," McCaskey repeated. That was a new one. "You think the escort might have been given a couple hundred bucks to have a cup of joe instead of visiting her client."

"Right."

"Did Wilson have a history of calling escort services?"

"Apparently," Tymore replied. "It was his way of keeping gold diggers out of his bed."

"What about last night?" McCaskey asked. "Do you recall which women he talked to?"

"He chatted briefly with Kendra and then Kat Lockley, who are on the senator's staff," he said. "He also talked with two congresswomen and a senator, Ken Link's daughter Jeanne, Wendy Fayette from the *New York Times*, and one of the waitresses. She's been cleared, though. She was still on cleanup detail when the woman arrived at the hotel. Now I have a question for you, Mr. McCaskey."

"Okay."

"What was General Rodgers doing there?"

"I don't know," McCaskey said. "That was a surprise to me. Why don't you ask Kendra?"

"I did. She wouldn't tell me. My guess is they want him to be involved in the USF Party in some capacity. Is that possible?"

"It wouldn't surprise me," McCaskey told him. "Off the record, I think he's looking to move on."

McCaskey felt a little deceitful not telling Tymore what he knew. But it was up to Rodgers or Hood to talk about the general's departure, not him. Trust was important, but it was trumped by loyalty.

"Now you tell me, Mr. McCaskey," Tymore said. "Why is Op-Center interested in this?"

"We are involved at the request of Scotland Yard," McCaskey told him. "It's a common reciprocal arrangement among international agencies."

"Why you and not the Metropolitan Police or the FBI?" Tymore asked.

"I know the Yard people from my years with the FBI," McCaskey replied. "It was just a favor. We did not expect to find anything."

"Can I quote you?"

"You can quote an unnamed source at Op-Center," McCaskey said.

Tymore agreed.

McCaskey obtained the phone numbers Tymore had collected. Though the reporter had already called the women who had talked to Wilson, McCaskey wanted to speak with them himself. They all denied having gone to see the billionaire, of course, though maybe they would tell McCaskey things they were unwilling to tell the press.

Rodgers phoned before McCaskey was able to place the first call. The general had just returned to Op-Center and was about to see Paul Hood. He asked McCaskey to join them.

"Sure," McCaskey said. "What's up?"

"Paul said you're running the Wilson investigation," Rodgers said.

"Right—"

"I want to talk about it," Rodgers said abruptly. "It could be a minefield."

Rodgers did not elaborate. McCaskey could not tell whether that had been a warning or a threat. He headed to Hood's office to find out.

Rodgers arrived moments ahead of McCaskey. Ron Plummer was just leaving. The silence exchanged by Rodgers and his replacement was actually heightened by the way they acknowledged each other, with a clipped first-name greeting and nothing more. The soldier and the diplomat never had much in common, but they had always gotten along. This was sad, but what made it worse was that McCaskey expected things were about to deteriorate.

"Ron did not want the job," Hood said to Rodgers as McCaskey shut the door. "I just wanted you to know that."

"Did he accept it?" Rodgers asked.

"For the good of Op-Center, yes," Hood said.

"Of course. We're all so damn selfless," Rodgers said. He folded his arms tightly and looked at McCaskey. Both men had remained standing. "Who are you working for now? The Yard?"

"Don't climb on my back, Mike," McCaskey said. "You know the drill. We help each other."

"We do?" Rodgers looked around. "I must have missed the lifeline you guys threw me."

This was a different Mike Rodgers than Darrell McCaskey had encountered that morning. Obviously, Rodgers had had time to think about what happened and was not very happy.

"Mike, those were my calls," Hood said. "Where to cut, who to shuffle, and who to help. If you want to vent, do it to me."

"It's not that clean, Paul," Rodgers said. "I've been offered a position with Senator Orr's new political party. The way this investigation is being handled could hurt us. And you."

"I don't understand," McCaskey said.

"People are going to regard your involvement as opportunistic," Rodgers told them. "Op-Center gets downsized, the director redefines its mission in a very public way, the cuts get restored."

"I hope you don't believe that," Hood said.

"I don't, but there are people who will," Rodgers said. "They may try to hit you again."

"So this is your lifeline to us?" McCaskey asked.

"Partly," Rodgers said. "I also want to protect the senator. The Wilson death is already big news. The Metro Police are on it. People expect that. I'm worried that when they find out Op-Center is also involved, we'll start hearing about international conspiracies."

"And you think that our involvement will kick things to another level," McCaskey said.

"Exactly," Rodgers said. "It will bring even more unwanted attention to the senator and his cause."

McCaskey saw Rodgers's point. The murder was already crime news and business news. This would make it spy news.

"Mike, what's the senator's take on Wilson's death?" McCaskey asked.

Rodgers pinned him to the wall with a look. "Are you asking as part of the investigation?"

"Nothing we talk about leaves this office," McCaskey replied sharply.

"The senator had no beef with the man," Rodgers said. "He didn't like his banking plans but was going to fight those politically."

"Does he think someone at the party may have been responsible?" McCaskey pressed.

"I really don't know," Rodgers said. "I didn't see anything unusual while I was there."

"I didn't realize you were there," Hood said. He seemed genuinely surprised.

"They asked me over for a meet and greet, and then made the job offer," Rodgers said.

"Now I see why you're uncomfortable about this," Hood said. "You'd be a great asset to any team."

"But we can't just drop this."

"Why? It's a police matter."

"We'll be sharing information with the Metro Police, and we can shift the bulk of our load to them over the next few days. Hell, we *have* to do that. Darrell is needed elsewhere. But Scotland Yard asked for our help. Darrell found the evidence. For better or worse, we have to show London and the world some follow-through."

"Or else?"

"Key alliances may be hurt, and we can't afford that now," Hood said. "We're going to need to outsource more foreign recon than before."

"You should also realize that the deeper you get, the more difficult it will be to ease out," Rodgers said. "There will be a turf war with the police, and then you'll have to see this through or come off looking weak. People will wonder why you were involved in the first place. They won't get the quid pro quo side of our business. They'll think you were grandstanding."

"Perhaps," Hood said. "I'm hoping there's a middle ground and that we can find it."

"You know, there might be a way to satisfy everyone with a minimum of fuss," McCaskey said. "Mike, how receptive do you think Senator Orr would be to meeting with me?"

"I don't know. To what end?"

"To show his goodwill. An interview would acknowledge Op-Center's role in this investigation. That could be our big, public flourish. It would allow me to tell the press and Scotland Yard that I met the man, found him blameless—I presume—and would like to hand this investigation to the police, where it belongs. We can still be the Yard's eyes and ears but from a distance."

"I don't know if the senator would have a problem with that, but his associate Admiral Link might," Rodgers said.

"Why?" Hood asked.

"He has openly wondered if this whole thing is a ploy to get our—I mean your—budget cuts restored," Rodgers said. "He might see this as a way for Op-Center to get attention."

"Is Link running the show?" Hood asked.

"No," Rodgers said. "But he was at the Company for years, and I would not want to invoke retaliation needlessly."

"If Link has it in for us, visiting the senator probably won't change things," McCaskey said.

"It might," Rodgers said. "He does not seem to be the kind of man who likes to be cornered."

"Who does?" McCaskey asked.

"My point is, Link has the influence and resources to get uncornered," Rodgers said.

"That's a potential problem," Hood admitted. "But we're in this thing now, and that's a *real* problem."

"How do you position it so that Senator Orr doesn't appear to be a suspect?" Rodgers asked.

"I'm not going over there to find out what he did, only what he might have seen and heard," McCaskey said. "We can even say he asked for the meeting. That would make him seem eager to cooperate."

Rodgers considered the proposal. "I'll call him," he said

after a moment. "Kat told me that Senator Orr is going to do *Nightline.* That may be a good platform to announce something like this."

"It would help everyone," McCaskey agreed.

The general excused himself. Hood and McCaskey exhaled.

"That was . . . strange," McCaskey said, after searching for a better word but not finding one.

"Yeah."

"I guess we're the enemy now."

"I didn't get that," Hood said.

"Oh? I heard a serious threat with Ken Link's name attached."

"That was an advisory," Hood said. "Mike is hurting, but he's looking out for Op-Center. My head is the only one that might interest him."

The men discussed other Op-Center business until Rodgers returned. He looked like a catcher who disagreed with an ump's call but knew better than to say so.

"I just had a conference call with Senator Orr and Admiral Link," Rodgers said. He regarded Hood. "The senator has declined to see Darrell but said he would meet with you as a courtesy."

"As a *courtesy*?" Hood declared.

"This is a criminal investigation, not a press conference," McCaskey said.

"The senator does not want to give the impression that he is being interrogated," Rodgers replied. "He told me he will gladly answer Paul's questions about the case but insisted that he does not have much to say."

"Right. And when I go there, this immediately becomes more about us than about him," Hood said. "It looks like I'm making a personal headline grab, which will call into question our motives—which Link has already done—and undermine everything Op-Center has or will contribute to the investigation."

"Mike, I just don't get it," McCaskey said. "I damn near agreed to exonerate the senator and back away. Why wouldn't he want that?"

"My guess is he isn't guilty of anything," Rodgers said.

Hood rested his elbows on his desk. He dug his palms into his eyes. "I think it was Twain who said that when all else fails, do what's right." He looked up. "Gentlemen, we were justified getting into this, and we have a valid reason to see it through. Mike, please thank the senator for us and tell him we hope it won't be necessary to accept his generous offer when the investigation is further along."

Rodgers did not respond. He looked at McCaskey, gave him a half-smile, and left the office.

"Not 'strange,'" McCaskey said when Rodgers was gone. "That was disturbing. How did we end up on different sides of the barricade?"

"I'm not even sure how the barricade got there," Hood said.

"I swear, I should have just ignored the goddamn wound under Wilson's tongue," McCaskey said.

"No!" Hood replied, a hint of anger in his voice. "That would have been a lot worse than disturbing, Darrell. When it becomes wrong to seek justice, we should all turn in our suits."

Darrell could not dispute that. But he was not ready to agree that the goal was more honorable than what it might take to get there: going to war against an old friend.

SEVENTEEN

Washington, D.C.
Monday, 7:22 P.M.

It was not supposed to happen the way it did. The death of William Wilson was supposed to be news for a day or two and then go away. It was supposed to be recorded as a heart attack, not a homicide. Now it was not going to go away, and she had to change the focus.

She dressed the same as last time, only this time she wore a scarf instead of a wide-brimmed hat. And big, dark sunglasses, pure Audrey Hepburn. All the fashionable people wore them at night. She went to another fashionable hotel, the Monarch on M Street NW, in the upscale West End district. She sat by a courtyard fountain, her back to the hotel, her feet on the ground, her purse and a package of Kleenex in her lap. She thought of the death of her father, something that always brought tears. She wept into one Kleenex and then another for practice. Then she stopped crying and waited. She told herself not to worry, everything was going to go down perfectly.

A white stretch limousine pulled up. A couple got out. She ignored them. They ignored her. A few minutes later, a cab arrived and two men emerged. One of them attempted to talk to her. He was a lobbyist for the recording industry. Close, but not worth the effort. She did not cry. She did not continue the conversation.

The third limousine was a black stretch. A gray-haired gentleman emerged with a young aide. The older man was about sixty and dressed in Armani. He was wearing a wedding band and a deep tan. He obviously lived in a sunny climate. He was tall and trim and apparently worked out.

She started to sob. With a glance her way and a tug on his cuff links, the older man excused himself from the younger man and walked over.

"Is there something wrong, miss?" he asked.

Southern accent. Deep south. He touched her shoulder. She looked at his hand and then at him. The hand appeared soft, except for chafing around the crook of the thumb. From a golf glove and too-hard grip, she imagined. There were three clear one-carat diamonds in the cuff link and a Rolex on his wrist.

"Thank you, but I—I don't want to trouble you," she said.

"It's no trouble to stop a pretty girl's tears," he replied.

She smiled up at him. "You're sweet. But really, I'll be all right just as soon as I find someone to teach my husband a lesson."

"Where I come from, looking after the honor of a lady is not only a duty, it is a privilege," the man said. "May I ask what the problem is? Perhaps I can help."

"I was here to meet a friend for drinks," she said. "I was sitting here, and he came in with one of his coworkers. He was all over her. He was supposed to be at a conference. He did not even see me." She started sobbing again.

The man handed her his handkerchief. It was monogrammed. "May I ask your name?" he said.

"Bonnie," she said.

"How utterly charming," he said. "I am Robert Lawless. Bob to my friends. If you like, we can talk about this further."

"Mr. Lawless—"

"Bob," he said softly.

"Bob," she said, "I appreciate your kindness, but I think I'll just sit here a while and then go home."

"To a scoundrel?"

"For now," she said. "I will see about having him relocated in the morning."

"I am not without connections here," Bob said, patting her shoulder. "Perhaps I can help. If you'd like, we can still have that drink."

She shook her head vehemently. "No! He's still here, and I don't want to see him again—"

"In my suite, then, if you like," Bob said. "I will be a gentleman."

The woman dabbed her eyes and looked into his. "Well . . . I don't feel like going home, and it is chilly."

"That is to be expected when you sit beside a fountain," he pointed out with a smile. "Your shoulder is damp with spray. We can set your coat out to dry."

She smiled back. "All right, Mr. Lawless—Bob. Thank you. I would be delighted to join you for a drink."

Bob walked back to his aide and finished up their conversation. He sent the young man off in the limousine, then returned. He offered her his arm. She put on sunglasses—to hide her bloodshot eyes, she said—then took it. Less than two minutes later they were in his penthouse suite.

They sat in the living room, and he poured drinks from the minibar. He removed her damp jacket for her. He sat on a separate chair, though he did move it over to be close. She asked what he did. He said he was one of the largest commercial real estate brokers in the Carolinas. He told her he spent a great deal of time in Washington lobbying for tax incentives so that companies would stay in the United States instead of moving to Mexico or the Far East.

She felt bad. Bob Lawless was her kind of guy, except for the fact that he obviously had a wife and did not care. But she was here, and they needed this kill.

He had moved in closer while he was speaking and fixed her with his pale blue eyes. She responded to his "gentlemanly" advance by crying and then taking his hand for support and allowing him to put his arm around her. He kissed her damp cheek. She turned and hugged his neck and put her hands behind his head. She let her fingers loose in his longish hair, and he began kissing her neck. Without breaking their connection, she slid from her chair and bent over him, still holding him tight.

He was sitting and she was standing. She put her lips gently against his ear and continued to kiss it while she released her embrace and moved around him.

"You are a wonderful man, Bob Lawless," the woman whispered as she shifted behind him.

"And you are a beautiful woman," he replied. "One who should never know this kind of pain."

"You are so sweet, so gentle."

She sniffled hard to show that her tears were coming to an end. Then she eased her right arm around his throat. She slid her fingertips gently along his throat to the left, so that her forearm went across the front.

"Your neck, your shoulders, they're so strong," she said.

"That comes from a lot of golf and tennis," he told her. "I also work out with a trainer."

"It shows," she said. Her eyes ranged over his torso. "Broad shoulders, graceful motion, strong hands."

Her fingers moved to his ear. A moment later, his chin was near the crook of her arm.

"I like outdoor games," she said. "Indoor, too."

"Oh? What kind?" he asked slyly.

Suddenly, the woman pulled her forearm back toward her, hard. Before Bob could react, she put her left hand against the left side of his face and pushed to the right. That drove his throat deeper into the wedge of her elbow.

This particular choke hold blocked the air supply instantly and completely. It also cut off the flow of blood to the brain. Unconsciousness typically came in less than ten seconds. That was not even enough time for the skin of the neck to bruise.

Bob Lawless gasped silently while tugging and then

clawing desperately at her arm. He kicked out with his unscuffed Ferragamos as the seconds lengthened. The shiny black shoes moved like windshield wipers, in and out, in and out, before falling to the plush plum carpet. An instant later, Bob's shoulders drooped, his arms went slack, and his head rolled to the right.

Cautiously, the woman relaxed her hold. Bob's head dropped forward, his breathing barely audible.

"What kind of games do I like?" the woman said. "The kind where I make the rules."

The woman went to a lamp and angled the shade so the light hit Bob in the face. Then she retrieved her purse from a nearby coffee table. She removed the syringe and the handkerchief he had given her. She used the cloth to grip his tongue, raising it and working the needle underneath She poked the tip into the large vein at the root and injected ten milliliters of potassium chloride. Then she stepped back. She watched, listened as his respiration went from shallow to none.

She tucked the handkerchief and syringe in her purse, retrieved her jacket, then undid one of the buttons of Bob's shirt. She slid her right hand inside and felt his chest. There was no heartbeat. She stood back.

"Sorry, Bob," she said. "But at least you died advancing a cause you believed in."

Bob had removed her scarf. She used it to wipe fingerprints from the solid surfaces she had touched—the drinking glass and the wooden armrests of the chair. Then she slipped it back on her head. The woman removed a pair of white gloves from her purse and put them on, along with her sunglasses. She left the room and returned to the elevator, careful to keep her face downturned. All that the cameras in the elevator would see was her jacket and the top of her head.

Just like the night before.

Hopefully, no more killings remained.

EIGHTEEN

Washington, D.C.
Monday, 8:30 P.M.

Darrell McCaskey came by to see Rodgers after the meeting with Hood. He invited Rodgers for a drink but the general declined. He said he needed to be alone, to think about the job offer from the senator. In fact, Rodgers did not feel like socializing with anyone from Op-Center. It was nothing personal, but the odor of disloyalty hung about the place and its people. Rodgers hoped it would pass. He liked McCaskey and Bob Herbert. But he needed to get away from it now. He spent a few hours cleaning his office, deleting personal files from his computer, and storing them on disks.

He reached his ranch-style home in Bethesda, Maryland, at seven-thirty. He removed his jacket and dropped it over the arm of the sofa. Then he poured a drink and sat down at the small dining room table. As he went through the mail, he sipped the small "medicinal dose" of Southern Comfort, as his grandfather used to call it. It was exactly what he needed to heal his wounded soul.

The mail was all catalogues and bills, no letters. Not that Rodgers was surprised. He could not remember the last letter he received. He remembered what it meant to get letters in Vietnam, to read words that had made a journey from hand to hand. It was immediate and intimate, like looking over someone's shoulder as they gave something of themselves. Opening an envelope that contained an offer for a 0 percent credit card or discount coupons from the local strip mall did not have the same effect.

Then something nearly as good happened. Rodgers got a call from Kat Lockley. She was not calling about business.

"I'm sorry I did not get to see you before," she said. "It was a *very* press-intensive day. And it's not over. We've got *Nightline* coming up."

"I understand completely," he said. "Are you going with the senator to the *Nightline* broadcast?"

"Actually, I'm not. I had a meeting outside the office about the convention. He went with his attorney, David Rico. Dave had some concern about what Koppel might ask and wanted some ground rules about the homicide."

"Understandable."

"So, since I'm free, and since it looks like we're going to be working together, I was wondering if you felt like grabbing dinner or a snack or a drink," she said.

"Actually, dinner is a good idea," he replied. "I didn't have time for lunch. Where are you?"

"In my car, on Delaware Avenue."

Rodgers thought for a moment. "How about Equinox, 818 Connecticut Avenue NW?"

"Perfect," she said. "American cuisine."

"That's why I suggested it," Rodgers said. "I'll be there in thirty-five or forty minutes."

"I'll be at the bar with a vodka martini," she said. "By the time you get there, it will be my second."

"I hear that," Rodgers said.

He hung up, left his own unfinished glass in the sink, snatched his jacket from the sofa, and headed out. The call from Kat was more healing than the Southern Comfort. It was reassuring to feel part of a team, especially when a woman was right there in the huddle. It occurred to him that he did not even know if she was married, engaged, dating, or straight. Right now, the camaraderie was more important.

The roads to D.C. were lightly trafficked, and Connecticut Avenue NW was virtually empty. Rodgers made the drive in a half-hour flat. The dark bar was crowded with staffers from the White House, which was nearby, along with a cross section of Washington power brokers. Kat was at the end of the bar, talking to a slender, very attractive woman. The woman was holding a small beaded purse in her left hand and a glass of red wine in her right.

"Mike, I'd like you to meet Lucy O'Connor," Kat said as he approached. It was loud in the bar, and Kat had to shout to be heard. No wonder nothing ever stayed a secret in Washington.

The woman put her drink on the bar. "Delighted," she said as she shook Rodgers's hand.

"Lucy writes about the Hill for the *American Spectator* and has a syndicated radio show," Kat said. "How many markets now?"

"Forty-seven," she said.

"Impressive," Rodgers said.

"Not compared to what you have done," Lucy said.

Rodgers rolled a shoulder. "I was in the wrong places at the right time."

"A true hero, taciturn and modest," Lucy remarked. "But since you've very happily fallen in my lap, General Rodgers, tell me, in as few words as you like. Is Op-Center busy redefining its mission?"

"If having your budget whacked is redefining, I suppose the answer is yes," Rodgers replied.

"I heard about the cuts, but that isn't what I meant. I'm talking about the Wilson investigation."

"Wow, that's really the talk of the town, isn't it?" Rodgers asked.

"*Everything* is the talk of this town," Lucy said.

"The Wilson investigation is a fluke," he said.

Rodgers leaned past the reporter and ordered a Samuel Adams. He hated being pushed, and he hated being pushed by journalists even more. They attacked the front door, the back door, the windows, and when that did not work, they crawled under the front stoop and waited like snakes.

"Is that what you two are here to discuss?" Lucy asked.

"Good guess, but no," Kat told her.

Lucy frowned. "You're not going to tell me it's purely social."

"Actually, it is," Rodgers said as the bartender handed him his beer. "I was at the senator's party last night. Ms. Lockley wanted to meet me and called. Here I am."

"Why were you at the party?"

"Free food," Rodgers said.

Lucy smiled. "All right, General. I won't press. But Kat? I want a half-hour window if there's any news. That will give me time to put it on my web site."

"And give you bragging rights for being the first," Rodgers said.

"That's what gives a reporter heft," Lucy replied. "You remember those days, don't you, Kat?"

Kat said she did and agreed to give Lucy a scoop if there was one to be had. The reporter left the bar to scout for leads elsewhere. Kat picked up a shopping bag that was beside the stool, and Rodgers escorted his date and his beer to the restaurant atrium for dinner.

"Sorry about all that," Kat sat as they were seated. "She got there right before you did, so there was no time to disengage. I hope it wasn't too painful."

"Define 'too.' "

"Enough to make you not want to work with us," Kat said. "We have to be much more accessible than the key people at Op-Center."

"It will take getting used to, but I'll survive," Rodgers said. "All I need to do is keep up that Gary Cooper facade."

"That may be even more appealing," Kat pointed out.

"Maybe, but at least there are only two words to the

script," Rodgers said. " 'Yup' and 'nope.' I can handle that. But how about we do what we told Ms. O'Connor. Keep this social."

"Good idea," she said, just ahead of a smile that was the first one he could recall seeing.

"Anything interesting in the bag?" Rodgers asked.

"A present and my Nikes," Kat said. "Heels get tiring."

"I can imagine," he said. "You want to change? I won't say anything."

"Not appropriate in here. When I leave."

"So tell me. How did you come to work with the senator?" Rodgers asked.

"Well, as you probably gathered from Lucy, I used to be one of them," she said. "I graduated from Columbia and was hired by the *Wall Street Journal* as a reporter for the Washington Bureau."

"Were your folks reporters or politicians?"

"They were New York City cops. Both of them. So was my older brother. The Lockley family defined the word *tough*."

"Was there any pressure for you to go into law enforcement?"

"Not directly." She laughed. "Unless you consider taking martial arts and gun safety classes instead of ballet and playing with dolls to be pressure. I didn't mind, though. We did it as a family."

"Sounds pretty well-adjusted," Rodgers said.

"It was."

"Then where did journalism come from?"

"Our other family activity was watching the news on TV," Kat said. "The local news always had a lot of police stories, and I loved watching the reporters. They got to hang with police officers and firefighters and soldiers, so I started doing my own newscasts with our video camera and interviewing my folks and their friends. I loved it, and it stuck."

The waiter came over, and they took a moment to look at the menu. They decided to order several appetizers and share.

"So," Rodgers went on. "Did you go directly from the *Journal* to becoming the senator's press secretary?"

"Pretty much," she said. "I made some stabs at getting into TV, but you need connections, fangs, or both. All I had was an interest in reporting news. Dad and the senator were old buds. When I was assigned to cover Don Orr's last campaign, he offered me a job. He said it wasn't nepotism. He told me I had 'the goods.' "

"You do," Rodgers said.

"Maybe." She shrugged. "I figured if nothing else, I'd pick up TV connections for the future."

"Smart. Looks like you anticipated everything."

"Not quite," she said. "In a high-profile position like this one, you have to watch everything you say *and* everything your boss says." She gestured toward the bar. "As you saw back there, self-censorship is a constant process, and you suffer a complete loss of privacy. I did not appreciate the degree to which that would happen."

"Maybe you need to come up with an alter ego," Rodgers suggested. "Get a wig, a pair of sunglasses, black lipstick."

"I have all of those." She laughed. "It's my Goth side."

"Pardon?"

"Goth. Gothic. You know—vampires, black lace and leather, sharpening your teeth with a file and dying your skin white."

"People do that?" Rodgers asked.

Kat nodded. "It's a large and growing subculture."

"I had no idea."

The age difference of some twenty years suddenly became very apparent to Rodgers. He still thought the rock group KISS was over the top. At the same time, Rodgers's respect for Senator Orr grew. The Texan was even older, yet he had dared to hire a twenty-something who brought different ideas to the staff. Though it *was* alarming to think of vampires as a potential voting bloc.

"It's funny," Kat said as the food arrived. "I'm the journalist, yet you're the one asking the questions."

"I don't have access to a dossier of your entire life," Rodgers pointed out.

"Touché," she said, smiling again.

The two talked a little about Rodgers and then about the problems of mounting a national campaign. It was an open, intelligent talk. Rodgers did not know if it had been part of Orr's plan, but by the time they were finished, the general had decided to accept the employment offer.

While they were having coffee, Lucy O'Connor returned. She was making notes in a PalmPilot as she weaved through the crowded restaurant and made her way directly to the table. Upon arriving, she fixed her eager eyes on Kat.

"There's been another killing," she said breathlessly.

"Who?" Kat asked. She seemed unusually alarmed. Or maybe she was tired of talking to reporters.

"A big shot Southern realtor named Robert Lawless," Lucy said, reading from the PalmPilot. "A woman went to his hotel room—at the Monarch, this time—and left a few minutes later. Sometime between, she apparently poked him under the tongue with a hypodermic. The only difference between the Wilson and Lawless incidents is that this killer went up with him."

"Did the security cameras get anything?" Rodgers asked.

"Same as yesterday," Lucy replied. "A woman whose features were hidden, this time by a scarf and sunglasses."

"How did you hear about it?" Kat asked.

"Someone in hotel security saw the woman in the elevator, thought she looked suspicious, and decided to check on Mr. Lawless. I was in the bar, networking, heard the fuss."

"But they didn't hold the woman," Kat said.

"They were a few steps too late," Lucy said. "She got off on the mezzanine, not in the lobby, and walked out a side door. The good news, I guess, is that it seems to take your soiree out of the spotlight. Lawless wasn't on the invite list."

Kat looked at her watch, then excused herself. She said she was going outside to call the senator. This was something he should know before he taped the show. "I owe you," she said to Lucy as she left.

"I'll want a comment from the senator," Lucy said.

Kat nodded as she walked away. The reporter smiled and took the seat across from General Rodgers. The thirty-something woman had short blond hair, pale skin, thin red lips, and a hungry look.

There were all kinds of vampires in Washington.

"Lucky you were there," Rodgers said.

"My middle name is Kay," the reporter said. "My folks gave it to me so I could add it to Lucy whenever I wanted."

"Cute," Rodgers said.

"So, General," Lucy said. "What about these rumors that Op-Center is being phased out?"

"Intelligence fund reapportionments are cyclical," Rodgers said. "Op-Center got a boost five years ago, now they're being cut back. They're still beefier than they were when they started."

That was longer than "nope." Mike Rodgers was proud of himself—but only for a moment.

"They?" Lucy said.

That was a slip. Rodgers should have been more careful.

"General, are you going to work for Senator Orr and the USF?" Lucy asked. "Is that why you were at the party last night?"

"Nope," he said.

"Nope?" Lucy said, her mouth twisting.

"Nope." Words were a reporter's oxygen supply. Cut it off, and they died.

"Sir, I am on your side, *their* side. I can help. The more leads I get, the more credibility I have, the more favorable press the senator gets. Are you sure there's nothing you want to tell me?"

"Yep," he said.

She frowned. She reached into the PalmPilot carrying case and handed him a business card. "When you feel like talking, call me first."

He tucked the card in his shirt pocket. He said nothing, though he did smile politely.

Kat returned then and said that the news had reached the senator right after he left.

"How did he hear about it?" Rodgers asked.

"From *Nightline*," she replied. "They wanted him to know that they were going to go easy on the questions about Wilson because of this."

Lucy got up to give Kat the seat. "Well, I'm going to get online and coin a name for our serial killer before someone else does. It will make an incredible book title one day."

The reporter left while Rodgers and Kat finished their coffee.

"Well, that was a strange end to a very unusual day."

"Strange in what way?"

"It started with me denying that Op-Center would ever fake evidence to get publicity and ended with me sitting here wondering if a reporter would kill people to get a book deal."

The woman laughed. "Lucy is aggressive. But I don't think she's a killer."

"Was she at the party last night?"

"Yes," Kat said. "That was why she came over to me at

the bar. To guarantee continued terrific coverage of the USF for continued A-list status."

"Will you give it to her?"

"I said I'd talk to the senator," Kat said. "But I'll probably give it to her. Otherwise, she *might* become homicidal."

Kat insisted on picking up the tab, after which Rodgers walked her to her car. There was no sexual tension, which was fine with him. It had been a long day. He was looking forward to catching *Nightline* and going to bed.

And for the first time in his life, General Mike Rodgers realized how utterly, sadly accurate the maxim about old soldiers truly was.

NINETEEN

Washington, D.C.
Monday, 10:55 P.M.

Darrell McCaskey was sitting in bed, reading and waiting for Maria to finish taking a shower. His wife had spent most of the day with Ed March, helping him investigate the Malaysian connection. March had taken her to dinner to thank her. McCaskey had been checking on Orr party guests and had been unable to join them.

Maria had just entered the bedroom when the phone beeped. It was Dr. Minnie Hennepin.

"The police are bringing in another apparent hotel homicide," she told him. "They found the same kind of puncture wound as Mr. Wilson."

"Who was it?" McCaskey asked as he put his book on the night table. He reached for the TV remote control and put on the local news.

"A Southern businessman. That's all I heard."

"Do the police have any information about the killer?"

"Apparently they have no more information than they had on the first one," she said.

"Doctor, I appreciate the call," McCaskey said.

Maria lay down beside her husband. He kissed his wife, then cradled her while he checked his cell phone for messages. There were no missed calls. He rang his office phone and found no messages there, either. That was going to make his next step an extremely difficult one.

The death of the businessman, Robert Lawless, was the lead story on the news. They listened to an interview with

Lawless's aide and watched a video shot from the security camera of the woman emerging on the mezzanine. She was careful to hide her face from the camera.

"What does your gut tell you about all this?" McCaskey asked his wife.

"She's a professional."

"Yeah. This is not some angry escort turning against men."

"But what individual would have access to hypodermic needles and drugs?" she asked.

"Potassium chloride is readily available from chemical supply firms, and syringes are easy to come by."

"Did you learn anything from the party guests?" she asked.

"Unless we're dealing with a cover-up, all of the women had alibis," McCaskey said.

The phone rang as they were talking. McCaskey muted the TV and checked the Caller ID. It was Paul Hood.

"I assume you've heard," Hood said.

"Yes," McCaskey replied.

Maria took the remote and punched up the sound. McCaskey put a finger in his ear so he could hear.

"Not to be cold about it, but how does this impact us?" Hood asked.

"I was just thinking about that, and it looks like a lose-lose-lose situation," McCaskey said. "The Metro Police have not called to ask for our input. If we force it on them, we're going to come off as aggressive. If we don't, we'll appear weak. If we investigate independently, we'll seem isolated and high-handed."

"What if we officially bow out?" Hood asked.

"Bailing is our best option," McCaskey said. "Scotland Yard will squawk, but it's unlikely anyone will hear. The trick is what spin do we put on it?"

Maria poked his side. "You can't leave."

McCaskey frowned.

"You stand a better chance of finding her than the police," Maria went on.

"Hold on, Paul," McCaskey said. He turned to his wife. "Why do you think *we* can find her?"

"She is not a killer. She is an assassin."

"Why would an assassin go after a successful but relatively unimportant businessman like Lawless?"

"Exactly," she said.

"I don't follow."

"Unlike the death of William Wilson, this murder was an afterthought," Maria said. "Someone wanted Wilson out of the way, so they hired a very skilled individual who made it look as if he had died of natural causes. They did not want a murder. Otherwise, they could have hired a sniper to shoot him from Lafayette Park. When you destroyed that scenario, they were forced to target someone else, to make the Wilson death seem like the first high-profile strike of a hypodermic serial killer who was chasing down wealthy businessmen. Lawless happened to be the man she picked."

"What makes you think that Lawless was an arbitrary choice?" McCaskey asked his wife.

"Look at the dissimilarities in the approach to the death," the former Interpol agent told him. "William Wilson had bodyguards. The assassin had to approach him as a lover to get past them and make sure they stayed away. And because she was the lover of a high-profile individual, the hotel staff would have made a point of paying her very little attention. She came to the hotel, they did their business, she left—all of it relatively invisible. Tonight was different. Listen to these interviews," she said, pointing at the TV. "The woman spoke with another man in the courtyard but never looked up at him. The dead man's assistant noticed her, but she did not let him see her face. She was being very cautious."

"Right. She did not want to be identified, because she was waiting to kill him," her husband said.

"No. After the killing, she got off on the mezzanine," Maria said. "She had already cased out the hotel, knew how to leave with minimum visibility. Why do that and then go *back* outside and expose herself to all of this scrutiny? If Lawless had been the intended target all along, she could have posed as his wife or daughter and gotten into the room. She could have ambushed a housekeeper and taken a master key. She could have knocked on his door after he had gone in. Who would not admit a young woman? She could have used a syringe to inject hydrochloric acid into the lock to dissolve it. She took none of those safer routes because our assassin did not know Lawless was going to be her victim. Not until she spoke with him, found out he was successful enough to fit the serial killer motif she—or whoever hired her—had invented, and learned that he was staying in the hotel alone."

McCaskey was silent while he processed everything his wife had said. "You're saying that making this appear to be a pattern actually underscores the uniqueness of the first hit," McCaskey said.

"That is how I see it," Maria replied.

"It's possible," he muttered after a long, long moment. "Dammit, it really is. Brava, my love."

She smiled at him.

"Paul, did you hear any of that?"

"I did, Darrell, and I'm still processing it," Hood told him. "But tell Maria 'well done.' "

"Thank you!" she said from under her husband's arm.

"It sounds like we're going to have to stay involved with this, then," Hood said.

"Maybe even deeper than we were before," McCaskey said.

If Maria had nailed this, they were not looking at a

vengeful escort or industrial espionage. They were looking at something strongly reminiscent of what the FBI called an IOS, an improvised operational scenario. One in which the carefully devised plans for a strike team, undercover personnel, or sometimes both had to be quickly and effectively reconfigured because something had gone wrong.

An operation that was traditionally handled by seasoned intelligence personnel.

TWENTY

Washington, D.C.
Tuesday, 7:13 A.M.

Paul Hood had gone home for a long sleep, shower, then returned to Op-Center. He was wiped out from a day that was spent mostly with Ron Plummer, reviewing the restructuring of Op-Center. The investigation was also draining. It was not just a chess game but a chess game on multiple levels. Overinvolvement to help Scotland Yard might damage relations with the Metro Police. A concession to the police might weaken Hood's credibility not just with the Yard but with other intelligence agencies. Spending money on a non–core operation might hurt Hood's standing with the CIOC and with Op-Center employees who were going to be hard-pressed to do their existing jobs. In one sense, it was a hell of a challenge. In another, it was daunting and exhausting.

The previous afternoon had been so full that Hood did not have an opportunity to call his former wife. When he finally did have the time, it was nearly eleven P.M. Sharon would probably be asleep or with Jim Hunt. In any case, Hood preferred to talk with her when he was fresh. It helped him deal with whatever feelings of entitlement or bitterness she might spray his way.

Ironically, just before he phoned her, Matt Stoll called. He said that he understood the staff cuts and could do a lot of the maintenance work, paperwork, "the gruntwork" himself. But he said he needed at least another set of hands to help him. Cheap hands. "Monkey hands," he said.

There was something about that image which amused Hood. He knew a chimp they could hire.

He was disappointed with the crankiness in his soul, but the hurt was there and it wasn't going away. As long as he didn't communicate that to Sharon, no harm was done.

Sharon was rushed, as usual, when he called. She was going to work out, and her trainer—another addition to her new life—did not like it when she was late. She was also polite but formal, as Hood had come to expect. He got the words out quickly. Otherwise, he would have changed his mind about telling her that he had found an internship for Frankie Hunt.

"It's with Matt Stoll," Hood told her. "He'll be working on put-the-square-peg-in-the-square-hole stuff. Inventory and routing software and hardware upgrade notifications."

"Great," Sharon said. "Thanks."

She really did sound grateful. That made him uncomfortable. Sharon was happy because he was helping his goddamn *replacement.* There was a point at which a good soldier became an idiot. He felt he had crossed that.

"E-mail me his contact information," Hood told her, continuing because he had no choice. "I'll order an expedited background check, and we can go from there."

"Will do," she said. "Frankie is a good kid."

"I'm sure he is," Hood said pleasantly. It was filler, but he could not think of anything else to say. Anything civil, that is.

Since the children had already left for school, the call ended with a pair of unsentimental good-byes. Hood sat there for a moment, looking at the phone. He wanted to slam his fist on it but did not. The phone was not his enemy. He was. Mr. Cooperative, the mediator, the nice guy.

The idiot.

As with Senator Debenport the day before, an early-morning phone conversation ended with Hood feeling as if he had been someone's stooge. He hoped this did not become a pattern. It might make him insecure, and crises did not yield to men of caution. At the same time, Hood could not afford to become overly bold and push Op-Center deeper into areas where it had no legitimate business.

Both extremes were tested when Darrell McCaskey arrived. McCaskey came to see Hood with something that had been on his mind all morning: the name of the only individual who fit Maria's quick-sketch profile.

"Admiral Kenneth Link," McCaskey said. "He's a former head of covert ops with the CIA, he's got an anti-European agenda, and he knew where William Wilson was staying."

"Okay, so Link did not like the man's policies," Hood said. "What does he gain by removing Wilson?"

"I'm not sure," McCaskey admitted. "But I can't dismiss the possibility."

"Fair enough. Talk it out."

"A prominent Brit dies abroad after a sexual encounter," McCaskey said. "The Fleet Street tabloids are all over that. Wilson's death not only cripples and probably terminates the new banking venture, it affects the stock price of his company. The tawdriness of what happened hurts the value even more. In short, Wilson's death shuts down a potential threat to the American economy."

"Right," Hood replied. "But doesn't that help the current administration and not Senator Orr?"

"Just the opposite, I would think," McCaskey said. "If the rumors about Orr are true, he is going to come out and effectively promote a strong policy of isolationism. Wilson's death gives the senator a salacious, Eurocentric target, someone the president's endorsed successor can't hit."

"Because, like us, the president has overseas alliances to protect."

McCaskey nodded. "Orr wouldn't care about that. His only concern is the American electorate."

"That might also be a rival's concern," Hood said. "Someone could be looking to frame Link and stop a credible threat to the two-party system."

"It's possible," McCaskey admitted.

Hood shook his head. "One problem I have with your theory, Darrell, is that Wilson was as viable a target for Orr alive as he was dead. In fact, if Wilson were alive, his European banking operation might have won Don Orr even more support."

"But we're not talking about the senator," McCaskey reminded him. "We're talking about Admiral Link."

"I understand that. But I'm still not clear what he could possibly gain. Why would he want to hurt Orr's rhetoric by eliminating William Wilson?"

"That *is* the big question," McCaskey said.

"It's also one I'm not sure Op-Center needs to answer," Hood said. "We agreed to stick a finger in this for Scotland Yard. The more I look at it, the more it does not seem like a crisis."

"That depends on your definition of crisis," McCaskey said. "I see a person or persons who were able to move quickly when their killing was exposed. That suggests a conspiracy, one that may involve the office of a United States senator. Give me a little more time to research this, Paul. Let me take a closer look at Kenneth Link and Orr's staff."

"What about Mike?" Hood asked. "Would you involve him?"

"I'm not sure," McCaskey said.

Neither man said what was obviously on both of their minds. Would Mike give his loyalty to the old team or the new? Was it even fair to put him in that position?

A chess game with multiple levels, Hood thought.

Hood called Liz Gordon's office. She was not in yet, and he left a message for her to see him when she arrived. He wanted her to whip up a quick-sketch profile of Link. Then he turned to his computer and brought up the Senate's secure home page. The staff directory was accessible only to government officials. Hood looked up Orr's office staff. Admiral Link was not there, of course, since he was only involved in the United States First Party.

"Do we know anything about Katherine Lockley and Kendra Peterson?" Hood asked.

"A little," McCaskey said. He leaned over Hood, typed his password on the keyboard, and opened the file he had collected on Senator Orr's staff.

"Lockley was a journalist before joining Orr," McCaskey said, looking at his notes. "I checked her bylines, her college records. She checks out. Peterson was a Vietnam war baby, Marine dad, came to live here when she was a kid. She's a gymnast, a national champion in her early teens who missed out on the Olympics because of tendonitis in her fingers. She joined the Marines and managed to pass the physical, though the tendonitis returned, and she ended up working in Camp Pendleton on the DANTES program."

"Which is?"

"Not as ominous at it sounds," McCaskey told him. "It's the Defense Activity for Non-Traditional Education Support certification program. She pushed paper to make sure qualified Marines got a good shot at civilian jobs."

"Is that all she did?"

"It's the only job on record," McCaskey said. "When her enlistment was up, Ms. Peterson used her DANTES connections to get herself a job as a clerk in the U.S. embassy in Japan. That often means a spook."

"Did she pick Japan?"

"That was what the Military Outplacement Specialty Office came up with," McCaskey said.

"No obvious red flags there," Hood said. "Who else is on the senator's staff?"

McCaskey went through the remainder of the list and what he had gathered about each individual. No one stood out.

Hood sighed as McCaskey walked back around the desk. "I don't know, Darrell. You've shown me how Link is qualified to mastermind this but not a single reason why he would."

"Why was Wilson at that party?"

"According to the news reports, so that Orr's friends could make a connection, try to temper his plans," Hood said.

"Is that easier to believe than the fact that Wilson was being set up?" McCaskey asked.

"Frankly, yes. I don't see the trail of bread crumbs that leads from Wilson to Link. Senator Orr is wealthy, and he has extremely wealthy friends. They could have set up a program to challenge Wilson. In fact, that would have made a very strong campaign plank. Even if Link wanted to sabotage Orr's campaign for some reason, make it appear that he was behind the murder, why kill a second businessman? No," Hood said, "I don't see how they connect."

"Okay. Here's a reason Link might have wanted Wilson dead," McCaskey said. "Publicity for Orr. Guilty by innuendo, then exonerated by the second murder."

"Possibly."

"Or maybe Link is a sociopath who misses the thrill of undercover operations," McCaskey said. "I know I do."

"You were stopping transgressions, not instigating them," Hood pointed out.

"Whether you snort, smoke, or inject, danger is a tonic," McCaskey said. "Look, Paul. I don't know why he would do this. I only have a feeling that there's something here."

"How much time will you need to explore this feeling?"

"Forty-eight hours?"

Hood frowned. "Take a day and see where it leads. I can't promise you more than that."

"All right."

"You also have to decide about Mike," Hood went on. "Until I have his resignation, he's still working with us."

"What do you think?"

"Tough call. If he finds out, he'll think we couldn't trust

him. But he'd also feel obligated to tell Link. Best to give him plausible deniability for now."

"Good call. Speaking of calls, I'm going to let Maria know what's up. She might have some ideas."

"Good idea," Hood said. He thought for a moment. "Mike is an honorable man. He may not like what we're doing, but if he smells something wrong, he'll act."

McCaskey smiled.

"Did I miss something?" Hood asked.

"The smile, you mean? Yeah. You never leave us out to dry."

"You lost me," Hood said.

"You said that Mike may not like what *we're* doing," McCaskey told him as he turned to go. "You don't pass the buck, Paul."

Hood did not realize he had done that.

When McCaskey had gone, Hood went to his E-mail. He just stared at the monitor. He had just received another pat on the shoulder for being a good and responsible man. If Paul Hood was so good and responsible, how did he get to this place in life? Rationing McCaskey's hours like they were water in the desert, working as cabin boy on the Good Ship Sharon and Jim, playing defense instead of offense with the CIOC and the William Wilson investigation. When Hood was the mayor of Los Angeles, he used to feel that fighting the city council or one of his commissioners to a draw was unsatisfactory. Right now, a stalemate sounded sweet.

"Knock, knock."

Hood looked up. Liz Gordon was standing in the doorway. Her dark eyes were large and owl wise, framed on three sides by short brown hair. They were set in a wide, open face that invited trust.

"Come in," Hood said.

Liz entered.

"Have you ever heard of Admiral Kenneth Link, former head of covert ops for the CIA?" Hood asked.

"No," Liz said. "Former head? So what is he doing now?"

"Helping Senator Donald Orr launch the new USF Party."

"That's the one Mike is going to work for, correct?"

Hood snickered. "I'm glad to see the Op-Center grapevine hasn't been affected by cutbacks."

"There are cheap, unlimited minutes on that network," Liz joked.

"I saw an online news flash that Orr should be holding a press conference now," Hood said, looking at his watch. "The word is that Link will serve as Orr's vice presidential candidate. Darrell believes Link may be connected to the deaths of William Wilson and this other gentleman, Robert Lawless. I need a quick, rough profile."

"Sure, but I can tell you what it will probably look like," Liz said. "How long did he run covert ops?"

Hood looked up his file. "Twelve years."

"That's a long time," she said. "Did he go right from that job to this one?"

"Within a few months."

"Classic. How often do you hear about former presidents, generals, quarterbacks, and CEOs retiring and playing golf?"

"I don't know—though right now that sounds like a damn fine idea," Hood admitted.

"Precisely. People who run high-performance teams in pressure cooker situations get fried over time," Liz told him. "They rarely go back to that kind of operation. Chances are good that if Admiral Link got out, he did not jump back in. Would the killings have had an elective quality for him?"

"You mean, did it have to be Wilson and did it have to be now?"

Liz nodded.

"We're not sure. What about Link leaving intelligence

work and missing the risk factor? Darrell seems to think that might be significant."

"Moving from behind a curtain at the CIA to center stage in a national political campaign is a pretty big risk," Liz said. "Which brings us to the X factor."

"Which is?"

"A political ticket would be subjected to scrutiny by the press and public," Liz said. "Orr and Link have no control over where those eyes and fingers go probing. A man used to being in charge of things might want to set up a few sidelines that he could control, just to enjoy some familiar ground."

"Including something this bold?"

"Well—that's the unknown quantity," Liz explained. "I'll have a look at Link's file, but I'm not optimistic. A dual murder seems a little extreme for someone who just moved from an organization where that kind of activity was at least acceptable, if not encouraged."

Hood said he would E-mail the file to Liz. Before leaving, she asked if he was all right.

"Sure, why?" he asked, though he knew the answer.

"The situation with Mike," she replied.

"That wasn't easy," Hood admitted. "But hiring and firing are part of the job description."

"Does he know you're investigating his new colleague?"

"No. At least, no one told him. I don't know what he might surmise or suspect."

"So everything's under control here," she said.

Hood picked up a paperweight Alexander had made in the first grade. It was a blue and white glazed lump of clay that was supposed to be Earth. He held it in his fist. "I've got the whole world in my hand, Liz," he said.

"Like Atlas," she said.

"He had it on his shoulders," Hood pointed out.

"Like Atlas," she repeated.

Hood thought about that, then smiled. She got him. He put the paperweight down. "What do you do when you feel like your life and career are on a parallel course in the wrong direction?"

"That depends," Liz replied. She shut the door. "If you're patient, it's like moving around that globe. Learn what you can on the journey, enjoy the scenery, and eventually, you come back around."

"What if you feel like you're running out of fuel?"

"Ride the winds."

"I have been," Hood told her.

"And?" The psychologist moved toward the desk. "Talk to me, Paul."

Hood hesitated. He was not good at this. He did not like to complain or to seek help. But Liz must have sensed that something was wrong. The woman was responsible for keeping psychological files of the staff, and her antennae were always extended. Decisions made in these offices could affect millions of people. If Liz felt that someone were under too much stress, either personal or professional, she could order them to take time off. She had done that with Mike Rodgers after his Striker military unit was decimated in India.

"Truthfully, Liz?" Hood said. "I feel like those winds have been blowing me all over the damn place, mostly away from where I need to be."

"Do you know where you need to be?"

"Not doing this," he said. "Not cutting personnel and pulling back from missions. Not kowtowing."

"That's negative space," she said in a careful, nonjudgmental voice. "You can't define what you should be doing by what you're not doing." She leaned on the desk so their eyes were level. "First tell me this, Paul. Are we talking about home or about Op-Center?"

"Both," he admitted.

"So you feel like your backsliding in two areas."

"Yeah. At the same speed and gaining momentum."

"Do you wish you were back with Sharon?"

"No," he said without hesitation.

"Are you upset that she's getting her life together?"

Liz was Harleigh's therapist, so Hood was not surprised that she knew this.

"No," he answered truthfully.

"You said you were kowtowing. To Sharon?"

Hood nodded. "To her, to the CIOC, to Scotland Yard, and when you leave I'll probably feel like I was kowtowing to you."

"Then tell me to go."

Hood hesitated.

"The only way to stop backsliding is to dig down with your heels." She stood. "Do it, Paul."

"Okay. We're done," he said.

"Not good enough. That isn't an end. It's neutral."

"I don't see the difference," he confessed.

"I'm still here. I'm still talking, aren't I?"

Hood grinned. "Get out," he said sharply. "*Now*," he added.

Liz smiled. "One more thing?" she asked.

Hood could not tell whether or not this was a trap. "One," he said firmly.

"Everyone is disoriented and retrenching," Liz said. "Sharon, the intelligence community, the nation. You're being pushed, but it isn't personal—it's partly fear, partly a sense of renewal."

The intercom beeped. It was Bugs Benet's line.

Liz turned to go. "Don't be afraid to push back," she said. "Aggression externalized is preferable to aggression internalized."

"Isn't that how wars start?" Hood asked as the intercom beeped again.

"No," Liz said. "Was the American Revolution about tea? Was the Civil War about slavery?"

"In part—"

"Bingo. War is never about one thing," Liz said. "It's about one thing that was never addressed and became two things, then three, and finally exploded and consumed everything."

She was right. "Thanks, Liz," Hood said as he picked up the phone.

"Anytime," she said.

Hood nodded gratefully as he took the call. "What is it, Bugs?"

"Chief, the White House just called," Bugs said. "The president wants to see you in two hours."

"Did he say why?"

"No," Bugs said.

Being asked to see the president was not unprecedented. However, if Hood had any doubt about the wisdom of Liz's advice, it evaporated when he asked who else was going to be there.

"Senator Debenport," Bugs replied.

TWENTY-ONE

Washington, D.C.
Tuesday, 7:30 A.M.

With the flags of Texas and the United States as his backdrop, the dome of the Capitol between them, bright morning light causing his gray eyes to sparkle, Senator Donald Orr announced his candidacy for president. A crowd of some two-dozen supporters cheered. Half as many reporters recorded the moment.

Mike Rodgers stood well off to the side with Kat Lockley. He had called early to tell her he was going to accept the job offer and she told him Orr would appreciate having him at the announcement. Rodgers was glad to be invited. Admiral Link stood anonymously among Orr's supporters with Kendra Peterson. Explaining the presence of Rodgers or Link was not a concern. Kat had told the gathering ahead of time that there would be no questions. The press secretary had looked directly at Lucy O'Connor when she said that. Rodgers was not in uniform, and it was unlikely that any member of the press corps would recognize him, either as the deputy director of Op-Center or from the news coverage of the UN siege or the assault in India. Those stories had been about Op-Center, not about him. Rodgers had wanted to be here so he could see how his future boss operated in public. He was certainly impressed with the way Orr had handled himself in his two television appearances. Rodgers routinely taped both the *Evening News* and *Nightline* appearances on his digital recorder. The senator was a master of working the camera. He addressed issues directly and with clarity. When he was not speaking, he used a lowered eyelid, a raised brow, a slight pursing of the lips, or a slant of the head to express himself. Orr knew the difference between communicating and mugging.

"This will not be an ordinary campaign," Orr promised after making his introductory statement. "It will be inaugurated—and I use that term with an eye on the future," he said with a big wink, pausing for applause from his supporters. "It will be inaugurated under the banner of a new party with a new vision for the nation. The United States First Party, working for a new independence."

There were cheers and strong applause from supporters.

Kat leaned toward Rodgers. "That's the slogan," she said.

"I figured," Rodgers replied. "It's a good one. Yours?"

She nodded, then turned her attention back to Orr.

"Our independence will be built on a framework that already exists but has been marginalized by legislation and special interests: the Bill of Rights and the American Constitution. Other nations do not understand our passion for these documents. They do not understand our passion for the freedoms they protect. They are accustomed to being dominated by kings or czars or warlords. We threw off a foreign king. We will not tolerate the dictates of other nations. We will not put their needs above our own. We will no longer be part of a globalization process that finds our values and our way of life reprehensible."

There were more cheers and a few raised fists. Granted, these were the converted. But Rodgers liked what he heard. He could imagine that a majority of American voters would, too.

"Our party will be holding its first convention later this week in San Diego," Orr went on. "Just as the USF will not be an ordinary party, ours will not be a business-as-usual convention. The doors will be open to all. Everyone who attends will have a vote. That is the American way."

The group roared its approval.

Rodgers leaned toward Kat. "I assume you have a plan to fill the convention center," he said. "What are there, about ten thousand seats?"

"Twelve thousand," she said. "Four thousand people are being bused from Texas alone. We have a lot of support in Orange County less than an hour from the convention center—"

"John Wayne country."

"That's right. Our people there have organized a Freedom Freeway caravan to drive to San Diego," Kat told him. "That should bring us another three thousand. We have smaller groups coming from other parts of the country, and we believe individuals will come just to be part of something new and exciting."

"The press likes caravans of ordinary folks," Rodgers observed.

Kat smiled. *Like her namesake,* Rodgers thought.

Orr continued speaking. Rodgers just now noticed that he barely consulted his note cards. He had taken the time to memorize his speech. He was using the silences to make eye contact with the crowd.

"There may be voters in my great home state who feel abandoned by this change in party affiliation," Orr continued. "To those people I say, only the label has changed. The Texan is still a Texan. Don Orr is the same man. He is still a champion for the young who want to work and the elderly who don't want to retire. He believes that service to the nation, to its industry and its economy, should be honored. To those Americans who do not yet know me, I ask that you listen to what we have to say over the next days, and weeks, and months. We are not vainglorious politicians interested in power. We are not puppets controlled by special interest groups or special interest money. We are proud Americans who want to restore our nation to what it was and can be again. A country of scholars and adventurers. A land of bounty, not just in food and natural resources but also *ideas*. A launching pad of extraordinary new goals worthy of an exceptional people. A nation of justice and equality for the wealthy and those less fortunate, for the healthy and the infirm, for people of all ages."

"Leave no vote unharvested," Rodgers whispered to Kat.

"Perhaps, but the senator isn't pandering, General," Kat said. "He means it."

"I believe he does," Rodgers said. "In fact, I'm counting on it." The general was doing more than that. He was responding to it. Whether it was his own situation with Op-Center or a general frustration with bureaucracy, politics, and a fragmented national focus, he was becoming enthusiastic for the first time in years.

"And finally, a few words to our friends abroad," Orr said. "United States First does not mean United States *only*. We believe that a strong and vital America is essential to the health and prosperity of the world. But we believe our role should be as a beacon, not as a bank. We will be trailblazers, not nursemaids. The world is best served by a United States of America that is not a crutch but a foundation, strong and unshakable. This is the platform of our party, one that is designed to serve the proud people of our nation. Ladies and gentlemen, I thank you for your gracious attention today and in the days to come. God bless you all, and God bless these United States."

As the crowd cheered, Kendra maneuvered the senator from the podium and reporters. Questions were being shouted about William Wilson, but they were being ignored. Kat was making notes in a PalmPilot about who was asking the unfriendly questions. Those reporters would probably find access to the senator restricted until that was no longer an issue.

Link had gone ahead to a waiting sedan. Kendra tucked the senator into the back of the black limo and slid in beside him. When they drove off, Rodgers followed Kat toward a table where beverages and snacks were available. They grabbed two cups of coffee before the reporters came by, then walked slowly across the lawn behind the Capitol.

"You know, if a major party candidate had said all that, they'd call it bluster and rhetoric," Rodgers told her.

"That's the difference between Senator Orr and the others," Kat said. "Do you disagree?"

"Not a bit. I found it inspiring," Rodgers said.

"Really?" Kat asked.

"Yeah. Especially the part about people not getting retired."

Kat smiled. "You know, I didn't even think of that."

"I am curious, though. Why was Kendra running interference over there instead of you?"

"We wanted to make the senator's departure seem like a security concern rather than blocking the press," she said.

"That makes sense," Rodgers said. *At least in an image-sensitive Washingtonian way.* "Meanwhile, what's happening with the Wilson matter?"

"You mean did the other murder take the pressure off?" she asked. "Somewhat, though a few reporters privately wonder if we were responsible for both."

"Were you?"

"Oh, absolutely," Kat replied dryly. "This whole thing is like a homicidal '*House That Jack Built.*' This is the candidate who hired a killer to slay the realtor to cover the assassination that got him the attention for the campaign that Kat built." The young woman shook her head. "There are always—*always*—going to be three groups of reporters and commentators. Those who think you're guilty of something, those who think you're innocent, and those who think the topic is a sideshow. You only need the last two groups to stay in the race."

"As far as public relations are concerned," Rodgers said.

"Right. It doesn't help if you're actually guilty."

Lucy O'Connor caught up to the two. She looked tired. Rodgers noticed the red light on her microcassette recorder was on. The tape was still turning.

"Good morning," the reporter said. "That was a terrific speech."

"Thanks. I'll tell the senator you thought so," Kat replied.

"Is anything new, on or off the record?" Lucy asked. She looked at Rodgers, and he looked at her. She repeated the question with her eyes.

"Apart from the senator running for president of the United States? Nothing," Kat said. "What are you hearing?"

"A lot of backlash from the rush-to-judgment mentality everyone had yesterday," Lucy replied.

"Did people really think Senator Orr was behind the assassination?" Rodgers asked.

"I would categorize it as a perverse hope," Lucy replied.

Rodgers shook his head. "*Perverse* is a good word."

"A story like the Hypo-Slayer is where above-the-fold by lines and book deals come from," Lucy added. "Speaking of stories, General, are you ready to tell me what you're doing here?"

"There will be a press release at the appropriate time," Kat told her. "You will have it early, of course."

"Any word on a likely running mate?" Lucy asked. "I noticed Kenneth Link was here."

"The ticket will not be announced before the convention," Kat said.

"Come on, Kat. Off the record. I promise."

"Sorry," Kat replied.

Lucy turned to Rodgers. "What about the Op-Center investigation, General Rodgers?"

"What about it?"

"I hear that a gentleman named Darrell McCaskey is on his way over to talk to Admiral Link."

"What?" Kat said. She stopped, took her cell phone out, and speed-dialed the admiral's number.

"How do you know that?" Rodgers asked.

"Friend of mine with the postal police was talking to him. McCaskey wouldn't tell him what it was about. Ed thought I might know." Lucy smiled. "He wanted to help."

Kat had turned her back to the others. She was only on the phone for a few seconds when she snapped it shut. "I'll see you later," she said to Rodgers and Lucy, and hurried off.

"*Come on*, Katherine," Lucy said, running after her. "I just gave you a major heads-up—"

"I know that, and I appreciate it."

"Show me!"

"When I can," Kat promised.

That did not make Lucy happy. Rodgers started after Kat, and Lucy tugged his arm. "General, I can help you," she insisted.

"Thanks."

"It doesn't work like that," Lucy said, giving him another tug. "You have to help me, too."

Rodgers withdrew his arm and started walking after Kat. Lucy followed him. Her persistence did not bother him. That was her job. What frustrated him was something that was roiling in his gut.

"General, *talk* to me. Just tell me what you're doing with Senator Orr. Are you working for him or for Op-Center?"

"What do you think?"

"I think that if you were working for Op-Center, Kat would have known about the Darrell McCaskey interview," she said.

"Makes sense," he said.

"I know. That's a direction, but it isn't a story. Give me something I can use. Anything. A lead, an off-the-record observation, a quote I'll attribute to an anonymous source—"

"The Hypo-Slayer," Rodgers said.

"Beg pardon?"

"Is that what you came up with last night when you said you needed a name for the killer?"

"Yes," Lucy said. "It was the best I could do before deadline."

"It's good," he said.

"Thanks. Now, how about it? Lend me a hand here."

Rodgers stopped. "You know what? I'm out of the hand-lending business. It's nothing personal, but I helped Japan. I helped the United Nations. I helped the entire Indian subcontinent. Do you know what it got me?"

"Not a lot of personal press."

"I don't care about that," he said. He was about to cross the fail-safe point but did not care. "It got me downsized."

"You were released from Op-Center?"

"Released is what you do to a wounded condor or a seal with a coat of crude oil. I was canned, Lucy."

"Jeez. General, I'm so sorry. May I quote you?"

"Why not? You can also quote me as saying that loyalty is missing in action, along with honor and integrity. Not just at Op-Center but throughout society. Real service is rewarded with lip service, and opportunists are calling the plays. I've been invited to join the senator's team in some capacity to try to change that. I plan to accept because I trust in the American people to see the difference between arrivistes and people of character and principle. Close quote," he added.

"Would you mind if I asked Paul Hood to comment?"

"No," Rodgers said. "But Lucy?"

"Yes?"

Rodgers hesitated. He wanted to tell her not to make him sound bitter. However, he did not know how to say that without acknowledging that he *was* bitter.

The reporter seemed to read his thoughts. "Don't worry," she said. "I'll make it come out right."

Rodgers smiled softly.

Lucy thanked the general and left. Rodgers stood there for a moment, not sure how he felt. He had not planned to say those things, but then he had not planned on being downsized, either. Or losing Striker in the field. What was it Trotsky had said? The more time you have to plan, the more mistakes you'll make. This came from the heart.

Rodgers jogged after Kat. He wanted to let her know what he had done, though he did not think she would mind. His comments were not about Orr; they were about Mike Rodgers and Op-Center. Besides, there was a benefit to what he had just done.

He was with them now, mind and soul.

TWENTY-TWO

Fallbrook, California
Tuesday, 5:45 A.M.

For Tom Mandor, it was about the money. For Wayne Richmond it was about the money, but it was also about the danger. That was why he had gone to Alaska to drive a rig. That was why he came back to work as muscle.

At five A.M., he had left his cabin and had walked a quarter mile east, into the cold, dark hills. He did that once or twice every week in the late spring, summer, and early fall. That was when the peak was a place of perfect danger. Here, Richmond could confront as much danger as he wanted. He chose more than he needed just to test himself. Life *should* be a constant series of trials. It was the only way to grow, to *be* alive rather than simply act it. It was a way of controlling your adversaries and, thus, have a measure of control over your own life.

Wearing high tan western boots and carrying a finely honed Bowie knife, Richmond walked through the windy predawn darkness. He was dressed in a heavy denim jacket and black leather gloves to protect him from the near-freezing temperatures. Here, nearly four thousand feet up, there was even occasional sleet and snow. As he neared the ledge, he saw the dimly lit tops of white clouds a thousand feet below. Above there were still only stars and navy blue sky. When the sun finally began to rise over the sharp, curving ridge and warmed the rocky ledge, danger also wakened. That was where the diamondback rattlesnakes lived.

The snakes nested in a line of boulders right at the edge of a cliff. Each season there were hundreds of them to be harvested. The first light of dawn woke the poikilotherm quickly, raising its blood temperature to the temperature of the new day. The triangular-headed snakes, anywhere from one to three of them, would move out in search of field mice, wild hares, early birds, or any small animals they could devour. It was not necessary for them to see their prey, which was why they could hunt before the sun had fully risen. The pits on the head of the rattlesnakes sensed the warmth of a living creature while their extended tongues could taste the prey on the air, the equivalent of Richmond smelling cooking in the kitchen. It allowed the snakes to pinpoint prey with deadly accuracy. An average adult diamondback was four to five feet long and could leap nearly that far.

The snakes were the color of dirt, invisible to the casual observer until their distinctive rattle warned potential attackers away. It sounded like the buzzing of a large hornet unless the snake was coiled to give it height and striking distance. That position raised the rattle completely off the ground, making it sound more like a pepper grinder. The coiled position also brought the snake's head up in two or three seconds.

The diamondbacks were defensive rather than offensive creatures. Typically, they minded their own business and sought to avoid confrontations with larger animals like bobcats, coyotes, and humans.

That was why Richmond liked to poke them first with the end of his fifteen-inch blade. He did not want them to shy from a confrontation. He usually crouched and touched the tip of the knife to the tail. Most of the time the snakes moved away. If they did, he circled widely and blocked their retreat. He forced them to coil, which gave him the fight he wanted.

This morning, as Richmond sat on a rock and watched

the dawn, he saw two snakes emerge from the rocks. One was fully grown, and the other was about ten inches long. Parent and offspring, out for a hunt. The smaller snake stopped behind a rock and curled into a tight spiral. It obviously was not happy with the chilly wind. The other snake continued to move away from the nest.

Diamondbacks are born live, and Richmond figured the smaller one to be about two weeks old. There were probably more in the nest. They would feed on whatever insects passed by, perhaps click beetles. Richmond decided he would kill them both, starting with the youngster.

Richmond moved from the large, cold rock. He did not carry a cell phone on these excursions. If he were careless enough to get bitten, Richmond felt that he deserved to die. Besides, calling 911 would be pointless. By the time an ambulance or helicopter reached him, he would be dead. The venom would instantly cause hemolysis, the destruction of red blood cells, preventing tissue oxygenation. That caused the major organs to shut down. He would be dead within ten or fifteen minutes.

The smaller snake sensed his approach. It moved closer to the rock, uncoiled, and slid onto the opposite side. Richmond smiled. He put the sole of his right boot on the top of the rock. It was a pyramid-shaped rock about a foot high and relatively flat. He waited until the tail disappeared then tipped the rock over. It landed on the snake, pinning it in the center. The tongue shot in and out and the tail wriggled angrily, but it was helpless. Richmond checked to see where the other snake was. Its beaded skin reflected the first yellow rays of sun as it moved from the ledge. The creature was intent on feeding, not on aiding its spawn. Richmond stepped on the rock, putting his weight on it, to make sure the smaller snake was truly pinned. Then he went around front, crouched in front of it, and drove the knife straight down into the tapered area behind its head. The head dropped off, the tongue still flicking for several moments as the black soil swallowed the blood seeping from its body.

Richmond wiped the knife blade on the dirt. Then he rose and went after the other snake.

That was when he heard it. Richmond turned back to the ledge. He crouched and listened.

There was a fire road to the east, a narrow, rain-rutted dirt path he could use to escape in case the only paved road were ever blocked by a blaze. Below it, about two thousand feet down, was a housing development. Occasionally, people hiked here to look out over the valley. They rarely walked up this early to watch the sunrise because they would have had to set out in the dark. But once in a while they drove out to see the sunrise. What he had heard sounded like a car.

Richmond moved toward the fire road. There was a Jeep parked on a landing. The vehicle was black with a gold star on the side. There was a lone occupant, a sheriff's deputy. He probably had the night shift and had come up here before heading home. The deputy opened a thermos.

The lawman would be up here for a few minutes at least. That was good. Richmond had an idea. He doubled back, slipping the bowie knife into the leather sheath attached to his belt and removing his windbreaker as he walked. He passed the dead snake, lying on the ground muddied with its blood. He continued after the larger one. His eyes moved slowly from side to side. He paid special attention to stones and underbrush.

The snake was in a narrow gully, cut by erosion and filled with rocks that had washed down the slope. There was a gopher hole hidden among the small stones. The snake was going to warm itself on the rocks while it waited for breakfast to emerge. At least, that was apparently the snake's plan. Richmond had a different idea. He walked alongside the gully and lay his windbreaker on the rocks. He knotted the ends of the sleeves, spread them out flat, then went back behind the snake. Scooping up a handful of stones, he began tossing them at the reptile one at a time. They hit the animal in the tail and body, and it moved ahead, rattling. Richmond followed. He continued to pelt the snake, driving it toward the windbreaker. As he expected, the snake crawled into the only shelter nearby: one of the two sleeves. Once the creature was inside, Richmond quickly grabbed the sleeve at the armpit. The snake had tried to coil itself inside. As a result, it was completely within the sleeve. Richmond carefully folded the body of the jacket around the sleeve so the diamondback did not slip out. Then he put his left hand around the sleeve and moved it toward the snake's head. He held tight as the snake squirmed to get loose, its body twisting and undulating inside the sleeve. When the diamondback finally relaxed, Richmond untied the mouth of the sleeve with his right hand. If he released the head, the snake would drop free. Richmond then wrapped his right hand around the rattle. The creature was now his silent prisoner. Without removing his hands, Richmond hugged the windbreaker toward his belly and walked forward. Having the snake beside him, a captive, was almost like carrying a gun. The snake was just as potent, just as feared. Even better, Richmond realized, was that the snake would take the blame for the killing.

Richmond reached the rocky ledge. The sun was well above the distant mountains now. In the distance, a trio of hawks had begun to search the hillsides for small animals. He never tired of watching them circle as their wings and tail feathers shifted this way and that as they rode the changing thermal currents. Whenever a bird saw a potential meal, it called to the others, then pulled in its wings and plummeted like a lawn dart. Unlike the defense-minded snakes, the offense-oriented birds were nature's most perfect hunting machines.

Defense and offense, Richmond thought. What looks inherently dangerous on the dirty ground is not. What seems graceful and beautiful in the blue heavens is lethal. Appearance is rarely an accurate yardstick for danger.

Richmond started down the fire road toward the Jeep. The driver's side window was open.

"Good morning, Deputy," Richmond said as he approached.

The deputy glanced into the side mirror. "Morning, sir." He regarded Richmond a moment longer. "Are you okay?"

"Yes, why?"

"Looks like you got your arm bundled up."

"No, no, I'm just collecting birds' eggs for my aviary," he smiled. He was speaking in a soft, fair voice. Laying a trap was part of the fun.

"Collecting eggs—with a bowie knife?" the deputy asked.

"That's for snakes," Richmond said as he reached the window.

"I thought so, though I suggest next time you bring a firearm. Carrying anything larger than a pocket knife is a felony."

"But not a handgun?" Richmond said.

"No, sir."

"Lord bless the NRA," Richmond said.

The deputy took a swallow of coffee, then replaced the cup on top of the thermos. He was wearing a wedding band. He could not have been more than twenty-six. Richmond wondered if he came up here to slack off in secret or to contemplate the universe. Was he deciding whether to leave his wife or wistfully remembering how they used to come up here at night to make out? Richmond tried to guess how far ahead this young man had planned his life. To the next day? To the next promotion? To his first or next child?

"I'm Wayne Richmond, by the way," the man said.

"Andy Belmont," the deputy said. He extended his

hand, then withdrew it when he remembered the bundle of eggs. "Pleased to meet you."

"Likewise," Richmond replied. "I walk here often, but I haven't seen you here before."

"I was transferred from Southwest Station last week," Deputy Belmont told him. "I thought it would be a good idea to familiarize myself with the area in case I'm ever called up here."

"Good thinking," Richmond said. "Tell me, Deputy, is this the start or end of your shift?"

"The end," the deputy said. "I get the morning babysitting chores so my wife can go to work. Then her mother relieves me so I can go to sleep."

"Really? It must be difficult, working different hours like that."

The deputy smiled. "I don't know. It sort of makes us appreciate the time you do have together."

"I guess that would be true," Richmond said. He looked down at the young man's exposed lap. All he had to do was empty the windbreaker sleeve and grab the radio from the deputy's left shoulder. It was within easy reach, by the window. Deputy Belmont would die where he sat.

The deputy put his thermos in the cup holder between the seats. He turned his headlights back on. "Have a good day, sir, and don't forget about the knife."

Richmond had bent forward to talk to the deputy. He straightened so that his waist was even with the window. "Thanks. I won't."

He stood back. The deputy waved as he started down the path. Richmond nodded after him. And with his fingers tightening around the snake's neck, he twisted it in a complete circle. The snake, which had begun wriggling again, trembled for a moment and then was still. Richmond shook the sleeve lightly. The snake did not move. He dumped it from the sleeve and jumped back.

The snake hit the ground and lay there. It was dead.

Richmond left it for the crows, then turned and started back toward the ledge.

The day had begun better than Richmond could have imagined. Two snakes were dead, and he had spared a deputy. Three lives had been his. More, if he counted the wife and child.

To risk or not, to kill or not. Choice was the heart of control, control was the engine of power, and power was the key to a rewarding life. Wayne Richmond did not know how rewarding the rest of his life would be. But this day, at least, had begun very well indeed.

TWENTY-THREE

Washington, D.C.
Tuesday, 9:44 A.M.

Darrell McCaskey was not what his FBI coworkers would have described as "badge heavy." He did not bully suspects, subordinates, or anyone else. But when he wanted results, he usually got them. He was earnest. And if the earnestness failed to register, there were always his squared shoulders, unyielding eyes, and commanding manner.

McCaskey was dressed in a leather jacket instead of his usual tweedy blazer. He felt the battered old bomber jacket looked street-smart, a little more intimidating. He arrived at the Russell Senate Office Building and showed his Op-Center ID to the security guard. McCaskey instructed the young woman not to call ahead. He wanted to send a signal to the admiral. This was an investigation, not a fishing expedition. McCaskey would be courteous and respectful during the interview, but he would not be servile. The Bureau referred to this as the LAT approach—legal authority tactics. Suspects had rights under the law. So did police and Bureau interrogators.

McCaskey walked quickly to the senator's office. The receptionist directed McCaskey to the conference room. Political parties are not permitted to have unelected representatives working on federal property. There were no regulations governing unaffiliated advisers.

Admiral Link had just returned from the press conference and was checking E-mails on his laptop. He appeared slightly unsettled.

"You don't waste time," Link said without looking up from the computer.

"Not when I'm on the taxpayers' clock," McCaskey said.

"Civic responsibility. A sad exception, not the rule," Link said. "Would you like coffee or tea, Mr.—?"

"McCaskey, and no thanks," McCaskey interrupted. He took a notebook from the inside pocket of his jacket. "I just wanted to ask you questions about some of your activities at the Company."

Link smiled. "I have two things to say, Mr. McCaskey. First, you're aware that I am not permitted to discuss any of the work I did, even with a member of an intelligence service."

"Technically, that isn't true."

Link finally glanced up. "What do you mean?"

"The standard CIA employment agreement says that a former employee may not reveal information that might compromise ongoing operations," McCaskey said. "You signed such an agreement without riders. I checked. My questions involve personnel you may have worked with who are either no longer with the Company or may be assigned to the D.C. area."

"You abrogate the spirit of confidentiality, Mr. McCaskey."

"People have said worse things about me, sometimes in English," McCaskey replied. "What is the second thing you wanted to say?"

"Sidestepping the question of whether you or anyone else has reasonable cause to insist on this interview, I'm curious," Link said. "By what chartered authority is Op-Center here to question me?"

"By the International Intelligence Cooperation Act of 2002," McCaskey replied as he sat at the table across from Link. "A British national has died, Scotland Yard has requested an investigation, and we were the agent they selected. By law, I am permitted to ask questions of potential witnesses to the crime or events leading up to it. The senator agreed to an interview with Director Hood, which establishes his understanding of the validity of the IICA. Do you object to my questioning you?"

"Yes, and I also question your interpretation of the law," Link said. "But I'll give you the benefit of the doubt—for the moment."

"Thank you. Admiral Link, have you personally hired anyone for the United States First Party?"

"No," Link replied.

"Have you recommended anyone for a staff position, paid or interned, for the United States First Party?"

"Eric Stone, the young man who is managing the convention," Link said. "That's Eric with a *c*."

"How do you know Mr. Stone?" McCaskey asked as he wrote the name in his notebook.

"He was my assistant at the Company. Eric is a very good organizer."

"Does he have field experience?"

"As a certified public accountant," Link replied. "Chicago office."

"Have you hired or recommended anyone else?" McCaskey asked.

"Not yet."

"What about the senator's staff?" McCaskey asked.

"I brought in Kendra Peterson," Link said.

"How do you know her?"

"She was a field agent based in Japan but working in North Korea and Taiwan," Link said.

"One of yours?"

"Yes. Strictly ROO."

ROO was *recon only operative*. However, McCaskey knew that even passive field agents were sometimes used in offensive operations. There was a case in Russia in 1979 when CIA operative Genson Blimline had been exposed by a Soviet mole. Rather than pull him out, the Company sent an observer in to watch the men who were sent to watch him. When they moved against Blimline, the ROO moved against them. Both the ROO and Blimline were able to get to a safe house in Moscow.

"Ms. Peterson's name came up as a possible contact when Striker went over there," said a voice from behind McCaskey. "I can get you that file."

McCaskey turned. Mike Rodgers was standing in the conference room doorway.

"May I come in?" Rodgers asked Link.

"Absolutely," Link replied.

Rodgers entered. His eyes were fixed on McCaskey. "What's the latest on the witch-hunt?"

"I wouldn't call it that," McCaskey replied.

Rodgers did not reply.

"Mr. McCaskey, if you have more questions, would you please get to them?" Link said. "I have real work to do."

Link's smugness was starting to piss McCaskey off. "Admiral, this is a serious inquiry," McCaskey said. "It would be a mistake to think otherwise."

"Sir, *you* are taking it seriously, which is not the same thing," Link told him. "But then, I have an advantage you do not, Mr. McCaskey."

"And that is?"

"I know that I am innocent of any wrongdoing or complicity in wrongdoing. Now, what's your next question?"

As much as McCaskey disliked Link, he reminded himself that he was here to get information, not to make a new friend.

"Are you aware of anyone who might possess the skill to talk their way into a man's room, kill him by lethal injection under the tongue, and leave virtually undetected?" McCaskey asked.

"A woman, you mean."

"Or a man who might have trained a woman."

Link acknowledged the correction with a nod. "Only Kendra."

"That woman is a font of hidden talents. Where did she get her training?" McCaskey asked.

"From the United States Marines," Link said. "She spent several months as a 91-W, a health care specialist. She had to transfer out because of a problem with her fine motor skills."

"Related to tendonitis?" McCaskey asked.

"I don't know," Link said. "Would you care to ask her?"

"Not at present," McCaskey said. He wanted time to research Kendra's file before talking to her.

"You may not get another chance," Link advised him.

"Why not?"

"Because when you're finished here, I intend to see that neither you nor anyone else from Op-Center get back in," Link told him.

"That sounds like a warning and smells like guilt."

"Only to a group of very desperate intelligence operatives," Link said. "Paul Hood is already having difficulties with the CIOC. Senator Orr can see that he has a great many more."

"Oh? Under what theory of Congressional authority?"

"Harassment of a private citizen," Link told him. "Look, Mr. McCaskey. I don't want to be difficult. We're on the same team. Two businessmen have been murdered, and I would like to see their killer found and punished. But you have very odd suspicions about me and no evidence. Now you want to heap some of that vague conjecture on Kendra Peterson. I will ask her to join us in the spirit of cooperation, not because I believe the interview to have merit or cause. I would take that opportunity while the spirit is willing."

McCaskey looked from Link to Rodgers. "No, Admiral. If I want something from Ms. Peterson, I will be in touch."

Link laughed. "I haven't decided whether you're confident, proud, or obtuse, Mr. McCaskey. But you *are* self-righteous. If I have not made it clear, you will not be coming back."

McCaskey rose. "Thank you for your time, Admiral." He looked at Rodgers. "I'm sorry this has been difficult for you, Mike."

Rodgers did not reply with words. His hard expression was enough to convey his anger.

McCaskey looked back at Link. The admiral had already turned his attention back to his laptop.

"One more thing, Admiral," McCaskey said.

"All right." He did not look up.

"How do you feel about Mr. Wilson's death?"

"Inconvenienced and torn," Link replied without hesitation. "A man enjoyed the senator's hospitality, returned to his hotel, and was murdered. That's a sad, lawless, unjustifiable act. But he happened to be an individual whose economic ideas would have been detrimental to our nation. You can see my dilemma."

"Some people would call it something else. A motive."

"If only the world were so black-and-white," Link said, "men like you would be ringmasters instead of sweeping up after the elephants. I'll tell you one last time, Mr. McCaskey. You are misguided and doing both yourself and your organization a disservice."

McCaskey showed himself out of the senator's office. He wondered if Link were being sincere. Years at the CIA had given the man one hell of a poker face. And he had been extremely forthcoming about Kendra's background. That is not something a guilty man was likely to do. McCaskey also wondered if he himself *was* being stubborn—"obtuse," as Link had put it—by not interviewing Kendra Peterson now. McCaskey decided he was not. He wanted to have a look at photographs from the party, at photographs from Kendra's file. He wanted to compare them with the indistinct pictures from the surveillance cameras. If there were no similarities, McCaskey might not have any reason to talk to her. Besides, if he had accepted, he would have been probing blind. He also would have been surrendering Op-Center's authority by acknowledging Link's control. Either Op-Center had the right to seek this information, or they did not. If Senator Orr could stop them with a phone call, McCaskey might as well give up the investigation now.

The former FBI agent put the process aside for now to consider the data. Senator Orr had three former CIA employees on his staff. Admiral Link had spent several years at the Company. He knew a few good people. This could be nothing more than that. Yet at least two of those people, Link and Kendra, had the skills, opportunity, and probably the resources to have targeted, cornered, and executed William Wilson and Robert Lawless. Link's caustic dismissal aside, his dislike of the man's fiscal policies could have moved him to murder. McCaskey knew of at least two instances when business concerns were said to have inspired CIA-organized TDs—terminal directives, the euphemism for assassinations. Patrice Lumumba, the first democratically elected leader of the Congo, was assassinated in January 1961 to protect American and Belgian business interests. In 1979, South Korean President Park Chung Hee was shot by CIA-backed personnel who feared that the economic boom was putting the nation too deeply in debt to Japanese lenders.

Perhaps William Wilson had been planning to contribute substantial monies to a USF rival. Scotland Yard might be able to find out for him. That would have rid both the party and the United States economy of a potential threat.

McCaskey did not have a lot of information. But he did

have more than when he arrived. For all of Link's bluster, the interview was a success. The only thing he had not anticipated was the presence of Mike Rodgers. The men had a lot of history between them, and he hoped they could get past this.

If not, McCaskey would survive. He was only an agent of policy, not the one who designed it.

Paul Hood was the man in the crosshairs.

TWENTY-FOUR

Washington, D.C.
Tuesday, 10:00 A.M.

It was a warm, clear day, and the world around him white and blue. Hood's eyes went from the gleaming monuments that dominated the Washington skyline to the clear sky that dominated the monuments. Many of the city's significant landmarks were visible from the White House, enhancing the already strong sense that this was the center of the globe.

Hood pulled into the heavily barricaded parking area on the north side of the White House. Being outside, warmed by the sun, Hood should have enjoyed a burgeoning sense of well-being. He did not. President Lawrence and Senator Debenport belonged to the same centrist section of the same party. Between them, they controlled Op-Center's charter and Op-Center's funding. If the two men had an agenda, Hood had no avenue of appeal. What he did not know was whether Lawrence and Debenport had called him here to expand the downsizing of Op-Center or whether they wanted him to work on some partisan intrigue.

On one level, it did not matter. Whether it was a mugging or a hazing, Hood knew it would hurt.

Hood passed through the security checkpoint at the west gate. Since he was not carrying anything, that meant a wand search from the security guard. A Secret Service agent met Hood at the security vestibule and escorted him to the office of the president's executive secretary. Senator

Debenport was already in the Oval Office. Hood was told to go right in.

Debenport was standing with his arms folded. President Michael Lawrence was seated on the edge of a desk that had once belonged to Teddy Roosevelt. That was the spot from which the president preferred to conduct meetings. He stood just over six feet four inches tall. This put him eye level with most of the people who came to see him. The president's sharp blue eyes shifted from Debenport to the door as Hood walked in. Lawrence's expression was warm and welcoming. The two men had always enjoyed a good rapport. That bond was strengthened over a year before, when Op-Center protected the president from a coup attempt. Unfortunately, politics were governed by a single rule: "*What can you do for me now*?" If Hood and Op-Center were a liability, the president would be hard-pressed to help them.

"Paul, thanks for coming," the president said, extending his hand.

"My pleasure," Hood replied diplomatically. It was not as if he had a choice. He turned to Dan Debenport. "Good morning, Senator."

"Paul," the senator replied.

Debenport was a slope-shouldered man of average build. He had thinning straw-colored hair and a quick smile. He was not smiling now.

The president gestured to a chair. Hood sat. The president returned to the edge of his desk. Debenport remained standing.

"Please tell Mr. McCaskey it was a hell of a piece of detective work, finding that wound under William Wilson's tongue," the president said.

"I will, and thank you, sir."

"I second that, Paul," Debenport said. "Are there any new developments?"

"Off the record?" Hood asked. He was tempted to ask Debenport if he and the CIOC were impressed enough to reinstate the budget cuts. But he had a politician's sense that there was another reason he was here.

"Everything we say here now is off the record," the president said.

"Well, we did a sketchy profile of the killing scenarios," Hood said. "There is a very sketchy fit with Admiral Kenneth Link. Darrell is talking to him now."

"An ambush interview?" Debenport asked.

"More or less," Hood said. "We may not have a lot of time on this, and Darrell did not want to be stonewalled."

"Good thinking," the president said.

That made two compliments back to back. Hood was convinced that the president wanted something.

"Going to talk to Link is a very encouraging development," Debenport said. "Is there any suggestion that Senator Orr might have been involved?"

"Senator, we're not sure whether there was anything for Donald Orr to be involved *with*."

"You probably need to find that out," Debenport replied.

That was unexpected. It was also a potential violation of district privacy statutes. "If it becomes necessary, and if Op-Center has the manpower to spare, we will," Hood told him.

"That's just the point," Debenport said. "It *is* necessary to expand the investigation."

"On what grounds?" Hood asked. He did not like where this was headed. "Do you have additional information?"

"Not as such," Debenport replied.

"Then—I'm confused."

Debenport paced for a moment before continuing. "Don Orr announced this morning that he will be running for president on the United States First Party ticket. Did you hear any of the senator's speech?"

"No," Hood answered.

"Don Orr intends to promote an extreme form of isolationism," Debenport went on. "It may sound appealing to voters, but it will be terribly destructive."

"The United States cannot disentangle itself from the global economy and international resources," the president said. "Even if we wanted to replace oil with nuclear or solar power and make all our computer and automobile components stateside, the tooling up period would take years."

"It would also be extremely expensive," Debenport added. "Union workers and factories are not inexpensive."

"All right," Hood said. "Senator Orr is misguided. I'm still not clear what justification Op-Center has to involve him."

"Paul, the senator is not only misguided, he is dangerous," Debenport said. "Voters, God bless them, tend to respond positively to protectionist ideas, however unworkable they are."

"That's their prerogative, God bless 'em," Hood pointed out. "Using a legitimate investigation to fling mud is also dangerous."

"Well, there you get into the question of rights versus responsibility," Debenport replied. "Consider the judge who overrules a jury that has been manipulated by a skilled attorney. A skilled politician can do the same thing. He can sell a catastrophic agenda. We need to take dramatic steps to undermine a seditious platform."

"What's wrong with debates?"

"You were in politics," Debenport said. "It's very difficult to fight someone who is selling feel-good tonics in a red-white-and-blue package. It usurps patriotism and unplugs the brain by appealing to the soul."

"Look, Paul," the president said. "We don't think the United States First Party has a chance of winning this election. But we believe that Senator Orr can rally the unions, the unemployed, and a chunk of the middle class and take twenty-five to thirty percent of the vote. Neither I nor the vice president is running. That means whoever wins will be a new president and quite possibly a minority. They will also have the senator stuck in their side, pushing his policies."

"Will you be running, Senator?" Hood asked.

"I have not yet made that decision," Debenport replied.

Anything that was not a firm no meant yes, and even those were subject to revocation.

Hood shook his head. "Senator, Mr. President—you're working hard to convince me that something wrong is right. What if I don't agree?"

"Then we get someone who does agree," Debenport replied flatly. "Nothing personal, Paul."

"Oddly enough, I believe you," Hood said.

"Also, we strongly disagree that what we are asking is wrong," the president told him. "Orr is the one who is being immoral. He is using the flag for a power grab. We are trying to prevent him from dismantling a successful national and international economic balance. You know me, Paul. Whoever wins, I will be going back to American Sense. I would not be involved in this if I did not believe in it."

American Sense was a Washington-based think tank the president had founded between his two terms. The nonpartisan organization was a well-respected source of geopolitical expertise.

"Answer this, Senator," Hood said. "Did the CIOC downsize Op-Center so we would be more inclined to take this assignment?"

"Do you believe that?" Debenport asked. "Because if you do, nothing I say will change your mind."

Hood laughed. "That's an old ploy, Senator, avoiding a question by suggesting it's out of line."

"There was a confluence of events," Debenport replied. "This was one way the momentum could turn."

"I guess it's better to be an opportunist than a conspirator," Hood said.

"Paul, *that's* getting personal," the president warned. "Senator Debenport has already said that he does not want to cause you distress. There's a proposal on the table. Either you accept it or reject it. There are no hard feelings either way."

"You mean, sir, I could go work for your think tank?"

"You would be an asset."

"Think of this another way, Paul," the senator said. "If this undertaking is a success, the new president might consider you for a different post. An ambassadorship, perhaps."

That should not have been unexpected. Embassies were political coin, the medium for payback. They were the ultimate pedestal for a bureaucrat, and Hood was surely that. Still, when he heard the proposal—the hypothetical phrasing was simply the language of barter—everything changed. Against Hood's will, his indignation deflated. He no longer viewed cooperation as capitulation. It was part of the job.

It was business.

"Let me talk to Darrell when he gets back," Hood said. His voice was low and conciliatory. "I'll see what he found out and where he thinks this can go. Then I'll call you, Senator."

"It sounds as if we have an understanding," Debenport said hopefully.

Hood did not want to say yes. "I understand," he replied.

"We can accept that for now," the president interjected. "When do you expect to hear from him?"

"I'll call him on the drive back. If he is finished with the interview, I will call the senator immediately."

"Sounds good," the president said. He offered his hand to Hood. "Paul, I know this is not easy. But I believe we all want the same thing. A prosperous and secure United States of America."

"We do," Hood agreed. He wanted to add, *With the Bill*

of Rights intact. But he did not. And he knew, then, that he had agreed to help them.

Hood left the Oval Office in something of a daze. Debenport was right. The men *did* have an understanding. Not that this plan was perfect or legal, only that it would go forward. Maybe it would move by inches at first, but it would proceed because there was no clearly defined ethic.

In an ideal world, men would fight ideas with other ideas, Hood told himself. But this was far from a perfect world. Every weapon in the sociopolitical arsenal had to be used.

Including rationalization? Hood asked himself.

Is that what this was?

On one level, what the senator and the president had asked him to do *was* wrong. They wanted him to broaden a legitimate but still very young investigation. They wanted him to pepper it with innuendo, to create gossip and not justice. Yet on another level, while their reasons were political, their argument was not wrong. It did not matter whether Donald Orr's vision was heartfelt or manipulative. It was impractical at best, dangerous at worst.

Hood reached his car. It was hot from sitting in the sun. In a way that was fitting. He had just made a pact with the devil.

Hood had been seduced intellectually and professionally. Though he hated himself for succumbing, he had to be honest: he was not surprised. Hood had felt distant from Op-Center, from friends, from his family for so long that it was nice to be plugged into *something*.

And there was something else, something the one-time golden boy mayor of Los Angeles did not like to admit. Idealism was great in theory but unwieldy in practice. In the end, Hood was like the world itself: a compromise; a surface of attractive, sun-hungry green and inviting blue concealing a hot, muddy interior; an imperfect paradox.

Hood turned on the car, cranked up the air-conditioning,

and set the secure cell phone in its dashboard holder. He slipped on the headset and autodialed Darrell McCaskey's number. As he pulled from the parking area, Hood did one thing more.

He prayed that McCaskey found just one reason to continue the investigation.

TWENTY-FIVE

Washington, D.C.
Tuesday, 10:44 A.M.

"How did it go, Darrell?"

After punching in the number, Hood grabbed a can of Coke from a cooler under the glove compartment. He always kept one there for emergencies, beside an ice pack he replaced each morning. The caffeine helped him focus. Once in a while he also reached for the ice pack. That was for meetings that ran too long, got too loud, and went nowhere. Presidential meetings were invariably very direct.

"The interview went all right," McCaskey said. "Mike was there, which was rough. He is not happy."

"No one is," Hood said. He could not concern himself with Mike Rodgers right now. "What about Link?"

"I have to say, Paul, the admiral was pretty forthcoming. The nutshell: Link did not like William Wilson and does not care that he's gone."

"Not a surprise but also not damning," Hood said. He took a long swallow of Coke. Motives could be elusive and misleading. He wanted to stick to the mechanics of the assassination itself. "Is there any evidence that Link has the assets to carry off these kinds of missions?"

"Evidence? No. Potential? Yes. Link has two former Company people on staff. One is a guy named Eric Stone, who is running the convention. He was Link's assistant and supposedly is a very efficient organizer. The other individual with intelligence credentials is the senator's executive assistant, Kendra Peterson. It turns out Kendra had medical training in the Marines."

"That's not in her file, is it?" Hood said. His head was still in the Oval Office, on the decision he had to make. Dossier data was swimming, anchorless, in his memory. He took another hit of Coke.

"No, it isn't," McCaskey said. "Kendra spent several months working in health care but left because of tendonitis in her hands. Presumably, the affliction was temporary. If a disability had been noted in Kendra's record, it might have impacted her career in the military and afterward. The staff sergeant probably let her transfer without remarking on what was a very brief tenure."

"Or her medical experiences may have been deleted more recently by a really efficient organizer who had access to them," Hood pointed out.

"It's possible. The point is, one of the first skills Kendra would have learned over there was how to give an injection," McCaskey said.

"I'll have Matt Stoll run a comparison on images captured by the security camera and at this morning's press conference," Hood said. "That may tell us if Ms. Peterson goes on the suspect list. What was your impression of Link himself?"

"He's very confident and a bit of a bully," McCaskey said. "He also made it clear that he feels extremely inconvenienced by our investigation. It's difficult to tell whether he's guilty or whether he just resents the hell out of our probe."

"Or he may just have it in for Op-Center," Hood said. The NSA and the NCMC had experienced a few run-ins over the years, including the exposure of former operative Ron Friday as a double agent. "If you had to guess, which is it?"

"That's tough to say, Paul. Link definitely views the investigation as politically motivated," McCaskey said. "He thinks Op-Center is using it to try to roll back the budget cuts. Truth is, I think we're going to hear a lot of that as long as we're involved in the Wilson killing."

"When have we ever worried about what people think?" Hood asked. It was ironic, though, Hood thought. Link could end up being right for the wrong reasons. "I'm going to get Matt Stoll working on that image comparison. What are the codes for the hotel image files?"

"WW-1 and RL-1," McCaskey replied. "I'm going to call Bob Herbert and pick his brain, then pop over to the British embassy. I rang George Daily. He's setting up a conference call with their security chief here. He was going to see if the Brits have anything on file about Wilson being watched, stalked, or threatened."

"Good idea. We'll talk more when you get back."

Hood hung up and called Bugs Benet. He asked him to access the online news photo services. He wanted images of Kendra Peterson, including this morning's press conference. They should be appearing online by now. Hood asked to have the pictures sent to Stoll's office along with Darrell's image files on the Wilson and Lawless killings. When he reached the office, Hood went directly to Matt Stoll's office.

The corridors were unusually quiet. There were fewer personnel, of course, and those who were there did not seem to be making eye contact with Hood. Maybe it was his imagination. Or maybe it was a variation on what they learned in elementary school. If they did not look at the teacher, they would not get called on. If they did not look at the director, they would not be fired.

Matt Stoll's office was different from the others in the executive level. The computer wizard had originally set up the Computer and Technical Support Operations in a small conference room. Hood had always intended to move the CATSO, but Stoll quickly filled the room with a haphazard arrangement of desks, stands, and computers. As Op-Center's computing needs grew, Stoll simply added to the original disarray. Within a few months, it would have been too much trouble to move it.

There were now four people working in the rectangular space. Stoll and his longtime friend Stephen Viens, Op-Center's imaging expert, worked back to back in the center of the room. Viens had previously managed the spy satellite access time schedules at the National Reconnaissance Office. Whenever the military or a spy agency needed images from space-based resources, they scheduled it through Viens. After Stoll's old college mate was scapegoated for a black ops funding scam, Hood hired him.

Before yesterday morning, three other individuals had worked in this office: Mae Won, Jefferson Jefferson, and Patricia Arroyo. Seven other technical experts worked in an adjoining office. Stoll had been asked to lay off five of the techies and one of these three people. He had selected Patricia Arroyo, who had the least seniority. She and the others were gone within the half hour. That was standard procedure in government agencies. Otherwise, disgruntled personnel could sabotage equipment or programs or walk off with sensitive material. Hood had made an exception in the case of Mike Rodgers. That was not a chance he could take with the others.

Hood greeted the solemn group and told them why he was there. Stoll did not wait for Bugs to send him pictures. He went to a raw news feed from one of the networks, grabbed images of the press conference, and isolated Kendra Peterson. He opened Darrell's files of the hotel security camera images. He opened his 3-D ACE file and left-clicked each of the images to drop them in the file. ACE stood for Angular Construct and Extrapolation, a graphics program Stoll had written. It created 3-D images based on a very little amount of information. Though it could not construct an entire face from a nose, it could show the nose from all angles. These could be superimposed over other photographs to see if they matched.

The only distinctive images they had of the assassin showed gloved hands, a chin, and a portion of one ear. Everything else was under a hat, a scarf, in boots, or beneath loose-fitting clothes. Even the skin color was unreliable. Kendra was a very light-skinned Asian woman. The woman in the elevator had a dark chin, but that could have been caused by the shadow of the hat.

"This lady sure knew what she was doing," Viens said. He had walked over to have a look.

"Darrell figures she cased the hotels before going in," Hood said.

"I don't think so," Viens said. "At least, not in the way that you're thinking."

"Why not?"

"She knew where the cameras were, and she apparently knew what kind of lens they were using," Viens said. "She would not know that simply by eyeballing the cameras, since they were probably behind a two-way mirror."

"What kind of lens *were* they using?" Hood asked.

"The elevator at the Hay-Adams was using a thirty-seven millimeter wide-angle lens," Viens told him. "It foreshortens the center of the image and distorts the periphery so you can cover one hundred and eighty degrees of vision."

"A fisheye lens," Hood said.

"Colloquially, yes," Viens replied. "Elevator security uses either regular or wide-angle lenses, depending on the size of the carriage, the lighting in the corners, and whether the hot spot for crime is in the doorway or in the corners. There are also privacy issues about camera placement. Some counties will only allow a straight-down view on the top of the head. The way our lady is standing, the brim of the hat is positioned to block as much of the camera's view as possible."

"I'm still not sure what you're saying," Hood told him. "Wouldn't you stand the same way regardless of the lens?"

"No," Viens said. "A regular lens would not have fattened the brim to cover the nose this way. It's very likely that our assassin saw actual security images generated by this camera."

While the men spoke, Mae Won made a phone call.

"And it probably was not Ms. Kendra Peterson," Stoll declared. The thumbnail 3-D constructs were complete, along with the superimpositions. There were some two-dozen pictures. Stoll set up a slide-show presentation of the full-size images. "There is a match total of six percent based on available security cam viewing surface of seven percent of her anatomy."

"Does that mean there is not enough to go on or that she is not the one?" Hood asked.

"It isn't her," Stoll declared. "We have a series of click points," he said. He used the cursor to highlight parts of the visible physiognomy. "There are small bulges in bone, cartilage, flesh, even minute wrinkles. Some of them we can see, some of them we can extrapolate from the shadows. Ninety-four percent of these two faces is dissimilar in just the small area we can see. Unless she had facial surgery, the woman in the elevator can't be Ms. Peterson. And she did not have surgery, since I took a few of the older images that Bugs sent over and compared them to the lady at the press conference this morning. Those are identical."

"Mr. Hood?" Mae Won said.

"Yes?"

"Hay-Adams security says they only save those camera images for two days," the young woman said as she hung up the phone. "They already did their own comparison of the images. I thought if we scanned that picture library we might see which of the women went to the hotel."

"Can't we find out who visited the security office?" Stoll asked. "Politicians have benefits in the hotel ballroom. They must send advance security teams to check out the cameras."

"Actually, Darrell has already looked into that," Hood said. "The Hay-Adams does not keep a record of visits by Congressional advance staff. Even if they did, that might not help us. There could be a chain of people involved in passing information to the actual assassin."

"Including Ms. Peterson, if she is involved in any of the senator's security," Stoll pointed out.

"Possibly," Hood agreed.

The phone beeped. Mae Won answered it. "Sir, it's for you," she said to Hood. "It's Bugs."

"Tell him I'll be back in a minute," Hood said. "Matt, we still need to ID the woman in the photographs. Is there any way to construct a face from what we have? Bone structure from the chin, a jawline, anything?"

Stoll shook his head. "Not with any software I have."

"What about mug shots?" Viens asked. "The FBI has a file online. It might be worth comparing the chin we have with those."

"We might as well, though I don't think our assassin is a contract killer," Hood said.

"Why not?" Viens asked.

"Because they were too smart to end up on a camera," Hood said. "I doubt they have ever been inside a police station."

"This is weak," said a voice from behind.

Hood turned. Bob Herbert was in the doorway.

"What is weak, Bob?" Hood asked amiably. This was not the time to get defensive. Herbert was still in a volatile mode, and they had a case to solve.

"I've been sitting here listening to you guys play Junior Crimestoppers." Herbert rolled his wheelchair into the office. "You should have folded your intelligence chief into this, people. I've known hookers who were too smart to get caught on security cameras. That doesn't de facto make them potential assassins."

"Our intelligence chief removed himself from circulation yesterday," Hood remarked. "I thought it was best to let him return on his own. I'm glad he has. What's your take, then?"

"I talked to Darrell a few minutes ago, and my take is simple," Herbert said. "The killer has to fit two criteria. Otherwise, he isn't the killer. First, who stands to gain by Wilson's death? Second, who has the chops to pull it off? The only guy we have on that short list is Link. That leaves us two options. One: we waste resources looking for people who may *also* fit the criteria. Or two: we lean on Link with everything we can muster. Squeeze him like a lemon and see if we get juice. If not, *then* we move on."

"How would you squeeze him?" Hood asked.

"Thanks for asking," Herbert said. "We have to do what we used to do with suspected moles or double agents. We go right up and say, 'We think you're a rat. We're gonna be all over you until you crack.' Invariably, they look to get the heat off themselves. I believe these guys did that once by killing Robert Lawless. If we lean on Link, he'll either do that again or shut his operation down. In any case, he'll have to contact his cohorts to do that. When he does, we'll be all over them."

The room was emphatically silent.

"Who would make that call?" Hood asked.

"Darrell just did," Herbert replied. "That's why Bugs was calling you. To tell you that Darrell was on the line."

"It was the right decision," Hood remarked.

"He knew you'd think so," Herbert said.

"What did Link say?"

"He thinks you're desperate, and this proves it," Herbert replied. "Darrell told Link he was wrong. It was all the usual back-and-forth up-front bluster. Just like the United

Nations. The real work is going to take place behind the scenes. Darrell has Maria on the way to help. Matt's poking around computer files to find out more on Stone."

"Sounds good," Hood said.

"Yeah. Thanks. I'll let you know what turns up," Herbert said.

The intelligence chief turned and left the room. Hood let him go without comment. The silence was even deeper now. Hood broke it by thanking the team and leaving. Stoll hurried after him.

"Chief?" Stoll said.

Hood turned. "Yes, Matt?"

"Bob was a little out of line there—you handled that well."

"Thanks."

"But the truth is we're hearing a lot of conflicting things about Op-Center and the CIOC," Stoll said.

"Hearing from whom?"

"Okay, we're not actually hearing it," Stoll said. "We're sort of hacking it from Company and FBI internal E-mail."

"They should have used Mr. Wilson's firewalls," Hood said.

"They do," Stoll said.

"And you broke through?"

"Not exactly," Stoll told him. "There's a serious flaw in MasterLock, one that hackers would have had to plan ahead to exploit. Two years ago I sent E-mails to the agencies with a virus. A time bomb. What it does is lurk in the software and reset it to a previous systems checkpoint on my command. It's like sending the computer into the past for as long as I need, then restoring the current programs. If someone is on the computer, they are unlikely to notice."

"Matt, that's brilliant."

"Thanks. I figured the best way around increasingly sophisticated firewalls was to go in before they were raised.

The point is, according to internal E-mails, there are folks who say we're grandstanding by working on this Wilson thing, and others who say we're going down and desperate for attention."

"Neither of those is true," Hood said.

"Then what *is* true?"

"We were downsized, period," Hood told him. "Right now I'm working to see if we can't get some of our assets restored."

"Oh? What are the odds?"

"Pretty fair," Hood said. "I'll let all the department heads know when I have more information."

"Sweet. We could use a lift."

Hood gave the younger man's shoulder a squeeze, then went back to his office. He had never felt so torn in his life. His position made him unavailable for office gossip, let alone the gossip of other offices. Nor had Op-Center ever been a place where workers had a reason to gripe. There had been sadness and setbacks, but always due to missions. There was never a sense that the organization itself was in jeopardy. Certainly no one ever believed that Op-Center would be blindsided by the CIOC and other government agencies. Like Paul Hood, the National Crisis Management Center was the golden child of intelligence.

They thought.

Hood reached his office and shut the door. He stood inside, staring at his desk. If Hood accepted the president's offer, he would be participating in the spoils system he had always fought. His guiding principle would not necessarily be what was right but what was right for Op-Center. He would no longer be Pope Paul, as Herbert and the others sometimes called him in jest, but Apostate Paul.

But was *anything* so clear cut anymore? It did not matter whether the president was right or wrong about the threat Senator Orr represented. That was psychological spin-doctoring. What mattered was hanging on to men like

Matt Stoll and Darrell McCaskey. Hood would not like everything the new NCMC was asked to do. But this was not about his comfort zone. This was about preserving enough of Op-Center so that their important primary mission of crisis management could continue.

Hood went to the phone to call Senator Debenport. He would agree to the terms Debenport and the president had presented. He would ask for guarantees, not to be made an ambassador but to protect the existing staff.

He would make his deal with the devil.

TWENTY-SIX

Washington, D.C.
Tuesday, 11:50 A.M.

Kenneth Link sat alone in the conference room, reviewing a computer file of layout plans for the convention floor. Eric Stone had E-mailed a suggestion for the location of the podium. He felt the stand should be moved fifteen yards closer to the north side of the convention center. That put the speakers closer to the right when people entered the arena through the main gate. Link felt the change was gimmicky and declined to approve it.

Or maybe Link was just being contrary. He was not sure. The interview with Darrell McCaskey had left him in a sour mood. It had not gone the way he had anticipated. The admiral believed that by being forthright about his team and his dislike of Wilson, he would convince McCaskey of his innocence. Instead, something about their talk had caused Op-Center to harden its position. Link was a naval officer and a former head of covert operations for the CIA. He would not permit the tinsel-eyed former mayor of Los Angeles to hunt him. Or, even worse, to judge him.

Throughout his career, Link had always found the struggle between need and protocol, between expediency and restraint difficult to rectify. Right and wrong are subjective. Legal and illegal are objective. When the two forces are in conflict, which one should be followed? Especially when a legal wrong has the potential to rectify countless moral wrongs.

Link invariably put self-determination above regulations, which meant honoring *right* above *legal.* It meant more than that, though. Working in national defense was not a job for the fearful. It also was not a job for the unprepared. A man needed resources. Fortunately, Link had them. He was loyal to people, and people were loyal to him.

This matter of William Wilson should never have become the problem it was. Everything had been done the right way and for the right reasons. Looking under the man's tongue was on the medical examiner's checklist, but the tiny needle left no obvious trauma in the soft, veinal undertissue. Only someone who knew that anatomy well would have picked it up. Wilson's death should have been news for two days. After that, he would have been fodder for the weekly news magazines and monthly financial magazines for an issue or two. Most importantly, his banking scheme would have been forgotten. Others could have moved in with different opportunities for investors. Domestic opportunities that would be part of the USF platform. A program based on investments in American technology, manufacturing, and resources. A program that would have put money into the economy and given citizens deep and extensive tax benefits.

A program that would have really put the United States First Party on the political map.

In all their planning, no one had ever imagined that an intelligence service would get involved. Until this morning, Link had not thought they would stay in this for more than another day. He had thought the hiring of Mike Rodgers would discourage them, and the publicity about opportunism would be embarrassing. He had obviously underestimated Paul Hood. Link did not know if the investigation was a result of the man's fabled idealism, Hollywood-bred narcissism, or a combination of both. Regardless, the admiral could not let it get in his own way.

There were still actions to be taken, and Op-Center would interfere.

There was a point in intelligence and military operations when there was no longer any benefit to being clandestine. When a covert assassination fails, the strategy must shift to a Bay of Pigs scenario—albeit one that is designed to work. When the so-called architect group reaches that point, the question is no longer whether people suspect you did it but whether they can prove it.

Kenneth Link went to a floor cabinet in the far corner of the conference room. There was a safe inside. He opened it and removed a STU-3—a Secure Telephone Unit, third generation. He jacked the all-white phone into a socket behind a regular office phone on the conference table. The STU-3 looked like a normal desk set but with a crypto-ignition key that initiated secure conversations. This model interfaced with compatible cell phones, which is what he was calling now.

Bold action had to be taken. The action would be condemned, but it would also discourage others from pursuing Link. The police would look elsewhere for the Hypo-Slayer, as the media had taken to calling it. Before long, the investigation would all but disappear. The killer would not be found. The public would lose interest.

Besides, there would be other news to replace it.

TWENTY-SEVEN

Washington, D.C.
Tuesday, 12:10 P.M.

Mike Rodgers felt like Philip Nolan in *The Man Without a Country*. Whereas Edward Everett Hale's protagonist had been exiled for his part in the treasonous activities of Aaron Burr, Rodgers felt as if he had been banished by timing and circumstance. He was still employed by Op-Center, which had betrayed its charter. The general believed that Paul Hood was pursuing what the military described as a *directed service agenda*. That was a program masquerading as patriotism that was designed to help the branch itself, like starting a war to test new weapons or burn through old ordnance. Op-Center had a marginally legitimate reason to look into Wilson's death. Now they were pursuing it beyond that original mandate for self-serving reasons. Ironically, part of Rodgers understood those reasons. It had obviously hurt Hood to ask for Rodgers's resignation. He wanted to make sure there were no more firings. But part of Mike Rodgers also wanted to go to Op-Center and call Hood out, challenge him for the sludge he was flinging on Rodgers's new employer.

Instead, Rodgers sat down with Kat Lockley and Kendra Peterson and reviewed the plans for the convention as well as Senator Orr's platform. Now and then, they solicited Rodgers's opinion. The women were responsive to the handful of suggestions he made. The staff had spent so long knocking ideas around just between themselves, they were happy to have a new set of eyes. The experience was a good one for Rodgers. It was nice to be heard.

When the meeting was over, Rodgers asked Kat Lockley to lunch. She said she could get away in about a half hour. Rodgers said he would wait for her on Delaware Avenue. That lifted his spirits even more. At Op-Center, he had to remain detached from the women because he was the number-two man. He did not want to be emotionally involved with someone he might have to overrule or send into combat. It was pleasant to get in there and push around ideas, especially among young women who had energy and fresh ideas. And, yes, killer smiles. Bob Herbert had once described a meeting with young women at some university mock think tank as "PC."

"Not politically correct," Herbert said. "Pleasantly coercive."

This meeting was definitely PC.

On the way out, Rodgers bumped into Admiral Link. The future vice presidential candidate did not look happy.

"Is your friend Mr. McCaskey usually so bullheaded?" Link asked. "I don't mean that meeting," he added. "McCaskey called back to tell me we were going to see some rising tide on this investigation."

"What?" Rodgers said. "That doesn't sound like Darrell at all. Someone must be holding his feet to the flame."

"Is Hood usually this reckless?" Link asked.

Rodgers shook his head firmly. "This budget crisis must have really shaken him up. Do you want me to talk to him?"

"I don't think so—"

"I don't mind," Rodgers said. "I was thinking about going over there anyway and kicking up dust."

"No," Link said. "Hood is going to do what he wants. Let him. Why fight a battle we're going to win anyway?"

"Because I've got rockets in the launcher, and I've flipped open the safety cover," Rodgers said.

Link smiled. "Save them for the campaign, General. This is a sideshow. That's all it is."

Rodgers reluctantly agreed. There were times when he simply wanted to engage the enemy, and this was one of those times. Link thanked him for his support and went to see Kendra. Rodgers walked out to Delaware Avenue, sat on a bench, and let the sunshine wash over him. It was amazing how different the same sun felt in different parts of the world. It was searing in the deserts of the Southwest where he had once trained a mechanized brigade, impotent in the Himalayas, slimy in the humid Diamond Mountains of North Korea. It was full of warmth and vitamins in the South American plains, an outright enemy in the Middle East, and comforting here, like freshly brewed tea. Individuals and institutions had almost as many colors as the sun. Everything depended on the place, the day, and the circumstances.

There was a time when Op-Center had nourished Rodgers, too.

While the general sat there, he checked his cell phone for messages. There was one call from psychologist Liz Gordon, checking to see how he was, and one from Paul Hood asking him to call as soon as it was convenient. Hood sounded annoyed. Rodgers smiled. He could guess why. He speed-dialed Hood's direct line. Apparently, he was going to get his confrontation after all.

" 'Loyalty is missing in action, along with honor and integrity,' " Hood said angrily, without preliminaries. "Mike, did you give that quote to a reporter named Lucy O'Connor?"

"I did," Rodgers replied.

"Why?"

"Because it is true. And don't take it too personally, Paul. I told her it was missing everywhere, not just at Op-Center."

"How *I* take it doesn't matter," Hood said. "It's how the rest of the team takes it. Mike, I thought we had discussed the circumstances surrounding the budget cut, that you understood—"

"Paul, this is not just about me getting shit-canned," Rodgers said. "It's about this whole stinking investigation of Admiral Link."

"Stinking in what way?" Hood asked.

"It's harassment for gain," Rodgers told him.

"You know us better than that, dammit."

"I know Darrell better than that," Rodgers said. "I'm not so sure about you anymore, and I can't believe he did that without your okay."

"Yeah, I approved it," Hood told him. "Hell, I encouraged it, and with good reason. I didn't suggest the ramping-up, though. I shouldn't be telling you this, but that was Bob Herbert's idea."

"Bob?"

"Bob," Hood said.

That took Rodgers by surprise. It also stripped him naked. He looked around with slow, probing eyes. His gaze moved along the avenue, across the street, peered into parked cars and the windows of office buildings. Rodgers knew all the tails Op-Center used. He half-expected to see one of them watching him from behind a hamburger or a paperback book. The thought was also a disturbing reminder of how quickly an ally could become an adversary.

"Look, I'm not going to get into a howling contest in the press," Hood went on. "I told Ms. O'Connor that I disagree with your view and left it at that. But I do want to remind you that Op-Center is my first concern—"

"I have my dismissal to remind me, thanks," Rodgers interrupted.

"I thought you understood what went down," Hood said.

"I do. I thought *you* understood that I did not like it."

Both men snapped off the conversation. The crackling cell phone silence was heavy, but it did not hurt. Rodgers felt that Hood was out of line. As he sat there, his eyes continued to search for familiar faces. Aideen Marley, Maria Corneja-McCaskey, David Battat, some of the others that Rodgers himself had trained. His heart ached over what they must be feeling.

"Mike, we both want the same thing," Hood said. "Whichever way it goes, we want this to be over as soon as possible. So I'm going to ask you to cooperate by letting Bob's people work—"

"Christ, you don't have to ask that," Rodgers said. "I know the drill. Just don't put any of them on me."

"Of course not." Hood said. He sounded as though he had been wounded.

Too bad.

Rodgers clicked off the phone. He decided he was not angry with Bob Herbert. Yes, the intelligence chief was just doing his job. More importantly, though, Rodgers believed that Herbert had involved himself for the reasons Hood had stated: to put this crippled bird in the hangar. Unlike Paul Hood, Herbert was looking out for his friend's interests.

Rodgers tucked the cell phone back in his pocket. Because he was not technically on duty, he was not in uniform. It seemed strange wearing a blazer instead of his uniform. It was also liberating. Mike Rodgers and General Mike Rodgers had been the same person for so long, he was looking forward to discovering what it was like to be a civilian. Starting with having the freedom to talk back to a commander who had betrayed him.

Rodgers stopped looking for spies. He enjoyed the respite, and when Kat finally showed up, breathless but smiling, he knew he would enjoy his lunch as well. They set out toward a café with open-air seating, put their names on the waiting list, and talked about the morning. Rodgers let her out-gas as they rather unromantically called it in the military. But he made Kat promise that once they were seated, she would not discuss the campaign, the investigation, or anything else pertaining to Senator Orr. He wanted to hear about her life.

She agreed to tell him.

It was good to be a civilian but, more important, it felt good to be a man. Hood had done him a favor. He tried not to let his mind go to a place where it desperately longed to be, to a future where Senator Orr was President Orr and Mike Rodgers was the secretary of defense. A future where a spoils system appointee took over the CIOC from Senator Debenport. A future where the first act of the new chairman was to ask for Paul Hood's resignation.

Rodgers did not let himself go there because revenge was not a good primary reason to do anything. It caused rash, often counterproductive behavior, like the prizefighter who looked to put away a hated rival in round one and tired himself out.

Rodgers would take a more measured approach.

Revenge would not be an atom bomb. It would be fallout.

TWENTY-EIGHT

Herndon, Virginia
Tuesday, 12:11 P.M.

For more than a century, the Washington & Old Dominion Railroad was a lifeline to the nation's capital. Nicknamed the Virginia Creeper in honor of its speed—or lack thereof—the train moved northwest through Virginia to points beyond. The track still passes through the center of town, where an underground garage stands not far from the W&OD museum. Two hundred feet long by seventy-five feet wide, and fifteen feet deep, the garage used to have track over it. Now there is only high, wind-rustled grasses. Once covered by removable wooden slats, workers would use the garage to get underneath the cars and conduct repairs.

Today, the garage has a much different use. It is the workplace of Art Van Wezel. It is where the CIA employee runs three key facets of the black ops infrastructure, what he calls "ways, means, and most definite ends."

Commandeered by the OSS during World War II and covered with concrete, the Garage—that became its formal code name—was originally used as a secret listening post. Fifth columnists working in and around Washington, D.C., would often go into the countryside to meet fellow operatives or send radio messages to waiting submarines. Because of the wires already in place for the railroad, the OSS did not have to erect additional antennae. The rails also gave them train and hand car access to the entire region, allowing for furtive counterespionage activities. After the war, the Garage was transformed into a storage facility for equipment used by the successor to the OSS, the newly formed Central Intelligence Agency. During the Cold War, the CIA leadership used the garage for decatalogued weapons and chemicals. These were produced for the sole purpose of arming field agents. They were stored in the Garage because, officially, such armaments did not exist. In the 1980s, the CIA converted the Garage to a warehouse for covert ops equipment. It was staffed by two former navy men: Jason Harper and Art Van Wezel. When Harper retired, only Van Wezel remained.

Van Wezel was still there.

When Kenneth Link took charge of covert ops at the CIA, he spent a lot of time in the Garage. Part of that was spent organizing it into a world-class repository for new and specialized ordnance. Part of the time was also used to shift deactivated matériel from the Defense Supply Center in Richmond, Virginia, to the Garage. His rank gave him access to everything the navy was no longer using. Many of these weapons were prototypes that were either abandoned or actually went into production. Van Wezel made sure the weapons were kept in working condition. He also made sure that most of them were reported to have been destroyed. Link countersigned those reports. The admiral held on to them.

The admiral also held on to Van Wezel. Link made certain he was promoted to increasingly more lucrative pay grades. Link gave Van Wezel friendship and job security in an insecure world.

During Link's stewardship, the Garage appeared in fewer and fewer internal CIA memos. Over time, the warehouse virtually became Link's own private black ops repository and staging area.

The fifty-year-old Van Wezel was devoted to Admiral Link. Together, over the years, they built a small network of off-the-books counterespionage agents code named Mechanics. Most of them were former SEALs loyal to the former admiral. Today, the Mechanics remained on the Company's stealth payroll. But they were available to their friend and mentor for special jobs. They knew his heart, and they knew that it belonged to an uncompromising patriot. They recognized that Kenneth Link would never ask them to do anything that was not in the nation's best interests.

One of these people was Jacquie Colmer, a former captain on the admiral's staff. The thirty-six-year-old woman was fearless. When Link shifted to the CIA, he made certain that she was appointed the new navy liaison with the Garage. She and Van Wezel got together once a week to review inventory. That list was sent to Link, along with the whereabouts of the Mechanics. Jacquie also went out on the rare local jobs Link requested. Most of those were surveillance. A few were more hands-on.

Link had informed both Van Wezel and Jacquie about this new operation he needed done. The job was risky, and it was extreme. Both of the Garage veterans had grave reservations about the target. But they had read the newspapers. They understood what was at stake.

They would do what the admiral asked.

Van Wezel had two other functions at the Garage. One was intentionally visible. He maintained a small fleet of nondescript vehicles. These were "the means." The trucks and vans were owned and operated by the Herndon Road Services Company, a shell company controlled by the CIA. The HRSC rented vehicles to local firms in order to appear legitimate. Van Wezel wore white coveralls and could frequently be seen taking care of his half-dozen vehicles, washing and servicing them and waving to the locals when they passed.

Van Wezel's third job was to give operatives "the ways" to do their jobs. He maintained a large computer database of logos from utilities and local companies. He used these to make photo ID badges for the field ops. More often than not, he had the right one for the right job already at hand. He regularly checked the web sites of the firms to make sure the design had not changed.

For this particular mission, Van Wezel needed a badge for the Country-Fresh Water Corporation. The CFWC had a contract to provide water to the coolers in all local government agencies. He had called the CFWC, pretending to be the client, to make sure this was not a regular delivery day. It would be disastrous if the real provider showed up while Jacquie was there. Then he called the client to schedule a delivery for today. Van Wezel already had a badge prepared for another agent. It was an easy matter for him to put Jacquie's photograph on that ID. He also had a small sign with the CFWC logo. He slipped that into a frame on the side of the van. If the guard asked, this was a loaner while the real truck was being repaired.

Van Wezel was confident about the ways and means. He also had the "ends," one that was developed by the Air Force for air drops into power plants. It would accomplish the admiral's goal with a minimum of event-injuried allies. Despite their differences, the men and women of Op-Center were also Americans. Link had no desire to hurt them. He had only one objective: to stop them.

TWENTY-NINE

Washington, D.C.
Tuesday, 12:25 P.M.

Like dinner the evening before, lunch with Kat was a welcome respite from angry thoughts. She was a sophisticated young woman with an eye firmly on the future but also a critical eye on the past. She had not only been influenced by her police family, but her journalistic background had given her broad political exposure. Kat Lockley knew how the system worked. More importantly, the New York native obviously knew how to work the system.

"Being New Yorkers, how did you ever hook up with the senator?" Rodgers asked. "You said he was an old friend of your father. . . ."

"Army days. They drifted later, but never far or for long. When my dad was on the police force, he helped set up a program called Vacation Swap, when kids from the city went to some other place and vice versa," Kat said. "He and one of their other army buddies, Mac Crowne—a Park Avenue dentist, fittingly—took kids out to the Orr Ranch a couple of times a year. They were as different as could be, which is probably why they got along so well."

"Did you ever go?"

"A couple of times," she said. "Good thing, too."

"Why?"

"Senator Orr says he would never entirely trust a person who was uncomfortable around horses," she replied.

"The admiral does not strike me as an equestrian," Rodgers noted.

"He isn't. But he hunted sperm whales as a teenager in Newfoundland, before it was banned. That registered big on the Orr machismo scale."

"I hope the senator realizes I have nothing to offer along those lines—"

"But you do," Kat commented. "Tanks. Big beasts, difficult to tame. To the senator, tank warfare is like a medieval joust. Very manly."

"I see," Rodgers said.

Kat was absolutely a good person to have on the team. Experienced, enthusiastic, energetic. It was not just Kat, though. The entire conversation felt good. It was full of insights and compliments, camaraderie and hope. When it was over, Rodgers decided to go back to Op-Center and clean out his desk. Though he was still technically on the payroll, he wanted no part of the organization. He did not want to hold on to the anger Hood had made him feel. He would say his good-byes to those who wanted to hear them, and then Mike Rodgers would do exactly what Kat Lockley was doing: use the considerable experiences of his lifetime to look ahead. Rodgers could not imagine that Paul Hood would want or need him for anything over the next few days.

He walked Kat back to the office building, then drove out to Andrews Air Force Base—possibly for the last time. Mike Rodgers was not sentimental that way. Yet he did wonder if, on the whole, this had been a positive experience. So much good had been done but at an extraordinary cost. For himself, the sadness of the people he had lost would probably be stronger in his memory than the goals they had achieved. He also believed, as he had since Op-Center was chartered, that he would have done a better job running it than Hood had done. He would not go so far as to say that good things had happened in spite of the director. But he would say that Hood had not been as proactive as he would have been.

Hell, I was the one who assigned myself to the North Korea mission, Rodgers thought.

If he had not, Hood might have refused to let Striker act as aggressively as it did. His CIOC-friendly methods may have allowed Tokyo to vanish under a barrage of Nodong missiles. Waiting for approvals and charter revisions was the way to build a legal and clean-living entity, not necessarily the most effective one. It would be like soldiers in the field asking the president or secretary of defense to okay each maneuver. Rodgers always felt it was better to ask for forgiveness than for permission.

The air force guard standing near the elevator saluted smartly. Rodgers saluted back. Nothing in the young woman's eyes betrayed knowledge of what had gone on below. Perhaps she did not know. Op-Center's grapevine tended to grow, and remain, underground.

The initial discomfort of employees in the executive section had passed. They greeted Rodgers warmly as he made his way to his office. Rodgers told Liz Gordon and Lowell Coffey that he had decided to accept Senator Orr's offer and would be working on the campaign. Both wished him well. Rodgers did not know how he would respond to Hood if he saw him. The general could—and would—ignore his replacement, Ron Plummer. The political liaison had not won that job, it had been granted to him by default. That made Plummer neither enemy nor rival, just a man with a catcher's mitt. Paul Hood was a different matter. He was the one who had made the default call. Rodgers imagined everything from ignoring him to grabbing the front of his lightly starched white shirt, slamming him against a wall, and spitting in his wide, frightened eye. What stopped him, when they did meet, was the realization that Hood was finally doing what Rodgers had wished he would do for years: telling the CIOC to screw its own rules and doing what he thought was best for Op-Center. It was only too bad his newly found courage came at Admiral Link's expense.

Hood was talking to Bob Herbert in the intelligence chief's office. The door was open as Rodgers walked by. He offered only a peripheral glance inside. *Eyes on the future,* he reminded himself. Now that he thought of it, that mantra would make a terrific campaign slogan.

Neither man called after him nor hurried into the hallway. Rodgers felt relieved for a moment. There would be no confrontation with Hood. He would not have to listen to Herbert explain why he had joined the assault. Then Rodgers felt offended. *Who the hell are they to ignore me?*

He should have known Pope Paul better than that. The man was a diplomat, and diplomats could not leave situations unresolved. Even without the blessings of their governments, they usually employed back-channel routes to try to defuse crises. Maybe they needed to do good. Maybe they needed to meddle or to be loved. The motives were too complex for Rodgers to fathom. All he understood was soldiering. Until he came to Op-Center, that was all Rodgers needed to know. Inevitably, after the talks had broken down or bought only a temporary respite, it took spilled blood to grease the wheels of civilization.

Hood knocked on the open door as Rodgers was taking citations and photographs from the wall.

"I would like to change the date when I'm officially relieved of all responsibilities to Op-Center," Rodgers said. He did not look at Hood.

"When do you want to leave?"

"Today," Rodgers said. "Now." He put the framed pictures and documents on the desk then went and got two shoulder bags from a small closet in back. He stood behind the desk and carefully placed the mementos inside. He did it without sentiment or nostalgia about leaving. A soldier's life should be portable. The only item from his tenure here was a photograph of himself with Lieutenant Colonel Charlie Squires and Striker. It was taken after the team had been assembled, about two months before they went to North Korea.

"Is this how you want it to end, Mike?" Hood asked.

"You mean, without a parade or a twenty-one-gun salute?"

"I mean with this barrier between us," Hood said. "I want to give you that salute, Mike. Not just because you deserve to be honored but because Charlie once told me why it was created. Weapons were discharged to show that the military was granting safe passage to a trusted visitor."

"I told him that," Rodgers said wistfully. He could still see himself and the strapping officer sitting by the pool near the Striker quad when he asked about that. They had just come back from drilling and had heard a volley in the distance. "Twenty-one guns for the number of states in the union when the navy began the tradition. An old military tradition, just like something you reminded me of yesterday. Something I had overlooked for years."

"What was that?"

"We called it 'the faith and bullet rule' in Vietnam," Rodgers told him. "When you meet a politician, only put one of those in him."

"You know, Mike, tactics are easier when the objectives are clear, when you know what hill or town you have to take and what resources are available to do it. Politics is a war without rules of engagement or the immediacy of gunfire. Sometimes you don't realize you've been hit until days later or until you read it in the newspaper."

"I guess I should be grateful my executioner looked me in the eyes when he pulled the trigger," Rodgers replied.

"I did not say that," Hood insisted.

"Then I'm confused," Rodgers told him. "Are we talking specifically about us or are we having a philosophical discussion about what my grandfather used to call 'folly-tics'?"

"I'm trying to apologize," Hood said.

"For what? Firing me? Placing my new boss under a magnifying glass?"

"Neither. We've been over those. I'm sorry there's nothing I can do about any of it."

Rodgers buckled the first bag. Before he loaded the second, he regarded Hood. "That's another difference between soldiers and politicians," he said. "*No can do* is not in our vocabulary. Neither is *surrender.*"

"That may be," Hood said. Now there was a bit of steel in his voice. "I'll tell you this, though, Mike. If I had made a stand on these points that obviously offend your sense of honor, the battlefield would be hip deep with corpses. And I still would have lost the battle." Hood extended his hand. "I won't be offended if you don't shake it. I'll only be sad."

Rodgers had not yet started loading the second bag. He began putting the keepsakes inside.

"I can't," he said.

"You mean you won't," Hood said.

Rodgers snickered. "Politicians play with words, too." He held up his right palm. "I mean this hand just took down a photograph of a man who gave his life for this place. It can't, and won't, clasp the hand of a guy who was afraid to lose his job. And by the way, Paul. A battlefield littered with war dead is not the same as a job market having to absorb some bureaucrats. Don't ever compare them."

"I wasn't," Hood said. "I was only trying to connect with you somehow."

"Well, you failed."

"I can see that." Hood lowered his arm. "If you change your mind, the hand is still extended."

"I appreciate that."

"And I do wish you well," Hood added.

"I appreciate that, too," Rodgers said with a little more formality.

Hood left, shutting the door behind him. Rodgers looked around. The office seemed both bigger and smaller because of the naked walls. Men are small, but their deeds are large.

Rodgers did not regret what he had just done. Unlike Hood, he did not even feel sad. All he felt was a sense of pride that he had lifted himself from the battlefield and soldiered on. He finished packing the second bag, then went to his desk and removed the few personal items that were still there. A leather bookmark with the NATO logo, a letter opener from the king of Spain in gratitude for the way Striker had helped prevent a new civil war.

A memorial card from the service of Bass Moore, the first Striker killed in action.

Rodgers was convinced that he had done the right thing by rejecting Hood's hand. As he left his former office, the general was convinced of something else. That there was probably nothing on God's sweet earth that would ever make him rescind that decision.

THIRTY

Washington, D.C.
Tuesday, 2:18 P.M.

Though the military police would never acknowledge it, security was rooted in the two Ps: preparedness and profiling. It had to be done that way. The kids manning the gates and checkpoints at bases around the world lacked street smarts and experience. They required checklists.

Jacquie Colmer did not fit any of the terrorist profiles. She was fair-skinned, and she was a woman. That eliminated religious extremists and white supremacists. She was also disarming. She smiled a great deal, which terrorists tended not to do. Most were anxious young amateurs, fearful of being captured and disappointing their sponsors. Jacquie was not a novice. The key to successful penetration of an enemy target was what Jacquie had always called the *seduction factor.* Her job was not to muscle people into submission but to coerce them. She used femininity, compliments, small talk, and invigorating observations to make herself welcome. "*Look* at that sky!" she would say, or "*Smell* that rain!" She drew attention to the moment to hide what lay beyond.

While the Herndon Road Services Company was not the usual Country-Fresh Water Corporation vehicle, she had the proper documentation. The Andrews Air Force Base guard went through the antiespionage checklist, which he knew by heart. There were only containers of water in the back, and the front-to-back mirror view of the underside revealed nothing. The young, expressionless guard looked under the hood with a flashlight. He saw only the engine.

Jacquie was allowed to drive on.

The woman parked her van away from the sight line of the base sentry. She withdrew a hefty five-gallon container and hoisted it onto her right shoulder. She saw through the tinted glass that the guard booth inside the lobby was on the left side. She had made it this far. The guard by the elevator at the National Crisis Management Center would not give her much trouble. Especially a woman holding a large plastic bottle of water. A bottle that was tinted deep blue to make the water appealing.

And to hide what was in the neck of the bottle. What the tint did not conceal, Jacquie's glove and the bottle's neck did.

The sentry was a husky woman who held the rank of corporal. Her name tag said Vosa.

"Corporal Vosa, did you know that water coolers consume four billion kilowatt hours a year, which produces an annual level of pollution equivalent to the emissions of three-quarters of a million cars?" she asked the guard.

"I did not, ma'am," said the NCO.

Playing the nerd was also a useful tactic when one wished to get in and out of a place quickly. No one liked to talk to a chatterbox. They liked it less when they were addressed by name. It made the individual feel as though their privacy had been invaded even more.

The guard checked her papers quickly.

"It says here you have a delivery of eleven bottles," the corporal said. "You only have one."

"With me, right now," Jacquie replied. "The cart only holds ten. I figured I would take this one first, then go back for the rest. Easy before hard, that's my motto."

The guard called down to Mac McCallie in Ed Colahan's office. The CFO's group was in charge of supplies and the scheduling of deliveries. McCallie informed the guard that CFWC was indeed expected. The sentry used the remote keypad at her station to summon the elevator.

"That four billion kilowatt hours a year is three hundred million dollars worth of utility bills," Jacquie added. "You ought to mention that to your superiors. Not that I want to see these guys lose business, but I'm a taxpayer, too. Maybe we can help cut the military budget by eliminating water coolers."

"It's a thought, ma'am," the guard said charitably. She wrote out a pass and handed it to Jacquie. The delivery woman slapped the sticky ID on her Herndon Road Services delivery uniform.

The elevator door opened. Jacquie saluted casually with her left hand and walked on. "See you in a few minutes," Jacquie said.

The elevator took the woman downstairs, where she was met by McCallie. A former marine, judging from his posture. No one stood as straight and tight as the semper fi boys. He also offered to carry the bottle, another giveaway. She declined. He took Jacquie to the water cooler and stayed with her the entire time. She put the bottle beside the cooler, then went to go and get the other ten.

Which, of course, she would not be doing.

Jacquie went to the van. She drove away, waving to the guard as she left. He would not know she had failed to complete the delivery.

As she drove away, Jacquie pulled off the blond wig she was wearing. She allowed her long black hair to cascade out. In less than one minute a wristwatch-size timer inside the bottle cap would activate the flux compression generator that Art Van Wezel had placed in the long bottleneck. The FCG consisted of a tube stuffed with explosives inside a slightly larger copper coil. The coil would be energized by a bank of capacitors, creating a magnetic field. Five seconds later, the timer would detonate the explosives. As the tube flared outward, it would touch the coil and create a short circuit. The short circuit would cause the magnetic field to compress while reducing the inductance of the coil. The result would be an electric shock that broke free as the device self-destructed. The shock would only last a few microseconds, but it would produce a current of tens of millions of amperes.

The resultant electromagnetic pulse would make a lightning bolt seem like a flashbulb by comparison. It would turn Op-Center into an electronic graveyard. The pulse would also cover her tracks for her by erasing the videotapes fed by the security cameras. The military police and FBI would be looking for a talkative blond. One with blue eyes. She popped the colored contact lenses from her eyes and put them in the pocket of her uniform.

When Jacquie was a mile from the base, she pulled over on a narrow back street off Allentown Road. She was just a quarter mile from the Capital Beltway. It was important that she get there as quickly as possible. First, though, there were several things she had to do.

Jacquie slipped the water company signs from the sides of the van. She replaced them with signs she pulled from under the driver's side floor mat. They read, *Interfaith Good News Mobile*. She put a bow in her hair and a Bible on the passenger's seat. She placed a different license tag on the back of the van. The police would not think to stop her. No one would.

The wind was blowing hard, and she did not hear the blast when it came. But she knew the e-bomb had gone off. The rich blue sky over Andrews Air Force Base took on a brief, magnesium-white glow. It arced low just above and through the canopy of oak trees, a man-made aurora borealis that swiftly shaded to yellow, then green, then blue again as it vanished.

Jacquie smiled as she got back into the van. She drove to the highway, careful not to exceed the speed limit. She would return the van to Herndon, then stay in her house for several days. She would say she was sick with the flu while she waited to see the police sketch of the Op-Center bomber. She would be dieting while she was home. If the sketch happened to look like her now, it would not by the time she "got better."

Ironically, the government would benefit in one way because of what she had done.

The budget for water coolers would go way down.

THIRTY-ONE

Washington, D.C.
Tuesday, 2:37 P.M.

It sounded as though someone had popped a very large balloon. Hood's first thought was that one of Op-Center's emergency generators had exploded.

Paul Hood was sitting at his desk, his office door closed. He had been looking absently at the computer wallpaper, a crayon drawing of Los Angeles City Hall that Harleigh had done when she was four. He had been replaying the argument with Mike Rodgers, wondering if it could have gone differently, when he heard the burst from down the hall. It was loud enough to make him wince and to clog his ears for several seconds. A moment later the fluorescent lights above began to glow brightly. In front of Hood, the computer wallpaper was replaced by a strange, milky luminescence.

Hood rose slowly. As his ears began to clear, he heard coughing and shouts from beyond his closed door. He heard the people but nothing else. Not the hum of his computer nor the whir of the air conditioner or even the faint electric buzz of the coffee machine. Hood's left wrist felt warm. He glanced at his watch. The LCD was blank. So was the screen on his cell phone. He removed the watch. Faint ribbons of smoke curled from the battery compartment and also from the cell phone.

"No," Hood said. He suspected that what had hit Op-Center was not just a burned-out generator or a simple power failure.

He hurried to the door and opened it. The corridor beyond Bugs's cubicle was filled with wispy, yellowish smoke. The air was rich with the pungent aroma of ozone mixed with the foul smell of melted plastic. He later learned that these were from charred outlet plates, electric wires, and telephone lines.

Bugs was standing in the corridor, fanning away smoke, trying to see. He looked back when Hood emerged.

"What happened?" Hood asked.

"Something blew up in the lounge, I think," Bugs said. "I tried to call the gate to seal the perimeter, but the phones are fried."

"Emergency power is gone?" Hood asked.

"Everything."

"Do we know about casualties?"

"No."

"Are you okay?" Hood asked.

"Yes."

"Start getting people toward the stairwell," Hood said.

"Mike is doing that," Bugs said.

"Help him," Hood said.

"Sure," Bugs said. "Be careful."

Rodgers and Ron Plummer were the heads of the emergency evac team. The thought of them working together did not fill him with hope but with pride and respect. Differences among Americans always vanished when it mattered.

Hood gave Bugs a reassuring pat on the back just as Matt Stoll appeared from the mist. He was heading in the direction of the blast. Hood went with him.

"Can you tell me what happened?" Hood asked.

"We got kilned," Stoll said angrily.

"Sorry?"

"Superheated. The only thing I know that could do this is an e-bomb."

"Are you sure?" Hood asked.

"The glow of the lights, the monitors, is like a fingerprint. Nothing else could cause that."

"Was it inside the building or out?" Hood asked.

"Inside. I stopped by the Tank, and it was fine. I left Jefferson there to call for help. He was able to raise the front gate, which means they were not affected."

While all of Op-Center was secure, the Tank was the equivalent of an electronic fallout shelter. The conference room was protected from eavesdropping, hacking, and all manners of attack, including electromagnetic pulse. Stoll had designed it to be a large-scale Faraday cage, a hollow conductor that spread a charge along the outside of a system without producing an electric field inside. That would include a burst from an electromagnetic pulse. Ironically, Hood had believed that the only way they would be affected by an e-bomb is if an Air Force test at Andrews went sour.

Until now.

The smoke and the smell grew stronger as they neared the lounge. Stoll covered his mouth with a handkerchief, but Hood did not. The smoke was not too acrid, and he did not want to appear weak or impaired. That was important in a crisis. The men rounded a corner and entered the lounge.

The small room was clogged with yellow gray smoke. Without ventilation, it hung there, virtually impenetrable.

"Is anyone in here?" Hood shouted.

There was no answer.

"The smoke is from the explosive that triggered the EM burst," Stoll said. The portly scientist shuffled across the tile so he did not trip over any debris. While Stoll moved deeper, he waved his left hand to help clear the smoke. "The explosion was extremely low yield."

"How can you tell?" Hood asked. He was following behind, waving both hands and looking for victims.

"For one thing, the explosion did not have to be large to trigger the pulse. For another, I can see the base of the water cooler. The left side is gone. The bomb must have been beside it."

Hood saw a body. He knelt and bent close. Ugly, twisted pieces of the water cooler base were lodged in the man's chest. Blood stained his blue shirt thickly. He was not breathing.

"Who is it?" Stoll asked.

"Mac McCallie." Hood went to where he knew the candy and soda machines were. He fanned away the smoke. The vending machines were damaged, but not badly. Hood continued to feel his way around. There were upended tables and chairs, their legs twisted and surfaces peppered with shrapnel. From below. He felt the tops. They were spotted with blood. That meant they were still standing when McCallie was struck. Stoll was correct. The bomb was probably beside the cooler. Mac must have been here checking on the scheduled water delivery. Bloody damn government contracts like that were public information. Anyone could have gotten it. Hood took a slightly singed dishcloth from the sink and lay it gently across the dead man's face.

"This was designed to stop us, not kill us," Stoll said.

"Tell that to Mac," Hood said.

"Chief, I'm sorry," Stoll replied. "He was in the wrong place. All I'm saying is that whoever created this wanted to shut Op-Center down."

Jefferson Jefferson appeared in the thinning smoke of the doorway. "The base has been sealed, and an emergency rescue team is on the way."

"Thanks. Now get yourself out of here, but wait for the ERT at the top of the stairs," Hood said. "Tell them to come here."

"Yes, sir," the young man replied. He remained in the doorway for a moment looking at the body on the floor.

"Go," Hood said.

Jefferson turned and left. Hood heard his footsteps as he retreated. Except for distant voices and Matt's strained breathing, Hood heard nothing else. Op-Center seemed as lifeless as poor Mac. It was strange. He was able to compartmentalize the death of the man. It was a terrible event, but Hood would mourn later as he had Charlie Squires, Martha Mackall, and too many others. It was much more difficult to get his brain around the idea that Op-Center was a marble-silent tomb. This facility had given his life purpose, the only direction he seemed to have. Absent that, Hood felt as dead as Mac. Except he was still breathing.

Mike would say that means there's still hope, Hood thought. Maybe that would follow. Right now, all Hood felt was helplessness bordering on fear. He knew he had to get that under control. He had to focus.

Hood went over to Stoll. The computer scientist was squatting beside the jagged ruins of the water cooler and the adjoining debris field. Stoll had removed a penlight from his shirt pocket. He had taken it from an emergency supply kit in the Tank. He was examining the floor closely without touching anything. He looked like a boy studying an anthill.

"Does this tell you anything?" Hood asked.

"The bomb was not homemade," Stoll said.

"How can you tell?"

"They used eighteen-gauge clear sterling copper wire," he said through the handkerchief as he pointed with the penlight. "That gives an electromagnetic device a bigger pulse than standard twelve-gauge gold copper wire. But that is only true if the copper is free of impurities. A bomb maker needs some pretty sophisticated thermographic and harmonic testing equipment to qualify wire of that size."

"I assume the military has that capability," Hood said. "Who else?"

"A university laboratory, an aircraft or appliance manufacturer, any number of factories," Stoll told him. "The companion question, of course, is in addition to having the technical wherewithal, who would have the logistical chops to put an e-bomb inside a water bottle?"

"Or a reason," Hood said, thinking aloud.

"Yeah," Stoll replied, rising. "I don't imagine that Chrysler or Boeing has it in for us."

The emergency rescue team arrived then, their flash-lights probing the misty air. The smoke had achieved a consistency that made visibility a little easier. Mike Rodgers was the first man to enter. Seeing him, in command of the team and the situation, gave Hood a boost.

"Be careful where you step," Rodgers said. "This is a crime scene."

The four men who followed turned their lights on the floor. They walked carefully to the body of Mac McCallie and tried to revive him.

"Are you two all right?" Rodgers asked Hood and Stoll.

Hood nodded. "Did everyone get out?"

"Yes," Rodgers said. "Bob complained, but the blast killed all the electronics on his wheelchair, so he did not have much choice. The wheels locked when the servo-mechanisms got fried."

"Jesus, what about Ron Plummer?" Hood said, suddenly alarmed. "He has a pacemaker—"

"He's okay," Rodgers said. "We took him up with Bob. The med techs got to him right away."

"Thank God," Hood said. It seemed strange to thank God in the midst of this carnage. But Hood was grateful for that one bit of good news.

Hood, Rodgers, and Stoll moved aside as two of the rescue technicians carried Mac away on a stretcher. They moved quickly, even though there was no need. The other two ERT personnel went deeper into the facility to make sure there were no other injuries or individuals who might have been overcome by smoke.

"The base commander put a team to work getting a generator running," Rodgers said.

"Matt, how long until the computer monitors and fluorescent lights go dark?" Hood asked.

"It'll take another ten or fifteen minutes for the internal-system gases to lose the electromagnetic charge," Stoll said.

"We should probably get out of here, let the cleanup crew draw out the smoke," Rodgers said.

Hood nodded. The cleanup contingent of the ERT would be moving in with large potassium permanganate air purifiers. These big, fifty-pound units would clear eight hundred cubic feet of air per minute.

The three men headed toward the stairwell. Op-Center looked ghostly, with only the milky glow of the dying overhead lights and monitors.

"Matt, I don't suppose any of the hardware outside the Tank would have survived," Hood said.

Stoll shook his head. "Most of the files are backed up there, so at least the data is secure. But it's going to cost a bundle to replace the nuts and bolts. The computers, the phones, the PalmPilots, the CD and DVD data disks people were using. Even the coffeemakers and minifridges. Hell, we must have at least a thousand lightbulbs that are useless now."

"You've still got your team," Rodgers said. "And that includes me, Paul. I did not get around to changing the date on my resignation."

Hood was not a sentimental man, but that one choked him up. He thanked the general, though the sound came out more gulp than word.

"Getting back to who had the ability to pull this off," Stoll said, "I have to ask if either of you has any idea who might have done this."

Neither man spoke.

"I mean, it may not be the most tactful question to ask, but could it have been the guys we are investigating?"

"It could be any number of individuals or groups," Hood said. "Maybe the New Jacobins in Toulouse looking for a little revenge."

"Forgive me again, but that doesn't fit," Stoll went on. As ever, his pursuit of knowledge was chronically unencumbered by tact. "Like I said back there, this could have been designed to produce far more fatalities than it did. The New Jacobins and some of the other people we've crossed swords with would have been happy to reduce us all to binary digits."

"Matt's right," Rodgers said. "I know what it's like to lose a man, Paul, but this was designed as a flash-bang not as a kill shot. Someone wanted to blind us."

"Who?" Hood asked diplomatically.

The general did not answer. The question became rhetorical rather than leading. The men reached the narrow stairwell. They started up single file. Stoll was in the lead with Rodgers behind him.

"What we should do is plan to meet in the Tank as soon as possible," Hood went on. "Put all the possibilities on the table and cross-reference them with known modi operandi."

"I don't think we'll be able to go back down there today," Rodgers said. "Which is just as well, because I want to do some nosing around."

"Need any help?" Hood asked.

"No," Rodgers said firmly.

Hood left it at that. What was implied was far more important than what was said. Rodgers wanted to make sure that Op-Center's investigation of Admiral Link had not hit a nerve.

The men reached the parking lot on the south side of the building. There was a small picnic area with tables. Op-

Center employees stood and sat around them, alone and in very small groups. A few were smoking, even fewer were talking. It was strange to see no one using a cell phone or laptop. The blast had destroyed them all. There were misty clouds inside the cars parked nearest to the building. Their electronic components had also been burned out.

Most eyes turned to Hood when he emerged. The team knew, intuitively, that he would be the last man out.

Hood moved among the group to where Bob Herbert was sitting. He wanted to make sure his colleague was okay. Herbert said he was. He said it without emotion, which bordered on disinterest to Hood. But at least there was no anger. That was progress. Hood then told his team about Mac McCallie. There were a few moans of disbelief and several quiet oaths. Mac could be a severe pain in the butt who damn near counted every staple. But he was a professional who put in long hours. If employees needed something to do their job, he made sure they got it, ASAP. Hood also promised that they would find whoever had infiltrated their organization and planted the bomb.

The 89th Medical Group was stationed at Andrews, and ambulances began arriving to give each of the dozens of employees an on-site examination. Installation commander Brigadier General Bill Chrysler also arrived by staff car. Hood stepped from the group to meet him.

It was just now hitting the director that his facility had been e-bombed. Op-Center had been virtually destroyed. Hood felt violated, overwhelmed, and demoralized. Paradoxically, he was also starting to feel what Liz Gordon had once called "impotent rage," the desire to lash out in the absence of a target. Worse, he knew he had to stifle every one of those feelings. Unless the team was very lucky, this would not be a quick fix nor an easy one. And finding the perpetrator was not the only immediate problem. Hood also had to make sure that the CIOC or the press did not start positioning *this* as a publicity stunt or a grab for additional funding. He also had to make certain that the CIOC did not decide that it was easier to shut down Op-Center than to fix it. After what Hood hoped would be a brief meeting with Chrysler, his top priority would be to get in touch with Debenport and let him know that Op-Center was vigorously pursuing the investigation of the USF Party.

After all, they had something that they did not have before: a very personal reason.

THIRTY-TWO

Langley, Virginia
Tuesday, 3:44 P.M.

Darrell McCaskey had spent several unproductive hours at the British embassy and then at FBI headquarters. He had been looking for suppressed criminal records pertaining to any of his key players. He was searching, in particular, for someone who might have sold drugs or had a drug habit at one time. Someone who would have known how to inject William Wilson under the tongue.

There was nothing.

Dispirited, McCaskey was en route to Central Intelligence Agency headquarters in Langley, Virginia, when Maria called to tell him the news about an explosion at Andrews Air Force Base.

"Are there any details?" he asked.

"Only that eyewitnesses reported seeing a glow over the northwest corner of the base."

"That's where Op-Center is," McCaskey said.

"Which is why I phoned," she told him. "I tried calling Bob Herbert and Paul, but I only get a recording from the phone company saying there is a problem with the number I dialed."

McCaskey thanked her and tried calling them himself. He got nothing. He phoned the office of Brigadier General Chrysler and was told about the explosion. It appeared to be an electromagnetic pulse weapon. Everyone was still there except for Rodgers. McCaskey decided not to return.

If there were a plot against Op-Center, it was best to keep the resources disbursed. If there were a plot against the investigation, McCaskey refused to let this stop him. He had called in a favor with Sarah Hubbard, a friend at the Company's Central Intelligence Crime and Narcotics Center. McCaskey wanted to see a medical director at the Directorate of Science and Technology. There was an aspect of the murders that troubled him, and he needed answers. Hubbard said that Dr. Scot P. Allan was the man he wanted. She set up the appointment for four P.M.

McCaskey parked and went to the main entrance of the new headquarters building, a commanding white brick facade topped by a high, proud, hemispherical archway. The roof of the enclosed arch was made of panes of bulletproof glass. Compared to this showplace, Op-Center was downright homely. McCaskey went through the security checkpoint, where he was given a color-coded day pass to stick on his lapel. Then he waited for someone to come and get him. The former FBI agent felt a stab in his soul when he saw the sun slanting through the glass. The white stone gleamed, and there was a healthy sense of purpose to the men and women who moved through the corridors beyond. McCaskey thought of Op-Center and how badly the building and its occupants must have been wounded. He was glad, then, that he had not gone right back to Andrews Air Force Base. He needed time to process the fact that his home for the last six years had been invaded and disfigured.

A clean-cut young man arrived promptly to take McCaskey back to Dr. Allan's office. There was no conversation as the two men made their way along nondescript white corridors. This was the Central Intelligence Agency. People were trained to listen, not to speak.

Dr. Allan's book-lined office was toward the rear of a wing that included several laboratories, computer centers, and offices. Sports memorabilia was tucked between the volumes and hung on the wall between the diplomas. There were family photos in hand-painted frames, probably made by a daughter or son decades before. Compared to Matt Stoll's little tech hut, this was Mount Olympus.

Dr. Allan was a powerfully built, outgoing man in his late fifties. He had a long gray imperial beard at the end of a long face, full white eyebrows, and longish gray white hair. His brown eyes were dark with purpose. He looked like Uncle Sam dressed in a white lab coat with red stains on the sleeves. The all-American icon covered with blood.

"It's toluidine," the physician apologized, noticing McCaskey's gaze. "Working on a red dye." He did not tell him what it was for; this was the CIA. Allan motioned McCaskey to have a seat. He shut the door, then sat behind his desk. "I don't have a lot of time, Mr. McCaskey, but our mutual acquaintance said this was urgent."

"Yes, Dr. Allan. Thank you for seeing me."

"I had no choice," Allan informed him. "Ms. Hubbard wields a great deal of power here."

"She does?"

"Your friend controls the block of Redskins tickets." Allan smiled. "It's important to stay on her good side."

"She always had an angle."

"That is what government service is all about," Allan remarked. "Access and control. Now, what can I do for you?"

"Sir, I believe that Ms. Hubbard forwarded verification of my security clearance," McCaskey said.

"She did. She also told me that you were investigating the murder of William Wilson for the NCMC."

"That's right," McCaskey said.

"Speaking frankly, why did you want to see me? Do you suspect that someone here was involved?"

"Not someone who is presently employed here," McCaskey said.

"Good," Allan said. "I never discuss coworkers without their knowledge, especially with outsiders."

"We are part of the same team," McCaskey reminded him.

Allan just smiled.

"Doctor, I recall reading a top secret white paper about Company assassination policy in the 1960s," McCaskey went on. "It discussed the twenty-five-year-long moratorium instituted after the failed attempt to kill Fidel Castro using toxins in a cigar and poison in his beard."

"That is commonly known," Dr. Allan remarked.

"Yes. But there was a footnote I found interesting. It said that all of the Company's past and recent chemical attempts on high-value targets involved cyanide-based compounds. I need to know if that is true."

Dr. Allan suddenly seemed less relaxed. "Mr. McCaskey, the Redskins have a shot at the Super Bowl this year."

"I'm sorry?"

"I do not want to jeopardize my chances of seeing the game in person. That said, you are poking a finger in extremely sensitive areas."

"Sir, I know this is a very difficult question—"

"Difficult? You're asking me to explain what I may or may not do to abet murder," Dr. Allan said. "That is *not* a routine question."

"I appreciate that, but there is some urgency involved. Someone just attacked Op-Center—"

"What do you mean, attacked?" the doctor asked.

"They hit the place with an explosive device of some kind," McCaskey told him. "I have not been able to talk with my colleagues to get specifics. I'm guessing it relates to this investigation, and I need to find the people who are behind it. Any information you can provide may help."

Dr. Allan tapped his fingers anxiously on the desk for a few moments. Then he folded his hands. "Mr. McCaskey, I really wish you had not dropped this at my feet."

"I'm sorry, sir. But there it is."

"Yes," Allan said. He thought for another long moment. "Aw, hell. We're on the same team, Mr. McCaskey, and if you ever try to quote me, I'll deny everything. I think you are on the wrong trail."

"Why?"

"For one thing, the lethal injection described in the news accounts of Mr. Wilson's death. Potassium chloride is not a compound that we use for the purpose you just described."

"Do not or would not?"

"Both," Dr. Allan replied. "It just isn't anywhere on our radar. For the purpose of incapacitating an enemy, potassium chloride is too unpredictable. Individuals have different levels of tolerance. A dose that would kill one person might end up giving another nothing more than an irregular heartbeat."

"If that's true, why would someone have used it on William Wilson?" McCaskey asked.

"Three reasons. First, the compound is readily available online. Doctors routinely prescribe is as a counteragent for potassium depletion caused by high blood pressure medications. Finding out who ordered it, and from what national or international source, will be virtually impossible. Second, as you saw, potassium chloride is far more difficult to detect than cyanide. Third, the killer obviously had time to make certain the compound worked."

"Would you think a military medical technician would be familiar with its use?" McCaskey asked.

"Almost certainly."

"Do you happen to know, Dr. Allan, where on the human body field agents are told to give lethal injections?"

"In the muscles," he said.

"Not in veins?"

Allan shook his head.

"Why?"

"Muscle fiber has a very dense network of blood vessels and delivers drugs in just a few minutes," the physician told him. "The entry point is clearly visible, but that is the trade-off to a quick, efficient injection. That's another reason I do not believe your killer is a Company alumnus."

"I don't understand."

"Most of the people we send into the field are survivalists," Allan told him. "They are not scientists or doctors. Techniques are dumbed down as much as possible to give agents as little to worry about as possible. It is easier to inject an individual in the buttocks or thigh than in the arm or a more exotic spot, such as between the toes. An injection in the root of the tongue is relatively precise, not to mention dark and slippery. The person giving it cannot be a novice. In this case, maybe you should look for someone with dental training. The underside of the tongue is an entry point for a number of drugs used in oral surgery."

"I've already done that," McCaskey said. "Getting back to this question of novices, the Company has used precision assassins in the past. Poison in the tip of a blind man's cane, formaldehyde on a hero sandwich in a victim's refrigerator, even the abortive attempts on Castro."

"Yes, and those efforts against Castro are the *reason* today's killings are outsourced," Allan said. "Assassins can make millions of dollars a hit. Why would they work for salary and an inadequate pension?"

"Patriotism?" McCaskey asked sincerely.

"God and country cannot overcome greed," Allan replied. "When we engage in field work of this kind, it has to be successful. Often, it also requires plausible deniability, as you know. When we need it super clean, we go into a for-hire mode."

McCaskey had no more questions. But something the doctor just said did interest him. He stood. Allan also rose.

"Sir, I appreciate your time and counsel," McCaskey said.

The men shook hands across the desk.

"I am truly sorry it could not be more," Allan said.

"To the contrary," McCaskey told him. "This was very helpful, though I have to ask you, Doctor, to satisfy my own curiosity. What is it that drives you? Patriotism or greed?"

"Neither. I'm here for the difference in conjunctions," Allan replied.

"I don't follow."

"I asked myself that very question for years," Allan told him as they walked toward the door. "I deluded myself into thinking I came to work here out of civic spirit. Then I realized that, at the heart of it, I enjoyed more power than any other physician I know. I have power over life and death. That's *and,* Mr. McCaskey. Not *or.*"

The difference in conjunctions.

McCaskey left the doctor's office. He was glad to go. The office that had seemed warm and personal when he arrived now had a pall about it, a subtle chill, like the waiting room of a slaughterhouse. Murder was conceived here, plotted with cool, impersonal efficiency.

The young aide was still waiting outside the door to escort McCaskey back to the lobby. They walked in silence. This time, though, McCaskey's head was filled with noise. There was the sound of his own voice as he cherry-picked what had been said by Link and others. He played out an evolving monologue in his mind as he sifted through the last few days for clues.

He confronted his own shortcomings in his approach to the murder.

Maria always said her husband was naive. In a way, he was. He had always been an idealistic, self-denying G-man, Harry Hairshirt. In this instance maybe they were both right. Any crime could be approached two ways: with facts or with philosophy. McCaskey had been looking mostly at the facts. That was useful but narrow. A good commander could cover his tracks, as the assassin had done, but not his philosophy.

Greed versus patriotism versus power. One or more of those could well be the motive in this case, but to what degree and in what combination?

McCaskey had contemplated possible reasons behind Wilson's assassination, possibly a warning to investors that they should bank American. Perhaps the truth was much bigger than that.

Mike Rodgers had spent time with these people. The admiral himself was a military man. If Link were behind this, Rodgers might have thoughts about which of those values applied. McCaskey had to get in touch with him and the senator.

There was an out-of-service response from the general's cell phone, and no answer at his house. That left one place for McCaskey to try.

He slid into his car and headed toward Washington. McCaskey decided not to call Senator Orr's office but simply to go over. Rodgers might not like it, and the senator might like it even less. McCaskey had only two words for that, words he was prepared to back with his own show of greed and power.

Too bad.

THIRTY-THREE

Washington, D.C.
Tuesday, 4:10 P.M.

Mike Rodgers knew that he had already made a complete mental break from Op-Center. Since the Monday-morning meeting with Hood about budget cuts, Rodgers had not worried about unfinished NCMC business, about future activities, or about the operational status of his field agents.

After the blast, however, Rodgers suspected something else: that he had also divorced himself from Op-Center emotionally. He felt sad for the team members, who were hardworking and diligent, and for Mac's family, of course. But the carnage itself had not affected Rodgers. At least, not yet. Perhaps his brain had gone into survival mode. Ignore the pain, deal with the problem. Maybe, though, the blast was an outward expression of what he had already done inside. He had trashed Op-Center in his mind, angrily and violently. He had used a blowtorch to burn the place from every crease in his brain that might have cared. That was how Mike Rodgers had learned to deal with loss. It was cold, but it worked.

That did not mean Rodgers condoned this abhorrent attack. Therein lay the problem for him. If it were executed by a member of the Op-Center staff, the bombing was a repugnant way to manipulate policy. Rodgers did not believe Hood or any of his team were capable of doing that. If the bombing had been committed from without for political reasons, either by a domestic or foreign agency, the perpetrator would be uncovered. Someone would talk. Washington, D.C., had the most fertile grapevines this side of Northern California. Secrets were kept with the same care and sacred diligence as marriage vows.

And if Rodgers found out that anyone associated with Admiral Link or the USF Party had been responsible?

The general did not want to believe that. But if it turned out to be the case, Rodgers would make sure the perpetrators learned that truth and justice could not be suppressed. Not on his watch.

Rodgers did not remain in the parking lot with Paul Hood and the others. He spoke briefly with the base commander and Hood, then borrowed a Jeep to go into Washington. His own car had been one of those destroyed by the pulse. Rodgers felt a chill when he contemplated what had happened here. Electromagnetic pulse weapons were still in their infancy. The bombs were small, with a limited range. The problem developers faced was to generate a sufficiently wide-ranging pulse before the explosive trigger destroyed the weapon itself. But the impasse was nearly beaten, and within a year the Pentagon expected to deploy the first EMP devices. The navy would use the powerful microwave pulses of e-bombs to knock down antiship missiles; the army would pack pulse generators into artillery shells to neutralize the mechanized forces, field headquarters, and telecommunication capabilities of enemy troops; and the air force would load pulse weapons in bombers, fighters, missiles, and unmanned drones to shut down the infrastructure of enemy cities and take out aircraft. The latter could be particularly devastating. Unlike conventional explosives, which destroyed a plane in the air, an e-bomb would simply shut the engine off and drop the plane, its fuel, and its bombs on whatever was below. An enemy bomber taking off could be used to cripple its own air base. Tactical e-bombs could be fired air-to-air. A single fighter would be able to destroy entire enemy squadrons and their payload. Mini e-bombs, smaller than the one used against Op-Center, could become effective antiterrorist tools. In a properly shielded nuclear power plant, dam, or passenger aircraft, an electromagnetic pulse could be employed to shut down timers and thereby defuse bombs.

Of course, the reverse was also true. E-bombs could be used against American military assets and domestic infrastructure, just as it was today in Op-Center. Nuclear war had never really been an option. An EMP conflict, a war against binary digits, was probably inevitable.

And we may have just fought the first battle against ourselves, Rodgers thought. There was something unpleasantly biblical about that. It was a new world, and not necessarily brave. Combat would be waged via monitors and grids, not face-to-face or vehicle-to-vehicle. Maybe that was better for the psyche, and soldiers would be better adjusted. Post-traumatic stress would be reduced to a level of disappointment equal to losing a video game.

Rodgers wondered whether the senator's office had already heard what happened. Not that it mattered. A first reaction would not tell him whether or not they had been involved. He was more interested in going there, integrating himself in the activities of the late afternoon, and watching the people. Rodgers would be looking for exchanged glances when something about the attack was mentioned, or whispered phone conversations. Then there was the best information-gathering technique at all: the direct question. What was said was often less revealing than what was not said. His last talk with Paul Hood was evidence of that. The director of Op-Center knew exactly where Rodgers was going but did not offer advice. There was trust, caution, hope, and even gratitude in Hood's silence.

The senator's office seemed no different than it had been before. Kendra Peterson was standing outside her office, talking to an assistant. When the woman saw Rodgers, she stopped what she was doing and went to him. Her slender face reflected deep concern.

"General, did you hear about Op-Center?" Kendra asked.

"I was there," Rodgers told her.

"Sweet Jesus."

"How did you find out?" Rodgers asked.

Kendra took him by the elbow and led him to a corner, away from the intern pool. "The senator received a call from Dan Debenport at the CIOC."

"Why would Senator Debenport call here about that?"

"To say that he would request emergency funding so that Op-Center could continue to function," she replied. "Senator Orr is Chairman of the Senate Subcommittee on Short-Term Funding."

"That makes sense." Rodgers wondered if it was also a warning to Senator Orr that the investigation of William Wilson's death would continue. He could not understand why Debenport would be interested. Perhaps it was nothing more than backroom drama taking a turn in the footlights. "Is the admiral around?"

"Actually, he is not," she told him. "He left for a meeting with network producers about covering the convention. Do you need to talk to him? His cell phone is on."

"No, I'll talk with him later," Rodgers said. "What about Kat?"

"She's in. How well did you know the man who was killed?"

"Not very," Rodgers said. "He was a good man, a hard worker."

"That's a fine enough epitaph," Kendra said. "Do you or Director Hood have any idea who was responsible?"

"I don't, and if Paul Hood suspects anyone, he did not share that information with me," Rodgers told the woman.

"Is there a reason he would not?" Kendra asked.

"I'm sure Paul was preoccupied," Rodgers replied. He did not want to discuss the attack with Kendra. Not if there was a chance that she was involved. "What about you? Have you or the senator heard anything else?"

Kendra shook her head. "This is one of those things our country is going to have to watch out for more and more," she said solemnly. "The senator was saying that he wants to push for a new division of Homeland Security, one that would concentrate exclusively on the technology sector. He does not think he will have much trouble getting the funds after what happened today."

He could not tell whether Kendra had avoided the question or had instinctively and innocently slipped into stump speech mode. Just sell the preapproved ideas, nothing more. If you stick to the script, you cannot get into trouble.

"Well, that's always the way, isn't it?" Rodgers asked. "Get shot first, ask questions later."

Kendra smiled. "I like that."

"By the way, what are the senator's travel plans?"

"He is leaving for the convention tonight on his private jet," Kendra told him.

"Who else is going with him?"

"You're just full of questions," she observed. "I am going. Kat and the admiral will take a commercial flight tomorrow morning." She hesitated. "We had hoped you would be joining us in San Diego. Will that be possible now?"

"I don't know," the general replied.

"You're not part of the investigation, are you?" She added after a short pause, "Of the bombing, I mean."

"No. I am not."

His answer was as specific as her question. Kendra looked at him. She seemed to be waiting for him to elaborate, to say he was not part of any investigation. He did not want to lie to her so he said nothing. Yet once again, saying nothing was probably as informative as *Yes. I am.*

The woman smiled tightly, knowingly, then excused herself. Rodgers went to talk to Kat. He was annoyed with himself. He felt clumsy and exposed. He wondered how Darrell or Bob would have handled that differently.

Well, there is no turning this around, he told himself. *The only thing to do is move forward.*

Kat was in her office, on the phone, when Rodgers walked up. She smiled and motioned him in. Rodgers shut the door behind him and sat on the small sofa. A moment later, Kat hung up. She exhaled loudly.

"That was Lucy O'Connor—"

"Let me guess," Rodgers said. "She wanted to know if the senator had any reaction to the attack on Op-Center."

Kat nodded.

"Does he?"

"He thinks it's awful, as we all do," Kat said. Her warm eyes settled on his. "Were you at the NCMC at the time?"

Rodgers nodded.

"I'm sorry. Are you okay?"

"Surprisingly, yes. I lost my car and my work cell phone, and I'm guessing my credit cards got scrambled. But all of that can be replaced."

"I assume Hood and the others are pretty shaken."

"They're on autopilot, but they'll get through this," Rodgers replied. "I'm more interested in who was *behind* this."

"Of course. Any thoughts on that?"

He hunched forward. Now that Kendra was suspicious, there was no reason to be discreet. "I need to ask this, Kat, and I hope you'll keep it between us. But is there any chance that Admiral Link was involved?"

The woman did not seem surprised by the question. "A chance? Sure. A likelihood? No. Think what the admiral would stand to lose if he were caught."

"For what? Attacking Op-Center or having William Wilson killed?"

That one came out sounding more like an accusation than a question. This time Kat was openly disapproving.

"I surely hope you do not believe the admiral was involved in either of those," Kat said.

"I want to believe that," he said truthfully.

Kat's phone beeped. She answered. She listened for a moment, said she would be right there, then hung up.

"That was reception," she said. "Your friend Mr. McCaskey is here. He insists on seeing the senator."

"Let me talk to him," Rodgers said.

"We'll both go," Kat replied flatly.

Tension had descended like sleet, heavy and cold. The two walked through the office. Though it was nearly five o'clock, none of the workers was preparing to leave. Rodgers heard pizzas being ordered for dinner. There was excitement in the air, energy in the staff's activities, a sense of purpose on youthful faces. Here he was, embarking on a new career and trying to find out who bombed his old office. Yet he felt none of what these people felt. It was not a virtue of age but of attitude. For the first time in his life, Mike Rodgers did not know which side he was on.

McCaskey was pacing in the carpeted reception area. That was unusual. He was usually Mr. Patient.

"Hello, Mike," McCaskey said thickly. "I'd like to talk to you." He regarded Kat. "I also want to see the senator."

"That is not possible," she replied. "He is out."

"Then I'll go wherever he is," McCaskey told her.

"Don't waste your time," she said. "Senator Orr has already said he would only speak to your superior, and then as a courtesy, nothing more."

"My superior had his office fried—" McCaskey said.

"We were very sorry to hear that."

"I'll pass that along when I see Paul. Meanwhile, I want to discuss the attack with the senator."

"In what context? And by what authority do you come here and even make a demand like that?"

"Section 611 of the NCMC Operational Code," McCaskey replied. "I quote, 'If an ongoing operation is impeded by a tactical strike, the NCMC has the responsibility *and* the authority to investigate the person or persons who were a target of said operation.' Said operation is the investigation into the murder of William Wilson. Said target is Senator Orr. As the chief law enforcement officer for Op-Center, it is my duty to speak with him."

"From the start, Mr. McCaskey, I have believed this investigation to be politics, not police work," Kat said. Her gaze shifted from the former FBI officer to Rodgers. "General, you are still this man's superior. Would you, perhaps, suggest a less inconvenient and obvious avenue of harassment?"

"That is *not* what this is about," McCaskey insisted.

"No, not to you," Kat replied. "I believe you are an earnest man, a knight being moved on a chess board, convinced of his virtue but blind to the endgame. This whole thing, first the death of Wilson and now the attack on Op-Center, is clearly being hung on the senator by someone who does not want him to become president. *That* is what this is about. Hey, why don't you interview Lucy O'Connor? Her journalistic career is going to benefit a great deal from all of this."

"Ms. Lockley, I don't think I'm the one who needs a reality check—"

"Hold on, Darrell," Rodgers said.

"No, Mike. Someone hit us. I have the obligation *and* the right to question people who may have knowledge of the event."

"William Wilson was a guest at the senator's party!" Kat exclaimed. "That is the extent of his involvement with this situation!"

"Wilson was a guest just hours before he was murdered by someone who understood covert operations. That makes Admiral Link a suspect and throws a shadow on

Senator Orr," McCaskey said. "Ms. Lockley, I cannot make it any more concise than that."

"You'll have to," Kat replied. "The senator has made it clear that he will not see you."

"Darrell, why don't you let me handle this?" Rodgers said.

"Handle what? The investigation or getting me in to see the senator?"

"There is nothing *to* handle," Kat said. "This is a non-starter, Mr. McCaskey. The interview is not going to happen." She turned to go.

"Ms. Lockley, I am prepared to ask our attorney to seek a writ of mandamus. That will order Senator Orr to make himself available," McCaskey said. "If the writ is granted, and it will be, the senator will not be permitted to leave the District of Columbia until I see him."

"We have attorneys, too," Kat said over her shoulder.

"Darrell, I said I'll take care of this," Rodgers told him.

"Really? If you had helped before, we might have nailed the perps before Op-Center was tagged."

Rodgers moved McCaskey toward a corner, away from the receptionist. "That isn't fair," the general said.

"Like hell. You were off licking your thorny paw because Paul Hood hurt your feelings."

"Darrell, you're stressed. This is battle fatigue talking—"

"No. This is what I should have been doing from the start. Pushing. Maybe then the attack would not have happened."

"We'll never know. Look," Rodgers said. "I will go to San Diego with the senator and his staff. If they are involved, I will find out."

"Maybe."

"Okay, maybe," Rodgers agreed. "But pushing like this, in Washington, may not get you anything. Lowell is very good, but the senator has friends and influence. That's better."

McCaskey exhaled through his nose. "I've never played good cop, bad cop, Mike. I don't like manipulating people, or the law."

"That isn't what we're doing," Rodgers told him. "We're playing by the rules of the system."

McCaskey leaned closer. "Do you think they're involved?"

"I don't know. I belong to the school of innocent until proven guilty," Rodgers said.

"Your gut, Mike. Mine says yes. What does yours tell you?"

Rodgers looked into the main office. Kat was helping Kendra organize computer files for the trip. He could not tell if she was watching him. That was the great thing about the military. He knew who the enemy was.

"My gut tells me the same thing it told me before," Rodgers said. "To proceed with care, but definitely to proceed. I want the guys who hurt Op-Center as much as you do, Darrell. If they were responsible, I'll find out. I give you my word."

"What if I went with you?" McCaskey asked.

"That would be overkill," Rodgers said. "This needs to be finessed."

McCaskey sighed again. He seemed a little more temperate now. "You could have ordered me off. You didn't."

"I won't."

"When will you leave?"

"Kendra is leaving tonight with the senator and wants me to go with Link and his group tomorrow morning," Rodgers told him. "That should work. It will give me a chance to smooth things over with Kat."

"All right, Mike," McCaskey said. "I should probably

get over to Op-Center anyway. Do you know exactly how bad it was?"

Rodgers told him. McCaskey was sorry to hear about Mac but relieved and also surprised that there were no other casualties.

McCaskey left, and Rodgers went to make a phone call. He would use a pay phone, not one in the senator's office. He did not want the call to be logged. He no longer felt like the *Man Without a Country*. He felt worse, like a wayward apostle.

"*No man can serve two masters*," Rodgers reminded himself. Yet here he was, the man who prized loyalty above all, preparing to spy on his future colleagues to help his former teammates. Fortunately, there was another biblical quote that gave the general comfort: "*The righteous man escapes trouble, and the wicked man falls into it in his stead*."

Rodgers chose to believe that one. It was easy.

There was no other choice.

THIRTY-FOUR

Camp Pendleton, California
Tuesday, 2:21 P.M.

Two-star Marine General Jack Breen was listening to his voice mail when a name from the past appeared. Breen smiled. He remembered the name, all right. He remembered the day he first heard the name. It was February 18, 1991.

And he sure as hell remembered where he was when he first heard the name.

Their initial meeting was the result of a very unusual multiservice action in the first Iraq war. Then-Colonel Breen was the commander of a ten-man SWEAT "hogs" unit—Special Warfare, Elite Advance Troops. The men had been air-dropped into Iraq six days in advance of the planned main Marine invasion. An Iraqi transmission tower was located in a mountain four thousand feet northeast of the city of Ad Najaf. Breen's mission was to set up a satellite interface that would intercept Iraqi communications. Before the 2nd Marine Division moved in, Central Command wanted to know in which villages or underground tunnels enemy troops might be hidden. Those sites would be bombed ahead of time or avoided, if possible.

The SWEAT unit found one of those enemy bands. Or rather, the Iraqi band found them.

It happened in the foothills, at midnight, shortly after the Marines had landed. It was a cool night, in the midfifties, with a dry wind blowing down from the mountaintop. Because of the wind howling through their helmets, it was difficult to hear but not to see. All of the men were wearing khaki-and-green mountain camouflage uniforms and night-vision goggles. Four Marines were on parachute detail, burying the shrouds. The other six had formed a perimeter secure line. The PSL, which was actually a circle, sought to establish the outward parameters of the safe zone. They had landed on a gently sloping hill, with clear visibility below and short bluffs and boulders above. The high sites would need to be examined and secured before the group could proceed. Their target was on the opposite side of the mountain. Access was along a narrow dirt path, two thousand feet up, which girdled the peak. Satellite reconnaissance had revealed a cave toward the end of the route, near the tower. The men had until sunrise to reach it. The plan was to wait there until dark, then go out and set up the compact satellite dish. When the men were finished, they would retrace their steps, radio their base in Kuwait, and wait for an Apache to extract them.

The plan was changed by the United States Air Force.

The men had secured the area by 0027 hours. They were able to walk up the peak rather than climb, and moved in a relatively tight formation known as the flying geese. The point man of the wedge watched the ground for mines, the next two watched the terrain ahead, the next two watched the sides, and the next pair kept an eye on the skies. The two who followed covered the group, and the last man hung back to protect their flank. If they were attacked, they would drop and crawl in opposite directions to widen the wedge. It would be easier for the enemy to pick them off if they stayed in their close ascent phalanx.

The hogs were on the dirt path when Breen heard a whistle. It sounded like the wind. In fact, the noise was coming from a Sukhoi Su-7, a single-seat ground attack aircraft that was a standard tactical fighter-bomber in the Soviet Air Force for nearly forty years. Saddam had thirty of them in his air force, each armed with two 30 mm NR-

30 guns, seventy rounds per gun. Pylons under the wings carried two 742 kg or two 495 kg bombs or rocket pods.

This particular aircraft had been on patrol in what would later be known as the southern no-fly zone. The fighter was screaming toward the ground, illuminated by its own flames after taking a hit from a United States Air Force F-15E Strike Eagle. The F-15E had been searching for mobile Scud missile launchers and had not been informed about the Marine presence. Breen ordered the hogs to drop and cover, which was all they could do before the fireball ripped into the mountainside. It impacted well north of the Marines, about a quarter of a mile, but it sent flaming debris and rock in their path. Worse, the crash was sure to attract Iraqi troops.

Breen sent two men ahead to check the route, to see if there was some way to get around the wreckage. There was, but they would have to go back down the mountain and around the base. According to the topographic map, that would take them twice as long. They would be moving around in daylight.

Breen decided to try to complete the mission.

The mountain was steep in their present location, so they backtracked a half mile to a point where the map said they could walk down. Breen double-timed the unit, keeping the wedge formation as they descended. They slowed as they reached the base of the foothills, partly to conserve energy and partly to watch for shepherds or farmers who might be up early. Unfortunately, they were stopped by something they did not anticipate: the hogs found the mobile Scud for which the F-15E had been searching. It was sitting under an outcropping of rock, about three hundred yards below them. The tractor was hidden beneath a camouflage tarp. Iraqi soldiers were busy covering it with brush before sunrise.

Breen halted the unit. The men did not carry explosives, but they had M9 9 mm side arms and a single M249 light machine gun. They also had surprise. The hogs could probably take the Scud then slag it with fire in the fuel tank. However, the Iraqis might have time to call in backup. If the Marines were hunted, that could doom the primary mission, not to mention the team itself.

Reluctantly, Breen decided to continue with the original plan. However, he did break radio silence to call in the location of the Scud. Centcom agreed to hold off an attack until the hogs had time to get out of the area.

Unfortunately, it did not work out that way. The Iraqis had intercepted their signal. The Scud commander had no idea what had been said, but he had a good idea *why* it was said. He decided to relocate and called for air cover.

A joint dogfight, ground skirmish was not something Centcom wanted. It had the potential of becoming a flashpoint for the war before the coalition had a chance to put all its assets in place. Instead, the hogs were ordered to continue. The Scud would be dealt with by a mechanized army unit that was already in Iraq. The small tank group, nicknamed the Jolly Rodgers after their commander, was being prepositioned to help the 2nd Brigade move against the Iraqi 29th Mechanized Brigade's security zone. They had the satellite uplink and artillery range that would enable them to target and take out the Scud.

Breen and his hogs moved on to their target. Everything went well until the return trip. The Marines reached the cave early in the afternoon and hunkered down until sunset. Then they moved to the communications tower, spliced in the satellite interceptor, and went back along the original route. They had to circle wide around the still-smouldering wreckage of the Su-7, but the Iraqis did not see them.

Unfortunately, a sudden sandstorm had grounded the Apache fleet. The hogs had two choices. They could stay in the foothills and wait for as long as it took for flying conditions to improve, or they could hitch a ride back with a tank that was going to lead part of the charge into Iraq as the hidden Jolly Rodgers advance team picked off advancing Iraqi armor.

Breen did not want to ride back with army personnel, but it had been an arduous trek, they were very low on supplies, and there was no telling how long the sandstorm would last. He put the safety of his team above pride. The Marines agreed to a nearby rendezvous point and left after sunset. They connected at midnight, forty-eight hours after jumping into Iraq.

The man who drove the hogs back was then-Colonel Mike Rodgers. The Marines rode on the outside of the M1A1 Abrams. The trip took six hours, and it was the bumpiest, dustiest journey Breen had ever experienced. The men alternately sat and lay belly down on the rear of the turret or on the forward armor, over the fuel tank. They each had a canteen and foil-wrapped turkey jerky to sustain them. Even worse than the ride, though, was the fact that Colonel Rodgers was an absolute gentleman. He did not rag on the Marines for accepting a lift from the army. In fact, he commended the hogs for sticking to their planned objective instead of going for the trophy Scud.

"You saved a lot of lives," was Rodgers's final comment.

When they reached the staging area in Saudi Arabia, a Marine troop transport truck was waiting to take them to their own home base. Colonel Rodgers walked them to the vehicle.

"I'll see you when this is over," Rodgers said, saluting the Marine and then clasping his hand. "Where can I reach you?"

"Pendleton," Breen said. He grinned as his men climbed into the truck. "I'll probably be with the base chiropractor getting my back realigned."

It was then that Rodgers took his one and only jab at the Marines. "You semper fi guys are proud of your sea legs. I've always found a strong army ass to be much more valuable."

"We'll have to test that one day," Breen said. "What about you? Where are you going?"

"I've been overseas half my life. I'd like to find something stateside."

"Let me know where that is," Breen told him. "When we get together, dinner's on me."

"Not dinner," Rodgers told him. "Never dinner. I'm like Don Corleone. I hold out for favors."

"You've got it," Breen replied.

The men did get together after the war, right after Rodgers had accepted a deputy directorship at the newly formed Op-Center. They had a great night on the town in Washington with one of Rodgers's new coworkers, Bob Herbert. Op-Center picked up the tab. Rodgers never called in his chit.

Until now.

The voice mail message did not tell Breen what Rodgers needed, only that he might require intelligence-gathering support in nearby San Diego. Whatever it was, Mike Rodgers would get it. And when this little adventure was all over, General Breen would provide Rodgers with something he had been waiting fifteen years to give him: a high-speed ride on the bumpiest, wettest motorized rubber raft he could find.

THIRTY-FIVE

Washington, D.C.
Tuesday, 5:43 P.M.

At this moment, Alexander Hood's bedroom was more technologically capable than the bulk of Op-Center. That thought demoralized Paul Hood, though it was not as if they were starting from zero.

The exception was the Tank. Hood was there now. He was not helping to get the facility marginally operational. He was not helping the search-and-dispose team from Andrews look for other explosives. He was taking calls from officials and from friends. The president had called, followed by a chat with Senator Debenport. The senator asked if Hood thought the USF was responsible. Hood told him that possibility was being investigated. Debenport informed him that the CIOC was going to provide him with emergency reconstruction funds. Hood was appreciative, even though he knew why Debenport was getting him the money.

He spoke briefly with a reporter from the *Washington Post*, the only interview he gave, and with his occasional date Daphne Connors. Now Hood was talking with Sharon. His former wife had heard about an explosion from a friend at the Pentagon. She called to make sure Paul was all right.

"We lost one man and most of our electronics," Hood said.

"I'm sorry. Will you be able to get the facility running again?"

"That's being assessed now," Hood told her. "With enough money, though, anything can be fixed." He hesitated. *Except our marriage*, he thought. He wondered if Sharon noticed the pause and thought the same thing. Probably. She still knew him better than anyone.

"Is there anything I can do?" Sharon asked.

"Just let the kids know what happened," he said. "I'll try to call later." That, too, was probably the wrong thing to say. He used to say that all the time when they were married. The time they had been apart seemed to evaporate. It did not feel good. "I think the worst thing about this is that I've also seen the future, and it scares me," he went on quickly. "I can't imagine the fears our kids will have to live with."

"It sounds like you'll have to, if you're going to try to minimize them," Sharon replied.

Now *that* was different. A turnabout. Hood had expressed reservations about his job, and Sharon had encouraged him to work harder. It was as though the world itself had been rewired.

"I'll let the kids know you weren't hurt," Sharon went on. "I'll also tell Frankie that there may be a change of plans."

It took Hood a moment to remember who Frankie was. The intern. The son of his replacement.

"Don't tell him that," Hood said. "If he has a car that works and won't mind running errands, we can probably use him sooner rather than later."

"I'm sure he wouldn't mind," Sharon replied.

Hood thanked Sharon for the call and said he would get in touch with Frankie as soon as possible. In the midst of electronic chaos it was nice to be grounded by humanity. Ironically, that fact reflected something Mike Rodgers and Bob Herbert had been saying for years. Life, like intelligence operations, relies too much on electronics and too little on people.

Hood had written Frankie's cell phone number on a leather-bound notepad he carried in his shirt pocket. It had been a Father's Day gift from Harleigh several years before. Hood had not bothered to transfer the data to his computer. Another irony. Hood would have trouble digging the home number of his Russian counterpart Sergei Orlov from the data dump Matt Stoll had created in the Tank. But he possessed the number of intern Frankie Hunt.

Then again, Hood thought, *the way you've been handling crises lately, maybe you should give the kid your keys to the kingdom.* He could not do a worse job. He wondered what would happen if they turned over every aspect of government to newcomers for just a day or two. Would that bring their best or worst instincts to the fore? Would power destroy their innocence, or would they know, intuitively, to handle it with extreme care? Would they crush lives and careers simply because they could, because it was more convenient, more expedient than open debate, or would their angel natures guide them to higher ground?

Hood called Frankie, who said he could be available that night. Hood said the next morning would be fine. Frankie Hunt sounded wildly enthusiastic. He did not ask if there was any danger. He even addressed his new boss as "sir." Maybe Hood would not have to work as hard as he anticipated not to hold the "sins" of the father against the young man.

McCaskey came to see Hood while he was still on the phone with Frankie. Hood motioned him in. The FBI liaison had obviously taken a tour of the facility. He had been putting a lot of hours into the case and looked drawn. Now he looked a rung above beaten.

"By my soul, Paul, I do not want to find out that Americans did this to Americans," McCaskey said. "We don't make war on one another. Not anymore."

"Sure we do. We chew each other up with politics every day of every week," Hood said.

"Someone died here," McCaskey said. "That's different."

"I know, and I don't want to minimize that," Hood said. "But I've just been sitting here thinking how everyone in this town is a killer. Every damn one of us. We just don't use that word. We call it politics."

"Forgive me, Paul, but nuts to that," McCaskey said. "I believe that we're the good guys, Op-Center *and* most Americans. Our response mechanisms get triggered when something is wrong."

"Wrong by what yardstick?"

"This one," McCaskey replied, touching the left side of his chest.

Hood looked wistfully at McCaskey. He had not intended to discuss the new situation with his staff just yet. But maybe it was time. He shut the door of the Tank and returned to the conference table. He sat beside McCaskey.

"What if I told you that Op-Center's triggers had changed?" Hood asked.

"Changed how?"

"What if the only way the National Crisis Management Center can survive is by catering to partisan interests? By handling crises as before, but also by executing domestic black-ops activities?"

"Paul, what the hell are you talking about?" McCaskey asked. "What else happened that I don't know about?"

"We were hit with a different kind of bombshell," Hood told him. "It seems the president and Senator Debenport have decided that the USF represents a threat to this nation. They have requested that we use Op-Center and this investigation to stop Senator Orr."

"Are they insane?" McCaskey yelled. "This isn't the 1950s. I'd rather shut the door than—"

"Than do what, Darrell?" Hood asked. "Spy on Americans? The FBI and CIA do it all the time."

"With one difference," McCaskey said. "Reasonable

suspicion. We cannot use the investigation to impede a Constitutionally protected process."

"The problem is, we can," Hood replied. "It's a legitimate investigation—"

"Of a *homicide.* What you are suggesting is a completely different beast. It isn't ethical, Paul."

"Tell me which is the greater morality," Hood asked. "Do we let ourselves get squeezed a little so we can continue doing good in other areas? Or do we put up a Going Out of Business sign with our pride intact, allowing God knows how many crises to slip by Homeland Security?"

"That's an old argument, Paul. Does a commander sacrifice one life to save ten? What do you do for the greatest good?"

"It's an old argument because there is no clear-cut answer," Hood said.

"Sure there is. If you have to think about something in order to justify it, the thing is probably wrong."

"No," Hood insisted. "Sometimes you have to think about things because your initial instinct is to run. That's fear, not courage."

"That's rationalization."

"That's reality," Hood countered. "A reality in which Americans *do* fight Americans, whether we like it or not. Tell me, where does Darrell McCaskey end up if he walks out of here or the CIOC shuts us down? Back at the Bureau? At the Company, where national security is the meal and morality is the garnish? All you would be doing somewhere else is losing yourself in the system. The corruption would still be there. You just would not be able to see it."

McCaskey said nothing.

"We had it good," Hood said. "Maybe too good to last."

"We could tell them no."

"Sure. And do you think Debenport would get us funding to replace the equipment we lost?"

McCaskey just stared at his old friend. "I hear what

you're saying, Paul, but—forgive me—it still sounds like sophistry. I'm disappointed the president even put you in this position, after all you've done for him."

"He has his bosses, too. Every job has you shovel some shit. In this case, at least, we can still do our job. Maybe even better than before, because more money will be available to us."

"At what price, though?" McCaskey asked.

"Compromise," Hood said.

McCaskey shook his head. "I don't think I can go along with this."

"That's your choice," Hood said. He was sad but not surprised to hear that. "But it explains what I said before about dying. When I was at the White House this morning, I listened to Senator Debenport's bloody damn deal. I left, I had a long think, and I made my choice. But it cost me, Darrell. A part of my soul died before that electromagnetic pulse bomb was even detonated."

McCaskey looked as though his grip on the last rung had slipped. This was not how he had planned his life, how he ran his life.

"May I make a suggestion?" Hood asked.

"Please."

"Continue the work you were doing for the reasons you were doing it. We can worry about the rest of it later."

"Self-deception," McCaskey said.

"Will you feel better if a killer and possibly a bomber gets away?" Hood asked with uncharitable bluntness.

"That's a helluva choice," McCaskey said, his voice low, his eyes flat.

"Maybe it's just old age, but I can't remember a time when options were easy or clear."

McCaskey nodded gravely. "We agree on that, at least."

"I'll take it," Hood said with the hint of a smile.

"What I do not understand is how the hell we got here, Paul. Mike is gone, the building has been gutted, our integrity is no longer impervious. Even you would have to admit that."

"I do," Hood replied sadly.

Integrity had always been the center's hallmark. Integrity had also been Paul Hood's personal hallmark. Now, even if he draped an albatross around his neck and preached virtue like the Ancient Mariner, Hood would never have that quality again. What upset him more than the deal with Debenport was the fact that he had not seen this coming. He thought he was smarter than that.

"I'll have to get back to you on how we got here," Hood said. "Right now, I'm more concerned about where we are going and who is coming along. Can I count on you?"

"I'll finish what I started," McCaskey said.

"That's all I need. Thanks."

McCaskey headed toward the door. "I told Mike I would wait to hear from him before leaning any more on Orr and Link," he said. "In the meantime, I'm going to see if the Metro Police have anything. They've been concentrating their efforts on the second murder."

Hood nodded. "Thanks again," he added.

"Sure," McCaskey said.

The former FBI agent left, and Hood was alone once more. Alone in the Tank, the brain of Op-Center encased in its electromagnetically protected skull. Alone while his staff struggled to put the other organs together again. There was one, however, that Hood wondered if they would ever be able to retrieve. The one they needed almost as much as the brain: the heart.

THIRTY-SIX

Washington, D.C.
Tuesday, 6:31 P.M.

Darrell McCaskey picked up two things on his way to the Metro Police. The first was a cheeseburger. The second was his wife.

Maria had not asked to be involved in the investigation. But McCaskey knew she enjoyed getting her hands dirty, and in his mind this was as dirty as things got. Politics and murder. As old as Genesis. McCaskey did not tell her about Hood's conversation with Debenport. It was important that he convey the information objectively. He wanted her opinion, not her reaction to his own upset.

The murders were being investigated by the Metro Police First District Substation at 500 E Street SW. Lieutenant Robert Howell was leading the Focused Mission Unit, which consisted of four sergeants on loan from homicide.

McCaskey had phoned ahead. Howell said he would still be at the stationhouse when they arrived. He greeted the McCaskeys in his small, clean, second-floor office. The men had spoken on the phone the day before, after District Commander Charlie Alterman agreed to let Op-Center run the Wilson investigation. That meant Howell got to keep the case, which otherwise would have shifted from FMU to Homicide. The murder of Lawless was added to the FMU "dig," as they referred to forensics investigations, since the team had already been fielded.

There were photos of his parents and himself and framed diplomas from the Florida State University School of Criminology on the office wall. McCaskey was not surprised. The thirty-something lieutenant looked like a "college cop," as they used to call them in the FBI. He was a lean, clean-cut, tightly wound man with short red hair and deep-set eyes. His voice had the hint of a Southern accent. His white shirt was heavily starched so it did not wrinkle. Wrinkles suggested perspiration, and perspiration suggested worry or insecurity. Those were conditions that schooled detectives were taught to avoid. Howell did not sit until Maria had been seated. He was polite. That did not mean he would be cooperative. McCaskey had made his team look foolish and also had stolen their assignment.

As the men sat, Howell expressed both concern and genuine outrage about what happened at Op-Center.

"Officially or not, our resources are at your disposal," Howell said.

The detective's words gave McCaskey a whisper of hope. Men with vastly different interests could still find common ground in their response to horrific acts. Maybe the rest of what they did—the jockeying and the politics, the bargains made and assurances broken—was just not important enough to worry about.

"I very much appreciate your offer," McCaskey said. "Actually, I came by because I did not want you to think the attack has slowed our work on the Wilson case. It was based mostly on fieldwork, which is ongoing."

"Have you made progress?"

"Possibly," McCaskey said. "I'll be checking with one of my operatives in a few hours." He did not want to tell the detective about Mike Rodgers's full-court press against Orr's team. The job of the Metro Police was to protect and serve. The reality was they protected and served government heavyweights with special care. Their budget came from Congress. They would not appreciate Op-Center's more intrusive methods. "Do you have anything to freshen the mix?"

"We have what may be a nail polish and fiber sample from the second crime scene," Howell told him. "But that does not help because, first, Lawless may have picked those up somewhere else and, second, we do not have a suspect."

"Meaning there is nothing to compare it to," McCaskey said. "Where did you recover it?"

"From Lawless's silver-link watch band," Howell said. "It may have snagged the hem of her sleeve or lapel when he tried to defend himself."

"Do you have the specs?"

Howell nodded and went to his computer. He brought up the laboratory data. "The nail polish is a silky beige manufactured by a Chicago firm, Niles Polish. It's sold in shops nationwide, so it's unlikely we'll find the buyer. We cross-referenced charge card purchases with Senator Orr's guest list, but that turned up nothing."

"She probably paid cash," McCaskey said.

"That, and she could have done so anywhere in the country. As for the fiber, that is satin, navy blue, just like the dress we saw in the security camera video. The dye was manufactured by the Fuchun River Chemical Corporation of China, which does not tell us anything about the garment itself."

"One of those things did not come from the killer," Maria said. "Unless she has a terrible fashion sense."

"That was our conclusion," Howell said. "Mr. Lawless might have picked up the nail polish from a handshake or making a purchase. Hypodermic needles are easy enough to come by. We have been looking into individuals who would be qualified to have given both victims an injection. But there are over three hundred female dentists and hygienists alone in the metropolitan region. Then there are literally thousands of other medical doctors, nurses, even veterinarians. Besides, the killer might not even be from this area."

"I believe she is," McCaskey said. "I'm convinced the murder of Robert Lawless was organized quickly to cover our discovery that William Wilson was murdered. If that's true, then the assassin was still in the neighborhood."

"Reasonable," Howell said. The detective turned his pale poker face from the computer monitor. "Does the possible progress you mentioned a minute ago have to do with Senator Orr?"

"We would like to clear the senator if we can," McCaskey answered.

"Does that mean he or someone in his office is a suspect?" Howell pressed.

"No," McCaskey replied. If he had said yes, Howell would have informed the detectives on his team, and they would have told others. McCaskey did not want to be responsible for starting rumors. "Detective, I don't want to keep you from your dinner plans or family any longer than I have to. Are there any leads besides the nail polish and satin fiber?"

Howell shook his head. "I have to admit it has been tough getting off Go on this one. The security camera images have not helped, no eyewitnesses have come forward to tell us about the killer's movements, and our profiler has not found a hook to hang a psychological sketch."

"Did the medical examiner find anything unusual about Lawless's body?" McCaskey asked.

"Nothing," Howell said. "He died exactly as Wilson did."

"Was any hair recovered from either scene?" Maria asked.

"Plenty," the detective told her. "Blonde, brunette, black, red, white, even green. Hotel rooms are cleaned but not *that* thoroughly. We have thirty-seven different strands. Six of those match the housekeeping staff. We are checking with previous guests in the room. That will take time. If our killer was wearing a wig, that may make her untraceable."

As the detective was speaking, McCaskey suddenly flashed on something that made him want to kick himself. Hard. "Actually, Detective, now that I think of it, there is something the Metro Police could do for me. Do you have a computer I could borrow for a few minutes?"

"Sure. You can use mine," Howell said. He swung toward the keyboard. "Is there something I can look up for you?"

"Thanks, but I need to do this myself," McCaskey said. "Op-Center security."

"I see."

"We'll lock up, if you want to leave—"

"I can't do that," Howell said. "We have security procedures. But I will step outside."

"Thanks. I should only be five minutes or so."

The detective left without shutting the door. McCaskey went behind his desk.

"Shall I close it?" Maria asked, indicating the door.

"No," her husband replied. He typed in the address of the Op-Center web site which was backed up in a secure Tank. Thanks to software designed by Stoll, any subsequent addresses he typed into this remote keyboard would be unrecorded. He went to the District of Columbia personnel files. These were accessible to intelligence agencies in order to do quick security checks in the event of a crisis.

Maria stood behind him. "What was so important it had to be done now?" she asked.

"There is one woman I overlooked. Minnie Hennepin, the medical examiner. She would know how to give an injection *and* she would be in a position to overlook the puncture wound."

"She could also be an incompetent who got her high-paying job through—what is the word?"

"Patronage," McCaskey said. "That is certainly possible. We may know more after checking her background."

He accessed the medical examiner's file and read her curriculum vitae. "Red flag number one," he said. "She graduated from the University of Texas Medical School."

"So did thousands of other men and women," Maria said. "That does not mean anything."

"Do me a favor, hon? Don't play devil's advocate right now," McCaskey said as sweetly as possible.

"Why? You told me you needed extra eyes and another brain working on this problem."

"I do. But that doesn't mean shooting down everything I say."

"That was not everything. It was one thing."

"Okay," he said. "I'm sorry. Let's just drop it."

"If I say something contrary, will you think I am covering for her? Will I become a suspect then?"

"Don't be extreme," McCaskey said, looking back at his wife. "I was just thinking out loud. I don't want to hit a speed bump every time I open my mouth. Look, just forget I said anything."

"*You* are the one being extreme. I was simply pointing out that coming from Texas may be a false blip. Each of Senator Orr's senior staff members comes from a state of the union. Would they all be flags as well?"

McCaskey turned back to the computer monitor. He intended to let the subject drop. He hoped that she would, too. He did not want to explain to the Spanish-born lady that Texans shared a special bond, that they helped Texans, that he would not be surprised to learn that Senator Orr had promised her the surgeon general job if she helped him. Yes, it was a leap. But that was what detective work was about.

McCaskey heard Maria breathing heavily through her nose. He tried to ignore her as he continued to read. Following her internship at the Cambridge Medical Center in Minnesota, Dr. Hennepin went to work at the Walter Reed Army Medical Center Department of Clinical Investigation. She was eventually promoted to assistant chief and placed in charge of the team performing oversight of research involving human, animal, and laboratory-related studies. When Hennepin was passed over for directorship of the division, she filed a discrimination complaint with the medical center and the United States Equal Employment Opportunity Commission. Three weeks later, she went to work as the assistant medical examiner. Within the year, Dr. Hennepin had the top spot. There was no indication that anyone, Senator Orr included, had helped her. Of course, that was the kind of information that might be deleted if Dr. Hennepin were planning on becoming an assassin.

"Well? Did you find any other red banners?" Maria asked.

"Flags. And I'm not sure."

"I learned to give injections, too," Maria said testily. "My little sister Penelope is a diabetic."

"You were with me last night," McCaskey said. "Listen, hon. I said I'm sorry. Can we please just let it drop?"

"With pleasure," she said.

McCaskey could hear the angry pout in her voice. This was not going to be buried until he put a stake in its heart. And maybe that was his responsibility. Some of the useful speculation in this case had come from her. He closed the Op-Center site, turned back to his wife, and took her hands.

"Maria, I do need help, *your* help," he said. "We have a different idea what that entails, but I was wrong. I should have deferred to you."

"Are you just saying that?"

"No. I got defensive. This whole situation, this whole goddamn *week* has been a nightmare. Forgive me?"

Maria hesitated, but not as long as she would have if she were really angry. "All right," she said. "Then let me ask you something that I have been wondering."

"Shoot."

"Are you sure the killer was even a woman?" Maria asked.

"You mean, could it be a man dressed as a woman?"

"Yes."

"That was one of the first things I considered. I asked Detective Superintendent Daily whether Wilson's interests went in that direction. The Yard keeps track of such things about prominent citizens because potential blackmail could adversely impact the national economy. They also do not want the crown to be embarrassed by announcing a knighthood for someone who is trafficking pornography. They insist that Wilson is heterosexual."

"Wilson may not have known his date was a man," Maria replied. "Some of the 'women' who party at *Los Pantalones Para Vestir a Club*, in Madrid, are extremely convincing."

"That is a possibility," her husband agreed as he glanced into the hall. Detective Howell was hovering there like a buoy in rough seas. "Come on," he said, still holding his wife's hands. "Let's get coffee and think about a next step."

"I already have one, if you'll consider it," she said.

"I'm listening," he said as they left the office. He thanked Detective Howell and said he would be in touch.

Maria stopped before Howell returned to his office. "Detective, would we have access to your laboratory if we need it?"

"Of course." He went back to his office, wrote the number on a pad, and handed it to her.

"Thank you," she said. She put the paper in her back pocket. "I am not sure it will be necessary, but this is good to have."

The McCaskeys walked toward the stairwell.

"What was that about?" her husband asked.

"The dress is the key," Maria said as they started down the concrete stairs to the first floor.

"I agree. That's why I sent the security camera images to designers in the area, asked if they recognized it—"

"We will not learn the identity of whoever bought it," she said, shaking her head. "You said that yourself about the nail polish. What I am saying is that we need to find the dress itself."

"I have one man on that full-time. He had trash bins searched, fountains, and even a duck pond near the Hay-Adams dragged," McCaskey told her.

"It would not have been discarded," Maria said.

"How can you be sure?"

"Those were the first places you searched," Maria said. "Our assassin—"

"Is experienced," McCaskey said. "Fair assumption. Still, it might have been burned in a fireplace or stuffed in an incinerator."

"An incinerator is not a guarantee of total destruction," she said. "But I agree that it might have been consigned to a fireplace. Who among your potential suspects has one?"

"I don't know," he said. "Even if we find out, we would need a reason to get a warrant. 'They have a fireplace' is just not good enough."

"A warrant may not be necessary," she said. "We may not even have to go inside. Not yet."

"I don't follow."

"I know," she smiled. "You should learn."

"Ouch," he said.

"Let's go home," Maria said. "We will need to do a little research before going out again."

McCaskey agreed to the plan, but not just because debate would have been pointless and not because his wife was a sharp field op—something exhaustion and frustration had caused him to forget. It was simple math. A woman had sent the men of Scotland Yard, Op-Center, and the Metro Police into a dark alley with no discernable exit.

Maybe a woman was what they needed to get out.

THIRTY-SEVEN

San Diego, California
Wednesday, 7:01 A.M.

Short, stocky Eric Stone had always been ambivalent about history. He could not affect it, and whatever impact it was going to have had already occurred. Moreover, he did not believe people could learn from it or, failing that, were doomed to repeat it. There were always nuances that made events different. Caesar was not Napoleon who was not Hitler who was not Stalin. Anyway, what was important in one era did not matter now. How many people, old and young, could name one thing Calvin Coolidge had done? Or who he was, for that matter.

While tourists and visitors to the convention center gathered around the time line of San Diego, Stone went about his business. He checked booths where attendees received their badges, made sure the media was present and able to set up their gear, determined that there would be a sufficient number of buses to run delegates to and from the nearby hotels. He did not care that hunting peoples of northeast Asia had crossed the Bering Ice Bridge and migrated to the south to hunt caribou, bison, and mammoth some twenty thousand years ago. It did not matter to him that Juan Rodríguez Cabrillo was the first European to visit the region, sailing from Mexico into San Diego Bay in 1542 and claiming the region for Spain. It was unimportant that sixty years later, Sebastian Vizcaino sailed from Mexico and named the region after the Spanish saint San Diego de Alcalá. The natives could have been hunting dodos, the

Spanish men could have been French women, none of it mattered. The thirty-year-old was unapologetic about his interest in the present. That grew from spending time with his father, Phil, back in Indianapolis, when the fifty-year-old was dying from amyotrophic lateral sclerosis. Lou Gehrig's disease. Not just dying from it but being disintegrated by it. His limbs folding in on themselves as his muscles atrophied, his organs failing. In a lucid moment before he succumbed entirely to living decomposition, the elder Stone told his only son that he regretted so much in his life. Becoming a mechanical engineer instead of a painter. Not spending more time with Eric instead of bowling and drinking with the guys.

"I *had* a guy," the older man whispered. "The best guy." He touched the top of eighteen-year-old Eric's head with a hand whose fingers would not fully uncurl. "I could have had a better life."

That was the last thing Phil Stone had to say before the muscles of his face stopped working. He spent the last month of his life with his jaw hanging slack and his eyes staring at an aluminum bed rail and whatever memories he could find in his drug-hazed brain. Eric Stone resolved, then, to regret nothing. To live in the moment. That meant having power.

The elder Stone's illness devoured their savings and kept the young boy from graduating with any distinction. The only way he could get an education was by enlisting in the military. Having spent his life landlocked in the agricultural belly of the nation, he joined the navy, where he caught the eye of then–Rear Admiral Link. It was in San Diego, after the Persian Gulf War. There was a reception for the vice president of the United States at the Space and Naval Warfare Systems facility. SPAWAR provided more than half of the tactical and nontactical information management technology the navy used to complete its operational missions during the war.

To help pay the bills at home, Eric had worked as a waiter for a catering company. He was ordered to work the windy al fresco party. Something about his manner captured Link's attention. His intensity, perhaps. He handled a tray as carefully as he would nitroglycerin. The wind stirred the fabric of his dress blues, but he did not lose a single drop of champagne.

Eric Stone lived in the moment.

Link had Stone transferred to his own Department of Focused Sensing and Data Acquisition. This embraced intelligence-gathering operations through photographic, electromagnetic, acoustic, seismic, olfactory, visual, or other means. It relied on everything from satellites to aircraft to sensor fields arrayed on the ground in the form of probes and microtechnology. Stone went to work in the accounting division. At Link's request, he found ways to get better deals from suppliers so there was more money to spend on other things. There was no kickback, no padded invoices, no black-ops funding, no dishonesty. It was all about making FSDA/SPAWAR run more effectively. Link made sure that Stone got the schooling he needed. There was strong mentoring throughout the three years they were together.

SPAWAR was Link's jumping-off point to the Company. Before accepting their offer to run Far Eastern Intelligence from CIA headquarters, Link told Stone to get in touch with him when his hitch was up. Stone did that and went to work in the inspector general's office. There was an opening for an information system auditor, conducting efficiency analyses of CIA programs and activities. While Stone worked there, he attended classes in accounting at the University of Northern Virginia. He had his master's degree within three years. He transferred to Link's personal staff that same year, with GS-15 pay status and top-level security clearance. Stone's first job was making sure money reached field agents in Asia, which was Link's area of command. Within two years, Stone had become the admiral's executive assistant. The men did not socialize outside the office. On the job, however, they were as close as father and son, watching each other's backs in the shadow of a ruthless and complex bureaucracy and making sure the department ran smoothly.

Stone had never thought of the admiral as a political activist. Like the younger man, Link seemed to be absolutely focused on the moment, on whatever job needed to be done. It came as a shock when, six months ago, Link called him into his office and shut the door.

"Senator Donald Orr of Texas is going to be starting a new political party and making a serious run for the presidency," Link had said. "I'm going to find a way to work with him."

"Why?" Stone had asked.

The answer surprised him. "To stop him."

Link had met the senator at a Congressional Intelligence Planning Committee briefing several months before. The Texan was impressed with Link's grasp of the threat represented by terrorist cells relocating from the Philippines, Malaysia, and Indonesia to China. Implicit in the presentation was the notion that if Beijing could control international terrorism, it would give the Chinese a powerful tool to use against Western aggression. Paul Hood of Op-Center was also at that meeting, reporting on the recent efforts of the NCMC to try to contain Chinese expansion into the diamond market in southern Africa. Link had proposed a comprehensive "Quiet War" against Beijing, stirring student dissatisfaction from within, encouraging fringe provinces to move toward independence. Keeping the Chinese busy with domestic unrest would give them less time to worry about the United States and Europe.

The Quiet War was approved and funded. After the meeting, Orr took Link aside. He said he actually wanted to go further. He wanted to train CIA operatives to execute acts of terror in foreign capitals in what he called an "anti-civilian strike option." These ACSO units would attack the societal infrastructure with more devastating efficiency than terrorist attacks had been executed anywhere in the world. In a subsequent meeting, Link learned that half of the twelve-person CIP Committee was appalled at the notion of attacking civilian targets such as banks, communications centers, and landmarks. The other half thought there was merit to the idea and named a subcommittee of six congressional representatives to study it.

Link was horrified. It was one thing to monitor terrorists and take preemptive action against them. It was another thing to use that security apparatus to foster what Orr was calling "aggressive isolationism." But Link was too good an intelligence officer and too seasoned a bureaucrat to let Orr know what he was thinking. To the contrary. He encouraged Orr to talk. It was important to know what a potential opponent was thinking. Link resolved to take no steps against the top secret ACSO program until it moved from subcommittee to recommendation.

That never happened. The subcommittee decided the downside of ACSO made it too risky: the chance that a slip up could lead to the discovery that Congress had authorized strikes against civilian targets. Link was bothered that they did not react on moral grounds. It was all about personal preservation.

Orr accepted the setback with his courtly Texas grace, but he did not abandon the goal. ACSO and aggressive isolationism became obsessions with him. He privately enlisted Admiral Link in his crusade, assuming that a military man and intelligence director would see the wisdom of his goal.

Link confided in Stone that he did not. The admiral stayed close to Donald Orr because he wanted to know what the senator was planning. He believed Orr to be a dangerous man: a man with bad ideas and the charm to sell them.

It was a typically brisk morning on San Diego Bay. Stone's curly blond hair danced against his forehead. The salty sea wind was ribboned with the faint smell of diesel fuel. The unique gas-and-steel tang, the odor of latent warfare, was coming from the naval station just southeast of the convention center. The sounds of traffic moving along Harbor Drive mingled with the cries of sea birds and the roar of jets that landed every few minutes at the airport a few miles to the north. It was sensory chaos, but none of it bothered Stone. He was a source of calm in the midst of political and environmental anarchy. He had to be. What they did here would alter the course of world history.

An ironic destiny for someone who did not care to be a part of that stream, Stone thought. All the young man cared about was securing the goals Kenneth Link had set for them both. They were unusual ends, and it would take extraordinary means to get there. But they would succeed.

They had to.

Stone showed the security guard his pass and entered the convention center. A huge American flag hung on the south side of the room; the banner of the USF was suspended from the north side. Both were being steam-ironed to remove the wrinkles. Then they would be rolled and dropped when the convention got under way. Below them, rows of chairs were still being set up, their backs draped with gold and blue covers. Those were the colors of the convention. They signified a new dawn in a clear sky. The slogan of the convention was, "A New Day for America."

That it would be. But not in the way that Don Orr imagined.

Stone went to the podium to see how work on the sound system was progressing. Texas Congresswoman Nicolet Murat was there, waiting to run a sound check. Nicolet would be giving the keynote address the next day. She came from oil money and was in line to become Treasury secretary in an Orr administration. Stone smiled a crooked smile as he greeted Congresswoman Murat and her executive assistant. It was exciting to be part of a big machine with its parts and pieces nearly ready to engage. And not in the way its designer imagined.

The lopsided smile broadened.

How could dead history compare to rich, explosive *life*?

THIRTY-EIGHT

Washington, D.C.
Wednesday, 11:33 A.M.

The McCaskeys did not work very much when they got home.

They sat on the bed, pulled the laptop between them, and reviewed the list of possible suspects: Kendra Peterson, Kat Lockley, Dr. Hennepin. Mike Rodgers had mentioned a reporter, Lucy O'Connor, who covered Congress and arrived very soon after both murders. The McCaskeys had looked up her background. The résumé of everyone who had security clearance to the Capitol was filed online in the eyes-only section of the congressional web site. She wrote for the *American Spectator* and had a moderately successful syndicated radio talk show. She was a Pittsburgh native who had majored in communication at Carnegie-Mellon University.

"She also took their Interstellar Communication course and grabbed several credits from the Robotics Institute at the university's School of Computer Science," McCaskey remarked.

"What does that tell you?" Maria asked.

"She likes to think outside the coconut," he replied.

The couple went back to the police station. Howell's people had been doing some of the legwork they needed now. The Metro Police had obtained the addresses, license numbers, and make of car driven by each individual on their list of potential suspects. They also charted the location of security cameras closest to these people: parking garages, apartment lobbies, convenience stores, gas stations, banks, and traffic intersections. The latter were monitored for speeders and potential terrorists moving through the capital. Once the McCaskeys had these sites, they intended to go back out and visit them, borrow the tapes, and have a look for one of those women returning home after the crime.

They fell asleep instead. The days of youthful "forced march" crime-fighting were a thing of the past. The McCaskeys needed rest.

Maria got up at five-thirty the next morning. She showered, made coffee, then woke her husband. McCaskey was not happy to have passed out like that. He joined her in the kitchen at six-thirty. They had coffee and whole wheat toast. By seven o'clock, they were on the road.

McCaskey had not done patrol work since he was a debutant. That was Bureau slang for a first-year agent. He forgot how tiring it could be. Or maybe how much older he was. That aside, it was rewarding work made more so by Maria's enthusiasm. She loved police work and had an eye for detail unlike anyone he had ever met. She had decided that the killer would have driven from the murder sites. A woman alone, on foot, after dark, was likely to stand out. She might have been noticed from a bar or restaurant or by a passing motorist. That could have helped police determine her direction. If she had taken the Metro, she definitely would have appeared on a security camera. A taxi or limousine service was out of the question. Drivers paid attention to the people who got into their cars. Part of that was fear and part of it was bragging rights in case they happened to pick up a celebrity.

Assuming the killer was driving, she would have done so slowly. She would not have wanted to risk being stopped by the police. They might ask where she had been. If the killer had shared a drink with Wilson, the police might have smelled it and insisted on a sobriety test.

There were a great many assumptions in their scenario.

But experience, deductive reasoning, and good instincts could be as important to an investigation as facts, especially in a case such as this where there was very little hard data. McCaskey was thinking about that as they drove from site to site. His Op-Center ID got him access to the videotapes or digital records. None of them proved to be helpful. There was no sign of the cars they were looking for.

Maria was at the wheel. As McCaskey watched familiar storefronts and offices slip by, he had a troubling thought. A century ago, the booksellers, diners, attorneys, government offices, and banks would have been especially vulnerable to fire. Today, it was a new kind of fire that could destroy them. The kind that had crippled Op-Center. He wondered if there would ever be a time when people did not have to fear life as much as they feared death.

Not the way we do things now, he told himself.

Funds to fight these dangers were allocated by political need instead of by threat assessment. People like himself, Maria, and Detective Howell could not do the job America was counting on them to do.

"Do you think the killer might have rented a car?" Maria asked.

McCaskey looked at his wife. "I'm sorry?"

"The killer," Maria repeated slowly. "Do you think she might have rented a car?"

"I would be very surprised if she did," he said. "Assassins don't like to leave a paper trail."

"This assassin did not expect to be exposed," Maria pointed out.

"That is true."

"And she certainly would have gone in with a fake ID," Maria went on. "An experienced killer would have several, I'm sure."

"I suppose we can try that search if this doesn't get us anywhere," McCaskey said. "But there have got to be hundreds of rental facilities in the D.C. metro area. It will take days to visit them all, and what do we tell them when we do?"

"We show them pictures of all the women and see if they look familiar. Or better yet, we can see if any of them show up on security cameras. None of those women would have had a reason to rent a car."

"Yes, we could do that," McCaskey said.

That was another difference between today and his days as a rookie G-man. Twenty-odd years ago, at least a dozen agents would have been assigned to a case like this. Now there were two.

"Darrell, were you all right a minute ago?" Maria asked.

"Sorry?"

"You went away from me."

"Yes," her husband said. "I was thinking, that's all."

"What about?" Maria asked.

"The pork barrel," he said with a little laugh.

"Is that a restaurant?"

"In a manner of speaking," McCaskey replied. He loved his beautiful, sweet, Spanish wife. She was so worldly, so tough, and so very linear. "A person of influence takes a lunch tray to his senator and gets plates full of federal funds. It's another name for patronage."

"I see," Maria said. "It is the same as what bookmakers in Madrid call *el roulette del amigo*."

"That's exactly what it is. The roulette wheel of a friend," McCaskey said. "The fix is in, the outcome predetermined."

"Why were you thinking about that?"

"Because Op-Center was a victim of pork barrel politics. Maybe Paul is right, doing what he's doing. If we had played the system better, we would have more people looking for a killer. And that should be our bottom line, should it not? Protecting law-abiding citizens."

"That is my religion," she said simply.

"Well put." McCaskey looked out the window again. He noticed they were nearing Lafayette Park. "We're near the Hay-Adams. Why don't we go back there? Walk around, see if there is anything we may have overlooked."

"All right," she said.

That was the beauty of having married a cop. He might have to explain colloquial English to her, but he did not have to explain the intangibles of their lives and work. She got that.

They drove to the hotel, its tawny facade gleaming warmly in the morning light. They parked and decided to walk along Farragut North. The White House shone through the trees of Lafayette Park. McCaskey could see the press corps gathered in tents on the east side. The president was probably heading to the airport. It was too early in the week for Camp David. He remembered when the press looked for stories instead of handouts. There was a time when someone would have sniffed out the new relationship between the White House and Op-Center, exposed it, and not been afraid to write about it. Access to newsmakers. A different kind of pork barrel.

McCaskey took his wife's hand. She gave it an encouraging squeeze. She seemed to sense the frustration he was feeling with this case and with the situation at Op-Center.

"We'll get her," Maria said.

"Thanks. I believe that," McCaskey replied.

Maria stopped suddenly. She looked ahead. "No, I mean we *will* get her."

"I don't follow."

"I was just thinking about the assassin, what I would do if I had just killed someone at the hotel," Maria said. "I would be undistracted by conscience or the late hour. My only concern would be getting away quick and clean. That means I would be parked as close to the hotel as possible, on a relatively dark street."

"Of course."

"I would also have parked where there are the fewest eyeballs," Maria said. "Where would that be?"

"The side of the hotel by Lafayette Park," her husband said, "near where we parked."

"Yes. Darrell, do you think any of the White House reporters might have been there? Maybe one of them doing a live report for CNN?"

"Very possibly," he agreed. "But they would have been facing the White House, not the park."

"Perhaps they turned on their cameras early."

McCaskey looked in that direction. He did not think there was a chance of that, though he could not rule it out. Then something occurred to him. Something that made the pact with the devil suddenly seem more inviting.

"We may not need them," he said.

"Why not?"

"Because if the killer came this way, someone else may have gotten a good look at her," McCaskey said.

Without saying anything else, he borrowed Maria's cell phone and walked briskly toward the park.

THIRTY-NINE

Washington, D.C.
Wednesday, 11:54 A.M.

Yuri and Svetlana Krasnov might have imagined their own fate. They possessed the genetic Russian quality of dissatisfaction, inherited from their peasant parents. What they could never have imagined was the destiny of their son.

The young couple moved to the United States during the Cold War. They lived in Arlington, Virginia, and worked in the Soviet embassy. She was a stenographer, and he was a translator. Svetlana was also a cryptographer and helped to interpret intercepted military and governmental communiqués. Yuri translated messages from American-born spies. One morning, three months after arriving, they were approached by a CIA officer. He offered them a chance to work with the Agency. The agent wanted to know who was giving them intelligence so that the CIA could distribute disinformation to the Kremlin. In exchange, when it came time for the Krasnovs to be rotated back to the Soviet Union—after eighteen months, to make sure they did not become overly comfortable with the American way of life—they would be given asylum if they chose to stay. If their collaboration were ever discovered, the Krasnovs would immediately be taken into protective custody and relocated.

The couple had learned a great deal about the United States since moving here. They liked what they saw. What's more, they had a six-year-old daughter and four-year-old son and wanted them to grow up in a land of opportunity. A land without breadlines or restrictions on what they could say and think.

The Krasnovs were found out seven months later. A floater agent, one assigned to spy on spies, read a mole's report and resealed it before it was turned over to Yuri for translation. The deception was discovered. The Krasnovs fled. The family was relocated to Wisconsin and given the new last name Brown, chosen by Svetlana. She was a big fan of the *Peanuts* comic strip.

Young Fayina and her brother Vladilen grew up American, and no one could have been more of a patriot than Vlad. He joined the marines as soon as he turned eighteen and proved to be remarkably skilled with the M-14. His proficiency was the result of the years he had spent hunting with his father in the woods. Implicitly, the elder Brown wanted to be ready in case the KGB ever came looking for them. Fortunately, the collapse of the Soviet Union made that unlikely.

Vlad was so good with weapons that the Marines appointed him to a special reaction team at the Marine Corps Air Station in Iwakuni, Japan. As part of his assignment he was sent to Camp Foster, Okinawa, to train with the new Designated Marksman Rifle. The DMR was an urban combat rifle. Before being certified, Vlad had to be able to make a moving head shot from two hundred yards and hit a stationary thumbnail-size object from the same distance.

He placed number one at the base, and among the top 1 percent of all Marine marksmen nationwide. Shortly before the Iraq War, Captain Vlad Brown was reassigned to special duty at the White House. Along with two other men, Vlad spent his nights on the roof with infrared glasses, watching for potential attackers. His DMR was worn across his back in a loose leather sling. He could have the rifle unshouldered and aimed in less than three seconds. His orders were to report any suspicious movement within three hundred yards of the White House. Vlad wore a three-ounce video camera on his left shoulder, where it would not get in the way of his DMR. The camera relayed images to Secret Service On-site Command based in the West Wing. If the SSOC determined a threat was real, Vlad would be ordered to neutralize it.

The post was quite a journey for the son of Russian defectors, unthinkable a quarter century before. The young man took some ribbing because of his very Russian name, but not too much. That was the one area where Vlad Brown was self-conscious and extremely sensitive. Though the captain passed the monthly psych evaluations, which were required for armed individuals with presidential access, his fellow marksmen sensed his name was an area to avoid. There were some things team members picked up on that psychologists did not.

Vlad was rarely called to the White House during the day. Marksmen required seven or eight hours' sleep to be their sharpest and, besides, he did not like to be out much during the day. After seven months on the job, his eyes were accustomed to night, his body to the pleasant night air, his ears to the sounds of the evening and early morning. He did not want to do anything to upset that balance.

But the president's chief of staff said it was important, so Captain Brown put off going to sleep, called up a staff car, and had himself driven from the Marine Barracks at Eighth and I to the White House. Upon arriving, he went directly to the SSOC office and was introduced to Darrell and Maria McCaskey of Op-Center. The former Russian citizen felt an immediate empathy with Mrs. McCaskey. Obviously, she was not a native to these shores.

Secret Service Agent Stephen Kearns—the son of Greek immigrants—offered Vlad a seat in the small office. He declined. Mrs. McCaskey was standing, and the officer would not sit in her presence. Her husband introduced himself to Vlad. He looked as tired as the marine captain felt.

"Thank you for coming," McCaskey said. "Captain Brown, we are investigating the assassination of William Wilson at the Hay-Adams Hotel. I assume you've heard about it?"

"I have, sir."

"We understand from Agent Kearns that you wear a small video camera equipped with night-vision capabilities," McCaskey said. "We would like to look at the images from that night."

"We believe the individual we are seeking walked past the park, past your observation post," Mrs. McCaskey added.

"Agent Kearns, do you have any objection?" Vlad asked. Because of the cooperative arrangement between the Secret Service and the marines, dual releases were required before a third party could examine White House security tapes.

"Mr. and Mrs. McCaskey have been cleared by the office of the chief of staff," Kearns informed him.

"Then you have my permission, sir," Vlad told the Op-Center officer.

"Thank you," McCaskey said.

Agent Kearns had booted the digital videodisc on which the images were stored. The SSOC officer swung the monitor toward the McCaskeys. The couple must have friends in high places to have been given access to these images. Few people even knew they existed.

The image was time-coded and bookmarked in five-minute chunks. Kearns jumped directly to the times the McCaskeys wished to see. Vlad stood back while Darrell and Maria bent very close to the monitor and to each other. There was something touching about it.

A woman walked past the screen.

"Hold on!" Darrell McCaskey said. "Can you hold the image and enlarge it?"

Agent Kearns obliged. A blurry green image of a woman

filled the screen. She was walking away from the hotel toward Pennsylvania Avenue. Mr. McCaskey pointed at the monitor with his pinkie. He traced what appeared to be a faint smudge of dress beneath the woman's long jacket.

"See the line under the hem?" McCaskey asked his wife excitedly.

"Yes," Mrs. McCaskey said.

"What do you think?"

"That could be satin," she replied.

"Sir, if you give me a minute, I'll extrapolate the color information and sharpen the image," Kearns said.

"Please do," Mr. McCaskey said.

No one spoke as the computer did its job. Though the image was entirely in tones of green, the image processor was capable of matching a color to each particular shade. The saturation of green corresponded to the comparative brightness of a color. By removing the green and matching the remaining light intensity to a color, the image could be accurately colorized. At the same time, the computer scanned the picture to differentiate between legitimate information and pictorial noise such as blurred motion, video snow, and other artifacts. It removed these flaws by replicating information from adjoining pixels.

Within two minutes, the woman looked as if she had posed for a profile picture in daylight. The McCaskeys studied it for a minute, then asked Agent Kearns to print the image. He obliged. He handed the eight-by-ten to Mr. McCaskey.

"Do you recognize the individual?" Kearns asked.

"Yes," Mr. McCaskey replied. "Gentlemen, you have been of immeasurable assistance. Thank you."

Mrs. McCaskey smiled. It was formal but sincere. For Vlad, it was worth coming back to work. One day, when his assignment ended and the pressure of his job was behind him, Vlad hoped to find a woman like that. A woman with poise, intensity, and beauty.

The captain returned to his car and driver. Vlad had to admit it was encouraging how people from four nations had just worked together to solve the death of someone from a fifth country. There was probably a lesson in that for the United Nations and the world in general. But he was too tired to search for it. And maybe it was not worth analyzing. As Yuri used to say with a dismissive wave of his hand, "It's politics. My *keeshkee* cannot take it anymore."

Maybe the Krasnov gene pool and intestines were averse to chaos in general. It was lunch hour, and Vlad found the traffic disturbing. It was thick with growling buses, limousines, and Washingtonians who honked at tourists who slowed as they passed each familiar landmark. Vlad shut his tired eyes, and the comfort of darkness returned. Along with a troubling realization.

He shared a love of nighttime with someone else. Someone whose values were the antithesis of his own: the assassin.

Vlad nudged this thought from his mind. It was way beyond his pay grade. Besides, the gene pool that disliked chaos also gave him something else. Something with which there was no debating. A part of him that did not want to think about this: his *keeshkee.*

FORTY

Salt Lake City, Utah
Wednesday, 10:17 A.M.

Mike Rodgers was changing planes when he checked the personal cell phone he had bought to join the twenty-first century. He never took the phone with him to work, so it had been unaffected by the electromagnetic pulse. There was a call from Maria McCaskey and plenty of time to return it. The connecting flight to San Diego did not leave for another sixty minutes.

The flight from Washington had been routine. Routine for Rodgers, anyway. That invariably meant planning for conflict. The difference was that for the first time in his life, he was sizing up Americans. He was talking to Kat Lockley, trying to find out what she knew and what she might be hiding. Either she was very good at deception, or she was very innocent. He could not decide which. He was hoping it was the latter. In fact, he hoped this entire thing turned out to be a misunderstanding of some sort. Being away from Washington made him inherently less distrustful. The murderer of William Wilson was probably a former lover or a business rival. The EM attack on Op-Center may have been long planned, the timing coincidental. He still believed it was executed by a group or nation the NCMC had crossed. At least, Rodgers wanted to believe that. One of the failures of Homeland Security was that it presumed when the moat was drawn, only good guys remained in the castle.

Kat planted her ear to her cell phone the instant she left the plane. She said she had to talk to Eric Stone and to Kendra to see how everything was going. The senator had no plans for that morning. The convention opened in the evening, but the senator's big night was not until the next day. He would make a speech and then, on Friday, the convention would select a candidate. Kat said she wanted to make sure that everything was going as planned.

Rodgers walked away from where Kat was sitting. He went to a quiet corner at an empty gate and stood with his back against a wall. It felt good to stand after being in the crowded plane. People were rushing about, but the general felt disconnected from their urgency. He had always felt that way in combat, too. There was a tightrope strung between himself and the outcome, with potential enemies everywhere. He had to be very attentive to each step. This investigation was like that in a way because of what the outcome meant to him personally and professionally. Rodgers felt apprehensive as he punched in the number. He did not think Darrell or Maria was calling to find out if Kat had told him anything. Rodgers would have called from a phone on the airplane if he had intel. The call probably meant the McCaskeys had information for him. Maybe they had found the killer, an angry former employee or maltreated valet.

The information Darrell had was not what Mike Rodgers wanted to hear.

"A woman from your circle was at the second crime scene," McCaskey told him. "The time is right, and she was wearing a dress that matches the color of fibers found in the room."

Since this was an unsecured line, McCaskey would not tell Rodgers how he found that out, but the former FBI agent was a conservative man; he would not have made such a conclusive statement if he weren't sure.

"Who is it?" Rodgers asked.

"The reporter."

Lucy O'Connor. Rodgers felt relief, doubt, and renewed concern in quick succession. The relief was because the killer appeared to be outside the group. The doubt was because it seemed unlikely Lucy would have conceived the one murder alone, let alone a second murder and possibly the bombing of Op-Center. In the little time he had spent with Lucy, she did not seem to have the patience for murder. And concern because, if all that were true, Lucy had to be in league with someone. That still did not clear Link or his people.

"What about the hat with the big brim?" Rodgers asked. "Is that a match?"

"Not worn in this image," McCaskey said. "But it could have been stuffed into a shoulder bag."

That made sense. If she were caught on a security camera outside, there would be one less element to connect her to images from the hotel.

"What do you want me to do?" Rodgers asked.

"I think you should tell your traveling companion and see how she reacts," McCaskey said.

"I agree. We leave for San Diego in less than an hour. I'll try to call back before then."

Rodgers hung up. He flipped the phone shut and started walking toward Kat. She was still sitting there, her eyes fixed on nothing, her index finger in her open ear as she talked on the phone, conducting her business. But which business? And how was he going to find out? He was a soldier, not Morley Safer.

The seat beside Kat was open. Rodgers took it. She did not attempt to conceal what she was saying.

". . . only CNN talks to him before the press conference. That's the deal we made for a prime-time spot," Kat was saying. She was silent for a moment, her shoulders straight and stiff, her mouth a tight, unemotional line. Then she said, "I understand, Diane. But Larry was the only one who offered that. What about this: you get the first talk with the ticket. I would want ten minutes in the eight o'clock hour of the morning show." She was silent again. "Yes, an exclusive sit-down at the senator's home in Georgetown." Kat smiled slightly as she listened. "Good. I will present it to the senator, but I am certain it will be okay. Thanks. Say hi to Mike." Kat punched the Off button and slumped into the seat. "Well, this is what I worked for. Now I've got it."

"What is that?"

"A hungry press," Kat replied. "Before Wilson, Senator Orr was only on the radar of the all-news networks. Now everyone wants him, especially if they can shoot at the party house."

"Lucky break for us," Rodgers said.

Kat looked over. "I'm too busy for sarcasm."

"Okay. Let's try it straight up." Kat had given him a clean shot, and he decided to take it. Maybe that was the best way. "What do you say to Lucy O'Connor being at the Hay-Adams when Wilson was murdered?"

"I would say she was trying to get an interview," Kat replied. She speed-dialed another number.

"Or maybe trying to make news," Rodgers suggested.

"What are you talking about?"

Rodgers looked around to make sure no one was listening. For all he knew, Lucy O'Connor had been on their flight. "There is an image of Lucy leaving the Hay-Adams shortly after the murder. The dress she had on is the same color as the one the assassin was wearing."

Kat terminated the call. "That hardly makes her a killer or even an accomplice," she said. "Maybe they bought it off the same rack."

"That's a reach," Rodgers said.

"So is your idea of what constitutes a murder suspect," Kat said. "You've got a hungry reporter. A reclusive newsmaker. Of course she would be at the hotel after the party, trying to intercept him."

"You're defending her pretty adamantly," Rodgers observed.

"This is America. Lucy is still innocent. Besides, she doesn't deserve to be pilloried. Nor does Senator Orr," Kat said.

"Is that what you think is happening?" Rodgers asked.

"Yes. You or someone at Op-Center has obviously made up their minds that we are guilty of murder, or worse."

"No one has made that determination," Rodgers told her. "This is an investigation."

"Yours or Op-Center's?"

"Until my resignation takes effect, I am working for Op-Center by assignment and command of the undersecretary, Department of Defense Security Cooperation Agency," Rodgers replied.

"Then I suggest you get back to Washington and complete your assignment there," Kat said.

"For the record, I have spent most of my career in the field, protecting America and the rights of its citizens. I have condemned no one, either openly or in here," Rodgers tapped his right temple. "You, on the other hand, have made up your mind that I am out to get you. If that were true, I would have turned this over to Paul Hood and his bulldogs."

Kat's expression returned to neutral. She looked at her phone and tapped it in her open palm. "It sounded like an attack," she said.

"I'm a soldier. A lot of things I say come out like that."

"Not always." The young woman regarded Rodgers. Neutrality suddenly looked more like exhaustion. "General—Mike—I really don't know about what Lucy did or did not do. And I do not want to be defensive. It's just this whole thing has been a distraction at the worst possible time. Part of me believes it was designed that way by a person or group that does not want to see the senator become president or even have a voice in this election."

"Do you have any idea who that might be?"

"Sure. Every lobbyist and politician from the center to the left. Political rivals like Senator Debenport and Governor Jimmy Phyfe of Ohio, both of whom want President Lawrence's job."

"Do you have specific information that either of those men may be involved in the assassination?" Rodgers asked. "If you do, even if it's just a suspicion, this would be the time to tell me."

"There are rumors that Debenport and Lawrence are using the presidency to attract allies for partisan activities, but we have no proof of that," Kat told him. "Anything you can imagine is possible in Washington, but I don't even want to *believe* that."

Rodgers had always felt like a resistance fighter, risking his life to stop oppression. At the moment he felt like a collaborator, dirty and small. He moved closer. "You just said that anything you can imagine is possible. I have never done a lot of abstract thinking, Kat. I look at maps, at facts, at logistics. Since this thing started, I have been taking one small step at a time, just as I did whenever I led a unit against an enemy position. The difference is, I am accustomed to knowing who my opponent is. This is new ground for me and for Op-Center."

"For all of us," Kat said. "I have never been part of a murder investigation."

"At least your involvement is peripheral at best," Rodgers pointed out. "For that matter, the spotlight is on Lucy now, not any of your coworkers."

"I still do not believe she had anything to do with it."

"Why? Talk to me."

"Let me ask *you* something first," she said. "You've killed people. What does it take to do that?"

"Unless you're a textbook sociopath, all it takes is the first kill to commit the second and third," Rodgers told her.

"I don't understand."

"It's like skydiving or eating snake," Rodgers said. "You've already made the determination that it's something you need to do. What you need then is something to kick you over your gag reflex. One of my Strikers, Corporal Pat Prementine, had to think of a high school bully he hated the first time he lobbed a grenade."

"What did it take for you?"

"Economy."

"What?"

"Two weeks after I arrived, my platoon was doing recon in the southern region of the Central Plateau," Rodgers said. "We bumped into a large 'Cong encampment. They tried to surround us, and we knew we would have to punch hard and fast to secure an exit route. I was ordered to hunker down behind a rank-smelling tree trunk and cover a small clearing. I did. My soles were deep in muck, bugs crawled over my boots, and I was hot as hell. I heard gunfire start to crack in sporadic bursts. It was a hollow, distant, lonely noise that shut all the birds and insects up. I never experienced such silence once the shooting started. I knew the guys with guns would be coming my way soon enough, and I had to face the fact that I could die. I was okay with that. I made mental good-byes and said some quiet I-love-yous to my folks. While I was doing that, I saw an opportunistic target. Five 'Cong moved into position about two hundred yards away. They did not see me. I remember staring along my M1 thinking it wasn't fair to clock them from hiding, without warning. I even thought, *Hell. This is their home. What business do I have shooting them?* Then I saw one of them pull a bamboo stick grenade from a pouch. That was highly explosive, very deadly ordnance. I couldn't see our guys, but obviously Charlie could. Otherwise, he would not be going for the grenade. And at that moment it hit me. *If I tag him, he'll drop the pestle*—that's what the grenade looked like, a pharmacist's pestle—*and it will blow all five of them to snake food.* The 'Cong were crouching, and this guy stuck his head up for a last look. I had done the math, it worked, and I took the shot. It was clean, through his temple. The other four guys shouted and scrambled, I ducked behind the tree, and the pestle blew. I sat there with my back against the damp trunk as the smoke and the sharp smell of the explosive charge rolled by. I held my breath so I didn't start to cough and reveal my position to any backup they might have had. After about a minute, I swung around to look at the clearing. I saw a couple of 'Cong crawling through the smoke to try to find whoever had fired the shot. I picked them off."

"The second group was easier to kill?"

"Not just easier. Easy. Once you cross that line, you're not worried about damnation anymore."

"Like women and sex, I guess," Kat said.

"Killing. The male virginity," Rodgers said.

"Do you regret that experience?"

"How can I?" Rodgers asked. "It allowed me to do my job in Vietnam, in the Persian Gulf, and at Op-Center."

"A job whose legitimacy you questioned the first time you did it," the woman pointed out.

"I was nineteen."

"That did not make you wrong," Kat said.

"Okay," Rodgers said. "Now I'm the one who doesn't understand. Are you justifying what Lucy may have been involved in?"

"No. I'm questioning what appears to be your own convenient morality. Killing is okay in the first person, if you do it, but not if someone else does it."

Rodgers had opened himself up to Kat, hoping she

would do the same. He had not expected that response. He also did not appreciate it.

"You're looking at me like I'm holding a pestle in a clearing," Kat said.

"No. You already lobbed it," he replied.

"Touché," she said. "It was not my intention to attack you. I'm just trying to understand what drives the man who may be the next secretary of defense. But we're obviously getting ahead of ourselves. I do not know about Lucy O'Connor's activities that night, and I do not believe she is capable of what happened at the hotel or at Op-Center. I can only suggest that your people talk to her."

"I am sure they will," Rodgers said.

There was a poorly concealed threat in her comment about "getting ahead of ourselves." If Rodgers did not join the team, he would become a free agent.

"So where does that leave us?" Kat asked as she picked up the phone.

"I'm not sure," he admitted. "I feel like I've crossed a line here, but this is an unusual situation."

"I agree," Kat said. She crossed her legs and moved her right foot anxiously. "Let me make this really simple, because I still have calls to make. I want this relationship to work. You're an exceptional man, and you would be a great asset to the party and to our team. But the core group should be able to watch out for each other. We should not have to *watch* each other."

"I can't argue with that," Rodgers said. "That's why I said I am not sure where this leaves us." The way Kat was sitting then reminded him of seeing her on the bar stool at the Equinox in Washington. Her foot bouncing as it did now, Kat wired at the end of a long and stressful day. How much different the world and his own future seemed just a few days ago.

"You should let Admiral Link know," Kat said. "That's only fair."

"Sure. Just one more question, though," Rodgers said. "What would you do if you found out someone in the core group was behind this?"

"You're really pushing me, General."

"Would you watch their back?" he demanded.

"Until they were proven guilty, yeah," she replied. "This is America." She went back to her cell phone.

Rodgers walked over to a refreshment stand and ordered a black coffee. Thinking about the Equinox dislodged something in his memory. Something that had not seemed unusual at the time but did now. Rodgers took his black coffee and went back to the corner of the empty gate. He sat down, sipped the coffee for a moment, then took out his own cell phone. He called Darrell.

There was something Rodgers needed him to check.

Fast.

FORTY-ONE

Washington, D.C.
Wednesday, 1:29 P.M.

Darrell McCaskey was in the car with his wife. They were about to get onto 395 when McCaskey's phone beeped. It was Mike Rodgers. The general asked if anything was new.

"Maria and I just did a UPS on the reporter," McCaskey told him. "Her apartment, her car, and the radio station were clean." A UPS was an unsanctioned prescreen, meaning the two Op-Center agents had a look around without the benefit of a search warrant. That was necessary when law enforcement did not want an individual or group to know that new evidence had surfaced. Op-Center wanted time to get agents on her trail. Until then they wanted to make sure she continued talking to the same people as before. "We've got the Metro cops picking through the dump right now, looking for signs of the dress. We were about to join them."

"I don't think they'll find it," Rodgers said.

"Talk to me," McCaskey said.

"The night after the murder, I had dinner with my traveling companion," Rodgers told him. He was being nonspecific because of the unsecure line. "When I got there, she was talking with your target. My companion had a shopping bag. She told me it contained comfortable shoes, Nikes, which she never put on. She is wearing high heels now as well. I'm thinking—"

"She may have given her the dress for disposal after I exposed the crime," McCaskey said.

"Correct."

"That was the night of the second crime," McCaskey said.

"Also right."

"Got a name on that shopping bag?" McCaskey asked.

"*Groveburn*," Rodgers said. "Yellow plastic, red rope handles."

"We'll look into it at once," McCaskey said. "Maybe we'll get lucky and find the hypodermic there as well." He turned the car around and headed toward Kat's apartment on the corner of New Hampshire and N Street. "One more thing. What is her attitude about all of this, Mike?"

"She is acting more offended than guilty," Rodgers said. "If she is worried, she's being very cool about it."

"An operation like this would not hitch its wagon to a bunch of Jittery Janes," McCaskey said. "Mike, thanks for this. I'll leave a message if we find anything. Meanwhile, watch your back."

"Never been good at that, Darrell," Rodgers said. "Good or bad, the future's in front of you."

Rodgers hung up, and McCaskey handed the phone to Maria. "Mike is getting philosophical," McCaskey said. "That means he's worried."

"Mike is always worried," Maria said.

"True," her husband replied. "But most of that is usually on the surface. This is coming from inside."

McCaskey briefed his wife, who asked what he thought Rodgers might be worried about.

"That Kat could be guilty," McCaskey told her.

"Of what? Does he think she could have masterminded it?"

"I don't know if he believes that," McCaskey said. "My own feeling is that someone like Link had to be involved.

Not only because of the sophistication and coordination of the kills, but because it would be difficult to execute without someone covering for them inside Orr's office."

"Which brings me back to *why*," Maria said. "Could this really be all about money, about Wilson's plans for boosting European investments?"

"It could," her husband replied. "We'll know that when we talk to the people who did it."

"Assuming we get them," Maria said.

"We will," McCaskey said confidently.

"At Interpol Madrid, our success rate solving homicides was a little over sixty percent."

"We did a little better than that at the Bureau, but not enough," McCaskey said. "That was one reason I joined Op-Center. Results change when people like you, Mike, and Bob Herbert are added to the process."

"Your tactics also have changed," Maria pointed out. "We just did a break and enter."

"That is true, though I look at it as exploratory surgery. It sounds more benevolent than criminal."

"Sweetheart, there is nothing criminal about what we are planning," Maria said with absolute confidence. "We have a clear objective and will limit ourselves to that. Ms. Lockley will never know, unless we find something, in which case we will be in a position to step back and build a stronger case."

"We are still invading her privacy," he said. "We are still ignoring the Bill of Rights."

"What we are planning is less of a crime than those committed against Mr. Wilson and Mr. Lawless," Maria replied. "If we can stop a third homicide, then it is a risk worth taking."

"Obviously, I agree, or I would not be doing it," McCaskey said as he turned onto N Street. "But I am not going to pretend it is legal."

"To me, legal is less important than moral," Maria said.

"My conscience is not going to bother me tonight, whatever we find."

There was no explaining to Maria the American idea of personal rights. That was as pointless as arguing against Maria's logic. One was an absolute, the foundation of a national philosophy, the other was airtight. The only way to sidestep either was by embracing the other. McCaskey had made his choice.

The apartment building was a three-story, white brick structure. There was an outside door with a lock, a foyer for mail, and an inside door that led to the apartments. They would have to go through two locks before they reached the apartment. That would not be a problem. McCaskey carried a magnetic snap gun in his car. The original snap gun was developed in the 1960s so that law officers who were not trained lockpicks could open doors using something other than traditional raking techniques—that is, inserting a pair of picks and searching for the proper combination to turn the lock. The snap gun generated torque that simply muscled the lock back. It also tended to bend or destroy the lock, evidence that someone had forced their way in. The magnetic gun generated a powerful magnetic force in whatever direction the user indicated. It popped the lock and any interior dead bolts in an instant.

McCaskey and his wife approached the door. They had decided, if asked, that she was looking for an apartment and he was a broker. He put the point of the palm-size unit into the keyhole. He used his thumb to adjust the directional vector to the right. The lock opened immediately. The couple moved into the foyer, where they got a free pass. A resident was just coming out and opened the door. McCaskey dropped a pen and stooped to pick it up as the man passed. He did not want his face to be seen. Then McCaskey and Maria went inside. Since the elevator had a security camera, they took the stairs to Kat's third-floor apartment. There were five other apartments on the floor. While Maria watched the doors, her husband took a palm-size disk from his jacket pocket. He put it against the doorjamb. It was an ampere detector. If the door were wired with a burglar alarm, this would show current. He watched the digital readout. There was nothing. Although there could still be a motion detector inside, most urban apartments, especially newer buildings such as this one, had been prewired for perimeter entry. McCaskey used the snap gun to open the knob lock and dead bolt. McCaskey put the snap gun in his jacket pocket and removed a pair of leather gloves. He pulled them on so he would not leave fingerprints. The couple went inside.

The shades were drawn, and the apartment was dark. There was a small penlight attached to McCaskey's key chain. He flicked it on. Neighbors might know that Kat was away. He did not want them seeing lights behind the shades.

They were in a small corridor that led to the living room. McCaskey swung the light across the floor to look for pet hair. If Kat had a pet, she might also have a walker, someone to come by and take it out. He saw no traces of fur, nor did they hear anything. They started forward.

"I do not smell a fireplace," Maria said.

"I know," her husband replied.

They entered the living room. There was no fireplace there or in the master bedroom. They searched Kat's closets for the bag Rodgers had described.

"That's a good sign," Maria said after they had finished looking in the kitchen cabinets.

"Why do you say that?"

"Those are the kinds of bags women save," she said. "They make good gift bags or tote bags. Ms. Lockley had other bags in the broom closet. She obviously got rid of this one."

"Intriguing but circumstantial," her husband replied. He

looked around. He went to the bookshelf and pulled down her college and high school yearbooks. He flipped through them, looking for a name that might have come up during the investigation, a possible collaborator. There was none.

"We should have brought Matt to get into her computer," Maria said, pointing to a desk near the window.

"I'm sure that anything important is on a laptop, and I'm just as sure it is with her," McCaskey said.

He heard running water. It was coming from the kitchen. It was just the freezer. The ice maker was making ice.

"That's odd," he said.

"What is?" Maria asked, joining him.

"Ice makers only fill up when they're low."

He went to the stainless steel unit and opened the door. The engine was humming loudly, amplified by the close walls of the small kitchen. McCaskey flipped up the ice compartment. He dug through the new ice to the cubes below. He broke several chunks free and pulled them out.

"Damn."

Maria moved closer. "What is it?"

"There are blue stains in the ice," he said, holding a cube up to the freezer light. "See them?"

Maria nodded. "She had the dress in the ice compartment. That's a very good hiding spot."

McCaskey nodded. He set the ice down carefully on a shelf and used his pocket knife to poke around inside, just in case the hypodermic was there as well. It was not. That was probably in the milk, he thought only half in jest.

"If the dress was here this recently," McCaskey went on, "it means she may have taken it with her."

"Isn't that risky to have evidence on your person?" Maria asked.

"It would have been riskier to leave it here or to have destroyed it when you are on a short list of suspects," McCaskey replied. "Think about it. Where would the garment be safer than in the hands of airport security? My guess is she will dispose of it as far from the crime scene as possible."

Maria went back to the freezer. She stopped. Her husband smiled and handed her a spoon from the dish rack. He had wrapped it in a dish towel so they would not leave prints. She stuck it through the handle and pulled the door open, so as not to leave, or smudge, any fingerprints. She looked in the ice compartment.

"Why wouldn't she have taken out all the ice as a precaution?" Maria asked. "Dress fibers may have become stuck to them."

"That would have put them in plain view in the sink," McCaskey remarked.

"She could have washed them away."

"The FBI routinely checks drainpipes for evidence," McCaskey replied. "Whoever was behind this would surely have known that."

Maria made a face and looked down. She crouched. Her husband shone the light on the tile floor.

"Find something?" he asked.

"Maybe. Look at this," she said.

McCaskey squatted beside her. Maria was pointing to several slightly off-color stains.

"This limestone has no shine, which means it has not been sealed," Maria said. "The tile is extremely porous. It soaks up water."

"Okay. Some of the ice fell and was not picked up. It melted. It stained the limestone—"

"Darrell, the dampness stays in the tile for about an hour, then it evaporates," Maria told him.

"You're saying that someone was here within the hour," McCaskey said. He did not like the sound of that.

"It seems so," Maria said.

"It could have been a housekeeper."

"I don't smell any cleaning agent," Maria said.

"There's pineapple smell—"

"An air freshener," Maria said, pointing back at the bathroom. "I saw it earlier when we looked in the bedroom."

Damn, she is good, McCaskey thought. But that still did not convince him. It was still a big leap from a few damp spots on the floor to someone having been here in the last hour. McCaskey looked up. The ice dispenser in the freezer door was directly overhead. He ran his gloved finger along the inside of the plastic lip. "It's moist. The stains could have come from dripping condensation."

"That is possible," Maria agreed. "It is also possible that Ms. Lockley is being framed."

The realization was like a punch in McCaskey's gut. If it were true, it meant something else as well. Something that became clear when they heard movement in the hallway.

They had been set up.

FORTY-TWO

San Diego, California
Wednesday, 11:53 A.M.

It had been a two hour flight from Salt Lake City. Kat did not talk to Rodgers the entire time. He was not surprised, but he was inconvenienced. If she were innocent of wrongdoing, they should be talking about who might be involved. Instead, she just worked on her laptop and shut him out.

Rodgers checked his cell phone voice mail as soon as they deplaned. There was a long message from McCaskey. It was not very encouraging. McCaskey's urgency was underscored by the fact that he was not being circumspect, even though this was an open line.

"Mike, we found dye from what we believe to be the dress in Kat's ice dispenser," McCaskey said quickly. "We believe that someone was here in the last hour, perhaps to remove the dress. If they didn't, Kat may have packed it in her luggage. You have to find out. Tell her what happened here. Make her tell you what she knows. If she really knows nothing, someone may be framing her. Meanwhile, we've been baited and bagged. I can hear the police in the corridor. They are waiting for the superintendent to let them in. If we've been picked off, that means the attack on Op-Center was almost certainly tied to this case. Three men have died so far because of this. Don't underestimate these people. I'm going to leave Paul a message in the Tank. If you find out anything, coordinate through him. Take care, buddy."

Rodgers had stopped walking without realizing it. He stood near the gate as passengers rushed past him, as the world moved around him, as events unfolded that affected him. Yet he felt as though he were not a part of any of it. He put the phone away and looked around for Kat. She was well ahead of him. There was only one exit from Terminal One, and he rushed to catch up with her. They walked past the security checkpoint together.

"We really have to talk," Rodgers said.

"I know."

"No. You don't."

"This is not a good fit," she said.

"I agree. Where I come from, we follow the laws of the land."

She rolled her eyes. "That mantra is getting tired."

"How about a shot of caffeine, then," he said. "Either you were involved in a couple of murders or someone may be trying to pin them on you."

"Yeah. Op-Center."

"No!" Rodgers exclaimed. "Just listen to this."

"To what? Another one of your convoluted theories?"

"No!" Rodgers said. He pulled out his cell phone as they reached the baggage area. While they waited beside the nearest of the three carousels, Rodgers accessed McCaskey's message. He handed her the phone. With an expression that was more contemptuous than interested, she listened to the message. When it was finished, she fired Rodgers a look.

"Your people entered my apartment?" she said with a voice like sharp steel. "Did you know this was going down?"

"I thought they might," he admitted.

Kat smiled tightly. "That's worse," she said. "Much worse. The fact that you knew and didn't tell me."

"We can deal with that later," Rodgers said.

She shook her head. "You and I have nothing to deal

with at all," she said. The steel had superheated and turned molten. "I will take this entire matter up with our attorneys back East." She turned away.

"That is not going to work," Rodgers said, grabbing her arm.

She yanked it away. "If I get loud, airport security won't give a red hot damn about your rank, General."

"You won't do that," Rodgers said. "The papers will want to know what it was all about. I'll tell them."

She relaxed her body but not her expression. The carousel started to turn behind her. "What do you want?"

"I need to convince them of your innocence."

"Them or yourself?"

"Both," he said.

"Since my word is not good enough, what gets me an acquittal?"

"First, what happened to the *Groveburn* bag?" he asked.

"I left it at the office for Lucy."

"Why? The night you had it, you told me your Nikes were in it."

"They were," Kat said. "I also told you it contained a gift. Lucy wanted me to hold it so her boyfriend didn't find it. They live together."

Rodgers could not remember if she said it contained a gift. Maybe she had. "Is it still at the office?"

"I'm in San Diego," Kat said. "How the hell would I know?"

"You can call," Rodgers said.

"Right now."

"Yeah."

Kat's jawline tightened as she took out her cell phone. She called the senator's receptionist and asked about the bag. A moment later, she hung up.

"Lucy came by for it shortly before nine this morning," Kat said.

"After you left the apartment," Rodgers said. "She could have put it inside."

"Right. She just flew in the window like Peter Pan," Kat said. "Was there anything else?"

"Yes. When we get to the hotel, I want to be there when you empty your luggage," Rodgers said.

"Boy, you're pushing this."

"Sorry. I need to know that the dress is not here."

"I could have put it somewhere else, like a safe-deposit box."

"If necessary, we'll get to that later."

"And when you don't find anything anywhere, Op-Center will come up with some other idiotic notion to implicate me," she said. "The admiral is right. Your people are good at that."

That was it. Now she had gone too far. "Our people? You don't know us at all, Kat," Rodgers said. "We're good Americans, part of Senator Orr's America. We have died so people like you can shoot off your mouth. I asked for your help before, and you didn't want to give it. So, yes. We went behind your back. We found a problem, and I presented it to you. And by the way, it looks like someone ratted out 'my people.' The police apparently followed them into your apartment."

"Do you think the police were watching them?" Kat asked.

"Doubtful," Rodgers said. "They know McCaskey is former FBI and that he might have spotted a tail. More than likely they were watching your place."

"Why? How would they have known?"

"I'm guessing that whoever may have put the dress in your freezer, then removed it, tipped them off. Presumably, that someone is Lucy."

"So Lucy O'Connor picked the bag up, put the dress in the ice compartment so it would stain the ice, then removed it," Kat said. "Just so your guy would find the dye and blame me."

"It looks that way," Rodgers said.

"Why?"

"I don't know."

Luggage started sliding down the ramp. Kat turned to the carousel. Her indignation was gone, replaced by introspection. Rodgers stepped beside her.

"You really *are* puzzled by all this," Rodgers said.

"Puzzled, angry, distracted, and trying to get a bead on who is playing who," Kat said. "I know someone is."

"That's true. And accepting that there is a problem here is a start."

"I've known Lucy for years," she said. "I cannot believe she would do this. Hell, I looked in that bag. There was a gift, all wrapped up."

"To make sure you wouldn't open it," Rodgers said.

"Maybe."

Kat reached for her luggage. Rodgers helped her with both bags. His own followed quickly. They went to the taxi stand and stood under a cloudless, rich blue sky. A cool wind blew from the harbor. Rodgers looked toward it. He saw the statue of Charles Lindbergh that stood outside the terminal. It was ironic: a bronze statue of an aviator, and it was free of birds. The world surely was out of kilter.

The line was short, and they were hotel bound within a few minutes. Kat did not speak, and Rodgers did not push her. He would rather have a willing ally than a reluctant one. Five minutes later, they were at the Bay Grand, a mile from the convention center. The lobby was crowded with conventioneers and press. Rodgers and Kat went to the USF registration table and picked up their keys and ID at the VIP station. They were on the same floor, just below Orr's penthouse. The elevator was packed, and the silence between Rodgers and Kat continued. A young reporter from the *Washington Post* recognized the general from the coverage of the United Nations attack. Rodgers said he was here in an advisory capacity to Senator Orr. The reporter asked for a comment about the attack on Op-Center. Rodgers said it was abhorrent. He declined to say more. It was fascinating to him how the other conversations in the small carriage winked out as the journalist asked his questions. The delegates did not handle eavesdropping with the slick, multitasking skill of a Washingtonian. A veteran politician or journalist or society kingpin could be at a restaurant or party and not miss a syllable of his own conversation while skimming half a dozen others that might be going on around him. It was not a talent Rodgers had ever admired. He preferred the wide-eyed silence of his fellow passengers.

Kat turned to him when they reached her door. Rodgers's room was two doors beyond it.

"I still think this whole thing is ridiculous. There is some other, very simple explanation," Kat told Rodgers. "But if you want to go through my luggage, I won't stop you."

"Thanks. But there is something I want more than that," he replied. "I want your help. I want to find out if anyone on the USF team is behind these crimes."

Kat laughed humorlessly. "General, I just said I thought this was ridiculous. Why would I want to be part of it?"

"You're already part of it," he pointed out.

"Because some former G-man busted into my apartment and found blue ice?" she asked. "Because the police may have been following him and are likely to arrest him? Detective Howell is a friend of our office. He was not happy to see the case turned over to Op-Center."

That remark took Rodgers by surprise. "What do you mean, he's a friend of your office?"

"The detective admires Senator Orr. He did not approve of the way hearsay had become Op-Center's marching orders," she said.

"Has Howell been promised anything?" Rodgers asked. "Directorship of the FBI, anything like that?"

"No, though the defense secretary post might be vacant real soon."

Rodgers ignored the dig. "Are you sure he has been offered nothing?"

"Yes. Some people do things out of principle."

"In D.C., very few. You happen to be talking to one of the two I know."

"Am I?" She inserted the key card in the lock. "The man *I've* gotten to know, General, is suspicious bordering on paranoid. I'm beginning to wonder how you ever passed the Op-Center psych evaluation."

"We're paid to be paranoid," he replied. "That's what allows people like you to sleep nights."

"I sleep fine," she said as the green light flashed. She opened the door.

"How is Howell when he calls? Comfortable? Surreptitious? Vague?"

"Cautious," she replied. "*That* is certainly not uncommon in Washington."

"I'm missing something here," he said. "Some connection. Was Howell in the navy?"

"I don't know," Kat said as she hefted her bags into the room. She turned on the light and held the door open for a moment. Kat had obviously had enough. "Was there something else?" she asked. "You want to frisk me, go through my luggage?"

"You have anything to hide?" he asked, nodding at the bags.

"I'm not hiding anything from you right now," she said contemptuously.

Rodgers hesitated. Even if he found the dress it wouldn't prove anything. The luggage was brought to the airport in one van. Someone could have placed it there. "General Rodgers, please call if you need something.

Something that has to do with the USF. That is, if you're still interested in working with us."

Rodgers looked at her. Her bright eyes were sad as she shut the door. He started toward his own room. He noted the stairwell was right beside his room with a security camera above it. He wondered if Link had put him here on purpose, so the admiral could watch him.

Rodgers hoped not. He hoped a lot of things. He hoped he was wrong about Howell. Maybe the Metro Police detective was just sucking up to someone in power. That was prevalent in D.C. But then why would he have been watching McCaskey? Professional jealousy? A turf war? Or maybe he was just watching Kat's apartment and happened to see McCaskey go in. Howell may have known about the reporter being at the hotel that night.

Chances were good he would not be able to talk to McCaskey. Instead, Rodgers went to his room, sat on the bed, and entered a stored number on his cell phone. There was only one person he trusted to figure this one out.

The other man of principle Rodgers knew.

FORTY-THREE

Washington, D.C.
Wednesday, 3:44 P.M.

Bob Herbert was delighted to hear from Mike Rodgers. It was the only familiar aspect in a suddenly surreal situation, and for a moment, just a heartbeat, it sounded and felt like old times.

"How am I?" Herbert said in response to Rodgers's question. "I'm sitting in the parking lot, breathing non–machine-filtered air, which I happen to prefer to that dry, metallic-tasting crud in the Tank, working on a laptop I borrowed from—get this—the head cook in the Andrews commissary cafeteria. I had to create my own files between the Tuesday lunch menu and the recipe for Brigadier General Chrysler's favorite pie. Which is cherry, if you were wondering. My calls are being routed to a cell phone belonging to Jason Shuffler in accounting. He was parked outside the hit zone, and it was in his car. A bonus to being a peon."

Herbert was rambling, and he knew it. But it had been a long, rough day with no time to vent. Under the best of circumstances there was no one he felt completely comfortable with other than Mike or Darrell, and Darrell was not available. So Mike got the first big hit. Herbert took a short breath to calm himself, sucked his self-styled debriefing back down, and went to the above-the-fold news.

"Meanwhile, the cops have Darrell and Maria at the precinct," Herbert told Rodgers. "They were arrested for breaking and entering."

"I heard."

"Darrell made his one call to Paul, who shipped Lowell over there to get him out. Paul briefed me. Anything new out there?"

"My sixth sense is tingling," Rodgers said. "I need to know more about Detective Robert Howell."

"Funny you should ask."

"Why?" Rodgers asked.

"I happen to have his dossier on the computer," Herbert said. "I was looking for something in his background, something we might use to help get Darrell and Maria out of the cooler."

"What possible tie could he have to Link or the senator?"

"Maybe he's just a senate groupie," Herbert suggested.

"That's what Kat said," Rodgers told him.

"But you don't believe her because—?"

"She said it."

"Great. But do you have a better reason?" Herbert asked.

"No. Like I said, just a feeling."

"Okay," Herbert said. He adjusted the screen so it was angled away from the sun. "The detective is not married, he did not come from Texas, he has a record that would make Baden-Powell jealous. He served in the coast guard and—"

"Not married," Rodgers said. "Is he divorced?"

"No."

"Girlfriend?"

"There's nothing in the file," Herbert said.

"Shit," Rodgers said.

"What?" Herbert asked.

"I wonder if it could be blackmail."

Herbert scowled. "That's a pretty big leap."

"I've been told I make a lot of those," Rodgers said. "Is there anything in the dossier that is listed as eyes only?"

"No."

"So it may not be part of his civilian record. Can you get Howell's military records? If I go through channels, it will take days."

"I can probably go through Andrews—"

"That will take time," Rodgers said. "We don't have that."

"—or I can ask Matt," Herbert replied. "He's working on getting things running downstairs."

"Please do," Rodgers said. "This is important."

"I'm all over it, like ugly on an ape," the intelligence chief told him. "I'll call you back."

"Thanks."

Like ugly on an ape? Herbert thought as he clicked off and called downstairs to the Tank. Either he was severely overtired or the fresh air was doing funny things to his head.

Herbert asked Bugs Benet to send Matt Stoll up to parking spot 710. Stoll was upstairs in five minutes. He was grateful for the fresh air.

"The smell of fried copper wire is still pretty thick down in the sulfur pit," the portly scientist complained.

Stoll accessed the United States Coast Guard secure personnel files in ten minutes. Shortly after that, he pulled up an eyes-only file for Lieutenant Robert Howell. It was from 1989, a formal report by a hearing officer regarding an incident on the newly commissioned cutter *Orcas* stationed in Coos Bay, Oregon.

"Holy Christmas," Herbert said as he read the file.

"What have we got?" Stoll asked.

"A Get Out of Jail Free card for the McCaskeys, for one thing," Herbert replied.

The intelligence chief thanked Stoll and sent the reluctant wunderkind back to the sulfur pit. He immediately got on the phone with Mike Rodgers. The "suspicious" Mike Rodgers. The big-leap-taking Mike Rodgers.

The correct Mike Rodgers.

FORTY-FOUR

San Diego, California
Wednesday, 1:00 P.M.

Eric Stone had told the reception desk to let him know when Mike Rodgers arrived. Stone had not met Rodgers. But Kat had called to say she was concerned about his loyalties. That amplified the discomfort Stone felt over the fact that the general was still working with the people who were investigating the USF. Rodgers was a patriot, but not of the extremist mold like Senator Orr. Stone wanted to have a talk with him. More importantly, he wanted to look into Rodgers's eyes and see where his loyalties lay. Stone was very good at reading expressions. It was a talent he discovered while working as a waiter. He knew the exact moment there was an opportunistic break in a conversation so he could offer a tray of hors d'oeuvres. He knew from partygoers' expressions, from the way their eyes moved, who liked their egg rolls crispy, their meat skewers rare, and who did not like sushi. He could tell from the vaguely embarrassed manner who was going to take more than one or two cocktail wieners. He evolved those skills working for Admiral Link, watching the fearful or indignant or occasionally dangerous expressions of the servicemen and dignitaries, politicians and civilians who came to visit. Mike Rodgers was an unknown quantity to him.

Until Stone saw him in the corridor of the hotel. The general was just leaving his room. Stone wanted to get a quick sense of what he was about. From appearances, Rodgers was one hundred percent military. Admiral Link was that way, too. But the admiral was offense, and this man was defense. Stone could tell from the set of his head. It was not upright but tilted back slightly, presenting the chin. He was expecting a blow, yet the square set of his shoulder said he was ready for it.

"General Rodgers?" Stone asked as he approached.

"Yes?"

"Eric Stone," said the young man.

"Pleased to meet you, Eric," Rodgers said.

Stone offered his hand. The general shook it firmly though not too hard. He was a man who did not have to prove his strength.

"Did you have a good trip?" Stone asked.

"Yes, thank you."

Rodgers is formal, guarded, Stone thought. He wondered why. "You know, General, I have a bunch of steaks on the grill right now, so I can only stay a minute. But I hope we will have a chance to talk before things get under way."

"I look forward to that," Rodgers replied.

"I also hope all of this will be a positive experience for you, a welcome distraction," Stone went on. "I heard what happened at Op-Center. Just terrible. How long before operations can be resumed?"

"They're running now," Rodgers replied.

"At full capacity?"

"Full enough," Rodgers replied. "Op-Center has always been about the people, not the technology."

"Heart, not hardware," Stone remarked.

Rodgers nodded once in agreement.

"That's good to hear. We believe in that, too," Stone said, raising a fist in a show of solidarity, "which is why the senator and the admiral are convinced you will be an enormous asset to the party and to a future Orr administration. I hope you are still enthusiastic."

"More than ever," Rodgers replied.

"Truly?" The general's tone seemed a little too affirmative. It almost seemed like a challenge or a threat.

"Don't interpret quiet observation as disinterest," Rodgers said. "Contemplation moves power from here," he held up a hand, "to here," he touched a finger to his temple. "It does not lessen a man's strength."

"Ah. That is the scholar talking," Stone observed. He knew that Mike Rodgers held a doctorate in world history. The general had obtained it after two combat tours of Vietnam.

"To tell the truth, Eric, it's more of the soldier in me," Rodgers said. "I have participated in a number of wars and conflicts. I learned that if one moves too enthusiastically, he could put his foot on a land mine."

"I guess I was lucky," Stone said. "When I wore my country's uniform, we were at peace. We were always wary but unafraid. We were also optimistic, whatever the situation, whatever the alert status."

"I am always optimistic," Rodgers assured the younger man.

"Really?" Stone clasped him on the shoulder and laughed. "Forgive me, General, but you look as though you came for a funeral."

Rodgers fixed his eyes on Stone. "Actually, this is not my funeral face," he said. "If you want to see that, you will have to be with me on Saturday."

"Saturday? What is happening then?" Stone asked.

"We bury Mac McCallie," Rodgers said. "He died in the e-bomb blast at Op-Center."

"Oh. I am sorry," Stone said, removing his hand. "I have been rather tied up here. I had not heard there were casualties."

That was a lie. Stone knew everything about the explosion he had ordered. And he was furious at himself for the funeral comment. It proved Rodgers's point about careless haste causing problems. It gave the general a moral victory.

It gave Mike Rodgers first blood.

"As for being unafraid, Eric, fear has never driven me to be cautious or watchful," Rodgers went on. His tone was more aggressive now. What had begun as Stone sizing up the general had been turned around, like a classic military counteraction. "The apparent lack of chaos does that. It is always there, hidden. Disraeli said that peace has occasioned more wars than the most ruthless conquerors. Peace makes us complacent. We stop looking over our shoulder. One job of any leader is to sniff out that lurking danger. To stir it up if necessary, to free it so it can be crushed."

"That sounds like warmongering," Stone said.

"It is," Rodgers replied proudly. "I have always felt it is better to flush out the enemy before he has a chance to power up."

"While you are sniffing and flushing, do you also look over your shoulder?" Stone asked. "Do you know what is behind you right now?" His own tone was slightly confrontational now, but he did not care.

"I do know what is there," Rodgers said. "A fire escape and a hotel security camera." He smiled. "I like to know where the exits are."

Stone did not like this conversation or the turn it had just taken. He could not tell if Rodgers was still being philosophical or whether he was baiting Stone with references to the chaos of the past few days. What Rodgers did not say was also informative. He had mentioned nothing about Op-Center's investigation or the arrest of Darrell and Maria McCaskey. He knew, of course. When Detective Howell arrested the couple, he noted that the last number dialed on McCaskey's cell phone belonged to Mike Rodgers. Stone wanted to find out more about that if he could.

Quickly.

"You know, General, this is not the conversation I expected to have the first time we met." Stone laughed. "But it does interest me. In fact, if you have a minute, all I need to do is grab my laptop from the room. Then we can go over to the convention center together. I would appreciate your input."

"I would prefer to meet you there," Rodgers said. "There are a few things I have to do first."

"I can wait if you'd like."

"Your steaks will burn," Rodgers said. "I'll catch up with you. Maybe we can have a drink later."

"I would like that," Stone replied.

The convention manager continued down the corridor to his room. As he opened the door, he glanced to his left. Rodgers went to Kat's door and knocked. He did not attempt to conceal it. Was that innocent or meant to inspire concern? Stone could not be sure, and that frustrated him. More than the conversation, Stone did not like the man himself. Rodgers had launched salvos from his moral high ground. When Link spoke, it was with persuasive authority. This man lectured, as if there was no correct opinion other than his own.

Not that it mattered. He had learned what he needed to learn.

Mike Rodgers was not an ally. And if he was not an ally, then moderate or not, war hero notwithstanding, there was only one thing he could be: an enemy.

FORTY-FIVE

San Diego, California
Wednesday, 1:16 P.M.

When Mike Rodgers was thirteen years old, a local Connecticut YMCA organized chess games against a local grand master. Rodgers got to play one of those games, and won. The reason he won was simple: apart from knowing how to move the pieces, Rodgers had no concept of chess strategy. As his opening move, he developed the pawn that sat in relative anonymity in front of the queen's rook. He liked rooks—or castles, as he preferred to call them. That sounded more militaristic. He liked their sweep, their power. He wanted to get them out of their corner and ready for the fray. The grand master responded with Sokolsky's opening. But Rodgers's unorthodox move, located so far from the center of the board, unbalanced virtually every classic attack pattern for black. The grand master resigned the match after sixteen chaotic moves.

As Rodgers knocked at Kat's door, he had to admit that what Eric Stone had just mounted was the clumsiest, most amateurish psy-ops probe he had ever experienced. In and of itself, it made Rodgers doubt that these people could be responsible for any kind of conspiracy. Yet, in a way, that was also what made them dangerous. They fit no profiles. They were unpredictable.

Kat answered the door. She was impatient, from her eyes to the cock of her hips. "Yes, General?"

"I need to talk to you," he said. He walked around her and entered the room.

"By all means," she said sarcastically. "Come in."

"Sorry, but I did not want to stand there discussing this with Eric Stone watching and possibly listening."

Kat let the door shut. "Why would Eric be listening? Could it be he is worried that you're a loose cannon, dangerous to have at the convention?"

"No. He thinks I am concealing information. And he's right."

"What information?"

"That Detective Howell is being framed, and Stone may be involved in that," Rodgers said.

"Framed how, and to do what?"

"He was tipped off to be at your apartment," Rodgers said. "As for how—about fifteen years ago, he had an affair with a fellow coast guard cadet."

"So he's gay. Who cares?"

"That isn't quite the entirety of it," Rodgers said. "The other young man obviously had second thoughts and claimed he was seduced. Howell took the rap. Because Howell had seniority, the affair was deemed consensual by virtue of force majeure, a mild reprimand, but it went on Howell's psych profile, which was sealed."

"Until someone opened it."

"Yes," Rodgers said. "Someone who had access to military files."

"Meaning Admiral Link."

"Perhaps," Rodgers admitted. "Since I doubt the admiral would tell us whether this is true, there is only one way to find out. We have to ask Detective Howell."

"Why do you need me to do that?" Kat asked.

"I am not convinced he is playing entirely on Op-Center's side," Rodgers said. "If I call him, he probably won't say anything. If you call, he may. Especially if you call saying that you decline to press charges against Darrell McCaskey and his wife."

"Why would I do that?" Kat asked. "They broke into my apartment."

"They did not really have a choice," Rodgers pointed out. "They thought you might be involved in this."

"And now they don't? *You* don't?"

"I am hoping you are not," Rodgers said. "This would be a good way to strengthen that hope."

"You know, I was supposed to be downstairs five minutes ago, meeting with reporters about the campaign," she said. "But you made me so upset I couldn't even do that. *Now* you want me to help you with this mad chase of yours. I really wish all of this would just go away."

"Me, too," Rodgers said. "I was supposed to be downstairs auditioning for secretary of defense. Instead, I'm up here begging you to help me fight a battle that is not even mine."

"Nor mine, General," Kat said. With an angry huff she walked to the bed and fished her cell phone from under her coat. "Let's be done with this damn thing. What is Howell's number?"

Rodgers pointed to the phone on the night table. "Would you mind using that one, on speaker? I would like to hear."

"Fine," she said. "Why the hell not? Let's really humiliate the guy."

Rodgers gave her the main switchboard of the Metro Police, which was the only one he knew. They put her through.

"Detective Howell, this is Kat Lockley," she said. "I'm on a speaker phone. General Mike Rodgers of Op-Center is here with me."

She made a point of emphasizing Op-Center, to show the general that she did not consider him to be on her team. Rodgers had taken many rough knocks in his career. He would survive this one.

"Ms. Lockley, I was going to call you," Howell said. "I

suppose you have heard we found two Op-Center agents in your apartment. We arrested them for breaking and entering."

"Yes. I do not think I want to press charges, however," she said.

"Pardon me?"

"We can discuss that later. Right now, the general feels there is something more important we need to talk about."

"What is that?"

"Please excuse me for asking, Detective, but General Rodgers says he has reason to believe that you are being blackmailed."

There was a long, guilty hesitation. Kat looked at Rodgers. She was sitting on the pillows beside the nightstand, and he was standing at the foot of the bed. The distance had seemed vast a few moments ago. Now it evaporated.

"General, I have another call," Howell said. "Can you give me a moment?"

"I can."

Whether there was or was not another caller did not matter. Rodgers gave him the "moment." Howell returned in under half a minute.

"What makes you think I'm being blackmailed?" Howell asked.

"Are you?" Rodgers asked.

"Would you answer my question, sir?"

"We wondered about the snare Mr. and Mrs. McCaskey walked into," Rodgers said. "The timing was too neat. Someone went to the apartment with evidence to frame Ms. Lockley, our team entered, then you showed up."

"You assume we were not watching the apartment."

"If you were, you would have nabbed the first person who went in," Rodgers pointed out.

"General, this is not a conversation I wish to have."

"I understand," Rodgers said. "But you have to understand something as well. Op-Center was attacked. A coworker died—"

"I know. I'm sorry."

"Others have died as well. We are going to stop this. I do not have to tell you what will happen if you are implicated in any way."

There was a soft snicker on the other end. "Who was the one just asking me about blackmail?"

"This is internal affairs followed by due process," Rodgers said. "That's very different."

"Detective, I have always thought highly of you. I need you to tell me something, truthfully," Kat said suddenly. "Is General Rodgers hallucinating, or am I the one who is not seeing reality? Am I involved with bad people?"

For the third time, Detective Howell was silent. Kat's brow creased, and her mouth sagged at the edges. Rodgers shifted his eyes to the painting over the bed. It was a lithograph of a Spanish vessel in San Diego Bay when it was still a Spanish settlement. There were people gathered onshore as a bumboat approached. The name of the painting was *Aguardar Noticias Del Hogar.*

Awaiting News from Home.

Rodgers marveled at how different the world was, how different life was, when people had to wait weeks for an answer to a question like that. It was the reason men of great wisdom and even greater instinct had to be put in the field.

"I think that answers my question," Kat said sullenly.

"Detective, talk to us," Rodgers said. "If Ms. Lockley is correct, let us help. Whatever this is, we can fix it."

"No," Howell said. "I made my choices. I will live with them. But I do want you to know that I had no idea Op-Center was going to get hit."

"Did the same people do it?" Rodgers pressed.

"I don't know," he admitted.

"What *do* you know?" Kat asked.

"Only that someone, a man, phoned one day."

"When?" Rodgers asked.

"Two and a half weeks ago. He had information about my service record that could have ended my police career if it were revealed. I was told the information would be removed from my record if I cooperated."

"What did this cooperation entail?" Rodgers asked.

"He didn't say," Howell replied.

Of course not, Rodgers thought. That might have made him an accomplice to murder, far less desirable than a career scandal. "What did he ask for when he *did* say?" Rodgers asked.

There was a final silence, but it was brief. "At first, just a level-one autopsy," Howell replied.

"What is that?" Kat asked.

"The body goes in and out, no fine-tooth comb," Howell said. "Your people wanted Wilson off the slab and out of the country, Ms. Lockley. They *said* it was to get attention from the senator as soon as possible. That sounded reasonable. It was apparently a heart attack. I saw no harm in helping to rush things along."

"You said 'at first,' " Rodgers pointed out.

"Yeah. I did that one as a favor. Then your Mr. McCaskey came along and found out it was murder," Howell said. "At that point, I had already committed a departmental infraction. I might have been able to smooth that one over. But then they hit me with the other thing."

"The service record," Kat said.

"This is a scary town," Howell said. "You both know that. I did not want to end up a small-town sheriff somewhere, and I hoped—no, I prayed—that Darrell McCaskey could smoke these boys out."

"He still can," Rodgers said. "Ms. Lockley isn't pressing charges. Let him go. Help him."

"How?"

"That depends. Did you get the sense that these crimes were part of a larger operation?"

"Probably," Howell said. "They told me I would be informed when my 'interface,' as they put it, was no longer required. I received no such notification."

"So more killings may be planned," Rodgers said. "Detective, are you able to contact them?"

"No. I don't even know who I was talking to. Their ID was blocked."

"It was someone who had access to your service record," Rodgers said.

"Correct."

"So that means it could have been Link," Rodgers said. He did not think the admiral was the point man, however. That would be too risky. "When was the last time you spoke with this person?"

"Just now," Howell said. "He wanted to know if anyone had been asking about the case."

"How recently is 'just now'?" Rodgers asked.

"Right before you called," Howell said. "I hung up on him to talk to you."

Rodgers felt a chill. It was not fear. It was like an electrical current flowing along his neck as his brain started making connections. He wished that he had a firearm. Or an EM bomb, something that would shut everything down until he could have a thorough look around.

"Detective, did you tell the man that we were on the other line?" Rodgers asked.

"Yes," Howell replied. "He asked."

"All right. I need two favors, Detective," Rodgers said. "I need you to release the McCaskeys."

"I cannot do that without the proper documents," Howell said. "I will fax them to Ms. Lockley—"

"There is no time for that," Rodgers protested. "Come on, Detective. You know they are not criminals. Call it a false arrest and let them go. Say they had permission to be on the premises."

"They did," Kat said impulsively. "I said it was okay."

"All right," Howell said. "What is the second favor?"

"If your guy calls back, try to find out who he is," Rodgers said. He started moving toward the door. "Let Darrell know."

"I will," Howell said.

"Thanks. Talk to you later."

Kat terminated the call as Rodgers jogged along the short entranceway. He stopped by the front door and listened. He heard nothing. Kat had followed. She stood at the other end of the small hallway.

"What's wrong?" she asked.

"I'm not sure. I want you to stay here," Rodgers said.

"Why?"

"Because I'm going out, and there may be trouble," Rodgers said. "If there is, I need someone who can bail me out."

"What kind of trouble?"

"I have no idea," Rodgers said as he cracked the door. "But there is one thing I do know. What happened in Washington was just the preliminary. The big show is going to be here."

FORTY-SIX

Washington, D.C.
Wednesday, 4:42 P.M.

There is an impunity that comes with being once-removed from danger. A lock on the door. A police officer on the beat. A man of influence standing between you and those who want to hurt you.

In each case, it is an illusion. Darrell McCaskey knew that from his years at the FBI. He was betting that the young and inexperienced Lucy O'Connor did not. Before the afternoon was over, she would.

McCaskey and his wife had been released from the holding cell at the First District Substation. Detective Howell personally drove them to their car, which had been taken to the DMV impound lot at 65 K Street NE. The detective called ahead to have it released and waiting.

Howell was surprisingly forthcoming about what had happened. McCaskey felt as though he had suddenly been drafted as father confessor. Not that he minded, as long as he did not have to keep any of the intelligence a secret.

McCaskey did not judge the man. Fear and self-preservation always colored people's reactions. On the FBI he had seen countless crimes of passion that were conceived, executed, and regretted within the space of five minutes. That did not absolve the perpetrator, but McCaskey understood the drive.

McCaskey was sitting beside his wife in the backseat of Howell's car. When the detective was finished, Mc-

Caskey asked him what he expected in exchange for his cooperation.

"A way back out," Howell said plaintively.

"That may not be so easy. When we get these people, you know they will finger you," McCaskey pointed out.

"I know they'll try," the detective said. "I've been thinking. I can pretty much cover my own actions. If you two will say that I was working undercover and feeding you information from the start, that will neutralize their charges."

"When you cornered us in the apartment, you did not give us the option to explain things to you," Maria said angrily.

"They had me on a leash," Howell said. "I'm sorry."

"If General Rodgers did not call, we would be standing in front of your district attorney right now instead of driving to our car," she went on.

"I would have found a way to make this go away," Howell said.

"You say that as if it is an upset stomach," Maria said. "This would have been with us the rest of our lives."

"Yes, but in fairness, you did enter the woman's apartment unlawfully."

"We picked a lock to get a leg-up on something big and ugly," McCaskey interjected. "On the Richter scale of crimes, that is one point zero."

"Look, I already said I screwed up," Howell told him. "Hell, I screwed up in the military, too, which is what got me in this fix. What I did then wasn't even a crime. The tribunal made it one to give some punk kid absolution for feeling guilty about consensual sex."

"A punk kid," Maria said. "You mean a boy? A man?"

Howell nodded as they pulled up to the lot. "I took the hit for him because I knew what he was going through. I cared about him. I could have appealed the decision, but I didn't. Then these bastards dig it out and throw it back at me. I felt—only for a moment, but that was long enough—that I had earned myself a free pass for one future misdeed. This one. If I thought it would grow into what it did, I would never have agreed to help them. It was wrong. If you help me, I can make amends through continued public service. I've done a damn good job till now. If not, I'll atone in prison, which doesn't help anyone." He looked back at McCaskey. "The blue line, Darrell. Stick with me on this one. Please."

McCaskey opened the door and stepped out. He walked around to the driver's side. Howell rolled down the window.

"If I did what you asked, I would not be able to look Mac McCallie's widow in the eyes," McCaskey told him. "I will fight for you, Detective, I promise. But I will not lie for you."

Howell's face flushed, but he did not reply. He simply rolled up the window and drove away.

Maria took her husband's hand. "You did the right thing," she said. "I am proud of you."

"Boy, I wish that made it all better." He sighed. He watched the detective's car as it turned the corner.

As afraid as Howell had been when he made that decision, McCaskey imagined it faded to insignificance beside the fear and loneliness he was feeling now. He wished there had been another way out. Maybe he should have bucked it up to Paul.

"Or maybe he should have behaved himself," Maria said.

"What?"

"I know you," Maria said. "You are standing there wishing this all could have been different. Detective Howell made his choices. People died. He has to live with the consequences."

"I know," McCaskey said. "You know, I love what I do, but I there are times I hate what I *have* to do."

Maria gripped his hand more tightly and gave him a quick, reassuring smile.

The couple went and got their car. They nosed into the thickening traffic of rush hour.

There was little McCaskey could do for Robert Howell but, ironically, there was still one thing he could do for Mac McCallie. And McCaskey intended to do it.

He would find and punish the people who put this tragedy in motion.

FORTY-SEVEN

San Diego, California
Wednesday, 2:02 P.M.

No sooner had Rodgers entered the hallway than Kat ran after him.

"General, I have work to do," she said. "I can't stay here."

"You have to," he said. "I don't know who is at risk and, more important, by helping someone, you may be an accessory to a criminal conspiracy."

"I cannot believe the senator is behind this."

"You cannot prove he is not," Rodgers said. "Please. I don't have time to debate this. I need to do some checking."

"I'll wait an hour," she said. "No more."

Rodgers did not answer. For all he knew, Kat Lockley would leave the room as soon as he was out of sight. Rodgers did not know whether she was truly blameless or just feigning innocence. Before heading downstairs, he stopped and pounded on Eric Stone's door. There was no answer. He did not know where the convention manager was or what he might be planning. There was a lot Rodgers did not know. Too damn much, in fact.

Rodgers took the stairs to the lobby. That was not a consideration for personal security. If McCaskey called, Rodgers did not want to be standing hip-to-hip with nosy USF delegates.

The general reached the courtyard, which was encircled by tall, slender palm trees and brilliantly lit by a peach-colored sun. People were moving in all directions, and cars were stacked two deep in the sweeping entranceway. This was not the way to find Eric Stone. He went back inside to the registration desk and asked if anyone there had seen him. They said they had not. Rodgers did not believe they would have been told to lie. Stone had not come this way. He thought of checking the hotel security camera but decided that knowing where Stone had been was not going to help him right now. Rodgers had to find out where Stone was going.

Rodgers went back outside. He looked over at the convention center. It was probably a circus by now, with conventioneers arriving for free lunch followed by the opening speeches. Mobile media vans were outside, recording the event. It might be possible to use their multiple camera feeds to try to spot Stone. Since it was all Rodgers had, he decided to give it a try.

"General?"

Someone was standing behind him. He turned. It was Stone. He was holding a walkie-talkie and wearing a smile. Faint but sharp-edged voices crackled from the handheld device, the cross-talk of convention workers.

There was a move in the chaos gambit, Rodgers thought. *An unexpected move that took control of the board.* What Rodgers did not know was whether it was the luck of a novice or the seasoned improvisational skills of a professional.

"I understand you were looking for me?" Stone said, smiling.

"I was," Rodgers said.

"What can I do for you?"

Rodgers looked around. "First of all, how did you know where I was?" the general asked. He was trying to spot the nearest surveillance camera or a tail.

"General, there was nothing conspiratorial." Stone laughed. "The desk supervisor said you went this way. I knew what you were wearing and got lucky."

Rodgers did not buy that. One of the hundreds of people surrounding them could have been watching him. Perhaps someone in a hotel window.

"So what is it you wanted?" Stone pressed.

Rodgers regarded the younger man. He looked at his posture, at his expression, at his hands. "I spoke with Detective Howell of the Metro Police in D.C.," Rodgers informed him. "He told me he is being blackmailed by someone in your camp. I want to know who and why."

"That's ridiculous," Stone said. "The detective bungled an investigation. He needed someone to blame. He picked us. Maybe someone is putting him up to it; maybe he has a personal vendetta. All I can tell you is that he is wasting our time. Now, if that is all you need to know—"

"No, there's more. I want to know what the endgame is."

"To elect a president," Stone replied. He frowned and looked around. "Where is Kat, by the way? Did you see her?"

"I saw her."

"She's supposed to be with reporters, talking about the campaign."

"She's taking some personal time," Rodgers said. He moved closer. "Talk to me, dammit."

"I am."

"No. You're playing. There's smug in your smile, in your eyes, but you're still lying to me."

"Excuse me?"

"Tension displacement. When you're wound tight, it has to come out somewhere. Your fingertips are white. You're squeezing that walkie-talkie like it's a rubber stress ball. The pressure of all those steaks, is that what it is?"

"Yes, General. Look, I'll have to talk to you some other time—"

"You will talk now," Rodgers said.

"What you're doing makes no sense, do you realize that?" Stone protested. "Think about it. If I were guilty of a terrible crime, would I stand here and confess to you? Do you think you're that good a bully?"

"I can be," Rodgers said.

"Security would have your face pressed to the asphalt in about ten seconds," Stone assured him. "And I would have you incarcerated for assault, with no sad sack detective to bail you out."

Rodgers's gaze sharpened. "How did you know that?"

"What?"

"That Howell let the McCaskeys go."

"I didn't," Stone said.

It hit Rodgers a moment before he heard it. Voices were shouting from the walkie-talkie, inarticulate in their shrill and overlapping communiqués.

Stone raised the unit. "This is Stone. What's going on?"

"Something happened," someone said.

"What?"

"The admiral," the speaker said. His voice was hesitant, uneasy. "He left the hotel from the back exit, but he never made it to the convention center."

"It's only a mile!" Stone said. "Have you called the driver?" he asked as he reached for his own cell phone.

"We did. There's no answer. The admiral doesn't answer his phone, either."

"Is security on this?"

"They called 911 and asked for an aerial search to see if they can find the limousine."

"Tell security I'll be right there," Stone said angrily. He speed-dialed a number as he started jogging back toward the hotel.

Rodgers followed, also running.

"Kat, it's Eric," he said after a moment. "Something has happened. I need you to get downstairs and run the press."

The men entered the lobby. Word of a possible abduction was spreading. People had stopped whatever they were doing and were looking around, asking anyone with a

Staff badge for information. Stone ignored them all as he rushed by. The men walked past the elevators to a corridor lined with shops. The rear entrance was at the end of the carpeted hallway.

As Stone briefed Kat, Rodgers examined the feeling he had experienced just before the walkie-talkie came to life. A sense that had suddenly changed Rodgers's perception of what he thought was beginner's luck, a chaos gambit.

He no longer believed that Stone was an amateur. Neither was his boss, whoever that was. Someone had profiled Rodgers. They had understood exactly how the general would act and react to everything they did. Stone knew that Rodgers would seek him out in San Diego. He knew that, after their first talk, after McCaskey's arrest, Rodgers would tell Kat to stay out of the way for a while. Stone also knew that when he finally presented himself to Rodgers, the general would push for information.

In short, the son of a bitch Stone had been stalling him.

FORTY-EIGHT

Washington, D.C.
Wednesday, 5:47 P.M.

The sun was sinking low, and there was a chill in the air. The odor of diesel fuel wafted thinly from the aircraft at the base. It reminded Herbert of when he and his wife, Yvonne, used to be at a military airfield in some foreign land, waiting to be airlifted to or from a mission for the Company.

The light, the smell, the taste of the air reminded him in particular of the field at the U.S. air base in Ramstein, Germany. That was where he and Yvonne had their last meal before heading to Beirut, where she died and he lost the use of his legs. They had gone to the base commissary, grabbed a couple of sandwiches and coffees, and took a card table onto the field. It was a little too windy for candles, so they used a menorah the quartermaster had in storage. It was the best grilled cheese and coleslaw Herbert ever had. Yvonne never looked more beautiful and heroic to him. What a role model she had been. Always pushing him and herself to do a better job. She was convinced that whatever they did in Lebanon could help to bring peace to the region.

It did, to the nearly three hundred U.S. troops who died in the embassy bombing. Including Yvonne.

It was difficult for Herbert not to crash, burn, and smoulder for hours whenever that day came upon him—typically by surprise, like a mugger. It could be a song

Yvonne might have been listening to on the trip over. It could be a feeling in the air, like now. Even the smell of grilled cheese took him back. All Herbert could do was swallow the awful lump, concentrate on what he was doing, and get the hell out of that bittersweet place. Yesterday's EM explosion made the feeling even more immediate.

Stopping bad guys usually worked. That was what Herbert was trying to do now. The problem at the moment was not just wrestling down memories of Yvonne but fighting off the desire to hurt Paul Hood. As his grandfather used to put it back in Mississippi, he wished he could "sock him in the snot box and shake loose some intelligence." The firing of Mike Rodgers offended him like nothing else in the past quarter century. When this was over, Herbert would have to decide if he could still work with the man. The way he was feeling, maybe he and Mike should open their own version of Murder, Inc. Something like, Revenge, Inc. He even had the slogan. "You pay, then *they* pay." That would give them both a chance to act out in grand style.

For now, though, he had to find out what he could about Lucy O'Connor. Darrell had called to say that he and Maria were headed to her apartment. If she was not there—and McCaskey did not expect her to be—he needed to know where she could have gone.

"There is one thing about her you should know," Herbert told him.

"What is that?" McCaskey asked.

"She was busted while she was a student at Carnegie-Mellon," Herbert informed him.

"For what?"

"Riding the horse," Herbert said.

"Lucy was a heroin addict?"

"That's what the Pittsburgh PD records say," Herbert said. "Did six months in the pokey, where she went through rehab."

"Impossible. That would have showed up on her background check," McCaskey said. "She never would have been allowed near Congress."

"Unless someone had the file buried and told her one day there would be payback," Herbert said. "A real-life Don Corleone."

"Orr or Link," McCaskey said. "So how did you find the record?"

"I didn't," Herbert said. "Routine check of her college years turned up a bust at the frat house where Lucy lived. Her name wasn't mentioned. I called one of the kids who did time. She said, hell, yeah, Lucy was with her in the clink."

"She would have known how to give the injections," McCaskey said. "That's one more reason to believe she is the killer."

"Most likely. You're an aspiring journalist who screwed up, someone rescues you, gives you all kinds of access—there are people who would kill to protect that," Herbert said. "There are people who have killed for less."

"True, though I'm not going to sign on to that until I talk to the woman," McCaskey said.

"I agree."

"Speaking of which, if we don't find her at home, you have any suggestions where we should try next?" McCaskey asked.

"I sent Stephen Viens over to the NRO," Herbert said. "He's got an hour on the Auto-Search program in the Domestic Surveillance Platform."

The DSP was a new Homeland Security satellite. It was located in a geostationary orbit and kept pointed on the metro D.C. area. It had the ability to pinpoint cars by shape, weight, and the specific configuration of the dashboard electronics. Once spotted, the onboard camera could zoom in to read the license number. If suspicious individuals were seen getting into a particular vehicle or renting a specific car, the DSP could find and track them with relative ease.

"How did Viens swing time on that?" McCaskey asked. "The DSP is Homeland's baby."

"All I know is that Paul made a call," Herbert told him. "He got us the hour."

"Impressive," McCaskey said.

"I guess someone figured they owed us one or else felt sorry for us," Herbert said. "Anyway, Ms. O'Connor drives a red Mustang convertible. If she is on the road, we will find her."

As Herbert was talking with McCaskey, he got an instant message on his borrowed laptop.

Viens1: We have your car. It is just crossing the Woodrow Wilson Memorial Bridge headed west.

"Darrell, we've got your perp," Herbert said. "She's on 95 crossing the river. She could be headed to the airport." The irony of Lucy O'Connor being on a bridge named W. Wilson was not lost on him.

"We're on 395 east now," McCaskey said. "I'll turn and go for an intercept. Can Viens stay with her?"

Herbert forwarded the question to Viens, who wrote back that the NRO's Homeland Security liaison, Lauren Tartags, said he could take the time, barring a crisis. Herbert told Viens to thank Ms. Tartags for her generosity. Op-Center's imaging expert wrote back:

Viens1: It's not kindness. She says she has no choice.

That was odd, but Herbert did not worry about it now. The intelligence chief told McCaskey to remain on the line. He said he would forward any new information immediately.

Through the open line Herbert could hear McCaskey and his wife conferring. The mutual respect he heard in the exchange made him smile. Maria was a tough, swashbuckling, headstrong, old-school law officer. She was the kind of cop who did not knock on doors but kicked them in. She was a perfect counterbalance to the more meticulous McCaskey.

He was happy for them. And he envied them.

Despite receiving data from the new satellite, Herbert felt as if he were back in the technological Stone Age. Before the electromagnetic blast, he would have been sitting in his office looking at the images being forwarded directly from the DSP. He could do that in the Tank, but that would mean hanging with Paul Hood. That was something he did not want to do right now.

Especially when he could still do his work out here and let the mechanized odor of the parking lot transport him to another time and place. To a point in his life when he had the best team a man could have, a wife who was his devoted personal and professional partner.

Maybe that was why Paul Hood did not understand the bad judgment call he had made. He never had an Yvonne in his life. He did not understand the meaning of *partnership*. Maybe that was why Herbert had judged Hood so harshly. Because he did have that perspective.

And here, in the breezy quiet, where memories took form in the dark shadows beside the buildings, he had her still.

FORTY-NINE

Washington, D.C.
Wednesday, 6:06 P.M.

Darrell McCaskey never thought he would be grateful for rush hour.

The highway was clogged in both directions as he picked his way through the slow-moving traffic. Herbert kept him posted on Lucy's progress. The two cars were converging, albeit slowly. As a precaution, McCaskey called Detective Howell to have someone go to Lucy's apartment. He wanted to make certain she was not there, that the person in the car was not a decoy. Howell dispatched a squad car without comment. His emotional neutrality was not surprising. It would not have served his cause to challenge the request or to attach it to demands or guarantees. The detective was still a professional.

As McCaskey got onto 95 heading east, he was informed that Lucy's apartment was empty. She was almost certainly in the car. A minute later, Herbert came back on the line.

"You're about two klicks shy of her position," he said. "If I can make a suggestion, she has no more exits between where she is and your current position. You can get out of the car and cross the guardrail north of Springfield—"

"I know the place," McCaskey said. "I can see it ahead."

The car was moving a little less than twenty-five miles an hour. He looked into the oncoming traffic as he hooked the phone on his belt. He left the line open.

"Maria, I'm going to intercept Ms. O'Connor and get

her to pull over," McCaskey said. "We'll wait for you on the shoulder. I need you to get off at the next exit and swing around."

"You are assuming she'll stop," Maria said.

"She will," her husband said. "If she doesn't brake willingly, I'll stop the car in front of her."

"What if she's armed?" Maria asked.

"I'll keep my mouth shut tight," he replied.

Maria frowned disapprovingly. "With a gun, not a hypodermic."

"I'll watch myself," McCaskey assured her. "Crossing the highway will be the tough part."

McCaskey did not usually crack wise in situations like this. Something about Maria's gravity had touched and amused him. This was not like Madrid, where they had been former lovers as well as grumpy and reluctant allies. This was not even like the stakeout for Ed March on Monday morning. This was the first case they had worked together since getting married. Maria was showing concern. He had wanted to try to minimize that.

He kissed her cheek as he put the car in park and opened the door. Maria maneuvered herself over the armrests and took the wheel. McCaskey ran in front of the car and waved an arm as he scooted across two lanes of traffic. Cars braked and horns whined. He swore as he reached the guardrail. The Mustang was about five hundred yards ahead, in the passing lane. He saw the passenger's side. She was traveling about twenty miles an hour, then suddenly stopped. McCaskey hoped that Lucy had not heard the commotion and saw someone coming toward her. He did not want her trying to get away on foot. She would have a considerable head start.

"Darrell, can you hear me?"

McCaskey snatched the phone. "Yeah, Bob!"

"We're getting a thermal spike from the DSP," he said.

"Meaning?" McCaskey asked just as he heard horns in

the oncoming lane. Cars around the Mustang were stopping. "Never mind," he said. "I can see it. She torched the damn thing!"

"What?"

"There's smoke coming from the closed windows!" McCaskey said. "She must have snuck out when the car stopped. Can you get a visual on her?"

"No," Herbert said. "We've got cloud cover on the natural-light camera."

"All right. Call 911. I've got to find her."

McCaskey started running. People who could not maneuver away from the Mustang were leaving their cars and hurrying away on foot. A man in a Ram 1500 had pulled off on the shoulder, five car lengths back. He was rushing over with a fire extinguisher. Just then, McCaskey saw red lights flash behind him. He turned and saw Maria standing on the roof of their car. She was tossing road flares, trying to get his attention. His wife must have noticed the smoke and stopped. She was gesturing toward the Ram. Through the smoke McCaskey could just make out someone climbing into the cab. That had to be Lucy. The Ram had a 5.7-liter HEMI Magnum engine. It was a truck with *cojónes*. The vehicle would take the driver through cars and off road with no trouble.

Flames curled from the tops of the windows of the Mustang. The Ram driver hit it with a blast from the fire extinguisher. As he did, the windshield cracked from the heat, the spiderweb pattern shooting out from the center. A fire started with a cigarette lighter and whatever was lying around should not have gotten so hot so fast. She must have used an accelerant—

She was going to the airport, McCaskey realized. She had sprayed the contents of an aerosol can, hairspray or deodorant, in carry-on luggage.

McCaskey jumped the rail and grabbed the man about

the waist and pushed him down just as the can itself exploded. It blew out the fragmented windshield and sent a small fireball rolling across the hood. Pieces of singed black Tumi luggage floated on the smoke like black snow. Former junkies might not be slick, but they knew household chemicals. They also knew how to distract the law.

McCaskey rose from the asphalt. "You all right?" he asked the other man.

"Yeah. Thanks."

McCaskey was bruised but intact. He jumped around the front of the burning automobile. The Ram was coming toward them, along the shoulder. He tried to get in the back of the pickup as it passed, but he missed it.

Maria did not.

His wife had gotten back into the car and jabbed her way through traffic. When she was just a few yards from the oncoming Ram, she drove the car hard into the guardrail. The metal did not break, but it bulged just enough to clip the fender of the Ram, tearing it free on the passenger's side. The chrome dug into the spinning front tire. At the same time, Maria accelerated against the guardrail, bending it more and locking the fender into the tire.

The Ram's 345-horsepower engine screamed as the driver tried to push through the impasse. Before she could succeed, McCaskey was at the driver's side door. He yanked it open and looked up at the face of desperation. He saw a woman who was crying so hard there was as much sweat along her scalp as there were tears on her cheeks. She was a woman so far over her pay grade that she was trembling all over, everywhere but her hands. Her fingers were bone white and locked around the steering wheel. She looked down at McCaskey.

"It wasn't going to be like this," she said, her voice an unsteady whisper. She looked back out the front window.

McCaskey climbed onto the step. He reached past her and turned off the ignition. With fire engines screaming behind him, it was difficult to hear. He leaned close. "What was not going to be like this?" he asked.

"They told me I would get exclusives," Lucy said. "That's all I wanted."

"Who said that?"

She did not appear to hear. "They said I was putting him to sleep. They said that was what they wanted. They wanted me to mess up his room, make it look as if he had partied hard. They said he would be discredited."

"Wilson, you mean," McCaskey said.

Lucy did not answer. McCaskey turned her face gently toward him. "You gave William Wilson the injection."

"Yes."

"So you would have exclusive access to stories?"

She looked into his eyes. "They told me he wouldn't be hurt. Not like Meyers."

"Who is Meyers?" McCaskey asked.

"Richard Meyers. He was my boyfriend. We were on the beach three years ago in Corpus Christi. I gave him a speedball. He died."

"They knew about this?" McCaskey asked.

"I ran."

"They found out?" McCaskey asked.

"Yes."

"So there was blackmail," McCaskey asked.

Lucy nodded once.

The young woman, a junkie, had been in Texas. Someone must have found out and kept that information for future use. For blackmail. These guys must have been building their plan, their operation, for some time. "What about Mr. Lawless?"

"I did that, too," Lucy replied. "I had to. They said they would turn me in if I didn't. And then I had to put the dress in Kat's apartment." Lucy started to cry. "I didn't want to hurt Kat. I like her."

"Who told you to do all that?" McCaskey asked.

"She told me I would have to write only good things about them or I would go to prison for murder," Lucy said. "I got stuck. I didn't know how to get out."

"Lucy, who did you speak with? Admiral Link? Senator Orr? Someone who works for one of them?"

"A woman."

"Do you know *which* woman?"

"No," Lucy said.

"What number did she call?"

"My cell phone," Lucy said.

"Okay," McCaskey said. "Now I want you to stay here. Someone will come for you. You have to believe I'm going to try to help you, all right?"

"All right," she said blankly.

McCaskey gave her a reassuring pat on the back of her tense hand. Then he stepped back onto the highway. The police were making their way through traffic. Maria was standing there. Behind her, the airbag of the car had inflated.

"Nice move," he said. "Are you hurt?"

"No. You?"

"No."

McCaskey kissed his wife on the forehead and reached for his cell phone. It was gone. Poor Bob was probably mad with concern and madder with confusion. McCaskey hurried ahead. He needed to get a phone so he could call the intelligence chief. He showed one of the police officers his Op-Center ID. The man loaned him his phone. McCaskey said he would return it later.

McCaskey did not call Bob Herbert's phone because the line was probably still open. Instead, he called the Tank. Bugs Benet answered. He asked Hood's assistant to have Herbert find out who called Lucy O'Connor's cell phone within a half hour of the murder of William Wilson.

"Will do," Bugs said. "How can we reach you?"

"Don't worry about me," he said. "Keep an ear to the ground for Mike." McCaskey wasn't being heroic, just practical. He had a feeling that whether he was about to resign or not, Mike Rodgers was the one who would have to carry this ball in for the touchdown.

FIFTY

San Diego, California
Wednesday, 3:45 P.M.

Inevitably, out of chaos comes order. The only two questions are when and at what cost?

Chaos evolved quickly in the hotel lobby, as it always does. One convention-goer carried it to three who carried it to nine. When chaos spreads, Mike Rodgers knew that the most important thing was not to try to contain it. Security had called the police, and reinforcements were on the way. Their presence would emphasize what was already an extraordinary situation and remove whatever remained of normalcy. That would merely put the same amount of tumult in a more confined space. And chaos tended to leap whatever firebreaks were placed around it. The task at hand was to eliminate the cause, not to contain the result.

The cause was shock about the apparent abduction of Admiral Kenneth Link and uncertainty about who did it or why. Mike Rodgers wanted to get on the problem right away. And not just to help eliminate the panic. Apparently, this was related to whatever the hell had started in Washington just four days ago.

Rodgers walked over to a relatively quiet corner near the magazine stand. He called the office of General Jack Breen at Pendleton. Breen said it was good to hear from his old friend.

"Where are you?" the marine general asked.

"San Diego," Rodgers replied.

"San Diego? I hear there's noise in that area. Yours?"

"Indirectly," Rodgers said. "Jack, I need air recon ASAP. Something with eyes *and* teeth. We believe Admiral Kenneth Link has been kidnapped from the hotel here."

"Details?"

"He was in a limo, that's all I know. I don't know what kind. I wouldn't trust anyone to give me the right information anyway," Rodgers said.

"I'm requisitioning an Apache on the e-command link as we speak," Breen said. "Do you think there will be a ransom request or is this a GAT?"

GAT was grab and terminate. It was a military adaptation of the Mafia acronym SAW, snatch and whack.

"I don't know, which is why we need to try to find the limo," Rodgers said. "Can they pick me up somewhere around here?"

"Roof of the convention center, ten minutes," Breen said. "What kind of manpower do you need?"

"Full suit?"

That was thirteen men. Breen said he would provide that.

"Perfect," Rodgers said. "I'll be there."

"We'll plan to cover the routes east," Breen said. "The police will have plenty of resources deployed north along 405 headed up to Los Angeles and south to Mexico," Breen said. "I doubt kidnappers would want to get into the traffic or border check along that corridor anyway."

"Agreed," Rodgers said as his phone beeped. That meant there was an incoming call. "General, I'll see your boys in ten." Rodgers jogged from the lobby as he switched to the other call. "Yes?"

"Mike, it's Darrell."

"Have you got something?" Rodgers asked.

"Yes. It sounds like you're running."

"I am," Rodgers told him. "I'm organizing recon. It seems Admiral Link was just kidnapped."

"He was? That's surprising."

"Why?"

"Because we just busted Lucy O'Connor," McCaskey told him. "She confessed to giving those men the injections. Within a half hour of the first, she received a call from Admiral Link's office phone."

"Who did Lucy talk to?"

"She doesn't know," McCaskey said. "Only that it was a woman."

"I'm not sure if that means anything," Rodgers said. "Anyone could have used his phone."

"Not without his authorization code," McCaskey said. "We checked. No one in the office has that except Link."

"Were there calls after the second incident?" Rodgers asked.

"No, they were being very careful then," McCaskey said. "The criminal nature of the first action had already been uncovered. The perps would have been much more cautious the next day."

"Would they really have been that cavalier about murder?" Rodgers asked.

"Yeah," McCaskey said. "They had plausible deniability. Lucy could have gone up there and done it for a story."

"Okay. But why do it at all? Does Lucy have any idea?"

"Lucy appears to be suffering from a mild form of narcosis, probably due to something in the barbiturate family," McCaskey said. "I used to see the same speech and slowed reactions in the street."

"Could someone on Orr's staff have been providing her with drugs?" Rodgers asked. "That might have provided them with leverage."

"We checked. She scored those on her own, an old connection. We found the guy through his parole officer."

"What's your guess, then?" Rodgers asked.

"You mean a unified theory?" McCaskey asked.

"As unified as you can be over an open line," Rodgers said.

"Mike, I wish I knew. Someone in the senator's office wanted the first victim dead. Then they killed some random tourist to make it look like the first murder was not related to the big man or his party. Our reporter friend was in it for perks and as a patsy, if necessary. If I said anything beyond that, I would be making pretty big assumptions."

"Make them," Rodgers said as he ran along Harbor Drive. The wide road bordered the bay. The convention center was just ahead. In the distance he heard the unmistakable bass thumping of an incoming helicopter.

"Mike, what is homicide or abduction always about? Power. Revenge. Jealousy. Money," McCaskey said. "At the Bureau we used to assign a team to each of those and follow it back to a source."

"I don't have a team," Rodgers said. "Hell, when this is over, I may not even have a job."

"I know."

"Darrell—a hunch. Give me something."

McCaskey sighed. "We're talking about a politician who is already wealthy, who has never had a scandal attached to his marriage, who has the respect of his colleagues. If he is behind it, I am guessing it is for power."

"And the admiral?"

"You know him better than I do, Mike," McCaskey replied. "But think about it. He has had control over intelligence. That is *real* power. He knows what it tastes like."

The sounds of the chopper and his own hard breathing made it difficult for Rodgers to hear. Since McCaskey had access to the national news and the FBI pipeline, Rodgers asked him to call at once if he heard anything about a ransom demand. Barring that, Rodgers said he would call as soon as he had a lead or even a new idea. The general vowed he would get one if he had to dangle Eric Stone from the open hatch of the Apache.

Which is not the worst idea you have had today, he told

himself. Assuming he could find the bastard. Stone had vanished within moments of the report.

Rodgers could hear the higher-pitched whir of the police helicopters moving along the San Diego Freeway. Two hovered above Lindbergh Field in case the limousine had gone there, and two more from the Harbor Patrol were moving out to sea. Perhaps the kidnappers intended to fly Admiral Link from the area. There were sirens on the Pacific Coast Highway, which paralleled Harbor Drive. Convention security personnel were running here and there, shouting into walkie-talkies and trying to keep order around the convention center itself. They were apparently being told to keep people in the area. Having another four or five thousand attendees in the streets would only complicate rescue efforts.

Rodgers reached the eastern entrance of the convention center as the Marine helicopter landed. He showed one of the security guards his USF ID as well as his Op-Center ID. He was allowed inside. A wide, sunlit, concrete-heavy gallery circled the massive convention area. It was thick with refreshment stands, media booths, and USF vendors. People were standing around, just as they were in the hotel lobby, trying to pick up information and voicing theories as to who might be behind this. "Damn foreigners" was the expression Rodgers seemed to hear most.

It would be ironic if that were the case. International enemies of the USF Party were something Mike Rodgers had not even considered. Or someone seeking revenge for William Wilson, perhaps?

No, Rodgers decided. *Something like this would have been planned for some time.* The abductors would have had to know Link's schedule, been able to get to the limousine driver and take him out, and had a hideout or escape route ready. The kidnappers would have made dry runs.

Rodgers started up the concrete stairs that led to the top

of the convention center. He was tired, but years of training with Striker had kept him in top physical condition. The door to the roof was a fire exit. It was unlocked. Rodgers stepped out. The chopper was about fifty yards away. Rodgers waved to the pilot, who acknowledged with a salute. The general ran toward the Apache, ducking into the heavy prop wash.

Suddenly, Rodgers stopped.

The abduction needed a plan, he thought.

Was the answer right in front of him? He looked out at the city from the top of the convention center. Red and blue police lights spotted the main roads and highways. Helicopters were being swallowed in the smoggy inland skies. A great security machine was in motion.

But would it be enough?

With renewed urgency, Rodgers resumed his sprint toward the chopper.

FIFTY-ONE

Washington, D.C.
Wednesday, 7:08 P.M.

Reluctantly, Bob Herbert had moved his laptop operation to the Tank. McCaskey had informed him about the latest developments and he wanted to be directly involved in the operation. Besides, the winds in the parking lot had picked up, and there was an unpleasant chill on his back. And, as the engineers from Andrews put it, they needed someone to test the elevator with a load inside. Everyone else was still using the stairs. The tech boys had been working on the lift for three hours and told him everything seemed to be functioning. None of them had ridden it yet because they did not have the proper security clearance. Most of Op-Center had been fried, but protocol was still protocol.

Before heading downstairs, the intelligence chief phoned Stephen Viens. The surveillance operations officer was still at the NRO. Herbert asked him to see if any of the navy satellites had picked up the limousine in back of Link's hotel. Security recon was pretty thorough in the region because of the naval station, the naval submarine base, and the many inland operations facilities such as Fleet Technical Support Center Pacific and the Intelligence and War-Sim Center in nearby Riverside County. Viens said he would report back if he found anything.

Herbert was happy to test the elevator. It was strange. He had ridden this elevator thousands of times, but this was the first time he paid attention to the sounds, to the little bumps and jolts. Were those mechanical groans of pain or the yawns of waking machinery? He was very aware of the thinness of the air, which was being forced in by a portable, battery-powered pump on the top of the carriage. In a way, the carriage reminded Herbert of how he had been after Beirut: hurt and shut down for a while, then struggling back into service. That was an advantage Herbert had over his Op-Center colleagues. The rebuilding process was miserably familiar territory to him.

The elevator was a little sluggish, but it reached the bottom of the shaft.

Better too slow than fast, Herbert decided.

He wheeled himself out, reached back inside to send the carriage upstairs, and headed to the Tank. The skeleton team at work throughout Op-Center was sharp and focused. That did not surprise Herbert. In a postcrisis situation, work was an intense, short-term involvement that kept trauma from settling in. It was like an emotional gag reflex. The full impact of what had happened would not hit these people until they put down the armor of responsibility.

Hood was the only other person in the Tank. The reunion was surprisingly relaxed, at least from Herbert's perspective. The intelligence chief had kept Hood up to date and had nothing to add. He plugged the laptop into the dedicated power source in the room and rebooted it. He wanted to be ready if Viens called with information. The map from Homeland Security showed traffic patterns, air lanes, and even possible terrorist targets such as nuclear power plants, electrical grids, dams, transportation centers, and shopping malls. Overlays with different access routes could be added to the image if necessary.

The McCaskeys arrived shortly after Herbert. They brought dinner, which was welcome. It marked the first real break anyone had enjoyed since the attack. In the case of the McCaskeys, it was the first real time-out they had enjoyed since the death of William Wilson. Hood asked about Rodgers. Both McCaskey and Herbert told him what the general was doing.

"I meant, *how* is he doing?" Hood asked.

"I think he is kind of in limbo, waiting to see how this all turns out," McCaskey told him.

"It is odd," Maria said. "Mike Rodgers is out in the real world, but you say he is in limbo. We are in a badly wounded facility, yet we are supposedly connected to the world."

"I suppose everything depends on your attitude," Hood replied.

"Knowing you have a job helps," McCaskey said.

"Elected officials and appointees learn to live with flux," Hood said. "I still say it's the inside defines the outside."

"You mean like us," Maria said. "The shell of Op-Center is broken, but we are still functioning."

"Exactly," Hood said.

Herbert did not involve himself in the conversation. He busied himself with taking bites from the roast beef club sandwich the McCaskeys had brought, pulling up a map of San Diego County on his laptop, and jacking his borrowed cell phone into the Tank system. As a rule, pep talks bored the intelligence chief. Herbert was self-driven. Usually because there was a throat he needed to get his hands around. That was all the motivation he needed. This particular conversation had a fringe of wide-eyed sanctimony that made him angry. Maria had her spouse alive and well and at her side. Hood still had an organization to run and a résumé that would keep him circulating through government employ as long as he wanted. It was easy for them both to be optimistic.

Maybe you really ought to join Mike out there, Herbert thought. *Start a consultancy of some kind, maybe for private industry. Security in a nonsecure age.* It was something to think about.

The call from Stephen Viens came before Herbert had to listen to very much more of the chat. He was surprised to hear from the surveillance operations officer so quickly.

"We just got a call from the California Highway Patrol, San Diego Command Center," Viens told the intelligence chief. "They found what they think is your missing limousine."

"What makes them think it's the one?" Herbert asked.

Herbert did not ask why the CHP had called the NRO. The Department of Homeland Security had linked all the nation's highway patrol offices into the NRO's Infrastructure Surveillance System. The ISS gave local law enforcement offices unprecedented access to observe possible terrorist activity through military, weather, and other observation-equipped satellites.

"The limousine was abandoned in a lot off Highway 163, which is just east of San Diego," Viens said. "The original driver was found tied up in the trunk. He said he was hit on the head in the hotel parking lot, and that's all he remembers. The kidnappers obviously switched vehicles. The CHP wants the NRO to look through the back-image log, see if they caught a parked vehicle in the area."

"How long will that take?"

"Not very," Viens said.

"What do you mean?"

"The satellites that watch Naval Base Coronado and the inland flight training center do not overlap," Viens said. "They follow Highway 15 east. It looks like the limousine pulled over in a blind spot. They are double-checking now."

And who would know that better than a former head of naval intelligence? Herbert asked himself.

"It is possible that the Interceptor-Three border patrol satellite picked something up, but that may be a little too far south to have seen this activity. The FBI monitors that one and is looking into it."

"I'll let Mike know," Herbert said. "Thanks, Stephen."

Herbert updated the others while he punched in Rodgers's number.

"Why would the admiral organize his own abduction?" Maria asked.

"That's the key, isn't?" Herbert said.

Rodgers picked up the phone. The general said he was just about to board the Apache but waited while Herbert briefed him. Rodgers listened without comment. With the sound of the helicopter pounding in the background, Herbert was not even sure Rodgers could hear.

"Did you get all that, Mike?" the intelligence chief asked when he was finished.

"I did," Rodgers said.

"Any thoughts?"

"Yeah. I think we've been had," Rodgers said. "Big time."

"In what way?"

"I'll let you know when I've checked something out," Rodgers told him. "I've got to run. I'll call you as soon as I can."

"Go get 'em," Herbert said and hung up. He lowered the phone and looked at the others.

"Go get who?" McCaskey asked.

"Mike didn't say," Herbert said. "He told me he'll call in thirty minutes or so. The only thing I know for sure is it's ironic."

"What is?" Hood asked.

Herbert replied, "That the man who is in the best position to put this one away doesn't really work for us anymore."

FIFTY-TWO

San Diego, California
Wednesday, 4:29 P.M.

The news of the abduction shocked Kat Lockley. It also concerned her. Senator Orr would never have organized that, and she could not imagine who would. Someone from the outside, perhaps. Maybe Rodgers?

That was not important right now. What mattered was the senator and his safety. After talking with Stone, Kat jabbed the elevator call button. While she waited to take the carriage to the penthouse, she phoned the senator and told him what had happened. She asked him to stay in his room and said she would be there in a minute or two. Senator Orr agreed, at least until security could be organized for him to go downstairs. He felt it was important to talk to his people as soon as possible, to let them know that he was all right and the convention would go on. Kat said she would see to that. Her second call was to Pat Simcox, head of security. She wanted to make sure he stayed at his post outside the senator's room and did not join the detail searching for Admiral Link. Simcox said he had no intention of leaving. He told her not to worry. If this were a plot against the USF, no one would get through to the senator.

She believed him. The truck driver turned security man was tough.

The elevator arrived, and guests streamed out. There were concerned looks and questions for Kat. She told them the senator was all right, then excused herself and entered. On the way up, she was joined by Kendra Peterson.

"Eric called to tell me what happened," Kendra said. "I just spoke with the senator. He said you suggested he stay put."

"I did. Is there a problem with that?"

"No," Kendra insisted. "I think that's a good idea."

"Good."

Kat was glad. She did not feel like having it out with Kendra over this issue. The elevator opened, and Kat went to the senator's suite. She knocked on the door, and it opened. She stepped through.

Into something she did not expect.

Pat Simcox was standing in the entrance of the suite. He was pointing a 9 mm Glock model 19 handgun at Kat Lockley. A Gemtech SOS silencer was fixed to the barrel.

Kat stopped. Her eyes snapped from the gun to Simcox's brown eyes. "Pat, what are you doing?" she asked.

"Welcoming you," he replied.

"Why the gun?" she asked.

"Just go in!" Kendra snapped.

Kat turned angrily. "What the hell are you doing?"

"We'll discuss that when Eric gets here," Kendra said.

Kat walked into the living room. Senator Orr was sitting on a divan near the terrace. He was staring ahead, his breathing shallow. His arms were hanging limp, his hands lying palm-up in his lap. There was a glass-topped coffee table in front of him. An open bottle of ginger ale sat beside a half-empty glass. The senator's bodyguard was standing nearby.

"Senator?" Kat said. "Is he all right?" she asked the bodyguard.

He did not answer. Kat ran to the senator's side and squatted in front of him. She took one of his hands in hers. It was cool. "Senator Orr, are you all right?"

"He can't answer," Kendra said. "Mr. Simcox put several drops of sodium thiopental in his drink."

"What is that?" Kat asked.

"A mild anesthesia," Kendra replied. "It should keep him still for about ninety minutes."

"Why?" Kat demanded.

There was a knock at the door. Kendra waited. The knock was followed by two others. Kendra opened the door to admit Eric Stone. The young man walked in. His expression was serious but unworried.

"How is everything?" he asked.

"Perfect," Kendra said. "What is it like downstairs?"

"Mild disorder and growing," Stone replied. He walked over to Simcox and took the gun. "Get him dressed please, Thomas."

"Yes, sir," the bodyguard replied.

"Thomas?" Kat said.

"Thomas Mandor," Stone replied. "A longtime acquaintance of Admiral Link."

"What is he, an assassin?"

"No, Kat. We do not want to kill the senator," Stone assured her. "We want to get him away from here and have a long talk about William Wilson and about the future. We want to make sure we all have an understanding."

Kat rose and approached Stone. He held up his free hand for her to stop.

"Eric, what is this?" Kat asked. "What are you doing?"

"We are helping to save the country," he replied.

"What are you talking about? The senator is a patriot. And what about Admiral Link? You know him—"

"The admiral is not the issue. What concerns me right now is Donald Orr," Stone said. "He is a killer, a belligerent nationalist who appeals to the basest fears of the electorate. He nurtures the kind of suspicion that will one day make us turn on ourselves, on anyone who is different than he is."

Mandor returned with a hat, sunglasses, and windbreaker. He began putting them on the senator.

"Please," Kat said. "Stop this. Stop before it's too late."

"We are." Stone moved closer to Kat. "My question to you is this. Will you come with us, or do we leave you here?"

"Come with you where?"

"That is not important," Kendra interjected.

"Away from here, ostensibly to keep the senator safe," Stone said. "Yes or no, Kat? Are you coming or staying?"

Kat looked at the gun. "You wouldn't shoot me. Not here, not now."

"No one will hear," Stone assured her. "Your answer, please."

The woman did not know what to say. The silent barrel of a pistol was more persuasive than Stone's arguments. The sight had a way of short-circuiting the brain and weakening the legs. It was one thing to believe in an ideal. It was quite another to perish for it. But there was a stubborn part of her soul that did not want to be bullied. Especially when she and the senator had worked so hard to get here.

The brief, internal debate was resolved a moment later when a third option presented itself.

One that no one had anticipated.

FIFTY-THREE

San Diego, California
Wednesday, 4:44 P.M.

The low hum, more tangible than audible, came upon them suddenly. The windows began to wobble before anything else. That caused the drawn drapes to shake. A few moments later, everyone felt the vibrations.

The nearly sixty-foot-long AH64-D Apache Longbow helicopter lowered itself sideways beside the hotel. The sun threw its stark shadow against the drapes. The Longbow looked like a mosquito, with its slightly dipped rotors and stubby wings set against a long, slender body, a large General Electric T700-GE-701 turboshaft engine mounted high on each side of the fuselage.

The helicopter rotated slowly so that its 30 mm automatic Boeing M230 chain gun was pointed toward the room.

"Christ in heaven," Stone muttered as the aircraft turned.

He started toward the door just as the knob and lock popped loudly, and the door flew in along the hinges. Mike Rodgers stepped through the acrid smoke of the C-4 blast. He was followed by a small complement of marines. The marines were all carrying MP5-N assault rifles. Several of them moved toward Thomas Mandor and Kendra Peterson. They directed the two toward the bedroom. Neither of Stone's companions protested. Two of the marines remained with Mike Rodgers.

"Put your weapon down!" Rodgers ordered as he

walked toward Stone. He had to shout to be heard over the beat of the Apache that had ferried them to the rooftop. Rodgers expected to be using it again shortly.

The USF officer hesitated, but only for a moment. He turned the gun from Kat to Senator Orr.

"Don't!" Kat screamed.

"You are leaving me no choice!" he replied.

"I am," she said. She edged toward the senator. "We can talk about your concerns. We've done that before, all of us."

"It's too late," Stone said.

"Eric, have you actually killed anyone?" Rodgers asked as the marines filled the room.

"No," he admitted.

"Then don't start now. I know you think there's no other choice. People in an emotional situation often think that. But it isn't true."

"You don't understand!" Stone said. He gestured angrily at Orr with the gun. "This man is evil!"

"This man is a United States senator, and you are not his judge!" Kat yelled.

Slowly, the woman sat beside Orr. She was obviously attempting to place herself between the handgun and the senator. That was a sweet gesture, but at this range, Stone would take both of them out before Rodgers could reach him. That left just one option, and the general did not want to use it.

"Kat is right," Rodgers said. "You may get jail time for whatever you've done till now, but it beats having these boys cut you down."

"You tell me not to kill by threatening to kill me?" Stone laughed. "You're as twisted as Orr!"

Rodgers continued to move closer to Stone. The young man was standing sideways, the gun aimed down. He scowled, angry, cornered. In hair trigger situations like this, it was important to be determined without being overly aggressive.

"Let's stop thinking about who can kill who," Rodgers suggested. He extended his left arm slowly and opened his hand. "Let's do as Kat suggested and talk this thing over. Give me the weapon so we can start to ratchet this thing back."

Stone said nothing. Often, that meant the individual was ready to capitulate. It was usually noticeable in a softening of the tension around the mouth and eyes, in the sinew of the neck. Unfortunately, none of that was happening here. The thumping of the helicopter probably was not helping Stone to think straight.

"I'll tell you what, Eric," Rodgers said. "I'm going to have Lieutenant Murdock, who is standing right behind me, get on the radio. He'll send the helicopter away. It will be easier to talk."

"I don't want to talk!" Stone cried. "I want to finish what we started!"

"What *who* started?" Rodgers asked.

"The admiral, Kendra, and myself."

"What did you start?"

"The counterprocess," Stone said. "That was the code name the admiral devised. It was his idea, and it was the *right* idea!"

The young man was under both internal and external stress. More than intent and desire, physical strain could cause the handgun to discharge. Rodgers had to take precautions. He held his right arm straight down, the index finger pointed toward the floor. That was a sign to the marines. If the general crooked his finger, that meant to ice the target. If he raised his arm again, it meant to stand down.

"Talk to me about the counterprocess," Rodgers said.

"It was conceived to work within the senator's plan."

"Like a virus or a mole," Rodgers said.

"Yes."

"What was the senator's plan?"

"To kill his enemies," Stone replied.

"That's a lie!" Kat shot back.

"Let him talk!" Rodgers cautioned.

Rodgers watched Stone's grip on the handgun. There was no change. The general continued to walk toward him.

Stone turned slightly to address Rodgers directly. "Killing William Wilson was Orr's idea," Stone said. "Kat fleshed it out. It was a way of drawing attention to a problem and solving it at the same time."

"The problem of anti-American economic activities," Rodgers said.

"Exactly."

"How do you know the senator was behind the killing of Mr. Wilson?" Rodgers asked. He wanted to draw Stone deeper into conversation, focused on him and not on the senator.

"Orr told the admiral, and the admiral told me," Stone said.

"Did you ask the senator yourself?" Rodgers asked.

"Why bother? He would have lied to me. Anyway, the admiral never lied. Not to me."

Rodgers was just a few paces away. "If this is true, I need you to tell me everything. Then I can pass it along to Op-Center."

"Op-Center!" Stone snarled. He turned a little more. "They were the ones who screwed this up for all of us—"

Rodgers saw an opening and took it. Stone had raised his arm slightly so the Glock was pointed away from both Donald Orr and Kat Lockley. Rodgers reached across Stone and grabbed the man's right wrist with his own right hand. He forced the gun toward the floor as he simultaneously swung his left hand toward the gun. Rodgers pressed left with his right hand, against the back of Stone's forearm, and right with his left hand. Stone's wrist snapped audibly. The gun hung loosely in his trembling fingers, and Rodgers snatched it.

The marines moved in. One of them secured Stone by pushing him facedown on the carpet. The other ran to look after Kat and the senator. He told Kat to call downstairs for the hotel physician. Rodgers picked up the Glock.

"You don't know what you're doing!" Stone said.

"Saving you from death by lethal injection, I think," Rodgers replied. He motioned for the marine to let Stone sit up. Then the general crouched beside him. "Where is Admiral Link?"

"I don't know," Stone replied.

"I don't believe you," Rodgers replied. "You were filibustering outside the hotel while his limo was being hijacked. You wanted to keep me from seeing anything."

"That doesn't mean I know where he went," Stone said.

Rodgers shook his head. "Don't you get it? The counterprocess is over. Whatever it is, whatever it was supposed to be, this whole thing is done. Cooked. The only way you save any part of your own ass is by cooperating."

"I believe that what we have done is right," Stone replied. "And I won't rat out my boss. Neither will Ms. Peterson."

"This gentleman says he will," said a voice from the bedroom door.

Rodgers looked over. The other male member of Stone's party was standing there. His short marine guard was behind him, the assault rifle lowered. There was something contrite in the manner of the big man.

"Who are you?" Rodgers asked, rising.

"Thomas Mandor, sir."

"What is your role in all this?" Rodgers asked.

"Just muscle," Mandor replied.

"He was hired by Admiral Link's staff, supposedly as a personal security officer for the senator," Kat said bitterly.

"I *was* hired by Mr. Stone, but to escort the senator to another location," Mandor said. "And I happen to know where Admiral Link is."

"I'm listening," Rodgers replied.

"My partner has him. If I tell you where they are, can we cut some kind of deal?"

"No," Rodgers said. "If you don't, I'll do my damnedest to make sure the state of California adds obstruction of justice to whatever else you may have done."

Mandor considered that for just a moment. Then he told Rodgers where Kenneth Link had gone.

FIFTY-FOUR

San Diego, California
Wednesday, 5:15 P.M.

Rodgers and his marine unit charged back up the stairs to the roof of the hotel. They left Stone, Kendra, and Mandor in the custody of the local police. The three were charged with assault, a felony weapons charge, and conspiracy to kidnapping. Kat remained with Senator Orr and the hotel physician. Rodgers had questions for Kat, but this was not the time or place to pose them. He needed more information and suspected that only Kenneth Link had it.

Thomas Mandor had directed them to a cabin in the mountains of nearby Fallbrook. The pilot phoned the address to the county sheriff. The marine explained that they needed to get to the site without the chopper being seen or heard, which meant landing some distance away. He said that he did not need backup, just a spotter, someone to point out the residence. The sheriff sent Deputy Andy Belmont ahead to meet them. He said the young man would be waiting in an open field at elevation 1963 feet, three miles due northwest of the Mission Road exit in the foothills of the Coastal Range. That was just a quarter mile or so from the target. The dispatcher said that Deputy Belmont was familiar with the area and also had met Mr. Richmond. He would be able to point out the cabin. The pilot was told to look for a black Jeep with a large white star on the hood.

The Apache flew over Highway 163 and then followed

15 east. The pilot kept the helicopter under five hundred feet. Navy fighter pilots trained along this corridor, and he did not want to risk a collision. He ascended when he reached the foothills. Rodgers was sitting behind the pilot, watching for the deputy's Jeep. There was one marine to his right and three more in the snug jump seats behind them. They were actually more like paddles, recent additions to the Longbows that allowed them to shuttle small special ops units into hostile territory. The seats, even the fixed ones, vibrated like those old quarter-fed motel beds, and removing the headphones was guaranteed to leave a passenger's ears ringing for a week. This was not an aircraft designed for comfort. As the pilot proudly put it, "The Longbow was built for roughing things up." In addition to the chain gun, the helicopter could be equipped with air-to-surface Hellfire missiles on four-rail launchers and air-to-air Stinger missiles. This particular Apache did not carry Stingers. Part of that was a virtue of the quick launch protocol the crew had used to reach Rodgers as quickly as possible. Part of that was to protect the civilian population in the event technical failure brought the chopper down.

The pilot spotted the Jeep first and swung toward it. He set the Apache down two hundred yards away. Rodgers opened the door and ran over. The deputy climbed from the Jeep and offered his hand.

"You must be General Rodgers," the deputy said.

"That's right."

"It's a pleasure, sir," Belmont told him. "What do you need from me?"

"Tell me about the target," Rodgers said.

"It's a traditional log cabin set back about three hundred yards from a ridge," the deputy told him. "There are oaks all around—a real firetrap, but shady. May I ask what's going on there?"

"Hostage situation," Rodgers replied. "What is the best way in?"

"Are you looking to surround and siege or charge it?" Belmont asked.

"We're going in."

"There are more windows on the north side, the ridge side," the deputy told him. "You'll be safer coming in from the south."

"Is there someplace closer to set down for extraction?"

"There's a three-acre clearing off the point, just above the cabin," Belmont told him. "Good surveillance point, too."

"Great. Can you walk us there?"

"It will be an honor," Belmont assured him.

Rodgers gave the deputy an appreciative clap on the shoulder, then ran back to the Apache. Gathering his team, Rodgers told the pilot to get airborne and remain over the field. As soon as the marines had secured the cabin, one of them would direct the pilot to the point. If Link were here, as Mandor had said, Rodgers wanted to get him into custody as soon as possible. The way people were getting drugged, the general wanted to make sure he had at least one live and conscious USF official.

Hopefully, it was one who could be convinced to tell him what the hell was going on.

FIFTY-FIVE

Fallbrook, California
Wednesday, 6:00 P.M.

Eric Stone had said that based on the photographs he had seen, the isolated mountaintop cabin reflected the personality of the owner. Like Michael Wayne Richmond, it was rough, uncomplicated, and a little dangerous.

The two-room structure was small and dark. The hardwood floors were warped from groundwater that percolated from below and the old, beamed ceilings were stained from seeping rain. The many framed oil paintings of trucks, done by Richmond, were lopsided due to regular seismic activity. In the front, the four-pane windows looked out on a thickly weeded field that ran to a private dirt road. In the back, the windows offered views of steep slopes spotted with huge, precariously balanced boulders. A strong Santa Ana wind caused the branches of oaks on the sides of the house to scratch the roof insistently.

There were field mice in the attic. They had become active since the sun started to set. There was mostly beer, processed meat, and cheese in the refrigerator. The bread was stale. When it was dark, Kenneth Link would send Richmond out to get real food. Richmond would take his SUV, not the van they had used to get here. That was in the freestanding garage. If anyone had seen Richmond transfer his "captive" from the limousine, investigators would not find the other vehicle. Certainly not before the next night, when Link would manage to get away. He would leave here while Richmond was placing a call to the press, claiming to represent Far Eastern extremists. That would represent the first blow against the USF. The last thing Americans wanted was to make new enemies among radical terrorists. His hands bound, Link would make his way down the mountain path. He would run, fall, and scrape himself to make it look as if the escape had been a daring one. When Link finally reached the freeway, he would be saved. Then, after a manfully short hospital stay, the admiral would address the USF convention. He would ask the attendees to pray for the well-being of Senator Orr. When that was done, he would sit down with Eric Stone. If Orr had agreed to retire from the USF, he would be released. If Orr refused to cooperate, there would be widespread mourning about his disappearance and presumed death. In either case, Kat Lockley and Lucy O'Connor would be implicated in the deaths of William Wilson and Robert Lawless. He had no doubt that Kat would fall on her sword to protect Orr. The only one Link felt bad for in all this was poor Lucy. She had been used. But then, she had let ambition fog her judgment.

Following Kat's murder confession, the USF would lose even more credibility with the voting public. Donald Orr would return to the senate and then, when his term was over he would retire. A few months from now no one would remember that the USF had ever existed.

Link and his abductor were both in the main room of the cabin. Richmond was in a rocking chair. He was sitting forward, not rocking. Link was in a frayed armchair. They had just turned on the local news. The kidnapping was the lead story. The reporter said that Senator Orr was reportedly in his suite, under guard. The USF spokesperson, a local organizer who worked for Stone, said he hoped that the senator would have a statement to make within the hour.

"I hope that isn't true," Richmond said. "Orr should have been hauled out of there by now."

"I'm sure he has been," Link replied. "Eric may not

have wanted to say anything yet. Perhaps he has not heard from Mandor."

"Yeah. Tom could be afraid to use the cell phone. Maybe he'll wait till he gets to Vegas."

"That phone is secure," Link said.

"They could have gotten held up somewhere, at a roadblock or something," Richmond said.

That, too, was not likely. The cover story was that the senator was being moved for his own safety. The police would have no reason, or right, to overrule Orr's own security chief.

"Why don't you call Mr. Stone?" Richmond suggested.

"I'll give him a little more time," Link replied. He continued watching the TV. There were interviews with shocked and worried convention attendees and with the chief of police. Link was pleased and proud that his own abduction had gone so well, and he took some comfort in that. He told himself the second half of the operation had also gone off, and it was the reporters who were behind. He switched to CNN to see how the national news services were playing this.

Link suddenly became aware of something. The mice in the attic had stopped moving around. Perhaps they had gone outside to forage for food. Or maybe there was a predator outside. This was the time of day when rattlesnakes came out to feed and coyotes and owls began their hunt.

Or maybe they had visitors.

A moment later, the windows on either side of the room shattered, and two canisters of CS tear gas exploded in the room.

FIFTY-SIX

Fallbrook, California
Wednesday, 6:16 P.M.

The effects of chlorobenzylidenemalononitrile gas are instantaneous. It inflames the soft tissue of the throat, causing it to burn and swell. Within seconds, victims begin to experience dizziness and acute nausea. And it causes the eyes to water and sting. Even if an individual could keep his eyes open, the finely dispersed particles hung in the air like a thick, slow-moving fog.

Rodgers and his marines were wearing goggles to protect their eyes. They did not bother bringing breathing apparatus from the Apache. They had determined that the winds up here would clear the room quickly once the windows were shattered. They would hold their breath and remove the occupants, carry them some distance from the cabin.

Approaching the structure had been easy. With the deputy's help, the men moved along the sides that had no windows. Lieutenant Murdock used a MiFOP, a miniature fiber optic periscope, to look into the room. A suction device the size of a large housefly contained a small camera. Once that was attached to the window, the user could back away to a secure location. The fiber-optic lens relayed an image to a receiver that was the size of a computer mouse. Each of the marines was able to study the room and the position of the occupants before moving.

While Rodgers and five of the men crept toward the front door, the other two men positioned themselves to hurl the gas. In less than a minute, Kenneth Link and his companion were outside. Two marines secured the kidnapper with double-lock handcuffs while Lieutenant Murdock called for the Apache to come to the ridge. Rodgers used a secure point-to-point radio to inform Jack Breen of the rescue. He told him not to notify anyone else until they were airborne. He did not want reporters converging on this site until after they had left. When Rodgers was finished, he borrowed a canteen from one of the marines. He indicated for two of the men to stand off to the side as he led the admiral toward a nearby tree stump. Link sat, and the general handed him the canteen. Wheezing, the admiral took a short swallow and then poured water into a cupped hand. He rinsed each eye in turn.

Rodgers was glad that he was not holding a weapon. He had a feeling he was not going to like what Link had to say.

"Thanks for the save, Mike," Link said.

"Not a problem."

Link blinked hard to clear his vision. "How the hell did you locate me?"

"The kidnapper had a partner," Rodgers informed him. "He told us where you were."

"I figured this guy could not have been acting alone," Link said. "Where did you find him?"

"In Senator Orr's suite," Rodgers said.

Link took a longer swallow of water. "Is the senator okay?"

"He's fine," Rodgers said.

"Good."

Rodgers crouched beside the stump. "He did not have you tied up in there," the general said.

"No," Link said. "He said he had a gun, that he would shoot me if I tried to get away."

"Admiral, why don't we mothball the bullshit and talk about what happened?" Rodgers suggested.

"Sure."

"No, I mean what *really* happened," Rodgers said.

"What do you mean?"

"I mean that Stone told us everything," Rodgers said.

"Oh? What did he tell you?"

"How all of this was a plot to stop Senator Orr's candidacy, an operation to kill the USF."

Link looked at Rodgers. "Did he?"

Rodgers nodded.

Link glanced around. The two marines were standing twenty or so yards behind him. The tall, yellow grasses hissed lightly, and wind filled the field with a low yawn that would mask their conversation. The admiral looked down.

If a man is lucky, there is at least one moment in his life that Rodgers called the cornerstone. It is when a man has to make a decision based on principle not on personal security. It was a single building block that shaped the rest of his life. It was a moment he would look back on with pride or with regret. Rodgers had seen cornerstones in combat, when the decision was typically more one of instinct than a deliberative process. Some men froze under fire, others put the risks behind them and charged. The ones who choked never got over it. The ones who acted felt like gods for however many decades—or seconds—remained of their lives.

Admiral Kenneth Link was facing a cornerstone. Rodgers could see it in his bloodshot eyes. He was trying to decide whether to finish the lie he had just begun, which he might or might not be able to make stick. Or whether to embrace the truth and acknowledge the war he had apparently been fighting.

"Did Stone tell you that Senator Don Orr and Kat Lockley planned the murder of William Wilson?" Link asked.

"He did."

"Do you believe him?"

"I'm not sure," Rodgers admitted. "Why would the senator and Kat have done that? And why would he have confided in you?"

"We were his staff, his close advisers," Link said. "And he felt that his plan left him bulletproof. As for why he would do it, hate, for one thing. Politics for another. Orr felt that a tawdry death, a heart attack in the middle of sex, would destroy not just the man but the head of steam people had built for his fiscal plans. He believed that having it happen right after the Georgetown party would call attention to the USF. It would give him a platform to enunciate the differences between himself and the other Euro-friendly presidential candidates."

"But Op-Center screwed that up."

Link nodded. "Orr did not anticipate that Darrell McCaskey would discover the puncture wound. The son of a bitch wanted attention, not a murder charge."

"If you knew this, why didn't you go to the police?" Rodgers asked.

"We did," Link said. "Detective Howell was reluctant to move against Orr without conclusive evidence."

"He could have seen the wound."

"That would not have implicated Orr," Link said. "Just Lucy, who was doomed anyway because she gave Wilson and Lawless the injections. Besides, Howell was being blackmailed—"

"The gay date rape charge."

"Yeah."

"You could have gone to the FBI, or given the information to Scotland Yard," Rodgers said.

"Lucy still would have taken the hit," Link said. "And if she pointed fingers, Kat would have been implicated. Willingly, I might add. She is devoted to the senator. Orr might have been splashed with blood by association, but maybe not enough to derail him. Which voters would have mourned an arrogant, successful, anti-American British entrepreneur? No, Mike. We needed to stop Orr permanently."

"And how would you have done that? By killing him?"

"If necessary," Link admitted. "You don't understand, Mike. I've been watching this guy since I was in naval intelligence. I used to sit in on hearings of the Senate Armed Services Committee. The man I saw in these meetings was not the benign Texan ordinary Joe he presented to the voters. He reminded me of Joseph McCarthy. Xenophobic, suspicious, aggressive. He said that whenever he went home, he took walks in the desert and had visions of what he thought America should be. 'Fortress America,' he called it. Our national borders not just secure but closed, our resources maximized, our enemies cut off from financial aid, crushed, or left to beat each other to death. What he was selling to the American public was a cleaner version of that. But I knew he intended to accomplish that by any means necessary."

"So he was McCarthy *and* Stalin," Rodgers said. "Neat trick."

"You don't believe me? Ask anyone who was at those meetings," Link went on. "Ultimately, I was the only one in a position to do something about it. I watched him with the help of Kendra and Eric. When the mood of the country turned isolationist and Orr saw a real opportunity to win the presidency, he took it. That was when we made our move as well."

"You got close to him in order to stop him."

"That's right," Link said. "I had two options. I could have taken him out before he hit Wilson, but that would have made him a martyr to like-minded isolationists. So we chose to let him hook himself, then just reel him in. At the Company we ran operations like this worldwide."

"I understand all that," Rodgers said. "What I don't understand is why you tried to run this on your own."

"How many people do *you* let in on a top secret operation?"

"That depends," Rodgers said. He was growing angry.

"If my option was to trust someone like Paul Hood or blow up his goddamn organization, I'd trust Paul Hood with my secret."

"But you were also working with Orr and Kat!" Link said. "You went out with her. We didn't know how you felt about them. If we told Hood, he might have told you, and you might have told the senator. You and I weren't exactly getting along, Mike. I was pushing to find out where you stood."

"Talking would have worked better."

"Maybe."

"Not *maybe,*" Rodgers snapped. "Your decision killed one of my people!"

"I'm always sorry about collateral damage!" Link shot back. "But politics is war, and in wartime, people die. Innocent people. I read your file, General. You have seen that firsthand. We're soldiers, and our primary job is to defend our nation. Sometimes decisions have to be made quickly. They have to be made by people under stress, by people who are trying to keep one eye on the endgame and one eye on the best way to get there. That is what I did."

"You rolled a tank over your own soldiers," Rodgers said.

"That happens, too, doesn't it?" Link said.

"In retreat, when the battle plan is in disarray," Rodgers said.

"Whatever disarray we experienced was Op-Center's doing!" Link said, raising his own voice. "We needed a few more days to carry this operation out, to make sure that Orr was stopped. I made a command decision about Op-Center. We used the EM bomb instead of conventional explosives because we *didn't* want casualties. Your man was not supposed to be in the room when it went off."

"Another indication that you made the wrong decision," Rodgers said.

"We stopped Orr, didn't we?"

"Sure." Rodgers motioned the marines over. "Can you stand, Admiral?"

Link rose. "Where are we going?"

"I'm taking you to the San Diego PD," Rodgers said. "This is for them to sort out with the D.C. Metro Police."

"Right. I would like to know one thing, though. You do understand what we did, don't you?"

The marines arrived, and the admiral suddenly seemed like a different man. It was not uncertainty in his voice, or regret. *Perhaps it was a hint of fear as the reality of his situation settled in.*

"Why does it matter what I think?" the general asked.

"Things didn't exactly work out the way I planned," Link replied. "I've got one hell of a drop in front of me. A lonely drop." He grinned uneasily. "You're a scholar. Who was it who said that solitude is great if you're a wild beast or a god?"

"Francis Bacon said that," Rodgers told him. The general moved in closer. "Admiral, I understand what you did. I just don't agree. A nation is defined by its laws, not by vigilantes and rogue operations. You hurt people to enforce your own vision of the greater good."

"What about saving the nation from a tyrant? You don't think that was a worthwhile goal?"

"It has been one of the greatest goals of some of the greatest men in history," Rodgers said. He was trying to give the admiral *something*. "I just don't agree that the shortest path is always the best one. The singular thing about this nation is that we make mistakes but invariably correct them. Maybe Orr would have become a political force. He might even have become president. But the national mood would have shifted. We are a rough and impatient people, but we ultimately do the right thing."

Link's grin turned knowing. "So you *would* have ratted us out to Orr, wouldn't you? Talking instead of pushing—is that what you would have preferred?"

Rodgers did not answer. He did not know.

"I am content, then," Link said. "I did the right thing."

The Apache had landed in the clearing, and Rodgers told the marines to escort the admiral toward it. The general followed them. He thought about Link's question as he walked.

He had a feeling he would be thinking about it for quite some time.

FIFTY-SEVEN

San Diego, California
Thursday, 8:33 A.M.

The Apache landed at Pendleton, where Link was handed over to the military police. They, in turn, made arrangements to have him transferred to the San Diego police. The charge, for now, was fraudulent claim of kidnapping. It was based entirely on Rodgers's report that Link had maintained the deception for roughly one minute after he had been rescued. It was a very minor charge, but it was all they had for now. More would follow after Eric Stone had seen an attorney and made his own statement. He and Kendra were also in custody of the SDPD.

After the admiral's arrest, Rodgers returned to Senator Orr's suite. Kat and the senator were still there. The senator had recovered somewhat and was lucid enough to thank Rodgers for his quick action.

"I hope you don't believe any of Eric's ranting," Kat said.

"Yes," Orr added. "I understand he was quite out of his head."

Rodgers said no, of course not. This was obviously a plot created by Admiral Link, who had a long-standing grudge against the senator. They agreed that Senator Orr would not attempt to speak to the convention until the next day. Kat went down and, from the podium, told the attendees that the situation was still being investigated but that Link had been recovered and Senator Orr would speak to them the next day. Rodgers went with her to make sure she did what she said she was going to do. While Orr rested, Kat went back to her suite to write Orr a speech. Hotel security was stationed outside their door to protect them against further attacks.

And to make sure they stayed in their rooms.

Meanwhile, Rodgers called Darrell McCaskey. Rodgers brought him up to speed and told him what he needed to tie this one up.

The following morning, at Rodgers's suggestion, he met Kat and Orr for breakfast in the senator's suite. There was a knock on the door, and Kat went to answer.

"I'm starving," she said with a big smile.

The smile crashed when she opened the door. Detective Robert Howell was standing there with a detective and six officers from the San Diego Police Department. He was holding two manila envelopes. The local detective stepped forward. She was a young woman with steely eyes and a gentle but insistent voice. She was also holding a pair of envelopes.

"Ms. Kat Lockley?"

"Yes."

"I am Detective Lynn Mastio. We have a warrant issued by Judge Andrew Zucker this morning in the county of San Diego ordering your detention on the suspicion of planning and abetting two acts of homicide."

Senator Orr stepped forward. He looked from Detective Mastio to Detective Howell. "Bob, does this young lady know who I am?"

"I do, sir," Detective Mastio replied. "You are Senator Donald Orr. I have a warrant for your detention as well, Senator."

"Detention?" Orr snapped. "Are you saying we are under arrest?"

"No, Senator. Formal charges will not be filed until we have had a chance to further review the evidence that has been presented, Senator," Mastio replied.

"We have a convention to run!" Kat said. "You have no right to walk in with accusations based on hearsay and interfere with our work."

"I'm sorry," Mastio told her. "We do have that right."

Orr turned back to Howell. "What the hell are you doing here?"

"I have extradition papers," Howell said. He raised the envelopes. "If you are arrested for crimes that may have been committed in our jurisdiction, we will be bringing you to D.C. for arraignment."

"This is the most outlandish and offensive thing I have ever heard!" the senator barked. "I am the one who was assaulted here! Link and his accomplices are the ones you should be talking to!"

Orr seemed anxious to turn away, to throw his position and reputation against the problem and make it go away. Howell seemed equally determined to prevent that. When Rodgers had called McCaskey to suggest the detective fly out, Op-Center's top law officer seemed eager to make that happen.

"I find it odd that neither of you asked who was murdered," Rodgers said, stepping forward.

"I assume this has to do with that idiot Englishman," Orr said.

"What this has to do with are the rights of a murder victim," Rodgers said.

"How dare you lecture this man about rights!" Kat yelled. "He defended his nation in Vietnam and has spent a lifetime legislating on behalf of citizens like us, improving the standard of living for all Americans and for women in particular."

"The senator's patriotism is not at issue," Rodgers said. "Robert Lawless was an American," Rodgers remarked. "What happened to his rights? Lucy O'Connor is an American woman. Did she have any idea what she was getting into?"

Kat turned on Rodgers. "You are the worst of them all.

We took you in when you had nothing. I was responsible for Lawless and for Lucy. The senator had nothing to do with this."

"Admiral Link tells a different version of the story," Rodgers said.

"Ms. Lockley," Mastio said, "would you please turn around?"

Kat glared at her. "What? Why?"

Mastio removed handcuffs from her belt.

"You're handcuffing us?" Kat screamed.

"Yes, ma'am."

"Detective, I am not going anywhere without my personal attorney," Orr said. "I will call him and wait here until he arrives."

"I'm sorry, Senator, but that is not how it works," Mastio told him. "You will have to come with us. All of you."

"This is ridiculous!" Orr huffed.

"No," Rodgers said. "*This* is the system you took a vow to uphold."

"You have the right to remain silent and refuse to answer any questions," Mastio said to them. "Anything you say may be used against you in a court of law—"

"Please don't do this to the senator," Kat implored. "His office demands some measure of respect."

"It's like a bank account, Kat," Rodgers said. "The more you invest, the more you earn."

As Mastio finished reciting the Miranda warning, Kat turned again and glared at Rodgers, then at the others. Fierce, angry glances from the senator and his aide were met with resolute looks from the others. It was only a moment, but it was like nothing Rodgers had ever experienced. This was not like political views or tactical opinions clashing in an office or command center. Those were about ideas, and they were expressed in words. This had become a primal, unspoken confrontation, something closer to the apes than to the stars.

The young San Diego detective broke the tension. She provided an edge of humanity, a touch of the dignity Kat had requested.

"Senator, Ms. Lockley, if you agree to come peaceably, I will remove restraints," Mastio said. "My officers will gather your things and bring them to the stationhouse."

She agreed. "The press is downstairs," Orr said. "Will I be allowed to speak with them?"

"Actually, Senator, we will be leaving through the underground delivery level," Mastio said.

"The basement?" Kat declared.

"Yes," the detective replied. "We do not wish to upset the senator's supporters and risk a riot."

"You deserve one," Kat said.

"*They* don't," Mastio replied, impatience flashing for the first time. "Innocent individuals might be hurt."

There was no further discussion. The senator went to put on a necktie. Kat stepped into the hallway. She grabbed a banana from the room service cart. It had arrived during the debate and was left behind. One of the police officers made sure she took only the fruit and not a knife or juice glass.

While they waited for the senator, Detective Howell took Rodgers aside. The men stood beside the foyer closet.

"General, I want to thank you for asking me to come out," Howell said.

"It seemed the place you should be."

"You know I screwed up on this," Howell said.

"I've heard rumors," Rodgers said. He smiled. "Just rumors."

"Thanks. I want you to know I'll make it right with the department," Howell said. "I'll resign or take a bust-down or whatever disciplinary action they want."

"Detective, I have a feeling your testimony is going to be important in this case," Rodgers told him. "You're going to take heat for what you did, and there's going to be exposure on aspects of your personal life. Whatever dues you need to pay will get paid. I would be surprised if the Metro Police asked for more than that."

"I hope you're right."

"People are pretty compassionate, when you get down to it. They'll understand the kind of crap you were under from the start. If you hang tough, you'll be okay."

"Thanks." Howell smiled. "Just having Darrell make the call meant a lot."

"He's tough but fair," Rodgers said.

The senator arrived, and the group left, save for three police officers. Hotel security was called, and under the eyes of two house detectives, the trio of officers packed up Senator Orr's belongings and had them taken downstairs. Then they went to the rooms of Kat Lockley, Kenneth Link, Eric Stone, and Kendra Peterson and did the same. The suitcases were placed in a police van and driven to the station.

Mike Rodgers did not join them as they closed up the suites. He had a job to do. Ironically, with everyone else gone, General Rodgers was in fact if not in name the ranking official of the USF. He decided to go down to the convention hall and address the attendees. Though he was not one for public speaking, he was remarkably calm as he stood at the podium and said simply that the events of the past day had forced the USF to reevaluate its launch plans. He suspected the senator would have a statement to make within the next day or two but had no additional information or insights to share at present. He did not answer questions shouted from those near the stage.

"As of now," he said in closing, "the party is over."

The double meaning did not appear to be lost on anyone. Slowly, thousands of people made their way to the street. Some went to their hotels to change flights, others waited for the downtown bars to open, and still others picked up discounted souvenirs from vendors.

By early afternoon, as word of the arrest and extradition of Senator Orr spread through the city, the USF banners were already coming down. Soon, all that was left of the USF were discarded state placards and crumpled flyers tumbling from overstuffed trash cans and blowing down the Pacific Coast Highway.

FIFTY-EIGHT

Washington, D.C.
Friday, 8:22 A.M.

It was a bittersweet meeting for all.

Stuffy, with a hint of smoke still hanging high in the air, the Tank was what it would never be again: home to all the surviving, original members of the Op-Center command team: Paul Hood, Mike Rodgers, Bob Herbert, and Darrell McCaskey. Hood had seen the men talking in the hallway and invited them in. Only Martha Mackall, who was slain in Madrid, was not present. Lowell Coffey, Matt Stoll, Ron Plummer, and Liz Gordon had joined later. All were involved in getting Op-Center running again. Coffey was talking to Senator Debenport about appropriations, Stoll and his team were installing new equipment, and Liz was talking to the staff to make sure there were no postpulse fears about being downstairs in a sealed environment, in a place where one of their coworkers had been killed.

Hood had expected there to be tension between himself and Rodgers, between himself and Herbert. Instead, there was a sense of triumph. Darrell McCaskey had started an operation that they had seen to the finish line, all of them carrying the load part of the way. Hood was glad that it was Mike who had gotten to carry it home. He deserved to go out with a victory. If Bob Herbert held any bitterness about the downsizing of Op-Center, he had put it aside for now. Or maybe it was forgotten. The Mississippi native was like magnesium: a quick, bright burn, and then it was over. Just a few months before, Herbert had been angry *at* Rodgers for taking on an intelligence unit after the disbanding of Striker.

Or maybe he is just exhausted from pushing his wheelchair around, Hood thought. Herbert had ordered a spare motor, phone, and computer from the base quartermaster, but they would not be delivered until the next day.

"Detective Superintendent George Daily is a very happy man," McCaskey said as they settled in around the conference table. He looked at Rodgers. "Mike is a hero in the London press."

"Maybe Scotland Yard will give me a job," Rodgers replied.

"Whatever you do, go someplace where there is a window that opens," Herbert said. He was fanning himself with an intelligence briefing from Andrews. Until his own division was functioning again, Herbert had to rely on data from other OSARs, offices of surveillance and reconnaissance. "The flyboy engineers said it could be a day or two before they get the motor working again."

"Don't believe them," Rodgers said. "Military engineers always say things will take longer than they should. That way, when everything is up and running, we think they're miracle workers."

"I thought I was cynical," Herbert said. "Someone's been in the military way too long."

"You know, you could always run for president," McCaskey said. "I hear the USF has an opening."

"That is not for me," Rodgers said.

"The job or the philosophy?" Hood asked.

"The mantle of Donald Orr," Rodgers said. "I don't think the USF will survive. If it does, it will be a fringe organization. If what Kenneth Link said about Orr proves correct, he will become a poster boy of the lunatic far right."

"It's very true," Herbert assured him. "Whatever job you take next, Mike, let me handle the due diligence. I looked at the minutes of some of those closed sessions

Link told you about, the ones Orr attended. USF should have stood for Under a Serious Fascist."

"Gentlemen, Link is a name I do not particularly want to hear right now," Hood interjected. "Not after what he did here."

"In the name of patriotism, no less," McCaskey said.

"The sick thing is, who can deny that Senator Orr was a threat?" Rodgers said.

"Me," Herbert said, raising his hand. "Who can deny that William Wilson was a threat to the American economy?"

"No one, but that doesn't justify murder," McCaskey said.

"Why not? We've fought wars over economic issues," Herbert said. "Lots of people died in those, all of it wrapped in flags and served with apple pie."

"So we should just kill people who threaten our wallets?" McCaskey asked.

"That is way too big a thought for me," Herbert said. "I'm in intelligence, not wisdom."

Rodgers smiled.

"Look, I'm not defending Orr," Herbert went on. "If nothing else, he was a coward for sending a gullible kid like Lucy O'Connor to do his crap work and lying to her about what would happen. He was a scumbag for blackmailing Detective Howell. All I'm saying is that this happens routinely as a matter of national policy. In that respect, Orr's mistake was that he was the only member of Congress to vote on the issue. If war had been declared on England and Wilson were the only casualty, this whole thing would have been legal."

"I always believed that one should try to fight harmful or restrictive policies with better, more creative policies," Hood said.

"Sure. And when that fails, guys like me come in and set it right," Rodgers said.

"Bingo," Herbert said.

"I don't know," McCaskey said. "My older sister used to take part in sit-ins and be-ins in the sixties. They were pretty effective."

"Very," Rodgers said. "They cut the aid and support me and my guys needed to beat the Vietcong," Rodgers grumbled. "Only at that, Darrell."

There was a short, uncomfortable silence. The sense of a bittersweet reunion had passed. The balance was way off now, even among the men who were remaining with Op-Center.

"I think we're all still a little close to this situation," Hood said. "We should probably table the political debate."

"I agree," Rodgers said. "I just came by to thank Darrell and Bob for their help on this, and also Maria. She did great."

"I'll tell her," McCaskey said. He regarded Rodgers for a long moment. "So. What are your immediate plans?"

"Professionally, I have none," Rodgers said. "Personally, there's something I have to do. A question I have to answer."

"Need help?" Herbert asked.

"I thought you were short on wisdom," Rodgers said.

"That was false modesty," he replied.

"No," Rodgers said. "It was something the admiral asked me while the marines were taking him away. One of those lady-or-the-tiger things that I want to think about. Preferably while I'm rock climbing or baking on a coastline somewhere."

"You earned those breaks," Hood said. He was hurt by the fact that Rodgers had singled out the help of the others but not him. It seemed petty. But he let it pass. Hood was not in Rodgers's position and did not know how it felt.

The meeting broke up, McCaskey and Herbert leaving to help reboot Op-Center. Hood and Rodgers stood. The general faced his longtime associate.

"Have you spoken with the president about what went down?" Rodgers asked.

"Late last night," Hood said. He hesitated. He wanted to say more about the new arrangement, solicit the input of a valued confederate. He decided against it. "The White House was happy and very appreciative."

"That's good." Rodgers said. "Is that all?"

"What do you mean?"

"You looked like you wanted to say something else," Rodgers said.

"No," Hood assured him. "No, I just remembered there's an intern who I need to check in with."

"An intern? After all this, you're worrying about an intern. Can you say 'micromanage'?"

"It isn't that," Hood told him. "He's the son of Sharon's new squeeze."

Rodgers made a face. "And you're taking him on?"

Hood nodded. He felt like the high school nerd who had joined another club because they needed a chess player or debater.

"Always a difficult tightrope to walk, isn't it?"

Hood smiled. "Hopefully, my low-yield form of diplomacy will work."

"That wasn't a knock earlier, about talk ending in combat," Rodgers said. "It was a lament. I don't like war any more than you do. I've lost too many friends."

"I know."

The general's eyes softened and moistened. For a moment, he seemed to be near tears.

"I also didn't want you to think I was ignoring you before, when I thanked Bob and Darrell for their help. One of the things I was thinking on the flight back was some of the decisions Orr and Link made. It isn't like the military, where you have a target and a limited number of ways to reach it. Where everyone in your unit is identically armed and trained and you know pretty much how they're going to react. There is nothing predictable and no one reliable in politics."

"Some of us try; most of us fail," Hood admitted.

"You tried harder than most," Rodgers said. "I haven't always bought what you were selling, and I've been pretty vocal about that. But I can't fault your efforts. I guess you were the right man for this job." He gestured behind him to indicate all of Op-Center. "You listen, your instincts are damn good, and you have a good heart. And, hell. You had the White House nipping at one ankle, me kicking at the other, and a bomb that tore a hole through your middle. You still got us through and beat the bad guys."

"We all did," Hood reminded him.

"You were the coach. You get first champagne."

"Thanks," Hood said. It seemed a frail word for what Hood felt. But the feeling behind it was sincere.

"Well, I'm going to get myself out of here," Rodgers said. "Start that long furlough."

"You earned it," Hood said. "And I hope you find the answer to whatever the question is. You know where to come if you need advice."

"Yeah," Rodgers smiled.

The men shook hands, then embraced. It was a tough good-bye. The men had been through loss and triumph together. This was the man who had saved the life of Harleigh Hood. Though Hood expected that they would see each other again, an era of shared victory and pain was ending.

Rodgers broke the embrace with a sharp salute, then turned and left. He walked quickly and proudly into an uncertain future.

Hood went back to the conference table. His own future was also cloudy. There was rebuilding to be done, not just at Op-Center but inside Paul Hood. He did not question the decisions that had brought them to this point, the loss of Rodgers and other staff members, as well as the new alliance with the White House. But Hood did regret them. He always would.

Hood did not know his own future, of course. But he hoped that Rodgers was right about one thing. Hood hoped that unlike Donald Orr and Kenneth Link, he knew the difference between what was moral and what was not. And that he had the strength to stand up for what was right. The coming weeks would be a test, not just for him but for Op-Center.

Suddenly there was a hollow cheer from somewhere along the air ducts. That was where the group of air force mechanics had been working. A moment later, cool air began to circulate throughout the underground complex. Whether the engineers had misled Herbert or whether they had worked a wonder was not important. Only one thing mattered: *Renewal*, Hood thought. *You can never write it off.*

Never.

Other Books by Steve Pieczenik

THE MIND PALACE
BLOOD HEAT
MAXIMUM VIGILANCE
PAX PACIFICA
STATE OF EMERGENCY

For more information on Steve Pieczenik,
please visit www.stevepieczenik.com and www.strategic-intl.com

THE #1 *NEW YORK TIMES* BESTSELLING SERIES

Tom Clancy's Op-Center

Created by Tom Clancy and Steve Pieczenik
written by Jeff Rovin

TOM CLANCY'S OP-CENTER	0-425-14736-3
TOM CLANCY'S OP-CENTER: MIRROR IMAGE	0-425-15014-3
TOM CLANCY'S OP-CENTER: GAMES OF STATE	0-425-15187-5
TOM CLANCY'S OP-CENTER ACTS OF WAR	0-425-15601-X
TOM CLANCY'S OP-CENTER: BALANCE OF POWER	0-425-16556-6
TOM CLANCY'S OP-CENTER: STATE OF SIEGE	0-425-16822-0
TOM CLANCY'S OP-CENTER: DIVIDE AND CONQUER	0-425-17480-8
TOM CLANCY'S OP-CENTER: LINE OF CONTROL	0-425-18005-0
TOM CLANCY'S OP-CENTER: MISSION OF HONOR	0-425-18670-9
TOM CLANCY'S OP-CENTER: SEA OF FIRE	0-425-19091-9

Available wherever books are sold or to order call 1-800-788-6262

b676

Tom Clancy's Power Plays

Created by Tom Clancy and Martin Greenberg
written by Jerome Preisler

TOM CLANCY'S POWER PLAYS: Politika
0-425-16278-8

TOM CLANCY'S POWER PLAYS: ruthless.com
0-425-16570-1

TOM CLANCY'S POWER PLAYS: Shadow Watch
0-425-17188-4

TOM CLANCY'S POWER PLAYS: Bio-Strike
0-425-17735-1

TOM CLANCY'S POWER PLAYS: Cold War
0-425-18214-2

TOM CLANCY'S POWER PLAYS: Cutting Edge
0-425-18705-5

TOM CLANCY'S POWER PLAYS: Zero Hour
0-425-19291-1

AVAILABLE WHEREVER BOOKS ARE SOLD
OR TO ORDER CALL:
1-800-788-6262

B677